Geoffrey Chaucer

The Canterbury Tales

An illustrated selection

rendered into modern English

by Nevill Coghill

Penguin Books Ltd, Harmondsworth,
Middlesex, England
Penguin Books, 625 Madison Avenue,
New York, New York 10022, U.S.A.
Penguin Books Australia Ltd, Ringwood,
Victoria, Australia
Penguin Books Canada Ltd, 2801 John Street,
Markham, Ontario, Canada L3R 1B4
Penguin Books (N.Z.) Ltd, 182–190 Wairau Road,
Auckland 10, New Zealand

This translation first published by Penguin Books 1951
Revised 1958
Reprinted with revisions 1960, 1975, 1977
This selection published in Great Britain by Allen Lane 1977
This selection published in the United States of America
by Penguin Books 1977
This selection published in Great Britain
by Penguin Books 1978

Copyright © Nevill Coghill, 1951, 1958, 1960, 1977
All rights reserved

Typeset in Monophoto Plantin
Made and printed in Great Britain

Penguin Books
The Canterbury Tales

Professor Nevill Coghill has held many appointments at
Oxford University, where he was Merton Professor of
English Literature from 1957 to 1966 and where he is now
Emeritus Fellow of Exeter and Merton Colleges. He was
born in 1899 and educated at Haileybury and Exeter College,
Oxford, and served in the Great War after 1917.

Penguin Books

FOR
Richard Freeman
Brian Ball
Glynne Wickham
Peter Whillans
Graham Binns

The Canterbury Tales

Introduction

Chaucer's Life

Geoffrey Chaucer was born about the year 1340; the exact date is not known. His father, John, and his grandfather, Robert, had associations with the wine trade and, more tenuously, with the Court. John was Deputy Butler to the King at Southampton in 1348. Geoffrey Chaucer's mother is believed to have been Agnes de Copton, niece of an official at the Mint. They lived in London in the parish of St Martin's-in-the-Vintry, reasonably well-to-do but in a humbler walk of life than that to be adorned so capably by their brilliant son.

It is thought that Chaucer was sent for his early schooling to St Paul's Almonry. From there he went on to be a page in the household of the Countess of Ulster, later Duchess of Clarence, wife of Lionel the third son of Edward III. The first mention of Geoffrey Chaucer's existence is in her household accounts for 1357. She had bought him a short cloak, a pair of shoes, and some parti-coloured red and black breeches.

To be page in a family of such eminence was a coveted position. His duties as a page included making beds, carrying candles, and running errands. He would there have acquired the finest education in good manners, a matter of great importance not only in his career as a courtier but also in his career as a poet. No English poet has so mannerly an approach to his reader.

As a page he would wait on the greatest in the land. One of these was the Duke of Lancaster, John of Gaunt; throughout his life he was Chaucer's most faithful patron and protector.

In 1359 Chaucer was sent abroad, a soldier in the egg, on one of those intermittent forays into France that made up so large a part of the Hundred Years' War. He was taken prisoner near Rheims and ransomed in the following year; the King himself contributed towards his ransom. Well-trained and intelligent pages did not grow on every bush.

It is not known for certain when Chaucer began to write poetry, but it is reasonable to believe that it was on his return from France. The elegance of French poetry and its thrilling doctrines of *Amour Courtois** seem to have gone to his impressionable, amorous, and poetical heart. He set to work to translate the gospel of that kind of love and poetry, the *Roman*

* For a rich account of this strange and fascinating cult I would refer the reader to *The Allegory of Love*, by C. S. Lewis, O.U.P.

9

de la Rose, a thirteenth-century French poem begun by Guillaume de Lorris and later completed by Jean de Meun.

Meanwhile he was promoted as a courtier. In 1367 he was attending on the King himself and was referred to as *Dilectus Valettus noster . . .* our dearly beloved Valet. It was towards that year that Chaucer married. His bride was Philippa de Roet, a lady in attendance on the Queen, and sister to Catherine Swynford, third wife of John of Gaunt.

Chaucer wrote no poems to her; it was not in fashion to write poems to one's wife. It could even be debated whether love could ever have a place in marriage; the typical situation in which a 'courtly lover' found himself was to be plunged in a secret, an illicit, and even an adulterous passion for some seemingly unattainable and pedestalized lady. Before his mistress a lover was prostrate, wounded to death by her beauty, killed by her disdain, obliged to an illimitable constancy, marked out for her dangerous service. A smile from her was in theory a gracious reward for twenty years of painful adoration. All Chaucer's heroes regard love when it comes upon them as the most beautiful of absolute disasters, an agony as much desired as bemoaned, ever to be pursued, never to be betrayed.

This was not in theory the attitude of a husband to his wife. It was for a husband to command, for a wife to obey. The changes that can be rung on these antitheses are to be seen throughout *The Canterbury Tales*. If we may judge by the *Knight's Tale* and the *Franklin's Tale* Chaucer thought that love and marriage were perhaps compatible after all, provided that the lover remained his wife's servant after marriage, in private at least. If we read the *Wife of Bath's Prologue* we shall see that she thought little of wives that did not master their husbands. What solution to these problems was reached by Geoffrey and Philippa Chaucer he never revealed. He only once alludes to her, or seems to do so, when in *The House of Fame* he compares the timbre of her voice awaking him in the morning to that of an eagle. His maturest work is increasingly ironical about women considered as wives; what the Wife of Bath and the Merchant have to say of them is of this kind. The *Wife of Bath's Prologue* and the *Merchant's Tale* are perhaps his two most astounding performances. By the time he wrote them Philippa had long been dead. It is in any case by no means certain that these two characters utter Chaucer's private convictions; they are speaking for themselves. One can only say that Chaucer was a great enough writer to lend them unanswerable thoughts and language, to think and speak on their behalf.

The King soon began to employ his beloved valet on important missions abroad. The details of most of these are not known, but appear to have been of a civilian and commercial nature, dealing with trade relations. We can infer that Chaucer was trustworthy and efficient.

Meanwhile Chaucer was gratifying and extending his passion for books. He was a prodigious reader and had the art of storing what he read in an almost faultless memory. He learnt in time to read widely in Latin, French, Anglo-Norman, and Italian. He made himself a considerable expert in contemporary sciences, especially in astronomy, medicine, physics, and alchemy. There is, for instance, in *The House of Fame* a long and amusing account of the nature of sound-waves. In literary and historical fields his favourites seem to have been Vergil, Ovid, Statius, Seneca, and Cicero among the ancients, and the *Roman de la Rose* and the works of Dante, Boccaccio, and Petrarch among the moderns. He knew the Fathers of the Church and quotes freely and frequently from every book in the Bible and Apocrypha.

Two journeys on the King's business took Chaucer to Italy: the first in 1372 to Genoa, the second in 1378 to Milan. It has always been supposed that these missions were what first brought him in contact with that Renaissance dawn which so glorified his later poetry. While he never lost or disvalued what he had learnt from French culture, he added some of the depth of Dante and much of the splendour of Boccaccio, from whom came, amongst other things, the stories of *Troilus and Criseyde* and the *Knight's Tale*. Chaucer's power to tell a story seems to have emerged at this time and to derive from Italy.

Meanwhile he was rising by steady promotions in what we should now call the Civil Service, that is in his offices as a courtier. In 1374 he became Comptroller of customs and subsidies on wools, skins, and hides at the Port of London: in 1382 Comptroller of petty customs, in 1385 Justice of the Peace for the county of Kent, in 1386 Knight of the Shire. He was now in some affluence.

But in December 1386 he was suddenly deprived of all his offices. John of Gaunt had left England on a military expedition to Spain and was replaced as an influence on young King Richard II by the Duke of Gloucester. Gloucester had never been a patron of the poet, and filled his posts with his own supporters. We may be grateful to him for this, because he set Chaucer at leisure thereby. It is almost certain that the poet then began to set in order and compose *The Canterbury Tales*.

In 1389 John of Gaunt returned and Chaucer was restored to favour and office. He was put in charge of the repair of walls, ditches, sewers, and bridges between Greenwich and Woolwich, and of the fabric of St George's Chapel at Windsor. The office of Sub-Forester of North Petherton (probably a sinecure) was given him. The daily pitcher of wine allowed him by Edward III in 1374 became, under Richard II, an annual tun. Henry Bolingbroke presented him with a scarlet robe trimmed with fur. Once more he had met with that cheerful good luck which is so happily reflected in his poetry.

He felt himself to be growing old, however; he complained that the faculty of rhyming had deserted him. No one knows when he put his last touch to *The Canterbury Tales*. He never finished them.

He died on the twenty-fifth of October 1400 and was buried in Westminster Abbey. A fine tomb, erected by an admirer in the fifteenth century, marks his grave and was the first of those that are gathered into what we now know as the Poets' Corner. The Father of English Poetry lies in his family vault.*

Chaucer's Works

The order in which Chaucer's works were written is not certain. Some have been lost, if we are to believe the list of them given at the end of *The Canterbury Tales* in the 'retractions' made by the poet. His main surviving poems are:

Before 1372 part at least of a translation of the *Roman de la Rose*, *The Book of the Duchess*, and the *ABC of the Virgin*.

Between 1372 and 1382 *The House of Fame*, *The Parliament of Fowls*, and most probably a number of stories or preliminary versions of stories that were later included in *The Canterbury Tales*.

The House of Fame and *The Parliament of Fowls* are longish allegorical fantasies of much humour and delicacy. They contain passages of that rich conversation in verse which it is one of Chaucer's peculiar powers to invent, and in both poems the poet himself appears in person as a plump simpleton, much as he does in *The Canterbury Tales*. It was his pose to regard himself with a mild mockery.

Between 1380 and 1385 *Troilus and Criseyde* and the translation of Boethius, *De Consolatione Philosophiae*, were completed. The latter is the main basis of most of Chaucer's philosophical speculations, especially those on tragedy and predestination, which underlie its twin, *Troilus and Criseyde*.

This poem is his first great masterpiece. He calls it his 'little tragedy' ('Go, litel bok, go litel myn tragedye'), but it contains much, especially in the character and conversation of Pandarus, that is highly comic and amusing. Its psychological understanding is so subtle and its narrative line so skilfully ordered that it has been called our first novel. It appears to have given offence to Queen Anne of Bohemia (Richard II's wife) because it seemed to imply that women were more faithless than men in matters of love. Chaucer was bidden to write a retraction and so in the following year (1386) he produced a large instalment of *The Legend of the Saints of*

---

* For a somewhat fuller account of Chaucer's life and poetry than can here be given, reference is offered to my volume, *The Poet Chaucer* (O.U.P.).

Cupid (all female), which is also known as *The Legend of Good Women*. He never finished it. His disciple Lydgate said later that it encumbered his wits to think of so many good women.

From 1386 or 87 onwards he was at work on *The Canterbury Tales*. There are some 84 MSS and early printed editions by Caxton, Pynson, Wynkyn de Worde, and Thynne.

These manuscripts show that Chaucer left ten fragments of varying size of this great poem. Modern editors have arranged these in what appears to be the intended sequence, inferred from dates and places mentioned in the 'end-links', as the colloquies of the pilgrims between tales are called.

If we may trust the *Prologue*, Chaucer intended that each of some thirty pilgrims should tell two tales on the way to Canterbury and two on the way back. He never completed this immense project, and what he wrote was not finally revised even so far as it went. There are also one or two minor inconsistencies which a little revision could have rectified.

Together the tales make a reasonably continuous and consistent narrative of a pilgrimage that seems to have occupied five days (16 to 20 April) and that led to the outskirts of Canterbury. At that point Chaucer withdrew from his task with an apology for whatever might smack of sin in his work. In this rendering, while omitting certain of the tales, I have followed the accepted order first worked out by Furnivall (1868) and later confirmed by Skeat (1894).

The idea of a collection of tales diversified in style to suit their tellers and unified in form by uniting the tellers in a common purpose is Chaucer's own. Collections of stories were common at the time, but only Chaucer hit on this simple device for securing natural probability, psychological variety, and a a wide range of narrative interest.

In all literature there is nothing that touches or resembles the *Prologue*. It is the concise portrait of an entire nation, high and low, old and young, male and female, lay and clerical, learned and ignorant, rogue and righteous, land and sea, town and country, but without extremes. Apart from the stunning clarity, touched with nuance, of the characters presented, the most noticeable thing about them is their normality. They are the perennial progeny of men and women. Sharply individual, together they make a party.

The tales these pilgrims tell come from all over Europe, many of them from the works of Chaucer's near contemporaries. Some come from further afield, from the ancients, from the Orient. They exemplify a large range of contemporary European imagination, then particularly addicted to stories, especially to stories that had some sharp point and deducible maxim, moral, or idea. Almost every tale ends with a piece of proverbial or other wisdom derived from it and with a general benediction on the company.

It was not considered the function of a teller of stories in the fourteenth century to invent the stories he told, but to present and embellish them with all the arts of rhetoric for the purposes of entertainment and instruction. Chaucer's choice of story ranges from what he could hear – such as tales of low life in oral circulation, like the *Miller's Tale*, that are known as fabliaux – to what he had read in Boccaccio, or other classic masters, or in the lives of saints. To quote Dryden once more, ' 'Tis sufficient to say, according to the proverb, that *here is God's plenty*.'

The present version of this master-work is intended for those who feel difficulty in reading the original, yet would like to enjoy as much of that 'plenty' as the translator has been able to convey in a more modern idiom.

NEVILL COGHILL

A Note to this Edition

This present selection of *The Canterbury Tales* is drawn from Nevill Coghill's modern English rendering, celebrated in Penguin Classics for more than twenty-five years.

The pictures have been carefully selected from medieval sources, not to illustrate *The Canterbury Tales* but to give the reader an impression of life and society in and around Chaucer's time. Fortunately for posterity many of the richly illuminated manuscripts which provided a pictorial contemporary history of the period have been carefully and lovingly preserved in collections and museums. Our indebtedness to those painstaking, often witty artists of bygone centuries, many of them monks cloistered in monasteries, and to those who preserved their work, is great indeed.

Because change in most things at the time was slow the selection of pictures has not been confined to the sixty or so years of Chaucer's life but embraces a more generous span of the fourteenth century and the first half of the fifteenth. Moreover it must be remembered that during this period England was closely linked with France and Flanders. The basis of English society had been laid by the Normans; the English kings were French in origin, as were the courtly traditions. During the Hundred Years War, which lasted throughout Chaucer's adult life, a large part of France was English by inheritance or conquest.

To appreciate some of the pictures it must also be remembered that many of the artists who embellished these ancient manuscripts were illustrating classical or religious themes. The charm of many of these pictures is that the classical and religious themes are placed by the artists in contemporary settings with which they were familiar. Thus we see the birth of St Edmund recorded in a cheerful medieval bedroom, or Troy being built by medieval builders using medieval building methods. The whole, including many pictures of domestic objects, armour, weapons, etc., provides a fascinating panorama of the way of life in Chaucer's time.

Thanks are due to Bridget Heal, Gerald Cinamon and especially Paul Bowden for the design of this book, to Nancy Winters, Member of the Society of Scribes and Illuminators, for the calligraphy, and to Enid and Bernard Moore for the picture research. Bernard Moore prepared the captions and the texts in the colour sections.

. . . I have translated some parts of his works,
only that I might perpetuate his memory,
or at least refresh it, amongst my countrymen.
If I have altered him anywhere for the better,
I must at the same time acknowledge,
that I could have done nothing without him. . .

JOHN DRYDEN on translating Chaucer
Preface to the Fables, 1700

And such as Chaucer is, shall Dryden be.

ALEXANDER POPE
Essay on Criticism, 1711

The Canterbury Tales

The Prologue

When in April the sweet showers fall
And pierce the drought of March to the root, and all
The veins are bathed in liquor of such power
As brings about the engendering of the flower,
When also Zephyrus with his sweet breath
Exhales an air in every grove and heath
Upon the tender shoots, and the young sun
His half-course in the sign of the *Ram* has run,
And the small fowl are making melody
That sleep away the night with open eye
(So nature pricks them and their heart engages)
Then people long to go on pilgrimages
And palmers long to seek the stranger strands
Of far-off saints, hallowed in sundry lands,

And specially, from every shire's end
In England, down to Canterbury they wend
To seek the holy blissful martyr,* quick
To give his help to them when they were sick.
   It happened in that season that one day
In Southwark, at *The Tabard*, as I lay
Ready to go on pilgrimage and start
For Canterbury, most devout at heart,
At night there came into that hostelry
Some nine and twenty in a company
Of sundry folk happening then to fall
In fellowship, and they were pilgrims all
That towards Canterbury meant to ride.
The rooms and stables of the inn were wide;
They made us easy, all was of the best.
And shortly, when the sun had gone to rest,
By speaking to them all upon the trip
I soon was one of them in fellowship
And promised to rise early and take the way
To Canterbury, as you heard me say.
   But none the less, while I have time and space,
Before my story takes a further pace,
It seems a reasonable thing to say
What their condition was, the full array
Of each of them, as it appeared to me,
According to profession and degree,
And what apparel they were riding in;
And at a Knight I therefore will begin.
There was a *Knight*, a most distinguished man,
Who from the day on which he first began
To ride abroad had followed chivalry,
Truth, honour, generousness and courtesy.
He had done nobly in his sovereign's war
And ridden into battle, no man more,
As well in christian as in heathen places,
And ever honoured for his noble graces.
   When we took Alexandria,* he was there.
He often sat at table in the chair
Of honour, above all nations, when in Prussia.
In Lithuania he had ridden, and Russia,
No christian man so often, of his rank.
When, in Granada, Algeciras sank
Under assault, he had been there, and in
North Africa, raiding Benamarin;

* For Notes see pp. 361–369

In Anatolia he had been as well
And fought when Ayas and Attalia fell,
For all along the Mediterranean coast
He had embarked with many a noble host.
In fifteen mortal battles he had been
And jousted for our faith at Tramissene
Thrice in the lists, and always killed his man.
This same distinguished knight had led the van
Once with the Bey of Balat, doing work
For him against another heathen Turk;
He was of sovereign value in all eyes.
And though so much distinguished, he was wise
And in his bearing modest as a maid.
He never yet a boorish thing had said
In all his life to any, come what might;
He was a true, a perfect gentle-knight.

    Speaking of his equipment, he possessed
Fine horses, but he was not gaily dressed.
He wore a fustian tunic stained and dark
With smudges where his armour had left mark;
Just home from service, he had joined our ranks
To do his pilgrimage and render thanks.

    He had his son with him, a fine young *Squire*,
A lover and cadet, a lad of fire
With locks as curly as if they had been pressed.
He was some twenty years of age, I guessed.
In stature he was of a moderate length,
With wonderful agility and strength.
He'd seen some service with the cavalry
In Flanders and Artois and Picardy
And had done valiantly in little space
Of time, in hope to win his lady's grace.
He was embroidered like a meadow bright
And full of freshest flowers, red and white.
Singing he was, or fluting all the day;
He was as fresh as is the month of May.
Short was his gown, the sleeves were long and wide;
He knew the way to sit a horse and ride.
He could make songs and poems and recite,
Knew how to joust and dance, to draw and write.
He loved so hotly that till dawn grew pale
He slept as little as a nightingale.
Courteous he was, lowly and serviceable,
And carved to serve his father at the table.

There was a *Yeoman* with him at his side,
No other servant; so he chose to ride.
This Yeoman wore a coat and hood of green,
And peacock-feathered arrows, bright and keen
And neatly sheathed, hung at his belt the while
– For he could dress his gear in yeoman style,
His arrows never drooped their feathers low –
And in his hand he bore a mighty bow.
His head was like a nut, his face was brown.
He knew the whole of woodcraft up and down.
A saucy brace was on his arm to ward
It from the bow-string, and a shield and sword
Hung at one side, and at the other slipped
A jaunty dirk, spear-sharp and well-equipped.
A medal of St Christopher he wore
Of shining silver on his breast, and bore
A hunting-horn, well slung and burnished clean,
That dangled from a baldrick of bright green.
He was a proper forester I guess.

There also was a *Nun*, a Prioress,
Her way of smiling very simple and coy.
Her greatest oath was only 'By St Loy!'
And she was known as Madam Eglantyne.
And well she sang a service, with a fine
Intoning through her nose, as was most seemly,
And she spoke daintily in French, extremely,
After the school of Stratford-atte-Bowe;
French in the Paris style she did not know.
At meat her manners were well taught withal;
No morsel from her lips did she let fall,
Nor dipped her fingers in the sauce too deep;
But she could carry a morsel up and keep
The smallest drop from falling on her breast.
For courtliness she had a special zest,
And she would wipe her upper lip so clean
That not a trace of grease was to be seen
Upon the cup when she had drunk; to eat,
She reached a hand sedately for the meat.
She certainly was very entertaining,
Pleasant and friendly in her ways, and straining
To counterfeit a courtly kind of grace,
A stately bearing fitting to her place,
And to seem dignified in all her dealings.
As for her sympathies and tender feelings,

Noblemen riding through the country were escorted by their squires, knights and men-at-arms, not only for their protection but to demonstrate their rank and authority. Here the Dukes of Exeter and Surrey are shown riding on a mission to Henry, Duke of Lancaster, probably the richest man in England. Chaucer wrote the *Book of the Duchess* to mark the death of Henry's daughter, Blanche, from the plague.

She was so charitably solicitous
She used to weep if she but saw a mouse
Caught in a trap, if it were dead or bleeding.
And she had little dogs she would be feeding
With roasted flesh, or milk, or fine white bread.
And bitterly she wept if one were dead
Or someone took a stick and made it smart;
She was all sentiment and tender heart.
Her veil was gathered in a seemly way,
Her nose was elegant, her eyes glass-grey;
Her mouth was very small, but soft and red,
Her forehead, certainly, was fair of spread,
Almost a span across the brows, I own;
She was indeed by no means undergrown.
Her cloak, I noticed, had a graceful charm.
She wore a coral trinket on her arm,
A set of beads, the gaudies tricked in green,★
Whence hung a golden brooch of brightest sheen
On which there first was graven a crowned A,
And lower, *Amor vincit omnia.*
  Another *Nun*, the chaplain at her cell,
Was riding with her, and *three Priests* as well.
  A *Monk* there was, one of the finest sort
Who rode the country; hunting was his sport.
A manly man, to be an Abbot able;
Many a dainty horse he had in stable.
His bridle, when he rode, a man might hear
Jingling in a whistling wind as clear,
Aye, and as loud as does the chapel bell
Where my lord Monk was Prior of the cell.
The Rule of good St Benet or St Maur
As old and strict he tended to ignore;
He let go by the things of yesterday
And took the modern world's more spacious way.
He did not rate that text at a plucked hen
Which says that hunters are not holy men
And that a monk uncloistered is a mere
Fish out of water, flapping on the pier,
That is to say a monk out of his cloister.
That was a text he held not worth an oyster;
And I agreed and said his views were sound;
Was he to study till his head went round
Poring over books in cloisters? Must he toil
As Austin bade and till the very soil?

Was he to leave the world upon the shelf?
Let Austin have his labour to himself.
    This Monk was therefore a good man to horse;
Greyhounds he had, as swift as birds, to course.
Hunting a hare or riding at a fence
Was all his fun, he spared for no expense.
I saw his sleeves were garnished at the hand
With fine grey fur, the finest in the land,
And on his hood, to fasten it at his chin
He had a wrought-gold cunningly fashioned pin;
Into a lover's knot it seemed to pass.
His head was bald and shone like looking-glass;
So did his face, as if it had been greased.
He was a fat and personable priest;
His prominent eyeballs never seemed to settle.
They glittered like the flames beneath a kettle;
Supple his boots, his horse in fine condition.
He was a prelate fit for exhibition,
He was not pale like a tormented soul.
He liked a fat swan best, and roasted whole.
His palfrey was as brown as is a berry.
    There was a *Friar*, a wanton one and merry,
A Limiter,⋆ a very festive fellow.
In all Four Orders⋆ there was none so mellow,
So glib with gallant phrase and well-turned speech.
He'd fixed up many a marriage, giving each
Of his young women what he could afford her.
He was a noble pillar to his Order.
Highly beloved and intimate was he
With County folk within his boundary,
And city dames of honour and possessions;
For he was qualified to hear confessions,
Or so he said, with more than priestly scope;
He had a special licence from the Pope.
Sweetly he heard his penitents at shrift
With pleasant absolution, for a gift.
He was an easy man in penance-giving
Where he could hope to make a decent living;
It's a sure sign whenever gifts are given
To a poor Order that a man's well shriven,
And should he give enough he knew in verity
The penitent repented in sincerity.
For many a fellow is so hard of heart
He cannot weep, for all his inward smart.

A peasant coaxes a reluctant horse drawing a harrow. The man behind carries a sling shot and a pouch full of stones. He has missed with his last shot.

Therefore instead of weeping and of prayer
One should give silver for a poor Friar's care.
He kept his tippet stuffed with pins for curls,
And pocket-knives, to give to pretty girls.
And certainly his voice was gay and sturdy,
For he sang well and played the hurdy-gurdy.
At sing-songs he was champion of the hour.
His neck was whiter than a lily-flower
But strong enough to butt a bruiser down.
He knew the taverns well in every town
And every innkeeper and barmaid too
Better than lepers, beggars and that crew,
For in so eminent a man as he
It was not fitting with the dignity
Of his position, dealing with a scum
Of wretched lepers; nothing good can come
Of dealings with the slum-and-gutter dwellers,
But only with the rich and victual-sellers.
But anywhere a profit might accrue
Courteous he was and lowly of service too.
Natural gifts like his were hard to match.
He was the finest beggar of his batch,
And, for his begging-district, paid a rent;
His brethren did no poaching where he went.
For though a widow mightn't have a shoe,
So pleasant was his holy how-d'ye-do
He got his farthing from her just the same
Before he left, and so his income came
To more than he laid out. And how he romped,
Just like a puppy! He was ever prompt
To arbitrate disputes on settling days
(For a small fee) in many helpful ways,
Not then appearing as your cloistered scholar
With threadbare habit hardly worth a dollar,

But much more like a Doctor or a Pope.
Of double-worsted was the semi-cope
Upon his shoulders, and the swelling fold
About him, like a bell about its mould
When it is casting, rounded out his dress.
He lisped a little out of wantonness
To make his English sweet upon his tongue.
When he had played his harp, or having sung,
His eyes would twinkle in his head as bright
As any star upon a frosty night.
This worthy's name was Hubert, it appeared.

   There was a *Merchant* with a forking beard
And motley dress; high on his horse he sat,
Upon his head a Flemish beaver hat
And on his feet daintily buckled boots.
He told of his opinions and pursuits
In solemn tones, and how he never lost.
The sea should be kept free at any cost
(He thought) upon the Harwich–Holland range;
He was expert at currency exchange.
This estimable Merchant so had set
His wits to work, none knew he was in debt,
He was so stately in negotiation,
Loan, bargain and commercial obligation.
He was an excellent fellow all the same;
To tell the truth I do not know his name.

   An *Oxford Cleric*, still a student though,
One who had taken logic long ago,
Was there; his horse was thinner than a rake,
And he was not too fat, I undertake,
But had a hollow look, a sober stare;
The thread upon his overcoat was bare.
He had found no preferment in the church
And he was too unworldly to make search
For secular employment. By his bed
He preferred having twenty books in red
And black, of Aristotle's philosophy,
To having fine clothes, fiddle or psaltery.
Though a philosopher, as I have told,
He had not found the stone for making gold.
Whatever money from his friends he took
He spent on learning or another book
And prayed for them most earnestly, returning
Thanks to them thus for paying for his learning.

This proud figure is a medieval knight in civil dress. His costume illustrates the sumptuous and elegant attire of the upper classes.

His only care was study, and indeed
He never spoke a word more than was need,
Formal at that, respectful in the extreme,
Short, to the point, and lofty in his theme.
The thought of moral virtue filled his speech
And he would gladly learn, and gladly teach.
    A *Serjeant at the Law* who paid his calls,
Wary and wise, for clients at St Paul's★
There also was, of noted excellence.
Discreet he was, a man to reverence,
Or so he seemed, his sayings were so wise.
He often had been Justice of Assize
By letters patent, and in full commission.
His fame and learning and his high position
Had won him many a robe and many a fee.
There was no such conveyancer as he;
All was fee-simple to his strong digestion,
Not one conveyance could be called in question.
Nowhere there was so busy a man as he;
But was less busy than he seemed to be.
He knew of every judgement, case and crime
Recorded, ever since King William's time.
He could dictate defences or draft deeds;
No one could pinch a comma from his screeds,
And he knew every statute off by rote.
He wore a homely parti-coloured coat
Girt with a silken belt of pin-stripe stuff;
Of his appearance I have said enough.
    There was a *Franklin*★ with him, it appeared;
White as a daisy-petal was his beard.
A sanguine man, high-coloured and benign,
He loved a morning sop of cake in wine.
He lived for pleasure and had always done,
For he was Epicurus' very son,
In whose opinion sensual delight
Was the one true felicity in sight.
As noted as St Julian was for bounty
He made his household free to all the County.
His bread, his ale were finest of the fine
And no one had a better stock of wine.
His house was never short of bake-meat pies,
Of fish and flesh, and these in such supplies
It positively snowed with meat and drink
And all the dainties that a man could think.

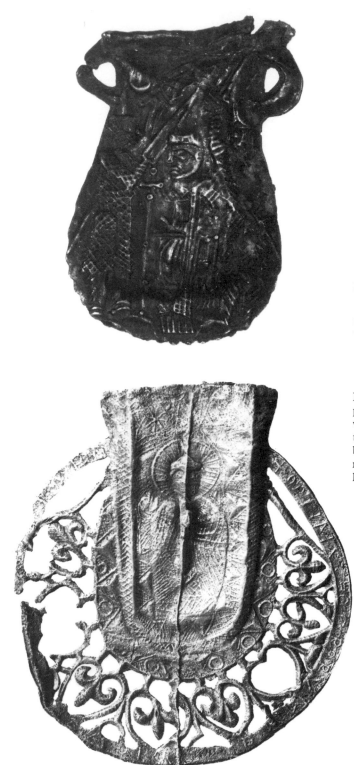

A pewter ampulla of the sort taken back from Canterbury by pilgrims. St Thomas was supposed to heal the sick and the ampulla would be filled with holy water.

Pilgrimages were an act of piety and pilgrims proudly recorded them by wearing the badges they obtained at the various shrines. Some of these badges are shown here. One represents St Thomas à Becket on horseback.

According to the seasons of the year
Changes of dish were ordered to appear.
He kept fat partridges in coops, beyond,
Many a bream and pike were in his pond.
Woe to the cook whose sauces had no sting
Or who was unprepared in anything!
And in his hall a table stood arrayed
And ready all day long, with places laid.
As Justice at the Sessions none stood higher;
He often had been Member for the Shire.
A dagger and a little purse of silk
Hung at his girdle, white as morning milk.
As Sheriff he checked audit, every entry.
He was a model among landed gentry.

    A *Haberdasher*, a *Dyer*, a *Carpenter*,
A *Weaver* and a *Carpet-maker* were
Among our ranks, all in the livery
Of one impressive guild-fraternity.
They were so trim and fresh their gear would pass
For new. Their knives were not tricked out with brass
But wrought with purest silver, which avouches
A like display on girdles and on pouches.
Each seemed a worthy burgess, fit to grace
A guild-hall with a seat upon the dais.
Their wisdom would have justified a plan
To make each one of them an alderman;
They had the capital and revenue,
Besides their wives declared it was their due.
And if they did not think so, then they ought;
To be called '*Madam*' is a glorious thought,
And so is going to church and being seen
Having your mantle carried like a queen.

    They had a *Cook* with them who stood alone
For boiling chicken with a marrow-bone,
Sharp flavouring-powder and a spice for savour.
He could distinguish London ale by flavour,
And he could roast and seethe and broil and fry,
Make good thick soup and bake a tasty pie.
But what a pity – so it seemed to me,
That he should have an ulcer on his knee.
As for blancmange, he made it with the best.

    There was a *Skipper* hailing from far west;
He came from Dartmouth, so I understood.
He rode a farmer's horse as best he could,

Scenes such as this were common
in the monasteries and convents
scattered through the country. Here
a semi-choir of minoresses, nuns of
the second order of Saint Francis
known as the Poor Clares, sing the
Divine Office (see also [6] in colour
section on Religion).

In a woollen gown that reached his knee.
A dagger on a lanyard falling free
Hung from his neck under his arm and down.
The summer heat had tanned his colour brown,
And certainly he was an excellent fellow.
Many a draught of vintage, red and yellow,
He'd drawn at Bordeaux, while the trader snored.
The nicer rules of conscience he ignored.
If, when he fought, the enemy vessel sank,
He sent his prisoners home; they walked the plank.
As for his skill in reckoning his tides,
Currents and many another risk besides,
Moons, harbours, pilots, he had such dispatch
That none from Hull to Carthage was his match.
Hardy he was, prudent in undertaking;
His beard in many a tempest had its shaking,
And he knew all the havens as they were
From Gottland to the Cape of Finisterre,
And every creek in Brittany and Spain;
The barge he owned was called *The Maudelayne.*
    A *Doctor* too emerged as we proceeded;
No one alive could talk as well as he did
On points of medicine and of surgery,
For, being grounded in astronomy,
He watched his patient's favourable star
And, by his Natural Magic, knew what are
The lucky hours and planetary degrees
For making charms and magic effigies.
The cause of every malady you'd got
He knew, and whether dry, cold, moist or hot;★
He knew their seat, their humour and condition.
He was a perfect practising physician.
These causes being known for what they were,
He gave the man his medicine then and there.
All his apothecaries in a tribe
Were ready with the drugs he would prescribe
And each made money from the other's guile;
They had been friendly for a goodish while.
He was well-versed in Aesculapius★ too
And what Hippocrates and Rufus knew
And Dioscorides, now dead and gone,
Galen and Rhazes, Hali, Serapion,
Averroes, Avicenna, Constantine,
Scotch Bernard, John of Gaddesden, Gilbertine.

Cathedral canons in their stalls.
A kneeling, tonsured priest on the
right holds a book before
the bishop who wears his mitre and
carries his crozier.

In his own diet he observed some measure;
There were no superfluities for pleasure,
Only digestives, nutritives and such.
He did not read the Bible very much.
In blood-red garments, slashed with bluish-grey
And lined with taffeta, he rode his way;
Yet he was rather close as to expenses
And kept the gold he won in pestilences.
Gold stimulates the heart, or so we're told.
He therefore had a special love of gold.

    A worthy *woman* from beside *Bath* city
Was with us, somewhat deaf, which was a pity.
In making cloth she showed so great a bent
She bettered those of Ypres and of Ghent.
In all the parish not a dame dared stir
Towards the altar steps in front of her,
And if indeed they did, so wrath was she
As to be quite put out of charity.
Her kerchiefs were of finely woven ground;
I dared have sworn they weighed a good ten pound,
The ones she wore on Sunday, on her head.
Her hose were of the finest scarlet red
And gartered tight; her shoes were soft and new.
Bold was her face, handsome, and red in hue.
A worthy woman all her life, what's more
She'd had five husbands, all at the church door,
Apart from other company in youth;
No need just now to speak of that, forsooth.
And she had thrice been to Jerusalem,
Seen many strange rivers and passed over them;
She'd been to Rome and also to Boulogne,
St James of Compostella and Cologne,
And she was skilled in wandering by the way.
She had gap-teeth, set widely, truth to say.
Easily on an ambling horse she sat
Well wimpled up, and on her head a hat
As broad as is a buckler or a shield;
She had a flowing mantle that concealed
Large hips, her heels spurred sharply under that.
In company she liked to laugh and chat
And knew the remedies for love's mischances,
An art in which she knew the oldest dances.

    A holy-minded man of good renown
There was, and poor, the *Parson* to a town,

Yet he was rich in holy thought and work.
He also was a learned man, a clerk,
Who truly knew Christ's gospel and would preach it
Devoutly to parishioners, and teach it.
Benign and wonderfully diligent,
And patient when adversity was sent
(For so he proved in great adversity)
He much disliked extorting tithe or fee,
Nay rather he preferred beyond a doubt
Giving to poor parishioners round about
From his own goods and Easter offerings.
He found sufficiency in little things.
Wide was his parish, with houses far asunder,
Yet he neglected not in rain or thunder,
In sickness or in grief, to pay a call
On the remotest, whether great or small,
Upon his feet, and in his hand a stave.
This noble example to his sheep he gave,
First following the word before he taught it,
And it was from the gospel he had caught it.
This little proverb he would add thereto
That if gold rust, what then will iron do?
For if a priest be foul in whom we trust
No wonder that a common man should rust;
And shame it is to see – let priests take stock –
A shitten shepherd and a snowy flock.
The true example that a priest should give
Is one of cleanness, how the sheep should live.
He did not set his benefice to hire
And leave his sheep encumbered in the mire
Or run to London to earn easy bread
By singing masses for the wealthy dead,
Or find some Brotherhood and get enrolled.
He stayed at home and watched over his fold
So that no wolf should make the sheep miscarry.
He was a shepherd and no mercenary.
Holy and virtuous he was, but then
Never contemptuous of sinful men,
Never disdainful, never too proud or fine,
But was discreet in teaching and benign.
His business was to show a fair behaviour
And draw men thus to Heaven and their Saviour,
Unless indeed a man were obstinate;
And such, whether of high or low estate,

An important functionary in the monasteries and religious houses was the cellarer. Here we see the cellarer of St Albans carrying the keys and purse which were the symbols of his office.

He put to sharp rebuke to say the least.
I think there never was a better priest.
He sought no pomp or glory in his dealings,
No scrupulosity had spiced his feelings.
Christ and His Twelve Apostles and their lore
He taught, but followed it himself before.
  There was a *Plowman* with him there, his brother.
Many a load of dung one time or other
He must have carted through the morning dew.
He was an honest worker, good and true,
Living in peace and perfect charity,
And, as the gospel bade him, so did he,
Loving God best with all his heart and mind
And then his neighbour as himself, repined
At no misfortune, slacked for no content,
For steadily about his work he went
To thrash his corn, to dig or to manure
Or make a ditch; and he would help the poor
For love of Christ and never take a penny
If he could help it, and, as prompt as any,
He paid his tithes in full when they were due
On what he owned, and on his earnings too.
He wore a tabard smock and rode a mare.
  There was a *Reeve*, also a *Miller*, there,
A College *Manciple* from the Inns of Court,
A papal *Pardoner* and, in close consort,
A Church-Court *Summoner*, riding at a trot,
And finally myself – that was the lot.
  The *Miller* was a chap of sixteen stone,
A great stout fellow big in brawn and bone.
He did well out of them, for he could go
And win the ram at any wrestling show.
Broad, knotty and short-shouldered, he would boast
He could heave any door off hinge and post,
Or take a run and break it with his head.
His beard, like any sow or fox, was red
And broad as well, as though it were a spade;
And, at its very tip, his nose displayed
A wart on which there stood a tuft of hair
Red as the bristles in an old sow's ear.
His nostrils were as black as they were wide.
He had a sword and buckler at his side,
His mighty mouth was like a furnace door.
A wrangler and buffoon, he had a store

A knight was unable to dress himself in his cumbersome and heavy armour and usually had the services of a squire for this; in this picture, however, the knight is being girded with his sword by a lady, in whose honour, perhaps, he is about to fight.

Of tavern stories, filthy in the main.
His was a master-hand at stealing grain.
He felt it with his thumb and thus he knew
Its quality and took three times his due –
A thumb of gold, by God, to gauge an oat!
He wore a hood of blue and a white coat.
He liked to play his bagpipes up and down
And that was how he brought us out of town.

    The *Manciple* came from the Inner Temple;
All caterers might follow his example
In buying victuals; he was never rash
Whether he bought on credit or paid cash.
He used to watch the market most precisely
And got in first, and so he did quite nicely.
Now isn't it a marvel of God's grace
That an illiterate fellow can outpace
The wisdom of a heap of learned men?
His masters – he had more than thirty then –
All versed in the abstrusest legal knowledge,
Could have produced a dozen from their College
Fit to be stewards in land and rents and game
To any Peer in England you could name,
And show him how to live on what he had
Debt-free (unless of course the Peer were mad)
Or be as frugal as he might desire,
And they were fit to help about the Shire
In any legal case there was to try;
And yet this Manciple could wipe their eye.

    The *Reeve*★ was old and choleric and thin;
His beard was shaven closely to the skin,
His shorn hair came abruptly to a stop
Above his ears, and he was docked on top
Just like a priest in front; his legs were lean,
Like sticks they were, no calf was to be seen.
He kept his bins and garners very trim;
No auditor could gain a point on him.
And he could judge by watching drought and rain
The yield he might expect from seed and grain.
His master's sheep, his animals and hens,
Pigs, horses, dairies, stores and cattle-pens
Were wholly trusted to his government.
And he was under contract to present
The accounts, right from his master's earliest years.
No one had ever caught him in arrears.

Westminster Abbey was founded by Edward the Confessor but the main parts, including the cloisters – the north walk is shown here – were built in the thirteenth and fourteenth centuries. Chaucer, who at the end of his life lived near the Abbey, must often have walked here.

(*Opposite*) A passageway in Penshurst Place in Kent which was built during Chaucer's lifetime by Sir John de Pulteney, a Lord Mayor of London who helped to finance the Hundred Years War.

No bailiff, self or herdsman dared to kick,
He knew their dodges, knew their every trick;
Feared like the plague he was, by those beneath.
He had a lovely dwelling on a heath,
Shadowed in green by trees above the sward.
A better hand at bargains than his lord,
He had grown rich and had a store of treasure
Well tucked away, yet out it came to pleasure
His lord with subtle loans or gifts of goods,
To earn his thanks and even coats and hoods.
When young he'd learnt a useful trade and still
He was a carpenter of first-rate skill.
The stallion-cob he rode at a slow trot
Was dapple-grey and bore the name of Scot.
He wore an overcoat of bluish shade
And rather long; he had a rusty blade
Slung at his side. He came, as I heard tell,
From Norfolk, near a place called Baldeswell.
His coat was tucked under his belt and splayed.
He rode the hindmost of our cavalcade.
 There was a *Summoner* with us in the place
Who had a fire-red cherubinnish face,*
For he had carbuncles. His eyes were narrow,
He was as hot and lecherous as a sparrow.
Black, scabby brows he had, and a thin beard.
Children were afraid when he appeared.
No quicksilver, lead ointments, tartar creams,
Boracic, no, nor brimstone, so it seems,
Could make a salve that had the power to bite,
Clean up or cure his whelks of knobby white
Or purge the pimples sitting on his cheeks.
Garlic he loved, and onions too, and leeks,
And drinking strong red wine till all was hazy.
Then he would shout and jabber as if crazy,
And wouldn't speak a word except in Latin
When he was drunk, such tags as he was pat in;
He only had a few, say two or three,
That he had mugged up out of some decree;
No wonder, for he heard them every day.
And, as you know, a man can teach a jay
To call out 'Walter' better than the Pope.
But had you tried to test his wits and grope
For more, you'd have found nothing in the bag.
Then '*Questio quid juris*' was his tag.*

Magic and Medicine - Trades and Professions

When Chaucer was a small boy bubonic plagues swept through Europe. In England the plague, known as the Black Death, claimed thousands of victims, and did much to change the face of the country, for whole villages ceased to exist and landowners were ruined. The picture (1) shows a priest, himself exposed to the disease, performing the last rites for some victims. Medical knowledge was very restricted and generally only the rich had access to it. For the great majority of people magic held out more hope. Sorcerers, witches, village wise women were often the doctors of the time, prescribing anything from love philtres to medicine, with often quite revolting ingredients. The doctors' prescriptions were rarely much better. Picture (2) shows a man consulting a sorceress who is supported by her grotesque familiars. Picture (3) illustrates more orthodox treatment. The patient is being bled, a medical practice which was to be a favourite resort of doctors for

centuries to come. Below (4) we see a patient submitting a flask of urine for inspection. The consulting room, with its sparse and uncomfortable furniture, gives a good impression of the interior architecture of the time. Pictures (5) and (6) come from the *Ellesmere Chronicle*, an edition of *The Canterbury Tales* published shortly after Chaucer's death. Each of the Tales is embellished with a picture of the character and we are thus indebted to the *Chronicle* for almost contemporary pictures of what Chaucer's pilgrims would have looked like. Picture (5) shows the Physician and (6) the Merchant.

The large picture (7) shows business being conducted in what is probably a goldsmith's shop of the period. The goods appear to be of high quality and the shop efficiently run, for a clerk is seated at the table recording the transaction as the shopkeeper bargains with the customer. The latter appears to be a

1

2
3

4

5

6

wealthy man and is accompanied by a servant to whom he has handed his purchases. The goods consist mainly of cups and flagons but hanging on a rod behind are other goods including a sword, belt and purse. Next (8) is a rather more humble shop – that of a mercer dealing in general wares. The customer is inspecting a mirror and it is amusing that the artist, incapable of showing the two objects in the mercer's hands as mirrors, makes the point by drawing the reflections of people who are not there. The next picture (9) shows the interior of a medieval apothecary's shop, the shelves lined with flasks containing mysterious medicines and elixirs. In picture (10) we see an artist painting three nude models. Not only is the easel practically identical with that of a modern artist but in his left hand the painter holds a palette and a maulstick, supporting his left hand precisely as artists do today.

Picture (11) epitomizes much of the social fabric of medieval times. It shows the warden of a guild examining apprentices who are seeking to be recognized as masters of their craft. The piece of work submitted at this test gave rise to the word 'masterpiece'. The guilds – many city halls, as in London, are still called guildhalls – had by Chaucer's time become rich and powerful and added to the development of a prosperous merchant class. The trade guilds played a vital part in establishing the high standards of craftsmanship which were typical of the period. A newcomer to a trade served an apprenticeship lasting for several years, usually living in his master's home. At the end of his indentures if he passed his test he became a journeyman, earning a daily wage. If his 'masterpiece' received the approval of the guild he became a master himself. The guilds had another important function, not only setting the standards to be observed by their members but fixing the prices to be charged for their wares. They also cared for the members and their families in distress. The guilds were often involved with the organization of pageants (of which the Lord Mayor's Show is a survival) and of the mystery or miracle plays in which, although bound up with the Church, lay the beginnings of theatre in England.

The merchant guilds also played a big part in the development of education, founding many of the schools which later were to become known as grammar schools. Although only a minority of the population of England could read or write there was developing a pronounced popular interest in education and reading and writing were no longer confined to priests and monks. Wealthy men were acquiring libraries and, more important, an interest in their contents, and most gentlemen had a few books. In his *English Social History*, G. M. Trevelyan says 'apart from books of piety, Latin classics taught at school, and heavy tomes of learning for real scholars the commonest types of reading among gentry and

12

burghers were chronicles of England and France in verse and in prose, endless romances in prose and in "rhyme doggrel" about Troy, King Arthur and a hundred other traditional tales. . . . Of lighter literature there was little except ballads, and they were more often recited or chanted than written or read.' But the actual writing and illustration of what books there were, for printing had of course not yet been invented, remained in the hands of scholars and scribes of varying degrees of competence, most of whom, if they were not professionals, had acquired a professional skill. Picture (12) shows a scribe seated in an ingenious chair equipped with a shelf for writing. In his right hand is a pen and in his left what is either a ruler to ensure straight lines or a knife to make erasures on the parchment.

The characteristic costumes
of the clergy—an abbot, a clerk
and a bishop

He was a gentle varlet and a kind one,
No better fellow if you went to find one.
He would allow–just for a quart of wine–
Any good lad to keep a concubine
A twelvemonth and dispense it altogether!
Yet he could pluck a finch to leave no feather:
And if he found some rascal with a maid
He would instruct him not to be afraid
In such a case of the Archdeacon's curse
(Unless the rascal's soul were in his purse)
For in his purse the punishment should be.
'Purse is the good Archdeacon's Hell,' said he.
But well I know he lied in what he said;
A curse should put a guilty man in dread,
For curses kill, as shriving brings, salvation.
We should beware of excommunication.
Thus, as he pleased, the man could bring duress
On any young fellow in the diocese.
He knew their secrets, they did what he said.
He wore a garland set upon his head
Large as the holly-bush upon a stake
Outside an ale-house, and he had a cake,
A round one, which it was his joke to wield
As if it were intended for a shield.
  He and a gentle *Pardoner** rode together,
A bird from Charing Cross of the same feather,
Just back from visiting the Court of Rome.
He loudly sang '*Come hither, love, come home!*'
The Summoner sang deep seconds to this song,
No trumpet ever sounded half so strong.
This Pardoner had hair as yellow as wax,
Hanging down smoothly like a hank of flax.
In driblets fell his locks behind his head
Down to his shoulders which they overspread;
Thinly they fell, like rat-tails, onc by one.
He wore no hood upon his head, for fun;
The hood inside his wallet had been stowed,
He aimed at riding in the latest mode;
But for a little cap his head was bare
And he had bulging eye-balls, like a hare.
He'd sewed a holy relic on his cap;
His wallet lay before him on his lap,
Brimful of pardons come from Rome all hot.
He had the same small voice a goat has got.

His chin no beard had harboured, nor would harbour,
Smoother than ever chin was left by barber.
I judge he was a gelding, or a mare.
As to his trade, from Berwick down to Ware
There was no pardoner of equal grace,
For in his trunk he had a pillow-case
Which he asserted was Our Lady's veil.
He said he had a gobbet of the sail
Saint Peter had the time when he made bold
To walk the waves, till Jesu Christ took hold.
He had a cross of metal set with stones
And, in a glass, a rubble of pigs' bones.
And with these relics, any time he found
Some poor up-country parson to astound,
On one short day, in money down, he drew
More than the parson in a month or two,
And by his flatteries and prevarication
Made monkeys of the priest and congregation.
But still to do him justice first and last
In church he was a noble ecclesiast.
How well he read a lesson or told a story!
But best of all he sang an Offertory,
For well he knew that when that song was sung
He'd have to preach and tune his honey-tongue
And (well he could) win silver from the crowd.
That's why he sang so merrily and loud.

Now I have told you shortly, in a clause,
The rank, the array, the number and the cause
Of our assembly in this company
In Southwark, at that high-class hostelry
Known as *The Tabard*, close beside *The Bell*.
And now the time has come for me to tell
How we behaved that evening; I'll begin
After we had alighted at the Inn,
Then I'll report our journey, stage by stage,
All the remainder of our pilgrimage.
But first I beg of you, in courtesy,
Not to condemn me as unmannerly
If I speak plainly and with no concealings
And give account for all their words and dealings,
Using their very phrases as they fell.
For certainly, as you all know so well,
He who repeats a tale after a man
Is bound to say, as nearly as he can,

A parish clerk, his aspersion in his left hand, sprinkles with holy water first the cook and her cooking pot, then the knight and lady and the table on which their meal is spread.

Each single word, if he remembers it,
However rudely spoken or unfit,
Or else the tale he tells will be untrue,
The things invented and the phrases new.
He may not flinch although it were his brother,
If he says one word he must say the other.
And Christ Himself spoke broad in Holy Writ,
And as you know there's nothing there unfit,
And Plato says, for those with power to read,
'The word should be as cousin to the deed.'
Further I beg you to forgive it me
If I neglect the order and degree
And what is due to rank in what I've planned.
I'm short of wit as you will understand.

Our *Host* gave us great welcome; everyone
Was given a place and supper was begun.
He served the finest victuals you could think,
The wine was strong and we were glad to drink.
A very striking man our Host withal,
And fit to be a marshal in a hall.
His eyes were bright, his girth a little wide;
There is no finer burgess in Cheapside.
Bold in his speech, yet wise and full of tact,
There was no manly attribute he lacked,
What's more he was a merry-hearted man.
After our meal he jokingly began
To talk of sport, and, among other things
After we'd settled up our reckonings,
He said as follows: 'Truly, gentlemen,
You're very welcome and I can't think when
–Upon my word I'm telling you no lie–
I've seen a gathering here that looked so spry,
No, not this year, as in this tavern now.
I'd think you up some fun if I knew how.
And, as it happens, a thought has just occurred
And it will cost you nothing, on my word.
You're off to Canterbury–well, God speed!
Blessed St Thomas answer to your need!
And I don't doubt, before the journey's done
You mean to while the time in tales and fun.
Indeed, there's little pleasure for your bones
Riding along and all as dumb as stones.
So let me then propose for your enjoyment,
Just as I said, a suitable employment.

And if my notion suits and you agree
And promise to submit yourselves to me
Playing your parts exactly as I say
Tomorrow as you ride along the way,
Then by my father's soul (and he is dead)
If you don't like it you can have my head!
Hold up your hands, and not another word.'
   Well, our consent of course was not deferred,
It seemed not worth a serious debate;
We all agreed to it at any rate
And bade him issue what commands he would.
'My lords,' he said, 'now listen for your good,
And please don't treat my notion with disdain.
This is the point. I'll make it short and plain.
Each one of you shall help to make things slip
By telling two stories on the outward trip
To Canterbury, that's what I intend,
And, on the homeward way to journey's end
Another two, tales from the days of old;
And then the man whose story is best told,
That is to say who gives the fullest measure
Of good morality and general pleasure,
He shall be given a supper, paid by all,
Here in this tavern, in this very hall,
When we come back again from Canterbury.

This picture of Chaucer comes from the Ellesmere Chronicle which dates from just after his death. It is probably an authentic likeness of the poet.

And in the hope to keep you bright and merry
I'll go along with you myself and ride
All at my own expense and serve as guide.
I'll be the judge, and those who won't obey
Shall pay for what we spend upon the way.
Now if you all agree to what you've heard
Tell me at once without another word,
And I will make arrangements early for it.'
   Of course we all agreed, in fact we swore it
Delightedly, and made entreaty too
That he should act as he proposed to do,
Become our Governor in short, and be
Judge of our tales and general referee,
And set the supper at a certain price.
We promised to be ruled by his advice
Come high, come low; unanimously thus
We set him up in judgement over us.
More wine was fetched, the business being done;
We drank it off and up went everyone

45

To bed without a moment of delay.
   Early next morning at the spring of day
Up rose our Host and roused us like a cock,
Gathering us together in a flock,
And off we rode at slightly faster pace
Than walking to St Thomas' watering-place;
And there our Host drew up, began to ease
His horse, and said, 'Now, listen if you please,
My lords! Remember what you promised me.
If evensong and mattins will agree
Let's see who shall be first to tell a tale.
And as I hope to drink good wine and ale
I'll be your judge. The rebel who disobeys,
However much the journey costs, he pays.
Now draw for cut and then we can depart;
The man who draws the shortest cut shall start.
My Lord the Knight,' he said, 'step up to me
And draw your cut, for that is my decree.
And come you near, my Lady Prioress,
And you, Sir Cleric, drop your shamefastness,
No studying now! A hand from every man!'
Immediately the draw for lots began
And to tell shortly how the matter went,
Whether by chance or fate or accident,
The truth is this, the cut fell to the Knight,
Which everybody greeted with delight.
And tell his tale he must, as reason was
Because of our agreement and because
He too had sworn. What more is there to say?
For when the good man saw how matters lay,
Being by wisdom and obedience driven
To keep a promise he had freely given,
He said, 'Since it's for me to start the game,
Why, welcome be the cut in God's good name!
Now let us ride, and listen to what I say.'
And at the word we started on our way
And in a cheerful style he then began
At once to tell his tale, and thus it ran.

The Knight's Tale

PART I

Stories of old have made it known to us
That there was once a Duke called Theseus,
Ruler of Athens, Lord and Governor,
And in his time so great a conqueror
There was none mightier beneath the sun.
And many a rich country he had won,
What with his wisdom and his troops of horse.
He had subdued the Amazons by force
And all their realm, once known as Scythia,
But then called Femeny. Hippolyta,
Their queen, he took to wife, and, says the story,
He brought her home in solemn pomp and glory,
Also her younger sister, Emily.
And thus victorious and with minstrelsy

I leave this noble Duke for Athens bound
With all his host of men-at-arms around.
   And were it not too long to tell again
I would have fully pictured the campaign
In which his men-at-arms and he had won
Those territories from the Amazon
And the great battle that was given then
Between those women and the Athenian men,
Or told you how Hippolyta had been
Besieged and taken, fair courageous queen,
And what a feast there was when they were married,
And of the violence of the storm that harried
Their home-coming. I pass these over now
Having, God knows, a larger field to plough.
Weak are my oxen for such mighty stuff;
What I have yet to tell is long enough.
I won't delay the others of our rout,
Let every fellow tell his tale about
And see who wins the supper at the Inn.
Where I left off, let me again begin.
   This Duke I mentioned, ere alighting down
And on the very outskirts of the town
In all felicity and height of pride
Became aware, casting an eye aside,
That kneeling on the highway, two by two,
A company of ladies were in view
All clothed in black, each pair in proper station
Behind the other. And such lamentation
And cries they uttered, it was past conceiving
The world had ever heard such noise of grieving,
Nor did they hold their misery in check
Till they grasped bridle at his horse's neck.
   'Who may you be that, at my coming, so
Perturb my festival with cries of woe?'
Said Theseus. 'Do you grudge the celebration
Of these my honours with your lamentation?
Who can have injured you or who offended?
And tell me if the matter may be mended
And why it is that you are clothed in black?'
   The eldest of these ladies answered back,
Fainting a little in such deadly fashion
That but to see and hear her stirred compassion,
And said, 'O Sir, whom Fortune has made glorious
In conquest and is sending home victorious,

48

We do not grudge your glory in our grief
But rather beg your mercy and relief.
Have pity on our sorrowful distress!
Some drop of pity, in your nobleness,
On us unhappy women let there fall!
For sure there is not one among us all
That was not once a duchess or a queen,
Though wretches now, as may be truly seen,
Thanks be to Fortune and her treacherous wheel
That suffers no estate on earth to feel
Secure a moment. Be assured that we,
Here at the shrine of Goddess Clemency,
Have watched a fortnight for this very hour.
Help us, my Lord, it lies within your power.
I, wretched Queen, that weep aloud my woe,
Was wife to King Capaneus long ago
That died at Thebes, accursed be the day!
And we in our disconsolate array
That make this sorrowful appeal to pity
Lost each her husband in that fatal city
During the siege, for so it came to pass.
Now old King Creon – O alas, alas! –
The Lord of Thebes, grown cruel in his age
And filled with foul iniquity and rage,
For tyranny and spite as I have said
Does outrage on the bodies of our dead,
On all our husbands, for when they were killed
Their bodies were dragged out – so Creon willed –
Into a heap and there, as we have learnt,
They neither may have burial nor be burnt,
But he makes dogs devour them, in scorn.'
    At that they all at once began to mourn,
And every woman fell upon her face
And cried, 'Have pity, Lord, on our disgrace
And let our sorrow sink into your heart.'
    The Duke, who felt a pang of pity start
At what they spoke, dismounted from his steed;
He felt his heart about to break indeed,
Seeing how piteous and disconsolate
They were, that once had been of high estate!
He raised them in his arms and sought to fill
Their hearts with comfort and with kind good will,
And swore on oath that as he was true knight,
So far as it should lie within his might,

Even kings and queens followed the common practice of sleeping in the nude. Although the picture suggests that this was so except for their crowns this was merely a device by the artist to convey their rank.

He would take vengeance on this tyrant King,
This Creon, till the land of Greece should ring
With how he had encountered him and served
The monster with the death he had deserved.
Instantly then and with no more delay,
He turned and with his banners in display
Made off for Thebes with all his host beside,
For not a step to Athens would he ride,
Nor take his ease so much as half a day,
But marched into the night upon his way.
But yet he sent Hippolyta the Queen
And Emily her sister, the serene,
On into Athens, where they were to dwell,
And off he rode; there is no more to tell.

    The figure of red Mars with spear and targe
So shone upon his banners white and large,
That all the meadows glittered up and down,
And close by them his pennon of renown
Shone rich with gold, emblazoned with that feat,
His slaying of the Minotaur in Crete.
Thus rode this Duke, thus rode this conqueror
And led his flower of chivalry to war,
Until he came to Thebes, there to alight
In splendour on a chosen field to fight.
And, to speak briefly of so great a thing,
He conquered Creon there, the Theban king,
And slew him manfully, as became a knight,
In open battle, put his troops to flight,
And by assault captured the city after
And rent it, roof and wall and spar and rafter;
And to the ladies he restored again
The bones belonging to their husbands slain,
To do, as custom was, their obsequies.

    But it were all too long to speak of these,
Or of the clamorous complaint and yearning
These ladies uttered at the place of burning
The bodies, or of all the courtesy
That Theseus, noble in his victory,
Showed to the ladies when they went their way;
I would be brief in what I have to say.

    Now when Duke Theseus worthily had done
Justice on Creon and when Thebes was won,
That night, camped in the field, he took his rest,
Having disposed the land as he thought best.

Itinerant performers – acrobats,
jugglers etc. were a familiar sight in
villages and market squares, and
travelled between the great houses
where they put on their acts for
the entertainment of the members of
the households. Here a tumbler
displays his agility.

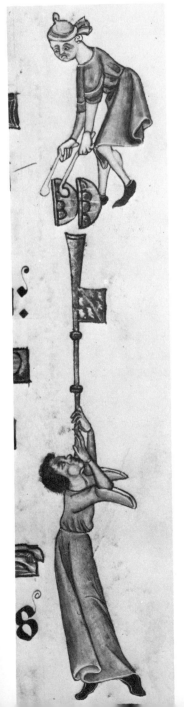

Chaucer wrote about 'pipes, trompes, nakers and clarionnes'. Here (top) are nakers – small kettledrums – and (below) a trumpet being played with verve.

Crawling for ransack among heaps of slain
And stripping their accoutrements for gain,
The pillagers went busily about
After the battle on the field of rout.
And so befell among the heaps they found,
Thrust through with bloody wounds upon the ground,
Two pale young knights there, lying side by side,
Wearing the self-same arms in blazoned pride.
Of these Arcita was the name of one,
That of the other knight was Palamon;
And they were neither fully quick nor dead.
By coat of arms and crest upon the head
The heralds knew, for all the filth and mud,
That they were Princes of the Royal Blood;
Two sisters of the House of Thebes had borne them.
Out of the heap these pillagers have torn them
And gently carried them to Theseus' tent.
And he decreed they should at once be sent
To Athens, and gave order they be kept
Perpetual prisoners – he would accept
No ransom for them. This was done, and then
The noble Duke turned homeward with his men
Crowned with the laurel of his victory,
And there in honour and felicity
He lived his life; what more is there to say?
And in a tower, in grief and anguish lay
Arcite and Palamon, beyond all doubt
For ever, for no gold could buy them out.
    Year after year went by, day after day,
Until one morning in the month of May
Young Emily, that fairer was of mien
Than is the lily on its stalk of green,
And fresher in her colouring that strove
With early roses in a May-time grove
– I know not which was fairer of the two –
Ere it was day, as she was wont to do,
Rose and arrayed her beauty as was right,
For May will have no sluggardry at night,
Season that pricks in every gentle heart,
Awaking it from sleep, and bids it start,
Saying, 'Arise! Do thine observance due!'
And this made Emily recall anew
The honour due to May and she arose,
Her beauties freshly clad. To speak of those,

Her yellow hair was braided in a tress
Behind her back, a yard in length, I guess,
And in the garden at the sun's uprising,
Hither and thither at her own devising,
She wandered gathering flowers, white and red,
To make a subtle garland for her head,
And like an angel sang a heavenly song.
    The great, grim tower-keep, so thick and strong,
Principal dungeon at the castle's core
Where the two knights, of whom I spoke before
And shall again, were shut, if you recall,
Was close-adjoining to the garden wall
Where Emily chose her pleasures and adornings.
Bright was the sun this loveliest of mornings
And the sad prisoner Palamon had risen,
With licence from the jailer of the prison,
As was his wont, and roamed a chamber high
Above the city, whence he could descry
The noble buildings and the branching green
Where Emily the radiant and serene
Went pausing in her walk and roaming on.
    This sorrowful prisoner, this Palamon,
Was pacing round his chamber to and fro
Lamenting to himself in all his woe.
'Alas,' he said, 'that ever I was born!'
And so it happened on this May day morn,
Through a deep window set with many bars
Of mighty iron squared with massive spars,
He chanced on Emily to cast his eye
And, as he did, he blenched and gave a cry
As though he had been stabbed, and to the heart.
And, at the cry, Arcita gave a start
And said, 'My cousin Palamon, what ails you?
How deadly pale you look! Your colour fails you!
Why did you cry? Who can have given offence?
For God's love, take things patiently, have sense,
Think! We are prisoners and shall always be.
Fortune has given us this adversity,
Some wicked planetary dispensation,
Some Saturn's trick or evil constellation
Has given us this, and Heaven, though we had sworn
The contrary, so stood when we were born.
We must endure it, that's the long and short.'
    And Palamon in answer made retort,

'Cousin, believe me, your opinion springs
From ignorance and vain imaginings.
Imprisonment was not what made me cry.
I have been hurt this moment through the eye,
Into my heart. It will be death to me.
The fairness of the lady that I see
Roaming the garden yonder to and fro
Is all the cause, and I cried out my woe.
Woman or Goddess, which? I cannot say.
I guess she may be Venus – well she may!'
He fell upon his knees before the sill
And prayed: 'O Venus, if it be thy will
To be transfigured in this garden thus
Before two wretched prisoners like us,
O help us to escape, O make us free!
Yet, if my fate already is shaped for me
By some eternal word, and I must pine
And die in prison, have pity on our line
And kindred, humbled under tyranny!'
     Now, as he spoke, Arcita chanced to see
This lady as she roamed there to and fro,
And, at the sight, her beauty hurt him so
That if his cousin had felt the wound before,
Arcite was hurt as much as he, or more,
And with a deep and piteous sigh he said:
'The freshness of her beauty strikes me dead,
Hers that I see, roaming in yonder place!
Unless I gain the mercy of her grace,
Unless at least I see her day by day,
I am but dead. There is no more to say.'
     On hearing this young Palamon looked grim
And in contempt and anger answered him,
'Do you speak this in earnest or in jest?'
'No, in good earnest,' said Arcite, 'the best!
So help me God, I mean no jesting now.'
     Then Palamon began to knit his brow:
'It's no great honour, then,' he said, 'to you
To prove so false, to be a traitor too
To me, that am your cousin and your brother,
Both deeply sworn and bound to one another,
Though we should die in torture for it, never
To loose the bond that only death can sever,
And when in love neither to hinder other,
Nor in what else soever, dearest brother.

A lady dresses her hair attended by
a maid with a mirror. In 'The
Knight's Tale' Chaucer, describing
Emily's beauty, writes:

Her yellow hair was braided in a tress
Behind her back, a yard in length, I guess.

Rather to further me in all, and do
As much in furthering me as I for you.
This was our oath and nothing can untie it,
And well I know you dare not now deny it.
I trust you with my secrets, make no doubt,
Yet you would treacherously go about
To love my lady, whom I love and serve
And ever shall, till death cut my heart's nerve.
No, no, you shall not, false Arcita! no,
I loved her first (O grief!) and told you so
As to the brother and the friend that swore
To further me, as I have said before,
So you are bound in honour as a knight
To help me, should it lie within your might;
Else you are false, I say, your honour vain!'
Arcita proudly answered back again:
'You shall be judged as false,' he said, 'not me;
And false you are, I tell you, utterly!
I loved her as a woman before you.
What can you say? Just now you hardly knew
If she were girl or goddess from above!
Yours is a mystical, a holy love,
And mine is love as to a human being,
And so I told you at the moment, seeing
You were my cousin and sworn friend. At worst
What do I care? Suppose you loved her first,
Haven't you heard the old proverbial saw
"Who ever bound a lover by a law?"
Love is law unto itself. My hat!
What earthly man can have more law than that?
All man-made law, all positive injunction
Is broken every day without compunction
For love. A man must love, for all his wit;
There's no escape though he should die for it,
Be she a maid, a widow or a wife.

  'Yet you are little likely, all your life,
To stand in grace with her; no more shall I.
You know yourself, too well, that here we lie
Condemned to prison both of us, no doubt
Perpetually. No ransom buys us out.
We're like two dogs in battle on their own;
They fought all day but neither got the bone,
There came a kite above them, nothing loth,
And while they fought he took it from them both.

Beheading by the sword.

And so it is in politics, dear brother,
Each for himself alone, there is no other.
Love if you want to; I shall love her too,
And that is all there is to say or do.
We're prisoners and must endure it, man,
And each of us must take what chance he can.'
    Great was the strife for many a long spell
Between them had I but the time to tell,
But to the point. It happened that one day,
To tell it you as briefly as I may,
A certain famous Duke, Perotheus,
Friend and companion of Duke Theseus
Since they were little children, came to spend
A holiday in Athens with his friend,
Visiting him for pleasure as of yore,
For there was no one living he loved more.
His feelings were as tenderly returned;
Indeed they were so fond, as I have learned,
That when one died (so ancient authors tell)
The other went to seek him down in Hell;
But that's a tale I have no time to treat.
Now this Perotheus knew and loved Arcite
In Theban days of old for many years,
And so, at his entreaty, it appears,
Arcita was awarded his release
Without a ransom; he could go in peace
And was left free to wander where he would
On one condition, be it understood,
And the condition, to speak plain, went thus,
Agreed between Arcite and Theseus,
That if Arcite was ever to be found
Even for an hour, in any land or ground
Or country of Duke Theseus, day or night,
And he were caught, it would to both seem right
That he immediately should lose his head,
No other course or remedy instead.
    Off went Arcite upon the homeward trek.
Let him beware! For he has pawned his neck.
What misery it cost him to depart!
He felt the stroke of death upon his heart,
He wept, he wailed. How piteously he cried
And secretly he thought of suicide.
He said, 'Alas the day that gave me birth!
Worse than my prison is the endless earth,

Drawing a long bow.
Drawing a cross bow.

Now I am doomed eternally to dwell
No more in Purgatory but in Hell.
Alas that ever I knew Perotheus!
For else I had remained with Theseus.
Fettered in prison and without relief.
I still had been in bliss and not in grief.
Only to see her whom I love and serve,
Though it were never granted to deserve
Her favour, would have been enough for me.
'O my dear cousin Palamon,' said he,
'Yours is the victory in this adventure.
How blissfully you serve your long indenture
In prison – prison? No, in Paradise!
How happily has Fortune cast her dice
For you! You have her presence, I the loss.
For it is possible, since your paths may cross
And you're a knight, a worthy one, and able,
That by some chance – for Fortune is unstable –
You may attain to your desire at last.
But I, that am an exile and outcast,
Barren of grace and in such deep despair
That neither earth nor water, fire nor air,
Nor any creature that is made of these
Can ever bring me help, or do me ease,
I must despair and die in my distress.
Farewell my life, my joy, my happiness!
    'Alas, why is it people so dispraise
God's providence or Fortune and her ways,
That can so often give in many a guise
Far better things than ever they devise?
One man desires to have abundant wealth,
Which brings about his murder or ill-health;
Another, freed from prison as he'd willed,
Comes home, his servants catch him, and he's killed.
Infinite are the harms that come this way;
We little know the things for which we pray.
Our ways are drunkard ways – drunk as a mouse;
A drunkard is aware he has a house,
But what he doesn't know is the way thither,
And for a drunk the way is slip and slither.
Such is our world indeed, and such are we.
How eagerly we seek felicity,
Yet are so often wrong in what we try!
Yes, we can all say that, and so can I,

In whom the foolish notion had arisen
That if I only could escape from prison
I should be well, in pure beatitude,
Whereas I am an exile from my good,
For since I may not see you, Emily,
I am but dead and there's no other remedy.'
   Now, on the other hand, poor Palamon,
When it was told him that Arcite had gone,
Fell in such grief, the tower where he was kept
Resounded to his yowling as he wept.
The very fetters on his mighty shins
Shine with his bitter tears as he begins,
'Alas, Arcite, dear cousin! In our dispute
And rivalry God knows you have the fruit.
I see you now in Thebes our native city
As free as air, with never a thought of pity
For me! You, an astute, determined man
Can soon assemble all our folk and clan
For war on Athens, make a sharp advance,
And by some treaty or perhaps by chance
Your lady may be won to be your wife
For whom, needs must, I here shall lose my life.
For, in the ways of possibility,
As you're a prisoner no more, but free,
A Prince, you have the advantage to engage
In your affair. I perish in a cage.
For I must weep and suffer while I live
In all the anguish that a cell can give
And all the torment of my love, O care
That doubles all my suffering and despair.'
   With that he felt the fire of jealousy start,
Flame in his breast and catch him by the heart
So madly that he seemed to fade and fail,
Cold as dead ashes, or as box-wood pale.
He cried, 'O cruel Gods, whose government
Binds all the world to your eternal bent,
And writes upon an adamantine table
All that your conclave has decreed as stable,
What more is man to you than to behold
A flock of sheep that cower in the fold?
For men are slain as much as other cattle,
Arrested, thrust in prison, killed in battle,
In sickness often and mischance, and fall,
Alas, too often, for no guilt at all.

An assortment of buckles and
hooks which embellished costumes
of the period.

Where is right rule in your foreknowledge, when
Such torments fall on innocent, helpless men?
Yet there is more, for added to my load,
I am to pay the duties that are owed
To God, for Him I am to curb my will
In all the lusts that cattle may fulfil.
For when a beast is dead, he feels no pain,
But after death a man must weep again
That living has endured uncounted woe;
I have no doubt that it may well be so.
I leave the answer for divines to tell,
But that there's pain on earth I know too well.
   'I have seen many a serpent, many a thief
Bring down the innocent of heart to grief,
Yet be at large and take what turn they will.
But I lie languishing in prison still.
Juno and Saturn in their jealous rage
Have almost quelled our Theban lineage;
Thebes stands in waste, her walls are broken wide.
And Venus slays me on the other side
With jealous fears of what Arcite is doing.'
   Now I will turn a little from pursuing
Palamon's thoughts, and leave him in his cell,
For I have something of Arcite to tell.
   The summer passes, and long winter nights
Double the miseries and appetites
Of lover in jail and lover free as air.
I cannot tell you which had most to bear.
To put it shortly, Palamon the pale
Lies there condemned to a perpetual jail,
Chained up in fetters till his dying breath;
Arcita is exiled on pain of death
For ever from the long-desired shore
Where lives the lady he will see no more.
   You lovers, here's a question I would offer,
Arcite or Palamon, which had most to suffer?
The one can see his lady day by day,
But he must dwell in prison, locked away.
The other's free, the world lies all before,
But never shall he see his lady more.
Judge as you please between them, you that can,
For I'll tell on my tale as I began.

Here the birth of somewhat
precocious twins is recorded. The
coffer or *huche* at the foot of the bed
was a familiar article of bedroom
furniture and was used to store
jewels and other valuables in what
was regarded as the most secure
room of the house.

A chest with the inside of the lid ornately decorated with shields and grotesque figures. It was probably made for a fourteenth-century Bishop of Durham who became Chancellor of England.

An oak chest of about A.D. 1400.

PART II

Now when Arcita got to Thebes again
Daylong he languished, crying out in pain
'Alas!' for never could he hope to see
His lady more. To sum his misery,
There never was a man so woe-begone,
Nor is, nor shall be while the world goes on.
Meat, drink and sleep – he lay of all bereft,
Thin as a shaft, as dry, with nothing left.
He pined away, his eyes were sunk and old,
Fallow his face, like ashes pale and cold,
And he went solitary and alone,
Wailing away the night and making moan;
And if the sound of music touched his ears
He wept, unable to refrain his tears.
So feeble were his spirits and so low,
And changed so much, one could not even know
Him by his voice; one heard and was in doubt.
And so for all the world he went about
Not merely like a lover on the rack
Of Eros, but more like a maniac
In melancholy madness, under strain
Of fantasy – those cells that front the brain.
Briefly, his love had turned him upside-down
In looks and disposition, toe to crown,
This poor distracted lover, Prince Arcite.
    But I shall take all day if I repeat
All that he suffered for the first two years
In cruel torment and in painful tears
At Thebes, in his home-country, as I said.
Now as he lay one night asleep in bed
The winged god Mercury, he thought, came near
And stood before him, bidding him have good cheer.
His sleep-imbuing wand he held in air,
He wore a hat upon his golden hair,
Arrayed (Arcita noticed) in the guise
He wore when closing up the hundred eyes
Of Argus, and he said, 'You are to go
To Athens. There shall be an end to woe.'
He spoke; Arcita started and woke up.
'Truly, however bitter be my cup,

To Athens I will go at once!' he said,
'Nor will I change my purpose for the dread
Of death, for I will see her. I can die
Gladly enough, if she be standing by.'
    He rose and snatched a mirror from its place
And saw what change had come upon his face,
The colour gone, the features redesigned,
And instantly it came into his mind
That being so disfigured and so wan
From the long sickness he had undergone,
He might, if he assumed a humble tone,
Live out his life in Athens unbeknown
And see his lady almost every day.
So, on the spot, he doffed his lord's array,
And dressed as a poor labourer seeking hire.
Then all alone, except for a young squire,
Who knew the secret of his misery
And was disguised as wretchedly as he,
He went to Athens by the shortest way
And came to Court. And on the following day
Arcita proffered at the gate for hire
To do what drudgery they might require
And briefly (there is little to explain)
He fell in service with a chamberlain
Who had his dwelling there with Emily.
The man was cunning and was quick to see
What work the servants did and which were good.
Arcite could carry water or hew wood,
For he was young and powerfully grown,
A tall young fellow too, and big of bone,
Fit to do any work that was ordained.
    Thus, for a year or two, Arcite remained
With Emily the bright, her page-of-state,
And gave it out his name was Philostrate.
And half so well beloved a man as he
There never was at Court, of his degree.
He was so much a gentleman by breed
He grew quite famous through the Court indeed,
And it would be a charitable notion
(They said) if Theseus offered him promotion
And put him to a service less despised
In which his virtues might be exercised.
Thus in a little while his fame had sprung
Both for good deeds and for a courteous tongue,

A game of chess in the peace and
quiet of a garden, while in the
background a gardener is at work.
Neat palings line the path and
a dog kennel is strategically placed
by the gate.

And Theseus took him and advanced him higher,
Made him his personal and chamber-squire,
And gave him money to maintain his station.
There came, moreover, men of his own nation
Secretly, year by year, and brought his dues.
He spent them cunningly, these revenues,
But honestly; none wondered at his wealth.
Three years went by in happiness and health;
He bore himself so well in peace and war
That there was no one Theseus valued more.
I leave him there in bliss, though bliss is brittle,
And turn to speak of Palamon a little.

In darkness horrible and prison tears
Poor Palamon had sat for seven years,
Pining away in sorrow and distress.
Who feels a two-fold grief and heaviness
But Palamon the love-constrained? He sits
As one that woe has sundered from his wits.
On top of that he was in prison, due
To stay there ever, not a year or two.

Who could make rhymes in English fit to vie
With martyrdom like that? Indeed, not I.
Let me pass lightly over it and say
It happened in the seventh year, in May,
The third of May (my ancient sources give
This detail in their fuller narrative),
Whether by accident or destiny,
For as events are shaped they have to be,
Soon after midnight, ere the sun had risen,
Helped by a friend, Palamon broke from prison
And fled the town as fast as he could go.
A drink had proved his jailer's overthrow,
A kind of honeyed claret he had fixed
With Theban opium and narcotics mixed.
The jailer slept all night; had he been shaken
He would have been impossible to waken.
So off runs Palamon as best he may.
The night was short and it was nearly day,
So it was necessary he should hide.
Into a grove that flanked the city's side
Palamon stalked with terror-stricken feet.
Here was, in his opinion, a retreat
In which he could conceal himself all day
And whence at nightfall he could make his way

Phlebotomy, or blood-letting,
being performed in medieval times
by a physician.

On towards Thebes and rally at his back
A host of friends all eager to attack
Duke Theseus. He would either lose his life
Or conquer and win Emily to wife.
That was his whole intention, fair and plain.
    I turn my story to Arcite again.
He little knew how close he was to care
Till Fortune brought him back into the snare.
    The busy lark, the messenger of day,
Sings salutation to the morning grey,
And fiery Phoebus rising up so bright
Sets all the Orient laughing with the light,
And with his streams he dries the dewy sheaves
And silver droplets hanging on the leaves.
And now Arcita, at the royal court,
Principal squire to Theseus, seeking sport
Has risen from bed and greets the merry day.
Thinking to do observances to May,
And musing on the point of his desires
He rode a courser full of flickering fires
Into the fields for pleasure and in play
A mile or two from where the palace lay,
And to the very grove you heard me mention
He chanced to hold his course, with the intention
To make himself a garland. There he weaves
A hawthorn-spray and honeysuckle leaves
And sings aloud against the sunny sheen
'*O Month of May, with all thy flowers and green,*
Welcome be thou, O fairest, freshest May,
Give me thy green in hope of happy day!'
    Quickly dismounting from his horse, he started
To thrust his way into the grove, light-hearted,
And roamed along the pathway on and on,
Until he came by chance where Palamon
Crouched in a bush, scarce daring to draw breath
Lest he be seen, in deadly fear of death.
He little thought Arcite had come in view,
God knows he could not have believed it true.
But it has well been said, for many a year,
'The fields have eyesight and the woods can hear.'
It's good to keep one's poise and be protected,
Since all day long we meet the unexpected.
    Little indeed Arcita, truth to say,
Thought Palamon was listening to his lay

Medieval weapons; *left to right :*
dagger, grillon, kidney and roundel.

Crouched in a bush and keeping very still.
Presently, when Arcite had roamed his fill
And sung his roundel, he began to brood
And fell at once into a sombre mood,
As do these lovers in their quaint desires,
Now on the spray, now down among the briars,
Now up, now down, like buckets in a well,
Just like a Friday morning, truth to tell,
Shining one moment and then raining fast.
So changey Venus loves to overcast
The hearts of all her folk; she, like her day,
Friday, is changeable. And so are they.
Seldom is Friday like the rest of the week.
    When he had sung Arcite began to speak,
Sighingly, sinking down as one forlorn.
'Alas,' he said, 'the day that I was born!
How long, O Juno, in thy cruelty
Wilt thou be harrying Thebes with misery?
Thou hast confounded those that played the lion,
The royal blood of Cadmus and Amphion!
Cadmus, the first of men to win renown
By building Thebes, or first in laying down
Her strong foundations, first to be crowned her king;
And I that share his lineage, I that spring
By right descent out of the royal stock,
Have fallen captive and am made a mock,
Slave to my mortal enemy, no higher
Than a contemptible, a menial squire!
Yet Juno does me even greater shame;
I dare no more acknowledge my own name.
Time was Arcita was my name by right;
Now I'm called Philostrate, not worth a mite!
Alas, fell Mars! Ah, Juno, stern of face,
You have destroyed our kin without a trace
Save for myself and Palamon, who dwells
In martyrdom, poor wretch, in Thesus' cells.
On top of this, to slay me utterly,
The fiery dart of love so burningly
Thrusts through my faithful heart with deadly hurt!
My death was shaped for me before my shirt.
You kill me with your eyes, my Emily,
You are the cause that brings my death on me!
All the remainder of my cares and needs
I'd rate no higher than a mound of weeds

64

Could I but please or earn a grateful glance!'
    And on the word he fell into a trance
A long, long time, then woke and moved apart.
    Palamon felt a cleaving in his heart
As of a cold sword suddenly gliding through.
He quaked with anger; hiding would not do
Now that he'd listened to Arcita's tale,
And with a madman's face, extinct and pale,
He started up out of his bushy thicket
And cried, 'Arcita! Traitor! False and wicked,
Now you are caught that love my lady so,
For whom I suffer all this pain and woe,
And of my blood – sworn friend – for so we swore
As I have told you many times before,
And you have cheated Theseus with this game,
False as you are, of a pretended name!
Let it be death for you or death for me.
You shall not love my lady Emily.
I, no one else, will love her! Look and know
That I am Palamon your mortal foe.
And though I have no weapon in this place,
Having escaped from prison by God's grace,
I doubt it not you shall be slain by me
Or else yield up the love of Emily.
You shan't escape me, therefore choose your part!'
    Arcite, however, full of scorn at heart,
Knowing his face and hearing what he said,
Fierce as a lion drew his sword instead
And answered him, 'By God that sits above,
Were you not sick, and lunatic for love,
And weaponless moreover in this place,
You never should so much as take a pace
Beyond this grove, but perish at my hand.
And I denounce all covenants that stand
Or are alleged, as between you and me.
Fool that you are, remember love is free
And I will love her! I defy your might.
Yet, as you are an honourable knight
Willing by battle to decide your claim,
Tomorrow, by the honour of my name
I will not fail you, nor will make it known
To anyone. To-morrow, here, alone
You'll find me as a knight, and on my oath
I shall bring arms and harness for us both;

And you shall have the right of choosing first,
Taking the best and leaving me the worst.
I'll bring you meat and drink, let that be said,
Enough for you, and clothes to make your bed.
As for my lady, should you chance to win
And kill me in this thicket we are in,
Then you can have your lady, as for me.'
And Palamon gave answer, 'I agree.'
And thus they parted at the coppice-edge
Until the morning. Each had given pledge.
    O Cupid, Cupid, lost to charity!
O realm that brooks no fellow-king in thee!
Well is it said that neither love nor power
Admit a rival, even for an hour.
Arcite and Palamon had found that out.
    So back to town Arcita turned about,
And the next morning, ere the day was light,
He filched two suits of armour by a sleight,
Fully sufficient for the work in hand,
The battle in the fields, as they had planned.
Alone as at his birth Arcita rode
And carried all the armour in a load.
There in the grove where time and place were set
These two, Arcite and Palamon, are met.
    Then slowly changed the colour in each face
Just as when hunters in the realm of Thrace
That standing in the gap will poise a spear
And wait for bear or lion to appear,
Then hear him coming, breaking through the branches,
And hear the swish of leaves upon his haunches,
And think, 'Here comes my mortal enemy!
It's either death for him or death for me.
For either I must slay him at this gap
Or he slay me, if I should have mishap.'
Just so these knights changed colour when they met,
Knowing each other and the purpose set.
There was no salutation, no 'Good day',
But without word or prelude straight away
Each of them gave his help to arm the other
As friendly as a brother with his brother;
And after that with spears of sharpened strength
They fought each other at amazing length.
You would have thought, seeing Palamon engage,
He was a lion fighting-mad with rage,

Arcite a cruel tiger, as they beat
And smote each other, or as boars that meet
And froth as white as foam upon the flood.
They fought till they were ankle-deep in blood.
And in this rage I leave them fighting thus
And turn once more to speak of Theseus.
    Now Destiny, that Minister-General
Who executes on earth and over all
That providence which God has long foreseen,
Has so much power that through the world might ween
The contrary, swearing by Yea and Nay,
It still would happen on a certain day
Though never again within a thousand years.
And certainly our appetites and fears,
Whether in war or peace, in hate or love,
Are governed by a providence above.
    This must explain why mighty Theseus found
A sudden wish to hunt with horse and hound
Especially the hart in early May.
About his bed there never dawned a day
But he was up and ready dressed to ride
With horn and hound and hunter at his side.
Hunting to him was such a keen delight
It was his ruling joy and appetite
To be a stag's destroyer, for the stars
Ruled he should serve Diana after Mars.
    Clear was the day, as I have told ere this,
And Theseus, bathed in happiness and bliss,
With fair Hippolyta, his lovely Queen,
And Emily, who was arrayed in green,
Rode out to hunt; it was a royal band.
And to the coppice lying near at hand
In which a hart – or so they told him – lay,
He led his gathering by the shortest way.
And pressing on towards a glade in sight
Down which the hart most often took to flight
Over a brook and off and out of view,
The Duke had hopes to try a course or two
With certain hounds that he had singled out;
And when he reached the glade he looked about.
Glancing towards the sun he thereupon
Beheld Arcita fighting Palamon.
They fought like boars in bravery. There go
The shining swords in circle, to and fro,

By the fifteenth century plate armour was replacing the traditional chain mail and the shield was becoming unnecessary. Some English knights brought their armour from abroad, particularly from Germany and Italy. Milan was famous for its armour, a suit of which is shown here.

So hideously that with their lightest stroke
It seemed as if they would have felled an oak.
What they could be he did not know, of course,
But he clapped spur at once into his horse
And, at a bound, he parted blow from blow,
And pulling out his sword he shouted, 'Ho!
No more on pain of death! Upon your head!
By mighty Mars the next to strike is dead,
The next to make a movement that I see!
Tell me, what sort of fellows may you be
That have the impudence to combat here
Without a judge or other overseer,
Yet as if jousting at a royal tilt?'
    Palamon answered quickly and in guilt,
'O Sir, what need of further word or breath?
Both of us have deserved to die the death,
Two wretched men, your captives, met in strife,
And each of them encumbered with his life.
And as you are a righteous judge and lord
Give neither of us refuge, and accord
No grace... Yet kill me first, in charity!
But kill my fellow too, as well as me.
Or kill him first, for little though you know,
This is Arcita and your mortal foe,
Banished by you on forfeit of his head,
For which alone he merits to be dead.
This is the man that waited at your gate
And told you that his name was Philostrate.
This is the man that mocked you many a year,
And you have made him chief equerry here.
This is the man who dares love Emily.
Now, since my day of death has come to me,
I will make full confession and go on
To say I am that woeful Palamon
That broke out of your jail feloniously.
And it is I, your mortal enemy,
That am in love with Emily the Bright
And glad to die this moment in her sight.
And so I ask for judgement and for death;
But slay my fellow in the self-same breath,
Since we have both deserved that we be slain!'
    And noble Theseus answered back again,
'This is a short conclusion. It shall stand.
Your own confession damns you out of hand.

A nun and a friar making music.
The nun is playing a shalm and the
friar a cittern, or lute, of somewhat
unusual shape.

I shall record your sentence as it stood;
There needs no torturing to make it good.
Death you shall have, by mighty Mars the Red!'
    On hearing this, the Queen began to shed
Her womanly tears, and so did Emily
And all the ladies in the company.
It seemed so very piteous to them all
That ever such misfortune should befall
Two gentlemen, that were of high estate,
And love the only cause of their debate.
They saw their bloody gashes gaping wide
And, from the greatest to the least, they cried,
'Have mercy, Lord, upon us women all!'
Down on their knees they then began to fall,
Ready to kiss his feet as there he stood.
    Abated in the end his angry mood;
Pity runs swiftly in a noble heart.
Though he had quaked with anger at the start
He had reflected, having time to pause,
Upon their trespass and upon its cause,
And though his anger at their guilt was loth
To pardon either, reason pardoned both.
For thus he argued: almost any man
Will help himself to love, if so he can,
And anyone will try to break from prison;
And then compassion in his heart had risen
Seeing these ladies weeping there together,
And in his noble heart he wondered whether
He should not show his clemency, and 'Fie,'
He thought, 'on lords who show no mercy! Why,
To be a lion both in word and deed
Towards a penitent is not to heed
His change of heart, and equal him with one
Proudly persisting in an evil done.
A lord will lack discretion among his graces
Who does not make distinction in such cases,
But weighs humility and pride as one.'
And, to be brief, his anger being done,
His eyes began to sparkle and uncloud
And having taken thought he said aloud:
'The God of Love! Ah, *Benedicite!*
How mighty and how great a lord is he!
No obstacles for him make any odds;
His miracles proclaim his power a God's.

Cupid can make of every heart and soul
Just what he pleases, such is his control.
Look at Arcita here and Palamon!
Both had escaped scot-free and could have gone
To Thebes and lived there royally; they know
That I have ever been their mortal foe;
Their lives are mine, they can make no defence;
Yet Cupid in the teeth of common sense
Has brought them here to die in melancholy!
Consider, is it not the height of folly?
What is so foolish as a man in love?
Look at them both! By God that sits above
See how they bleed! Are they not well arrayed?
Thus has their lord, the God of Love, repaid
Their services; these are his fees and wages!
And yet, in spite of that, they pose as sages,
These devotees of Love, as I recall.
But still this is the finest stroke of all,
That she, the cause of all these jolly pranks,
Has no more reason to return them thanks
Than I, and knows no more of this affair,
By God, than does a cuckoo or a hare!
Well, well, try anything once, come hot, come cold.
If we're not foolish young, we're foolish old.
I long have known myself what Love can do,
For, in my time, I was a lover too.
And therefore, knowing something of love's pain,
How violently it puts a man to strain,
As one so often caught in the same snare
I readily forgive the whole affair,
Both at the Queen's request, that on her knees
Petitions, and my sister Emily's.
But you shall swear to me and give your hands
Upon it never to attack my lands,
Or levy war on me by night or day,
But be my friends in everything you may.
I pardon you your fault. You are forgiven.'
  They swore as he had asked, and, having striven
To gain his patronage and further grace,
Were satisfied, and Theseus summed the case:
  'So far as riches go, and nobleness,
Were she a queen in question, or princess,
You would be worthy when the moment came,
Either of you, to marry. All the same,

Exposure to public humiliation was
an important feature of punishment
(e.g. stocks, pillories, etc.) in
medieval times. Here a woman
offender is paraded through the
streets in an open cart under
the eyes of the watching citizens.

Speaking as for my sister Emily,
The cause of all your strife and jealousy,
You are aware yourselves that she can never
Wed both at once, though you should fight for ever.
And one of you, come joy to him or grief,
Must go pipe tunes upon an ivy-leaf;
That is to say she cannot have you both,
However jealous you may be or loth.
And so, to put the matter in good order,
Let Destiny herself be your recorder
And shape your fortune. Listen to the close,
For here is the solution I propose.
   'My will is this, to make a flat conclusion
And end all counterpleading and confusion,
(And you will please to take it for the best)
That each shall take his freedom, east or west,
And without ransom or the threat of war;
And, a year later, neither less nor more,
Each shall return, bringing a hundred knights,
Armed for the lists and everything to rights,
Ready by battle to decide his claim
To Emily. To this I give my name,
My faith and honour, as I am a knight.
Whichever of you proves of greater might,
Or, more precisely, whether you or he,
Backed by the hundred knights allowed by me,
Can drive his foe to stake, or take his life,
To him I shall give Emily to wife,
To whom kind Fortune gives so fair a grace.
I'll build the lists upon this very place,
And God in wisdom deal my soul its due
As I shall prove an even judge and true.
There is no other way, let that be plain;
One of you must be taken or else slain.
And if this seems to you to be well said,
Think yourselves lucky, sirs, and nod your head.
That's the conclusion I've decided on.'
   Who looks delighted now but Palamon?
And who springs up rejoicing but Arcite?
And who could tell, what poetry repeat
The joy of all those present in the place
That Theseus had vouchsafed so fair a grace?
Down on their knees went everyone in sight
Returning thanks with all their heart and might,

War and the Feudal System

For most of Chaucer's life England was at war with France. In 1337 Edward III, whose mother was a French princess, claimed the throne of France and the Hundred Years War which followed lasted, broken by a few truces, until 1453. The poet was about six years old when the English won the famous victory at Crécy, led by the King's eldest son, the Black Prince. Scenes such as that in (1), with English ships packed with soldiers arriving at a foreign port, must have been a familiar sight, as were pre-battle conferences such as that shown in (2). There were many bloody battlefields during the war – the French dead at Agincourt in 1415 numbered 7,000. Looting was general and huge quantities of booty were brought back by the victorious soldiery. Picture (3) shows a pitched battle on foot, (5) a clash between mounted knights.

The fortified castles of the time were strongholds indeed and often could be taken only after a long siege. The walls were immensely thick and the gateways often protected first by the raised drawbridge behind which were the massive gates and behind them an iron portcullis. By the Middle Ages the battering ram was no longer of much use. Eventually its role was to be taken over by cannon, but meanwhile other devices such as the siege tower and the cat, or sow, were used. A cat, or sow, is shown in (6). It was a means of approaching the castle walls in order to mine them. The attacking force would dig under the wall which would then be shored up with timbers. These were later burnt to cause the wall to collapse. The defenders are here seen trying to destroy the cat by dropping heavy stones on the roof and by pouring boiling oil through holes punched by the man with a heavy pointed stake.

In (8) we see a captured knight, his helmet on a stick behind him, being dragged humiliatingly under the mocking gaze of ladies, and in (4) we are taken behind the scene of battle where the heavy sword of a knight is being re-sharpened on a grindstone. An important contribution to the early English

victories in the war, which resulted in English control of large parts of France, were the English long-bowmen (many of whom in fact came from Wales). Their deadly rain of arrows, fired with astonishing accuracy, wrought havoc among the French and brought about significant changes in the hitherto formal methods of warfare. One of the heroes of the Hundred Years War was the Black Prince and

1

it is remarkable that he was only sixteen years old when he led his troops to victory at Crécy. His effigy (7), surmounted by his heraldic achievements, can be seen in Canterbury Cathedral today. The king had no navy as such but battles at sea were frequent, indeed the first English victory of the war was at sea – in

10
11▶

the Battle of Sluys in 1340. The king's 'fleet' consisted of merchant ships provided by English sea-towns and we are given a vivid impression of one in (9), with trumpets braying from deck and crow's nest and archers in castellated turrets at bow and stern.

During Chaucer's lifetime the feudal system, introduced by the Normans, was gradually breaking up in England although its general structure continued for some time longer. A contributory cause was the Black Death which disrupted many manorial systems and strengthened the position of the serfs. In 1381

the knight's land or in his house or castle. They were also liable to serve the knight as soldiers, thus, ultimately, serving the king. The same system prevailed broadly throughout Europe and picture (10) shows villeins being instructed in the manor house before going out to their master's fields. Picture (11) shows reapers working under the direction of the lord of the manor's reeve or bailiff and is eloquent testimony to the lowly status of the villein. But by Chaucer's time the villeins were becoming progressively more independent and were receiving pay for their services. Also the

there was even a Peasants' Revolt led by Jack Straw and Wat Tyler. Under the feudal system the great barons were the vassals of the king and in return for his favours and particularly the land he gave them they accepted certain obligations including the provision of knights and men to fight for their royal master when needed. The barons in turn gave land to their knights who accepted similar obligations. The freemen and villeins who lived in the knight's manor were themselves granted land but their obligations were more down to earth. They were bound to work on

knight's obligation to provide men-at-arms for the king's service had been broken down by a system called *scutage* under which his vassals were allowed to pay a sum of money in place of each soldier they were supposed to provide. This enabled the king to hire mercenaries, so that many of the English soldiers who fought in the Hundred Years War were almost professionals.

Picture (12) depicts the execution of the captain of a renowned gang of robbers in Paris. It gives a good impression of the variety of costumes of the people.

Especially the Thebans, time on time.
Thus in good hope, with beating heart a-climb,
Each took his leave, and they began to ride
To Thebes and to her ancient walls and wide.

PART III

I judge it would be held for negligence
If I forgot to tell of the dispense
Of money by the Duke who set about
To make the lists a royal show throughout.
A theatre more noble in its plan
I dare well say was never seen by man.
It had a circuit of a mile about,
Well walled with stone; there was a ditch without.
Shaped like a circle there it stood complete
In tier on tier, the height of sixty feet,
So that a man set in a given row
Did not obstruct his neighbour from below.
    Eastward there stood a gate of marble white,
And westward such another rose to sight;
Briefly, there never was upon the face
Of earth so much within so small a space.
No craftsmen in the land that had the trick
Of pure geometry, arithmetic,
Portraiture, carving and erecting stages
But Theseus found him and supplied his wages
To build this theatre and carve devices.
And, to observe due rites and sacrifices,
Eastward he built upon the gate, above,
An oratory to the Queen of Love,
To Venus and her worship, and he dressed
An altar there; and like it, to the west,
In reverence to Mars he built a second;
The cost in gold was hardly to be reckoned.
Yet, northward, in a turret on the wall
He built a third, an oratory tall
And rich, of whitest alabaster, set
With crimson coral, to discharge the debt
Of worship to Diana of Chastity.
And it was thus that Theseus built these three
Temples in great magnificence of style.
    But yet I have forgotten all this while

From the *Roman de la Rose*, which
Chaucer translated into English,
comes this picture of a lady
admiring herself in a wall mirror,
the glass of which is convex in
shape.

To tell you of the portraits that there were,
The shapes, the carvings and the figures there
To grace these temples high above the green.
　　First, in the temple of Venus, you had seen
Wrought on the wall, and piteous to behold,
The broken sleeps and sighings manifold,
The sacred tears and the lamenting songs
And every fiery passion that belongs
To those that suffer love, the long-endured,
Their taken oaths, their covenants assured,
Pleasure and Hope, Desire, Foolhardiness,
Beauty and Youth, Lasciviousness, Largesse,
Philtres and Force, Falsehood and Flattery,
Extravagance, Intrigue, and Jealousy
Gold-garlanded with many a yellow twist,
That had a cuckoo sitting on her wrist.
Stringed instruments, and carols, feasts and dances,
Joy and display, and all the circumstances
Of love, as I have told you and shall tell,
Were in due order painted there as well,
And more than I can mention or recount.
Truly the whole of Citherea's Mount,
Where Venus has her dwelling above all
Her other playgrounds, figured on the wall
With all her garden in its joyful dress.
Nor was forgotten her porter, Idleness,
Nor yet Narcissus, beauty's paragon
In times gone by, nor doting Solomon,
Nor the unmastered strength of Hercules.
Medea and her enchantments next to these,
And Circe's too, and Turnus fierce and brave,
And rich King Croesus, captive and a slave,
That men might see that neither wit nor wealth,
Beauty or cunning, bravery or health
Can challenge Venus or advance their worth
Against that goddess who controls the earth.
And all these people captured in her noose
Cried out, 'Alas!' but it was little use.
Suffice these few examples, but the score
Could well be reckoned many thousands more.
　　Her statue, glorious in majesty,
Stood naked, floating on a vasty sea,
And from the navel down there were a mass
Of green and glittering waves as bright as glass.

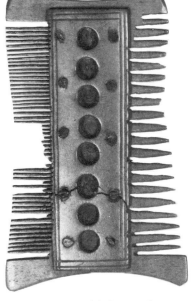

A bone comb with fine teeth on one
side and broad on the other.

In her right hand a cithern carried she
And on her head, most beautiful to see,
A garland of fresh roses, while above
There circled round her many a flickering dove.
    Cupid her son was standing to behold her
Fronting her statue, winged on either shoulder,
And he was blind, as it is often seen;
He bore a bow with arrows bright and keen.
    Why should I not go on to tell you all
The portraiture depicted on the wall
Within the Temple of Mighty Mars the Red?
The walls were painted round and overhead
Like the recesses of that grisly place
Known as the Temple of Great Mars in Thrace,
That frosty region under chilling stars
Where stands the sovereign mansion of King Mars.
    First on the walls a forest with no plan
Inhabited by neither beast nor man
Was painted – tree-trunks, knotted, gnarled and old,
Jagged and barren, hideous to behold,
Through which there ran a rumble and a soughing
As though a storm should break the branches bowing
Before it. Downwards from a hill there went
A slope; the Temple of Omnipotent
Mars was erected there in steel, and burnished.
The Gateway, narrow and forbidding, furnished
A ghastly sight, and such a rushing quake
Raged from within, the portals seemed to shake.
In at the doors a northern glimmer shone
Onto the walls, for windows there were none;
One scarce discerned a light, it was so scant.
The doors were of eternal adamant,
And vertically clenched, and clenched across
For greater strength with many an iron boss,
And every pillar to support the shrine
Weighed a full ton of iron bright and fine.
    And there I saw the dark imaginings
Of felony, the stratagems of kings,
And cruel wrath that glowed an ember-red,
The pick-purse and the coward pale with dread,
The smiler with the knife beneath his cloak,
The out-houses that burnt with blackened smoke;
Treason was there, a murder on a bed,
And open war, with wounds that gaped and bled;

Dispute, with bloody knife and snarling threat;
A screaming made the place more dreadful yet.
The slayer of himself, I saw him there
With all his heart's blood matted in his hair;
The driven nail that made the forehead crack,
And death stone-cold and gaping on his back.
  And in the middle of the shrine Mischance
Stood comfortless with sorry countenance.
There I saw Madness cackling his distress,
Armed insurrection, outcry, fierce excess,
The carrion in the undergrowth, slit-throated,
And thousands violently slain. I noted
The raping tyrant with his prey o'ertaken,
The levelled city, gutted and forsaken,
The ships on fire dancingly entangled,
The luckless hunter that wild bears had strangled,
The sow devouring children in the cradle,
The scalded cook who had too short a ladle –
Nothing forgotten of the unhappy art
Of Mars: the carter crushed beneath his cart,
Flung to the earth and pinned beneath the wheel;
Those also on whom Mars has set his seal,
The barber and the butcher and the smith
Who forges things a man may murder with.
And high above, depicted in a tower,
Sat Conquest, robed in majesty and power,
Under a sword that swung above his head,
Sharp-edged and hanging by a subtle thread.
  And Caesar's slaughter stood in effigy
And that of Nero and Mark Antony;

Reaping and gathering corn sheaves.

Though to be sure they were as yet unborn,
Their deaths were there prefigured to adorn
This Temple with the menaces of Mars,
As it is also painted in the stars
Who shall be murdered, who shall die for love;
Such were the portraits on the walls above.
Let these examples from the past hold good,
For all I cannot reckon, though I would.

    Mars in a chariot was carved, and clad
In armour, grim and staring, like the mad,
Above his head there shone with blazing looks
Two starry figures, named in ancient books,
Puella one, the other Rubeus.
The God of Battles was encompassed thus:
There stood a wolf before him at his feet,
His eyes glowed red, he had a man to eat.
Subtle the pencil was that told this story
Picturing Mars in terror and in glory.

    The Temple of Diana now, the Chaste,
Let me describe, and I shall use such haste
And brevity in what I now recall
As possible. The paintings on the wall
Were scenes of hunting and of chastity.
There I perceived the sad Callisto, she
Whom in her rage Diana did not spare
But changed her from a woman to a bear,
Then to a star, and she was painted so
(She is the lode-star, that is all I know;
Her son, too, is a star, as one can see).
There I saw Dana, turned into a tree*
(No, not Diana, she was not the same,
But Penneus' daughter, Dana was her name).
I saw Actaeon turned into a stag;
This was Diana's vengence, lest he brag
Of having seen her naked. There they show him
Caught and devoured – his own hounds did not know hi
Close by there was a painting furthermore
Of Atalanta hunting a wild boar,
And Meleager; there were others too
Diana chose to harry and undo,
And many other wonders on the wall
Were painted, that I need not now recall.

    High on a stag the Goddess held her seat,
And there were little hounds about her feet;

This effigy in a Yorkshire church of
John Gascoigne of Nasingcroft
shows in detail the fine quality of the
armour of the period.

Gilbert Marshal, 4th Earl of
Pembroke, whose effigy in Temple
Church, London, this is, is wearing
chain mail, but it failed to save him
for he was fatally injured in a
tournament.

Below her feet there was a sickle moon,
Waxing it seemed, but would be waning soon.
Her statue bore a mantle of bright green,
Her hand a bow with arrows cased and keen;
Her eyes were lowered, gazing as she rode
Down to where Pluto had his dark abode.
A woman in her travail lay before her,
Her child unborn; she ceased not to implore her
To be delivered and with piteous call
Cried, 'Help, Lucina, thou the best of all!'
It was a lively painting, every shade
Had cost the painter many a florin paid.

And now the lists were made, and Theseus
Who, at huge cost, had bidden them produce
These temples in a theatre so stately,
Saw it was finished, and it pleased him greatly.
No more of Theseus now; I must pass on
To speak of Arcite and of Palamon.

The day approached for trial of their rights
When each should bring with him a hundred knights
To settle all by battle, as I said;
So, back to Athens each of them had led
His hundred knights, all helmeted and spurred
And armed for war. They meant to keep their word.
And it was said indeed by many a man
That never since the day the world began
In all God's earth, wide seas and reach of land,
Had so few men made such a noble band
As in respect of knighthood and degree.
Everyone with a taste for chivalry
And eager, of course, to win a glorious name
Had begged to be allowed to join the game.
Lucky for those selected, so I say!
If such a thing should happen here to-day,
As you can well imagine, every knight
Who loves a lady and is game to fight,
Whether in England here, or anywhere,
Would certainly feel eager to be there.
Fight for a lady? *Benedicite!*
That would be something for a man to see.

And that was just the case with Palamon.
His knights had come and had been taken on;
Some were in coat of mail and others wore
A breastplate and a tunic, little more.

Some carried heavy plating, front and back,
And some a Prussian shield to ward attack;
Some cased their legs in armour, thigh to heel,
Some bore an axe and some a mace of steel
– There's never a new fashion but it's old –
And so they armed themselves as I have told.
Each man according to his own opinion.
 You might have seen arrive from his dominion
Mighty Lycurgus, famous King of Thrace;
Black was his beard and manly was his face.
To see the circling eye-balls of the fellow
Set in his head and glowing red and yellow!
And like a gryphon he would stare and rouse
The shaggy hair upon his beetling brows.
Huge were his limbs, his muscles hard and strong,
His back was broad, his bulging arms were long.
True to his country's custom from of old
He towered in a chariot of gold
And four white bulls were harnessed in the traces.
Over his armour, which in many places
Was studded with bright nails of yellow gold,
He wore a coal-black bear-skin, fold on fold,
Instead of surcoat, and behind his back
His fell of hair was combed and shone as black
As raven's feather, and a golden wreath,
Thick as your arm, weighted the head beneath.
It was immensely heavy, and was bright
With many precious stones of fiery light,
With finest rubies and with diamonds.
About his chariot, white enormous hounds,
Twenty and more, each larger than a steer,
And trained to hunt the lion and the deer,
Went following him. Their muzzles were fast bound;
Their collars were of gold with rings set round.
He had a hundred nobles in his rout
Armed to the teeth; their hearts were stern and stout.
 And with Arcita, so the poets sing,
Went great Emetrius the Indian king
On a bay steed whose trappings were of steel
Covered in cloth of gold from haunch to heel
Fretted with diaper. Like Mars to see,
His surcoat was in cloth of Tartary,
Studded with great white pearls; beneath its fold
A saddle of new-beaten burnished gold.

The ring was an important object
in medieval life. It could be not
only a token of affection between
lovers and others but a form of
credential or means of identification
and was sometimes thought to have
magical properties of protection.
Here a man presents a ring to a
lady – the artist has made sure, by
enlarging it, that it is recognized.

He had a mantle hanging from his shoulders,
Which, crammed with rubies, dazzled all beholders.
His hair was crisped in ringlets, as if spun
In yellow, and it glittered like the sun.
Aquiline nose and eyes with lemon light
And rounded lips he had, his colour bright,
With a few freckles sprinkled here and there,
Some yellow and some black. He bore an air
As of a lion when he cast a glance.
He was some twenty-five years old, to chance
A guess at it; a healthy beard was springing.
His voice resounded like a trumpet ringing.
He had a wreath of laurel on his head
For he was freshly, greenly garlanded.
And on his hand he bore for his delight
An eagle; it was tame and lily-white.
He had a hundred lords beside him there,
In all their armour (though their heads were bare)
And sumptuously decked with furnishings.
For take my word for it that dukes and kings
Were gathered in this noble company
For love and for the spread of chivalry.
Many a lion tame and spotted pard
Gambolled about this king of stern regard
And in this manner in their fine adorning
These lords came to the city on Sunday morning,
Round about nine o'clock, and lighted down.
      The noble Theseus led them through his town
(So it became him as a duke and knight),
And housed them each according to his right.
He feasted them and took great pains to please,
To honour and to set them all at ease,
And to this day it's said no human wit
However lofty could have bettered it.
      What minstrelsy, what service at the feast,
What gifts bestowed on greatest as on least,
How richly decked the palace, what the place
Ordained for first and last upon the dais,
What ladies loveliest in the dancing throng,
And which most exquisite in dance and song
And which to speak most feelingly of love,
Or what the falcons that were perched above,
And what the hounds that couched upon the floor –
Of all such questions I shall say no more

Than the result of it; I will not tease you,
Here comes the point, so listen if it please you.
    That Sunday night ere day began to spring
There was a lark which Palamon heard sing
(Although two hours before the day came on,
Yet the lark sang, and so did Palamon).
With holy heart and in a lofty mood
He rose on pilgrimage and he pursued
His path to Citherea, the benign
And blissful Venus, to her honoured shrine.
And in her hour, among the early mists,
He stepped towards her Temple in the lists
And down he knelt in humbleness and fear
With aching heart, and said as you shall hear
    'Fairest of Fair, O Venus, Lady mine,
Consort of Vulcan, Daughter of Jove Divine,
Giver of joy upon the heights above
The Mount of Citherea, by that love
Thou gavest to Adonis, heal my smart
And take my humble prayer into thy heart.
Alas! I have no language that can tell
The ravages and torments of my hell,
Which heart is all unable to bewray,
And I am so confused I cannot say
More than: "O Lady bright, that art aware
Of all my thought and seest my despair,
Consider this, have pity on my pain
As I shall ever struggle to maintain
Thy service, in so far as it shall be
Within my power to combat chastity."
There is my vow if you will tend my harms.
I am not one to brag of deeds of arms,
Nor do I ask for victory to-morrow,
Nor for renown; I neither seek nor borrow
Vainglorious praises or the proud profession
Of prowess, but would fully have possession
Of Emily, and die thy worshipper.
Choose Thou the means for this, administer
The ways, I care not how, whether it be
By my defeat of them, or theirs of me,
So that I have my lady in my arms.
Though Mars be god of battles and alarms
Thy power is so great in Heaven above
That if thou please I well may have my love.

And I will worship at thy shrine for ever;
Ride where I may, to thee my whole endeavour
Shall be in sacrifice and kindling fires
Upon thy altars. Yet if my desires,
Sweet lady, cannot please thee, end my sorrow
With death upon Arcita's spear to-morrow.
I shall not care when I have lost my life
Though he should win my Emily to wife.
This is the sum and purpose of my prayer,
Give me my love, sweet Goddess ever fair!'
    When Palamon had done his orison
He then did sacrifice with woe-begone
Devotion and with ceremonial rite
More than I now have leisure to recite.
And in the end the statue of Venus shook
And made a sign; and by that sign he took
His prayer had been accepted on that day,
For though the sign had hinted a delay
He knew for certain that his boon was granted,
And home he went at once, his soul enchanted.
    In the third hour after Palamon
Had sought out Venus for his orison,
Up rose the sun, and up rose Emily
And hastened to Diana's sanctuary,
Taking such maidens as she might require,
And they were ready furnished with the fire,
The incense and the vestments and a throng
Of other necessaries that belong
To sacrifices, horns of brimming mead,
As was the custom, all that they could need.
The Temple smoked and the adornments there
Glittered in beauty. Emily the fair
Joyfully washed her body in a well,
But how she did her rite I dare not tell
Save in a general way, though I for one
Think that to hear the detail would be fun.
If one means well why bother to feel queasy?
It's good for people to be free and easy.
Her shining hair untressed upon her cloak
They combed and set a crown of cerrial oak
Green on her golden head with fitting grace.
Two fires she kindled in the proper place
And did her rites, as he will find who looks
In Statius' *Book of Thebes* and other books,

Among the many attendants in a great house one of the most notable was the fool, or jester, who was licensed to say what he liked. Here we see a king with his jester who is carrying his bauble, his badge of office.

And when the fires were kindled she drew near
With piteous heart, and prayed as you shall hear:
  'O Goddess Chaste of all the woodlands green,
That seest earth and heaven and sea, O Queen
Of Pluto's kingdom, dark and deep below,
Goddess of virgins that from long ago
Hast known my heart, and knowest my desire,
As I may shun the vengeance of thine ire
Such as upon Actaeon once was spent,
Thou knowest well, O chaste omnipotent,
That I would be a virgin all my life
And would be neither mistress, no, nor wife.
I am, thou knowest, of thy company,
A huntress, still in my virginity,
And only ask to walk the woodlands wild,
And not to be a wife or go with child,
Nor would I know the company of man.
O help me, Goddess, for none other can,
By the three Forms that ever dwell in thee,*
And as for Palamon who longs for me
And for Arcita's passion, I implore
This favour of thy grace and nothing more;
Set them in amity and let them be
At peace, and turn their hearts away from me.
Let all their violent loves and hot desires,
Their ceaseless torments and consuming fires,
Be quenched, or turned towards another place.
Yet if thou wilt not do me so much grace,
Or if my destiny ordains it so
That one shall have me whether I will or no,
Then send me him that shall desire me most.
Clean Goddess of the chaste and virgin host,
Look down upon the bitter tears that fall
Upon my cheeks, O keeper of us all,
Keep thou my maidhood, prosper my endeavour,
And while I live a maid I'll serve thee ever.'
  The fires flamed up upon the altar fair
And clear while Emily was thus in prayer;
But all at once she saw a curious sight,
For suddenly one fire quenched its light
And then rekindled; as she gazed in doubt
The other fire as suddenly went right out;
As it was quenched it made a whistling sound
As of wet branches burning on the ground.

An iron spur with a savage rotating spiked rowel.

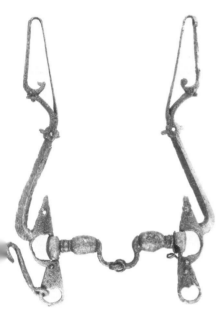

A curb bit of intricate design.

Then, from the faggot's tip, there ran a flood
Of many drops that had the look of blood.
　　Now at the sight she was so terrified
It almost drove her from her wits, she cried,
Not knowing what it was to signify,
For it was fear alone that made her cry,
She wept and it was pitiful to hear.
And then began Diana to appear,
With bow in hand, garbed as a Huntress,
And said, 'My daughter, cease your heaviness.
For thee the Gods on high have set their term,
And by eternal word and writ confirm
That thou shalt be espoused to one of those
That have for thee endured so many woes.
But unto which of them I may not tell.
Longer I cannot tarry, fare thee well.
And yet the fires of sacrifice that glow
Upon my altar shall, before thou go,
Make plain thy destiny in this for ever.'
　　And on the word the arrows in her quiver
Clattered together and began to ring
And forth she went and made a vanishing.
　　Wholly amazed at what had come to pass,
Emily thought, 'What can this mean? Alas!
O take me, take me under thy protection,
Diana, for I yield to thy direction!'
Then she went homeward by the shortest way
And that was all, there is no more to say.
　　Now in the hour of Mars next after this
Arcite rose up and sought the edifice
Of fiery Mars, to do beneath his banner
His sacrifice, as was the pagan manner,
In high devotion with a piteous heart,
And thus he said his orison apart:
'O thou strong God of War that art adored
In the cold realms of Thrace and held for Lord,
That hast of every monarchy and land
Of warlike men the bridle in thine hand,
And dealest them their fortunes by thy choice,
Accept my sacrifice and hear my voice.
And if my youth be such as to deserve
Thy favour, if my strength be fit to serve
Thy godhead, if I may be one of thine,
I pray thee then, pity this pain of mine.

'By that same suffering and burning fire
That long ago consumed thee with desire,
Having in use the incomparable flesh
Of fair free-hearted Venus, young and fresh,
Holding her in thine arms and at thy will,
–Albeit that once the time was chosen ill,
Seeing that Vulcan caught thee in his net
And found thee lying with his wife – but yet
By all the pain and passion of thy heart
Pity me too that suffer the same smart!
Thou knowest I am ignorant and young
And, as I think, more passionately stung
By love than any creature dead or living;
Little she thinks, in all the grief she's giving,
Of me, or cares whether I swim or sink,
And well I know ere she can learn to think
Kindly of me that force must have its place,
And well I know without thy help or grace
The little strength I have is all too slight;
Then help me, Lord, to-morrow in the fight,
Not only for the flames that burnt in thee
But for the fire that now is burning me.
Grant victory to-morrow to my sword!
Mine be the labour, thine the glory, Lord;
Thy sovereign temple I will honour above
All other places, it shall be my love
To work for thy delight, to use thy arts,
And hang my banner, yea, my heart of hearts
Above thy altar. All my Company
Shall do the same for ever, there shall be
Eternal fires burning before thy Shrine,
Nay further to this binding vow of mine,
My beard and hair, whose length and excellence
Has never suffered yet from the offence
Of razor or of shear, to Thee I give,
And will be thy true servant while I live.
Now, Lord, have pity on a heart so sore;
And give me victory, I ask no more.'
    His prayer was over, and the rings that hung
Upon the portals of the Temple swung;
So did the doors and clattered far and near,
At which Arcita felt the touch of fear.
The fires blazed, the altar glistened bright,
So that the Temple was suffused with light,

The illuminators of medieval
manuscripts would linger lovingly
and painstakingly over one capital
letter. Here is an elaborate letter B
with, in the upper part, a man
whipping a horse, and in the lower
a muzzled bear attacking its keeper.

A scented air rose upward from the ground.
Arcita lifted up his hand and found
More incense and he cast it on the flame
With other rituals. At last the frame
Of mighty Mars began to shake and ring
Its hauberk, and he heard a murmuring,
Low-voiced and dim, that answered '*Victory*';
And giving thanks and glorifying he,
Filled with the joyful hope that he would win,
Returned at once and went to seek his inn,
As happy as a bird is of the sun.
    Immediately an uproar was begun
Over this granted boon in Heaven above
As between Venus, fairest Queen of Love,
And the armipotent Mars; it did not cease,
Though Jupiter was busy making peace,
Until their father Saturn, pale and cold,
Who knew so many stratagems of old,
Searched his experience and found an art
To please the disputants on either part.
Age has a great advantage over youth
In wisdom and by custom, that's the truth.
The old may be out-run but not out-reasoned.
And Saturn stopped their argument and seasoned
Their fears, although it's not his nature to,
And found a remedy for this to-do.
    'My dearest daughter Venus,' said old Saturn,
'My heavenly orbit marks so wide a pattern
It has more power than anyone can know;
In the wan sea I drown and overthrow,
Mine is the prisoner in the darkling pit,
Mine are both neck and noose that strangles it,
Mine the rebellion of the serfs astir,
The murmurings, the privy poisoner;
And I do vengeance, I send punishment,
And when I am in *Leo* it is sent.
Mine is the ruin of the lofty hall,
The falling down of tower and of wall
On carpenter and mason, I their killer.
'Twas I slew Samson when he shook the pillar;
Mine are the maladies that kill with cold,
The dark deceits, the stratagems of old;
A look from me will father pestilence.
Then weep no more, for by my diligence

This Palamon, your dedicated knight,
Shall have his lady, as you swore he might.
Though Mars should help his champion, none the less
Peace must be made between you soon, I guess,
Although you do not share the same complexions;
That is what brings these daily insurrections.
I am your grandfather and, as before,
I'll do my best to please you; weep no more.'
   Now I shall cease to speak of Gods above,
Of angry Mars and Venus Queen of Love,
And tell you all, as plainly as I can,
The grand result for which I first began.

PART IV

Great was the festival they held that day
In Athens, and the lusty time of May
Put everyone so well in countenance
They spent all Monday at a joust and dance
And the high services of Venus. Yet
Because they knew that up they'd have to get,
And early too, to witness the great fight,
They went to bed betimes on Monday night.
   Next morning when the day began to spring
Clattering horse and noise of harnessing
Echoed through all the hostelries about.
Up to the palace cantered rout on rout
Of lords on palfreys, stallions, many a steed;
And what device of harness too indeed,
So rich and so outlandish, what a deal
Of goldsmith work, embroidery and steel!
Bright shields and trophies, headpieces and charms,
Great golden helmets, hauberks, coats of arms,
Lords on apparelled coursers, squires too
And knights belonging to their retinue,
Spears being nailed and helmets buckled strong,
Strapping of shields and lacing up of thong,
The work was urgent, not a man was idle.
The foamy steeds gnawing the golden bridle,
The armourers up and down and round about
Racing with file and hammer through the rout,
Yeomen on foot and commonalty come
With pipe and clarion, trump and kettle-drum,

Armed with short sticks and making such a rattle
It sounded like the blast of bloody battle.
The palace full of people up and down,
Here three, there ten, in all the talk of town
And making bets about the Theban knights.
Says one, 'He'll win'; another, 'Not by rights';
Some backed the man whose beard was black and squared,
Some backed the skin-heads: some the shaggy-haired;
Said one, 'There's a grim fellow, I'll be bound,
He has a battle-axe weighs twenty pound!'
And prophecy went seething round the hall
Long after day had sprung upon them all.
    Great Theseus was awoken out of sleep
By minstrelsy and noise about the keep,
But kept his chamber – a resplendent room –
Till the two Theban knights, to both of whom
An equal honour was done, were brought in presence.
    Throned in a window giving on a pleasance
Sat Theseus like a god in panoply,
And all the people crowded there to see
The Duke and offer him their reverence
And hear what orders he might issue thence.
A herald on a scaffold shouted 'Ho!'
Till all the noise was quieted below;
Seeing at last the people hushed and still
He thus declared the mighty Theseus' will:
    'Our Lord the Duke has in his high discretion
Considered the destruction and suppression
Of gentle blood, were he to jeopardize
The lives of those engaging under guise
Of mortal battle. Wishing none to die,
His Grace now purposes to modify
His ordinance. On forfeit of your lives
No sort of dart, no poleaxes or knives
May pass into the lists or be conveyed
Thither, no stabbing-sword with pointed blade
Be drawn or even carried at the side.
Further, no pair of combatants shall ride
More than one course with spears, descending thence
To thrust on foot only in self-defence.
If any man be injured, none shall take
His life; he shall be carried to the stake
That is to be ordained on either side,
And there conveyed by force he shall abide.

Another letter B, from the Luttrell
Psalter. Here a queen plays the
harp. Upper left a monkey seems to
be teaching an owl.

Brass rubbings from the tombs
of a fourteenth-century knight and
his lady. They are of Sir John
and Lady de Creke and are in the
church at Westley Waterless in
Cambridgeshire.

And should the principal of either faction
Be taken to the stake, or killed in action,
All fighting shall determine thereupon.
God speed you all, go forward and lay on!
With mace and long-sword you may fight your fill.
Now go your ways. This is his Grace's will.'
    The people rifted heaven with a shout
Of merriest good humour, crying out,
'God bless our Duke for doing what he can
To save the blood of many a gentleman!'
    Up go the trumpets and the melody,
Forth to the lists canter the company,
As they were bidden, to the city verge;
The streets were hung in cloth-of-gold, not serge.
    And like a lord the Duke began to ride
With these two Theban knights on either side.
Behind them rode the Queen and Emily,
And behind them another company
Of one or other according to their rank,
Threading through the city with the clank
Of hoof and armour to the lists that lay
Beyond. It was not fully prime of day
When Theseus took his seat in majesty.
Hippolyta the Queen and Emily
Were with him, other ladies ranked about,
And round the scaffoldage a seething rout.
    And westward, look! Under the Martian Gate
Arcita and his hundred knights await,
And now, under a banner of red, march on.
And at the self-same moment Palamon
Enters by Venus' Gate and takes his place
Under a banner of white, with cheerful face.
You had not found, though you had searched the earth,
Two companies so equal in their worth.
Never were two so splendidly arrayed
And there was none so wise as to have weighed
Which of them had the advantage of his foe
In valiance, age, degree or strength of show;
They were so equal one could only guess.
    In two formations they began to dress
And when the roll was called that all might see
Their number was not swelled by treachery,
The gates were shut, and then the herald cried:
'Young knights, now do your duty, show your pride!'

The heralds then withdrew, their work was done;
Out blared the trumpet and the clarion.
There is no more to say, but east and west
In go the spears in readiness, at the 'rest',
In go the spurs into the horse's side.
It's easy seeing which can joust and ride.
There the shafts shiver on the shields so thick;
One through his breast-bone feels the thrust and prick.
Up spring the spears to twenty foot in height,
Out go the long-swords flashing silver-bright,
Hewing the helmets as they shear and shred;
Out bursts the blood in streams of sternest red,
The mighty maces swing, the bones are bashed,
One thrusting through the thickest throng has crashed,
There the strong steeds have stumbled, down goes all,
Man under foot and rolling like a ball.
Another on his feet with truncheon pound
Hurtles a rider and his horse to ground;
One's wounded in the body, whom they take,
Spite of his teeth, and bear him to the stake
As was ordained, and there he has to stay;
One more is carried off the other way.
From time to time the Duke decrees a rest
To drink and be refreshed as they think best.
    Many a time our Thebans in the flow
Of battle met and did each other woe,
And each unhorsed the other. There could be
No tiger in the vale of Galgophy
Raging in search after a stolen cub
So cruel as Arcite with spear and club
For jealousy of heart to Palamon.
No lion is so fierce to look upon
In all Benamarin, and none so savage
Being hunted, nor so hunger-mad in ravage
For blood of prey as Palamon for Arcite.
The blows upon their helmets bite and beat
And the red blood runs out on man and steed.
    There comes at last an end to every deed,
And ere into the west the sun had gone
Strong King Emetrius took Palamon
As he was fighting with Arcite, still fresh,
And made his sword bite deeply in his flesh;
It asked the strength of twenty men to take
The yet-unyielded Palamon to stake.

Seeking a rescue, King Lycurgus coursed
Towards Palamon but was himself unhorsed,
And King Emetrius for all his strength
Was flung out of the saddle a sword's length
By Palamon's last stroke in sweeping rake.
But all for nought, they brought him to the stake;
Nothing could help, however hard he fought,
His hardy heart must stay there, he was caught
By force and by the rules decided on.

    Who clamours now in grief but Palamon
That may no more go in again and fight?
And when the noble Theseus saw this sight
He rose and thundered forth to every one,
'Ho! Stop the fight! No more, for it is done!
I will be true judge and no partisan.
The Theban Prince Arcita is the man
And shall have Emily, won by Fortune's grace.'

    A tumult of rejoicing filled all space
From every throat in such a caterwaul
It seemed as if the very lists would fall.

    What now can lovely Venus do above?
What is she saying, hapless Queen of Love?
Wanting her will her eyes were filled with mists
And shining tears fell down upon the lists.

    She cried, 'I am disgraced and put to shame!'
But Saturn said, 'Peace, daughter, watch the game.
Mars has his will, his knight has had his boon,
But, by my head, it shall be your turn soon.'

    The trumpeters with loudest minstrelsy
And the shrill heralds shouting frenziedly
Were in high joy of honour of Arcite.
But listen now and don't give way to heat,
See what a miracle happened thereupon!

    The fierce Arcita, with no helmet on,
Riding his courser round to show his face
Cantered the whole length of the jousting-place,
Fixing his eye on Emily aloft;
And her returning gaze was sweet and soft,
For women, speaking generally, are prone
To follow Fortune's favours, once they're known.
She was his whole delight, his joy of heart.

    Out of the ground behold a fury start,
By Pluto sent at the request of Saturn.
Arcita's horse in terror danced a pattern

And leapt aside and foundered as he leapt,
And ere he was aware Arcite was swept
Out of the saddle and pitched upon his head
Onto the ground, and there he lay for dead;
His breast was shattered by the saddle-bow.
As black he lay as any coal or crow
For all the blood had run into his face.
Immediately they bore him from the place
Sadly to Theseus' palace. What avail
Though he was carved out of his coat of mail
And put to bed with every care and skill?
Yet he was still alive, and conscious still,
And calling ceaselessly for Emily.

    Theseus, attended by his company,
Came slowly home to Athens in full state
Of joyous festival, no less elate
For this misfortune, wishing not to cast
A gloom upon them all for what had passed.
Besides they said Arcita would not die,
He would recover from his injury.
And then there was another thing that filled
All hearts with pleasure, no one had been killed,
Though some were badly hurt among the rest,
Especially the man with stoven breast.
As for the other wounds and broken arms
Some produced salves and some relied on charms,
Herb pharmacies and sage to make them trim;
They drank them off, hoping to save a limb.

    For such as these Duke Theseus did his best,
He comforted and honoured every guest
And ordered revelry to last the night
For all the foreign princes, as was right.
None were discouraged or in discontent;
It was a jousting, just a tournament.
Why should they be discouraged? After all,
It's only an accident to have a fall.
There is no shame in being borne by force,
Unyielded, to the stake by twenty horse,
Alone, with none to help – it must be so,
Harried away by arm and foot and toe,
And on a horse maddened by sticks and noise,
By men on foot, by yeomen and their boys.
There's nothing despicable in all this;
No one could ever call it cowardice.

An armoured knight brings a
message to his lord.

The Norman castle at Chepstow on the River Wye, on the border (the Marches) between England and Wales. This and similar strongholds were in use in Chaucer's time, for uprisings by the Welsh were a constant threat.

And therefore Theseus made proclamation
To stop all rancour, grudge and emulation,
That each side was as valorous as the other
And both as like as brother is to brother.
He gave them gifts, to each in his degree,
And for three days they held festivity.
Then he conveyed the Kings in solemn state
Out of his city, far beyond the gate,
And home went everyone by various ways
With no more than 'Good-bye!' and 'Happy days!'
 The battle done with, I may now go on
To speak of poor Arcite and Palamon.
Up swells Arcita's breast, the grievous sore
About his heart increases more and more;
The clotting blood, for all the doctor's skill,
Corrupts and festers in his body still,
That neither cupping, bleeding at a vein
Or herbal drink can make him well again.
The expulsive forces, known as 'animal',
Had lost their power to cleanse the 'natural'
Of poison, and it could not be expelled.★
His lungs began to choke, the vessels swelled.
Clotted was every muscle of his chest
By poison and corruption in his breast.
Nor could he profit, in his will to live,
By upward vomit or by laxative.
All, all was shattered and beyond repair,
Nature no longer had dominion there,
And certainly, where nature will not work,
Physic, farewell! Go, bear the man to kirk!
This is the sum of all, Arcite must die.
 And so he sent for Emily to be by,
And Palamon, the cousin of his heart,
And thus he spoke, preparing to depart:
 'Nothing of all the sorrows in my breast
Can now declare itself or be expressed
To you, O lady that I love the most;
But I bequeath the service of my ghost
To you, above all creatures in the world,
Now that my life is done, and banner furled.
Alas the woe! Alas the pain, so strong,
That I have suffered for you, and so long!
Alas, O Death! Alas, my Emily!
Alas the parting of our company!

A man hawking on foot. Falconry was not only a sport but a method of providing for the larder.

Alas, my heart's own queen, alas, my wife,
O lady of my heart that ends my life!
What is this world? What does man ask to have?
Now with his love, now in his cold, cold grave,
Lying alone, with none for company!
Farewell, my sweetest foe, my Emily!
O softly take me in your arms, I pray,
For love of God, and hearken what I say.
      'I have here, with my cousin Palamon,
Had strife and rancour many a day now gone,
For love of you, and for my jealousy.
And may Jove's wisdom touch the soul in me,
To speak of love and what its service means
Through all the circumstances and the scenes
Of life, namely good faith and knightly deed,
Wisdom, humility and noble breed,
Honour and truth and openness of heart,
For, as I hope my soul may have its part
With Jove, in all the world I know of none
So worthy to be loved as Palamon,
Who serves you and will serve you all his life.
And should you ever choose to be a wife,
Forget not Palamon, that great-hearted man.'
      Speech failed in him, the cold of death began
Its upward creeping from his feet to numb
The breast, and he was slowly overcome,
And further still as from his arms there went
The vital power; all was lost and spent.
Only the intellect, and nothing more,
That dwelt within his heart, so sick and sore,
Began to falter when the heart felt death.
Dusked his two eyes at last and failed his breath,
And yet he gazed at her while he could see
And his last word was 'Mercy . . . Emily!'
His spirit changed its house and went away
Where I came never – where I cannot say,
And so am silent. I am no divine.
Souls are not mentioned in this tale of mine,
I offer no opinion, I can tell
You nothing, though some have written where they dwell.
Arcite is cold. Mars guide him on his way!
Something of Emily I have to say.
      Palamon howls and Emily is shrieking.
And Theseus leads away his sister, seeking

To bear her from the corpse; she faints away.
Why tarry on her tears or spend the day
Telling you how she wept both eve and morrow?
For in these cases women feel such sorrow
When it befalls their husbands to be taken
The greater part seem utterly forsaken
And fall into a sickness so extreme
That many of them perish, it would seem.

Infinite were the sorrows and the tears
Of older folk and those of tender years
Throughout the town, all for this Theban's death.
Wept man and boy, and sure a wilder breath
Of lamentation never had been heard
Since Hector, freshly slaughtered, was interred
In Troy. Alas to see the mourning there,
The scrabbled faces, the dishevelled hair!
'Must you have died?' the women wailed. 'For, see,
Had you not gold enough – and Emily?'

No one could lighten Theseus of his care
Except his father, old Aegeus, there.
He knew the transmutations of the world
And he had seen its changes as it whirled
Bliss upon sorrow, sorrow upon bliss,
And gave his son instruction upon this:

'Just as there never died a man,' said he,
'But had in life some station or degree,
Just so there never lived a man,' he said,
'In all the world but in the end was dead.
This world is but a thoroughfare of woe
And we are pilgrims passing to and fro.
Death is the end of every worldly sore.'
On top of this he said a great deal more
To this effect, with wisest exhortation,
Heartening the people in their tribulation.

In time the thoughts of Theseus were astir
To find a site and build a sepulchre
For good Arcite, and how it best might be
Ordained to fit his honour and degree.
And in the end the place decided on
Was where Arcite first met with Palamon
In battle for their love, and there between
The branches in that very grove of green
Where he had sung his amorous desire
In sad complaint, and felt love hot as fire,

He planned a fire to make, in funeral
Observances, and so accomplish all.
So he commanded them to hack and fell
The ancient oak-trees and to lay them well
In rows and bundles faggoted to burn.
  Forth ride his officers and soon return
On swiftest foot with his commandments done.
And after this, Theseus appointed one
To fetch a bier and had it fitly clad
In cloth-of-gold, the finest that he had.
And in the self-same cloth he clad Arcite
And on his hands white gauntlets, as was meet,
He placed, and on his head a laurel crown
And in his hand the sword of his renown.
He laid him, bare his face, upon the bier,
And wept upon him, pity was to hear.
And that his body might be seen by all,
When it was day he bore him to the hall
That roared with mourning sounds in unison.
  Then came that woeful Theban, Palamon,
With fluttering beard and ash-besprinkled hair,
In sable garments stained with many a tear.
Yet, passing all in weeping, Emily
Was the most sorrowful of the company.
And that the service to be held might be

A mounted falconer. In falconry only the female bird was known as a falcon. The male bird was called a tercel.

The nobler, more befitting his degree,
Duke Theseus commanded them to bring
Three steeds, all trapped in steel and glittering,
And mantled with the arms of Prince Arcite.
Upon these huge white steeds that paced the street
First there rode one who bore Arcita's shield,
A second bore the spear he used to wield;
His Turkish bow and quiver of burnished gold
Was given to the third of them to hold;
Slowly they paced, their countenances drear,
Towards the destined grove, as you shall hear.
Upon the shoulders of the noblest men
Among the Greeks there came the coffin then.
Their eyes were red with tears, their slackened feet
Paced through the city by the master-street;
The way was spread with black, and far on high
Black draperies hung downwards from the sky.
  The old Aegeus to the right was placed
With Theseus on his left, and so they paced

Bearing gold vessels of a rare design
Brimming with honey and milk, with blood and wine;
And then came Palamon with his company,
And after that the woeful Emily
With fire in her hand, the custom then
Used in the obsequies of famous men.
    The solemn work of building up the pyre
Was done in splendour and they laid a fire
That reached to heaven in a cone of green.
The arms were twenty fathoms broad – I mean
The boughs and branches heaped upon the ground –
And straw in piles had first been loaded round.
    But how they made the funeral fires flame,
Or what the trees by number or by name
– Oak, fir-tree, birch, aspen and poplar too,
Ilex and alder, willow, elm and yew,
Box, chestnut, plane, ash, laurel, thorn and lime,
Beech, hazel, whipple-tree – I lack the time
To tell you, or who felled them, nor can tell
How their poor gods ran up and down the dell
All disinherited of habitation,
Robbed of their quiet and in desolation,
The nymph and dryad of the forest lawn,
The hamadryad and the subtle faun,
These I pass over, birds and beasts as well
That fled in terror when the forest fell,
Nor shall I say how in the sudden light
Of the unwonted sun the dell took fright,
Nor how the fire first was couched in straw,
Then in dry sticks thrice severed with a saw,
Then in green wood with spice among the stems
And then in cloth-of-gold with precious gems
And many a flower-garland in the stir
Of breathing incense and the scent of myrrh;
Nor how Arcita lay among it all,
Nor of the wealth and splendour of his pall,
Nor yet how Emily thrust in the fire
As custom was and lit the funeral pyre,
Nor how she fainted when they fed the flame,
Nor what she said or thought; and I shall name
None of the jewels that they took and cast
Into the fire when it flamed at last,
Nor shall I tell how some threw shield and spear,
Or what their garments by the burning bier,

Nor of the cups of wine and milk and blood
That others poured upon the fiery flood,
Nor tell you how the Greeks in mighty rout
Left-handedly went thrice and thrice about
The flaming pyre, and shouted as they drove,
And thrice they clashed their spears about the grove;
Nor yet relate how thrice the ladies wept
Nor who supported Emily and kept
Pace with her homeward, nor shall it be told
How Prince Arcita burnt to ashes cold;
Nor how the wake was held in the delight
Of funeral games that lasted all the night.
What naked wrestler, glistening with oil,
Made the best showing in his dangerous toil
I will not say, nor say how one by one
They all went home after the games were done;
But shortly to the point; for I intend
To bring my long narration to an end.
    In course of time, and after certain years,
Mourning had been accomplished and their tears
Were shed no more, by general consent.
And then it seems they held a parliament
At Athens touching certain points and cases;
And among these they dealt with certain places
With which to form alliances abroad
To keep the Thebans fully overawed,
And noble Theseus ordered thereupon
That summons should be sent for Palamon.
    Not knowing for what reason ordered back,
And still in melancholy suit of black,
Palamon came on this authority
In haste. Then Theseus sent for Emily.
    When all were seated there and hushed the place,
The noble Duke kept silent for a space
And ere he chose to let his wisdom fall
His eyes ranged slowly round about the hall.
Then with a sober visage and the still
Sound of a sigh, he thus expressed his will:
    'The First Great Cause and Mover of all above
When first He made that fairest chain of love,
Great was the consequence and high the intent.
He well knew why He did, and what He meant.
For in that fairest chain of love He bound
Fire and air and water and the ground

Two young knights bend the knee
to accept the commands of their liege
lord.

Of earth in certain limits they may not flee.
And that same Prince and Mover then,' said he
'Established this poor world, appointing ways,
Seasons, durations, certain length of days,
To all that is engendered here below,
Past which predestined hour none may go,
Though we have power to abridge our days.
I need not quote authority or raise
More proof than what experience can show,
But give opinion here from what I know.
    'Since we discern this order, we are able
To know that Prince is infinite and stable,
And any but a fool knows in his soul
That every part derives from this great whole.
For nature cannot be supposed to start
From some particular portion or mere part,
But from a whole and undisturbed perfection
Descending thence to what is in subjection
To change, and will corrupt. And therefore He
In wise foreknowledge stablished the decree
That species of all things and the progression
Of seed and growth continue by succession
And not eternally. This is no lie,
As any man can see who has an eye.
    'Look at the oak; how slow a tree to nourish
From when it springs until it comes to flourish!
It has so long a life, and yet we see
That in the end it falls, a wasted tree.
    'Consider too how hard the stone we tread
Under our feet! That very rock and bed
On which we walk is wasting as it lies.
Time will be when the broadest river dries
And the great cities wane and last descend
Into the dust, for all things have an end.
    'For man and woman we can plainly see
Two terms appointed; so it needs must be
– That is to say, the terms of youth and age.
For every man will perish, king and page,
Some in their beds and some in the deep sea,
And some upon the battle-field, maybe.
There is no help for it, all take the track,
For all must die and there is none comes back.
    'Who orders this but Jupiter the King,
The Prince and Cause of all and everything,

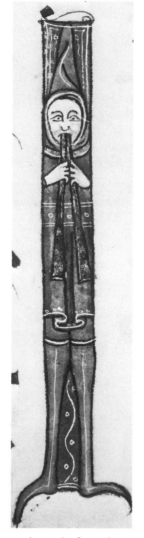

A decorative strip from the
Luttrell Psalter showing a man
playing on pipes.

Converting all things back into the source
From which they were derived, to which they course?
And against this no creature here alive
Whatever his degree may hope to strive.
    'Then hold it wise, for so it seems to me,
To make a virtue of necessity,
Take in good part what we may not eschew,
Especially whatever things are due
To all of us; his is a foolish soul
That's rebel against Him who guides the whole,
And it is honour to a man whose hour
Strikes in his day of excellence and flower,
When he is certain of his own good name
And never known in any act of shame.
And gladder should a friend be of his death
Where there is honour in the yielded breath,
Gladder than for a name by age made pale,
And all forgotten the heroic tale.
Then is the time, if you would win a name,
To die, upon the moment of your fame.
    'The contrary of this is wilfulness;
Why do we grumble? Where is the distress
If good Arcite, the flower of chivalry,
Departed in all honour, stainlessly
Set free from the foul prison of this life?
Shall those he loved, his cousin and his wife,
Murmur against his welfare, or suppose
He can return them thanks? Not he, God knows.
Offending so against him, they offend
Themselves, and are no better in the end.
    'So what conclusion can I draw from this
Except that after grief there should be bliss
And praise to Jupiter for all his grace?
So, ere we make departure from this place,
I rule that of two sorrows we endeavour
To make one perfect joy, to last for ever.
Then let us look, and where we find herein
The greatest grief let happiness begin.
    'Sister,' he said, 'it has my full assent,
And is confirmed by this my parliament,
That gentle Palamon, your own true knight,
Who loves and serves you, heart and soul and might,
And always has since first he saw your face,
Shall move you to feel pity, gain your grace

And so become your husband and your lord.
Give me your hand, for this is our award.
Let us now see your womanly compassion.
By God, he's a king's nephew! Were his fashion
No more than that of a knight-bachelor,
What with the years he served and suffered for
Your love (unless his sufferings deceive me)
He would be worth considering, believe me.
A noble mercy should surpass a right.'
   And then he said to Palamon the knight,
'I think there needs but little sermoning
To gain your own assent to such a thing.
Come near, and take your lady by the hand.'
And they were joined together by the band
That is called matrimony, also marriage,
By counsel of the Duke and all his peerage.
   And thus with every bliss and melody
Palamon was espoused to Emily,
And God that all this wide, wide world has wrought,
Send them his love, for it was dearly bought!
Now Palamon's in joy, amid a wealth
Of bliss and splendour, happiness and health.
He's tenderly beloved of Emily
And serves her with a gentle constancy,
And never a jealous world between them spoken
Or other sorrow in a love unbroken.
Thus ended Palamon and Emily,
And God save all this happy company!

                            Amen.

Words between the Host and the Miller

When we had heard the tale the Knight had told,
Not one among the pilgrims, young or old,
But said it was indeed a noble story
Worthy to be remembered for its glory,
And it especially pleased the gentlefolk.
Our Host began to laugh and swore in joke:
'It's going well, we've opened up the bale;
Now, let me see. Who'll tell another tale?
Upon my soul the game was well begun!
Come on, Sir Monk, and show what can be done;
Repay the Knight a little for his tale!'

    The Miller, very drunk and rather pale,
Was straddled on his horse half-on half-off
And in no mood for manners or to doff
His hood or hat, or wait on any man,
But in a voice like Pilate's he began*
To huff and swear. 'By blood and bones and belly,
I've got a noble story I can tell 'ee,
I'll pay the Knight his wages, not the Monk.'

    Our Host perceived at once that he was drunk
And said, 'Now hold on, Robin, dear old brother;
We'll get some better man to tell another;
You wait a bit. Let's have some common sense.'
'God's soul, I won't!' said he. 'At all events
I mean to talk, or else I'll go my way.'
Our Host replied, 'Well, blast you then, you may.
You're just a fool; your wits are overcome.'

    'Now listen,' said the Miller, 'all and some,
To what I have to say. But first I'm bound
To say I'm drunk, I know it by my sound.
And if the words get muddled in my tale
Just put it down to too much Southwark ale.
I mean to tell a legend and a life
Of an old carpenter and of his wife,
And how a student came and set his cap . . .'

    The Reeve looked up and shouted, 'Shut your trap!

Give over with your drunken harlotry.
It is a sin and foolishness,' said he,
'To slander any man or bring a scandal
On wives in general. Why can't you handle
Some other tale? There's other things beside.'
　　To this the drunken Miller then replied,
'My dear old brother Oswald, such is life.
A man's no cuckold if he has no wife.
For all that, I'm not saying you are one;
There's many virtuous wives, all said and done,
Ever a thousand good for one that's bad,
As well you know yourself, unless you're mad.
What's biting you? Can't I tell stories too?
I've got a wife, Lord knows, as well as you,
Yet for the oxen in my plough, indeed,
I wouldn't take it on me, more than need,
To think myself a cuckold, just because.
I'm pretty sure I'm not, and never was.
One shouldn't be too inquisitive in life
Either about God's secrets or one's wife.
You'll find God's plenty all you could desire;
Of the remainder, better not enquire.'
　　What can I add? The Miller had begun,
He would not hold his peace for anyone,
But told his churl's tale his own way, I fear.
And I regret I must repeat it here,
And so I beg of all who are refined
For God's love not to think me ill-inclined
Or evil in my purpose. I rehearse
Their tales as told, for better or for worse,
For else I should be false to what occurred.
So if this tale had better not be heard,
Just turn the page and choose another sort;
You'll find them here in plenty, long and short;
Many historical, that will profess
Morality, good breeding, saintliness.
Do not blame me if you should choose amiss.
The Miller was a churl, I've told you this,
So was the Reeve, and other some as well,
And harlotry was all they had to tell.
Consider then and hold me free of blame;
And why be serious about a game?

The Miller's Tale

Some time ago there was a rich old codger
Who lived in Oxford and who took a lodger.
The fellow was a carpenter by trade,
His lodger a poor student who had made
Some studies in the arts, but all his fancy
Turned to astrology and geomancy,
And he could deal with certain propositions
And make a forecast under some conditions
About the likelihood of drought or showers
For those who asked at favourable hours,
Or put a question how their luck would fall
In this or that, I can't describe them all.
    This lad was known as Nicholas the Gallant,
And making love in secret was his talent,
For he was very close and sly, and took
Advantage of his meek and girlish look.

He rented a small chamber in the kip
All by himself without companionship.
He decked it charmingly with herbs and fruit
And he himself was sweeter than the root
Of liquorice, or any fragrant herb.
His astronomic text-books were superb,
He had an astrolabe to match his art
And calculating counters laid apart
On handy shelves that stood above his bed.
His press was curtained coarsely and in red;
Above there lay a gallant harp in sight
On which he played melodiously at night
With such a touch that all the chamber rang;
It was *The Virgin's Angelus* he sang,
And after that he sang *King William's Note*,
And people often blessed his merry throat.
And that was how this charming scholar spent
His time and money, which his friends had sent.

　　This carpenter had married a young wife
Not long before, and loved her more than life.
She was a girl of eighteen years of age.
Jealous he was and kept her in the cage,
For he was old and she was wild and young;
He thought himself quite likely to be stung.

　　He might have known, were Cato on his shelf,
A man should marry someone like himself;
A man should pick an equal for his mate.
Youth and old age are often in debate.
His wits were dull, he'd fallen in the snare
And had to bear his cross as others bear.

　　She was a pretty creature, fair and tender,
And had a weasel's body, softly slender.
She used to wear a girdle of striped silk,
Her apron was as white as morning milk
To deck her loins, all gusseted and pleated.
Her smock was white; embroidery repeated
Its pattern on the collar front and back,
Inside and out; it was of silk, and black.
And all the ribbons on her milky mutch
Were made to match her collar, even such.
She wore a broad silk fillet rather high,
And certainly she had a lecherous eye.
And she had plucked her eyebrows into bows,
Slenderly arched they were, and black as sloes.

And a more truly blissful sight to see
She was than blossom on a cherry-tree,
And softer than the wool upon a wether.
And by her girdle hung a purse of leather,
Tasselled in silk, with metal droplets, pearled.
If you went seeking up and down the world
The wisest man you met would have to wrench
His fancy to imagine such a wench.
She had a shining colour, gaily tinted,
And brighter than a florin newly minted,
And when she sang it was as loud and quick
As any swallow perched above a rick.
And she would skip or play some game or other
Like any kid or calf behind its mother.
Her mouth was sweet as mead or honey – say
A hoard of apples lying in the hay.
Skittish she was, and jolly as a colt,
Tall as a mast and upright as a bolt
Out of a bow. Her collaret revealed
A brooch as big as boss upon a shield.
High shoes she wore, and laced them to the top.
She was a daisy, O a lollypop
For any nobleman to take to bed
Or some good man of yeoman stock to wed.

   Now, gentlemen, this Gallant Nicholas
Began to romp about and make a pass
At this young woman, happening on her one day,
Her husband being out, down Osney way.
Students are sly, and giving way to whim,
He made a grab and caught her by the quim
And said, 'O God, I love you! Can't you see
If I don't have you it's the end of me?'
Then held her haunches hard and gave a cry
'O love-me-all-at-once or I shall die!'
She gave a spring, just like a skittish colt
Boxed in a frame for shoeing, and with a jolt
Managed in time to wrench her head away,
And said, 'Give over, Nicholas, I say!
No, I won't kiss you! Stop it! Let me go
Or I shall scream! I'll let the neighbours know!
Where are your manners? Take away your paws!'

   Then Nicholas began to plead his cause
And spoke so fair in proffering what he could
That in the end she promised him she would,

A sight which would have touched the heartstrings of the Prioress for, said Chaucer, 'she used to weep if she but saw a mouse caught in a trap'. Another decoration from the Luttrell Psalter.

Swearing she'd love him, with a solemn promise
To be at his disposal, by St Thomas,
When she could spy an opportunity.
'My husband is so full of jealousy,
Unless you watch your step and hold your breath
I know for certain it will be my death,'
She said, 'So keep it well under your hat.'
'Oh, never mind about a thing like that,'
Said he; 'A scholar doesn't have to stir
His wits so much to trick a carpenter.'
    And so they both agreed to it, and swore
To watch their chance, as I have said before.
When things were settled thus as they thought fit,
And Nicholas had stroked her loins a bit
And kissed her sweetly, he took down his harp
And played away, a merry tune and sharp.
    It happened later she went off to church,
This worthy wife, one holiday, to search
Her conscience and to do the works of Christ.
She put her work aside and she enticed
The colour to her face to make her mark;
Her forehead shone. There was a parish clerk
Serving the church, whose name was Absalon.
His hair was all in golden curls and shone;
Just like a fan it strutted outwards, starting
To left and right from an accomplished parting.
Ruddy his face, his eyes as grey as goose,
His shoes cut out in tracery, as in use
In old St Paul's. The hose upon his feet
Showed scarlet through, and all his clothes were neat
And proper. In a jacket of light blue,
Flounced at the waist and tagged with laces too,
He went, and wore a surplice just as gay
And white as any blossom on the spray.
God bless my soul, he was a merry knave!
He knew how to let blood, cut hair and shave,
And draw up legal deeds; at other whiles
He used to dance in twenty different styles
(After the current school at Oxford though,
Casting his legs about him to and fro).
He played a two-stringed fiiddle, did it proud,
And sang a high falsetto rather loud;
And he was just as good on the guitar.
There was no public-house in town or bar

A set of keys with varying patterns of wards.

He didn't visit with his merry face
If there were saucy barmaids round the place.
He was a little squeamish in the matter
Of farting, and satirical in chatter.
This Absalon, so jolly in his ways,
Would bear the censer round on holy days
And cense the parish women. He would cast
Many a love-lorn look before he passed,
Especially at this carpenter's young wife;
Looking at her would make a happy life
He thought, so neat, so sweet, so lecherous.
And I dare say if she had been a mouse
And he a cat, she'd have been pounced upon.
    In taking the collection Absalon
Would find his heart was set in such a whirl
Of love, he would take nothing from a girl,
For courtesy, he said, it wasn't right.
    That evening, when the moon was shining bright
He ups with his guitar and off he tours
On the look-out for any paramours.
Larky and amorous, away he strode
Until he reached the carpenter's abode
A little after cock-crow, took his stand
Beside the casement window close at hand
(It was set low upon the cottage-face)
And started singing softly and with grace,
    '*Now dearest lady, if thy pleasure be*
    In thoughts of love, think tenderly of me!'
On his guitar he plucked a tuneful string.
    This carpenter awoke and heard him sing
And turning to his wife said, 'Alison!
Wife! Do you hear him? There goes Absalon
Chanting away under our chamber wall.'
And she replied, 'Yes, John, I hear it all.'
If she thought more of it she didn't tell.
    So things went on. What's better than 'All's well'?
From day to day this jolly Absalon,
Wooing away, became quite woe-begone;
He lay awake all night, and all the day
Combed his thick locks and tried to pass for gay,
Wooed her by go-between and wooed by proxy,
Swore to be page and servant to his doxy,
Thrilled and rouladed like a nightingale,
Sent her sweet wine and mead and spicy ale,

With their heads well protected from the sun these countrymen are engaged in scything and reap-hooking. The scythe looks much heavier and more cumbersome than the modern version. The man with the reap-hook carries a branched stick to hold back the vegetation as countryfolk do today.

And wafers piping hot and jars of honey,
And, as she lived in town, he offered money.*
For there are some a money-bag provokes
And some are won by kindness, some by strokes.
    Once, in the hope his talent might engage,
He played the part of Herod on the stage.
What was the good? Were he as bold as brass,
She was in love with gallant Nicholas;
However Absalon might blow his horn
His labour won him nothing but her scorn.
She looked upon him as her private ape
And held his earnest wooing all a jape.
There is a proverb – and it is no lie –
You'll often hear repeated: '*Nigh-and-Sly
Wins against Fair-and-Square who isn't there.*'
For much as Absalon might tear his hair
And rage at being seldom in her sight,
Nicholas, nigh and sly, stood in his light.
Now show your paces, Nicholas you spark!
And leave lamenting to the parish clerk.
    And so it happened that one Saturday,
When the old carpenter was safe away
At Osney, Nicholas and Alison
Agreed at last in what was to be done.
Nicholas was to exercise his wits
On her suspicious husband's foolish fits,
And, if so be the trick worked out all right,
She then would sleep with Nicholas all night,
For such was his desire and hers as well;
And even quicker than it takes to tell,
Young Nicholas, who simply couldn't wait,
Went to his room on tip-toe with a plate
Of food and drink, enough to last a day
Or two, and Alison was told to say,
In case her husband asked for Nicholas,
That she had no idea where he was,
And that she hadn't set eyes on him all day
And thought he must be ill, she couldn't say;
And more than once the maid had given a call
And shouted but no answer came at all.
    So things went on the whole of Saturday
Without a sound from Nicholas, who lay
Upstairs, and ate or slept as pleased him best
Till Sunday when the sun went down to rest.

This foolish carpenter was lost in wonder
At Nicholas; what could have got him under?
He said, 'I can't help thinking, by the Mass,
Things can't be going right with Nicholas.
What if he took and died? God guard his ways!
A ticklish place the world is, nowadays.
I saw a corpse this morning borne to kirk
That only Monday last I saw at work.
Run up,' he told the serving-lad, 'be quick,
Shout at his door, or knock it with a brick.
Take a good look and tell me how he fares.'

The serving-boy went sturdily upstairs,
Stopped at the door and, standing there, the lad
Shouted away and, hammering like mad,
Cried, 'Ho! What's up? Hi! Master Nicholay!
How can you lie up there asleep all day?'

But all for nought, he didn't hear a soul.
He found a broken panel with a hole
Right at the bottom, useful to the cat
For creeping in; he took a look through that,
And so at last by peering through the crack
He saw this scholar gaping on his back
As if he'd caught a glimpse of the new moon.
Down went the boy and told his master soon
About the state in which he found the man.

On hearing this the carpenter began
To cross himself and said, 'St Frideswide bless us!
We little know what's coming to distress us.
The man has fallen, with this here astromy,
Into a fit, or lunacy maybe.

I always thought that was how it would go.
God has some secrets that we shouldn't know.
How blessed are the simple, aye, indeed,
That only know enough to say their creed!
Happened just so with such another student
Of astromy and he was so imprudent
As to stare upwards while he crossed a field,
Busy foreseeing what the stars revealed;
And what should happen but he fell down flat
Into a marl-pit. He didn't foresee that!
But by the Saints we've reached a sorry pass;
I can't help worrying for Nicholas.
He shall be scolded for his studying
If I know how to scold, by Christ the King!

Get me a staff to prise against the floor.
Robin, you put your shoulder to the door.
We'll shake the study out of him, I guess!'
 The pair of them began to heave and press
Against the door. Happened the lad was strong
And so it didn't take them very long
To heave it off its hinges; down it came.
Still as a stone lay Nicholas, with the same
Expression, gaping upwards into air.
The carpenter supposed it was despair
And shook him by the shoulders with a stout
And purposeful attack, and gave a shout:
'What, Nicholas! Hey! Look down! Is that a fashion
To act? Wake up and think upon Christ's passion.
I sign you with the cross from elves and sprites!'
And he began the spell for use at nights
In all four corners of the room and out
Across the threshold too and round about:
 Jesu Christ and Benedict Sainted
 Bless this house from creature tainted,
 Drive away night-hags, white Pater-noster,
 Where did you go St Peter's soster?
 And in the end the dandy Nicholas
Began to sigh, 'And must it come to pass?'
He said, 'Must all the world be cast away?'
The carpenter replied, 'What's that you say?
Put trust in God as we do, working men.'
Nicholas answered, 'Fetch some liquor then,
And afterwards, in strictest secrecy,
I'll speak of something touching you and me,
But not another soul must know, that's plain.'
 This carpenter went down and came again
Bringing some powerful ale—a largish quart.
When each had had his share of this support
Young Nicholas got up and shut the door
And, sitting down beside him on the floor,
Said to the carpenter, 'Now, John, my dear,
My excellent host, swear on your honour here
Not to repeat a syllable I say,
For here are Christ's intentions, to betray
Which to a soul puts you among the lost,
And vengeance for it at a bitter cost
Shall fall upon you. You'll be driven mad!'
'Christ and His holy blood forbid it, lad!'

Feeding the poultry. The artist has added an amusing touch by putting one of the chicks on its mother's back. The woman carries her distaff under her arm.

The silly fellow answered. 'I'm no blab,
Though I should say it. I'm not given to gab.
Say what you like, for I shall never tell
Man, woman or child by Him that harrowed Hell!'*
    'Now, John,' said Nicholas, 'believe you me,
I have found out by my astrology,
And looking at the moon when it was bright,
That Monday next, a quarter way through night,
Rain is to fall in torrents, such a scud
It will be twice as bad as Noah's Flood.
This world,' he said, 'in just about an hour,
Shall all be drowned, it's such a hideous shower,
And all mankind, with total loss of life.'
    The carpenter exclaimed, 'Alas, my wife!
My little Alison! Is she to drown?'
And in his grief he very near fell down.
'Is there no remedy,' he said, 'for this?'
'Thanks be to God,' said Nicholas, 'there is,
If you will do exactly what I say
And don't start thinking up some other way.
In wise old Solomon you'll find the verse
"Who takes advice shall never fare the worse,"
And so if good advice is to prevail
I undertake with neither mast nor sail
To save her yet, and save myself and you.
Haven't you heard how Noah was saved too
When God forewarned him and his sons and daughters
That all the world should sink beneath the waters?'
'Yes,' said the carpenter, 'a long time back.'
'Haven't you heard,' said Nicholas, 'what a black
Business it was, when Noah tried to whip
His wife (who wouldn't come) on board the ship?
He'd have been better pleased, I'll undertake,
With all that weather just about to break,
If she had had a vessel of her own.
Now, what are we to do? We can't postpone
The thing; it's coming soon, as I was saying,
It calls for haste, not preaching or delaying.
    'I want you, now, at once, to hurry off
And fetch a shallow tub or kneading-trough
For each of us, but see that they are large
And such as we can float in, like a barge.
And have them loaded with sufficient victual
To last a day—we only need a little.

The waters will abate and flow away
Round nine o'clock upon the following day.
Robin the lad mayn't know of this, poor knave,
Nor Jill the maid, those two I cannot save.
Don't ask me why; and even if you do
I can't disclose God's secret thoughts to you.
You should be satisfied, unless you're mad,
To find as great a grace as Noah had.
And I shall save your wife, you needn't doubt it,
Now off you go, and hurry up about it.
　'And when the tubs have been collected, three,
That's one for her and for yourself and me,
Then hang them in the roof below the thatching
That no one may discover what we're hatching.
When you have finished doing what I said
And stowed the victuals in them overhead,
Also an axe to hack the ropes apart,
So, when the water rises, we can start,
And, lastly, when you've broken out the gable,
The garden one that's just above the stable,
So that we may cast free without delay
After the mighty shower has gone away,
You'll float as merrily, I undertake,
As any lily-white duck behind her drake.
And I'll call out, "Hey, Alison! Hey, John!
Cheer yourselves up! The flood will soon be gone."
And you'll shout back, "Hail, Master Nicholay!
Good morning! I can see you well. It's day!"
We shall be lords for all the rest of life
Of all the world, like Noah and his wife.
　'One thing I warn you of; it's only right.
We must be very careful on the night,
Once we have safely managed to embark,
To hold our tongues, to utter no remark,
No cry or call, for we must fall to prayer.
This is the Lord's dear will, so have a care.
　'Your wife and you must hang some way apart,
For there must be no sin before we start,
No more in longing looks than in the deed.
Those are your orders. Off with you! God speed!
To-morrow night when everyone's asleep
We'll all go quietly upstairs and creep
Into our tubs, awaiting Heaven's grace.
And now be off. No time to put the case

At greater length, no time to sermonize;
The proverb says, "Say nothing, send the wise."
You're wise enough, I do not have to teach you.
Go, save our lives for us, as I beseech you.'
   This silly carpenter then went his way
Muttering to himself, 'Alas the day!'
And told his wife in strictest secrecy.
She was aware, far more indeed than he,
What this quaint stratagem might have in sight,
But she pretended to be dead with fright.
'Alas!' she said. 'Whatever it may cost,
Hurry and help, or we shall all be lost.
I am your honest, true and wedded wife,
Go, dearest husband, help to save my life!'
   How fancy throws us into perturbation!
People can die of mere imagination,
So deep is the impression one can take.
This silly carpenter began to quake,
Before his eyes there verily seemed to be
The floods of Noah, wallowing like the sea
And drowning Alison his honey-pet.
He wept and wailed, his features were all set
In grief, he sighed with many a doleful grunt.
He went and got a tub, began to hunt
For kneading-troughs, found two, and had them sent
Home to his house in secret; then he went
And, unbeknowns, he hung them from a rafter.
With his own hands he made three ladders after,
Uprights and rungs, to help them in their scheme
Of climbing where they hung upon the beam.

Peasants gather and stack sheaves
of corn after the harvest. One of the
men seems to care for his hands
for he has a pair of gloves tucked in
his waistband.

He victualled tub and trough, and made all snug
With bread and cheese, and ale in a large jug,
Enough for three of them to last the day,
And, just before completing this array,
Packed off the maid and his apprentice too
To London on a job they had to do.
And on the Monday when it drew to night
He shut his door and dowsed the candle-light
And made quite sure all was as it should be.
And shortly, up they clambered, all the three,
Silent and separate. They began to pray
And '*Pater Noster* mum', said Nicholay,
And 'mum' said John, and 'mum' said Alison.
The carpenter's devotions being done,
He sat quite still, then fell to prayer again
And waited anxiously to hear the rain.

The carpenter, with all the work he'd seen,
Fell dead asleep – round curfew, must have been,
Maybe a little later on the whole.
He groaned in sleep for travail of his soul
And snored because his head was turned awry.

Down by their ladders, stalking from on high
Came Nicholas and Alison, and sped
Softly downstairs, without a word, to bed,
And where this carpenter was wont to be
The revels started and the melody.
And thus lay Nicholas and Alison
At busy play in eager quest of fun,
Until the bell for lauds had started ringing
And in the chancel Friars began their singing.

This parish clerk, this amorous Absalon,
Love-stricken still and very woe-begone,
Upon the Monday was in company
At Osney with his friends for jollity,
And chanced to ask a resident cloisterer
What had become of John the carpenter.
The fellow drew him out of church to say,
'Don't know; not been at work since Saturday.
I can't say where he is; I think he went
To fetch the Abbot timber. He is sent
Often enough for timber, has to go
Out to the Grange and stop a day or so;
If not, he's certainly at home to-day,
But where he is I can't exactly say.'

Potters exercised their wit and
ingenuity on designing jugs with a
variety of motifs. A medieval jug.

Less dignified are these droll,
grotesque pitchers for water or wine.

Absalon was a jolly lad and light
Of heart; he thought, 'I'll stay awake to-night;
I'm certain that I haven't seen him stirring
About his door since dawn; it's safe inferring
That he's away. As I'm alive I'll go
And tap his window softly at the crow
Of cock – the sill is low-set on the wall.
I shall see Alison and tell her all
My love-longing, and I can hardly miss
Some favour from her, at the least a kiss.
I'll get some satisfaction anyway;
There's been an itching in my mouth all day
And that's a sign of kissing at the least.
And all last night I dreamt about a feast.
I think I'll go and sleep an hour or two,
Then wake and have some fun, that's what I'll do.'
    The first cock crew at last, and thereupon
Up rose this jolly lover Absalon
In gayest clothes, garnished with that and this;
But first he chewed a grain of liquorice
To charm his breath before he combed his hair.
Under his tongue the comfit nestling there
Would make him gracious. He began to roam
To where old John and Alison kept home
And by the casement window took his stand.
Breast-high it stood, no higher than his hand.
He gave a cough, no more than half a sound:
'Alison, honey-comb, are you around?
Sweet cinnamon, my little pretty bird,
Sweetheart, wake up and say a little word!
You seldom think of me in all my woe,
I sweat for love of you wherever I go!
No wonder if I do, I pine and bleat
As any lambkin hungering for the teat,
Believe me, darling, I'm so deep in love
I croon with longing like a turtle-dove,
I eat as little as a girl at school.'
'You go away,' she answered, 'you Tom-fool!
There's no come-up-and-kiss-me here for you.
I love another and why shouldn't I too?
Better than you, by Jesu, Absalon!
Take yourself off or I shall throw a stone.
I want to get some sleep. You go to Hell!'
'Alas!' said Absalon. 'I knew it well;

Towns and Buildings

John Lydgate was an English poet, for a time a monk, who described himself as a disciple of Chaucer. He wrote an imaginative account of the siege of Thebes which he called *The Story of Thebes*, and by a 'merry conceit' added himself to Chaucer's pilgrims and his story of Thebes to *The Canterbury Tales*. The illustration (1) below shows him among some of the pilgrims. In the background is a typical medieval walled town. It is Canterbury itself with the cathedral in the upper right corner.

Most towns and cities at the time were surrounded by walls for the defence of the citizens within, and the remains of such walls and the city gates are still to be seen in many places, including Canterbury. The illumination opposite (2) shows the Tower of London and behind it London Bridge as Chaucer's pilgrims would have seen them. Indeed those pilgrims from London itself or from north of the capital would have had to cross the bridge to reach the Tabard Inn in Southwark, the starting point of

1

2

3

4

5

their pilgrimage. The miniature appears in a medieval manuscript, *The Poems of Charles, Duke of Orleans*, and records his 25 years' 'imprisonment' in the Tower after his capture at the Battle of Agincourt and while he was waiting for the considerable ransom appropriate to an exalted French prince to be paid.

Picture (3) shows the Great Hall of Penshurst Place in Kent as it is today and was substantially when it was built in Chaucer's time by Sir John de Pulteney. It is typical of the main chamber of a great feudal house with its high vaulted timber roof up to which the smoke from the open brazier in the centre would rise. A raised dais with the high table was where the lord and his family ate their meals, the inferior members of the household being seated below. Fine timber screens concealed the entrances. More modest, but solid and charming to modern eyes, is the timbered house (4). It still stands in Southampton and is now a public house, but the exterior has been painstakingly restored. It would have been the house of an

official or comfortably-off merchant and suggests the growth of a prosperous merchant class and the beginning of the decline of the feudal system.

More elegant is the courtyard in (5). The external staircase leads to the principal rooms on the first floor; in the foreground is the well, the water supply for the household. The roofed gallery connects the apartments on the next floor, and already the utilization of roof space by the introduction of dormer windows can be seen. During Chaucer's time significant changes in building were taking place. The gradual pacification and unification of the country, which began under King Edward I, were making less necessary the grim castles which had uncomfortably housed the wealthy families, and cannon as used in the Hundred Years War made these defensive buildings less effective. Wealthy families began to prefer the more comfortable, unfortified manor houses such as Penshurst Place. An exception to this trend was the handsome castle at Bodiam in Sussex (6), shown with its moat frozen over. Some 30 miles from Canterbury, it was actually built during the Hundred Years War while Chaucer was still alive. It was designed as a protection against a possible French invasion, for, although it is now well inland, at that time it commanded the mouth of the River Rother, which was a navigable river flowing through part of south-east England. Internally this area was one of the safest and most settled in the country, but about the time Bodiam castle was built three south-coast towns were actually sacked by the French.

Medieval building methods can be seen in (7). As was the practice at the time artists would illustrate religious and classical themes by drawing partly on their imagination but largely on familiar habits and surroundings, however incongruous. This picture illustrates a classical theme but the builders are medieval builders using medieval methods. The bottom picture (8) shows Canterbury Cathedral today. The building was begun in the eleventh century and the cathedral was partly rebuilt and added to during the Middle Ages, but with the exception of the central perpendicular tower—Bell Harry—erected 100 years later—it is much as Chaucer's band of pilgrims would have seen it at the end of their journey. The deed shown in (9) is the lease of a house in the garden of the chapel of St Mary in Westminster, London, which Chaucer signed in 1399.

True love is always mocked and girded at;
So kiss me, if you can't do more than that,
For Jesu's love and for the love of me!'
'And if I do, will you be off?' said she.
'Promise you, darling,' answered Absalon.
'Get ready then; wait, I'll put something on,'
She said and then she added under breath
To Nicholas, 'Hush . . . we shall laugh to death!'
    This Absalon went down upon his knees;
'I am a lord!' he thought, 'And by degrees
There may be more to come; the plot may thicken.'
'Mercy, my love!' he said, 'Your mouth, my chicken!'
    She flung the window open then in haste
And said, 'Have done, come on, no time to waste,
The neighbours here are always on the spy.'
    Absalon started wiping his mouth dry.
Dark was the night as pitch, as black as coal,
And at the window out she put her hole,
And Absalon, so fortune framed the farce,
Put up his mouth and kissed her naked arse
Most savorously before he knew of this.
    And back he started. Something was amiss;
He knew quite well a woman has no beard,
Yet something rough and hairy had appeared.
'What have I done?' he said. 'Can that be you?'
'Teehee!' she cried and clapped the window to.
Off went poor Absalon sadly through the dark.
'A beard! a beard!' cried Nicholas the Spark.
'God's body, that was something like a joke!'
And Absalon, overhearing what he spoke,
Bit on his lips and nearly threw a fit
In rage and thought, 'I'll pay you back for it!'
    Who's busy rubbing, scraping at his lips
With dust, with sand, with straw, with cloth, with chips,
But Absalon? He thought, 'I'll bring him down!
I wouldn't let this go for all the town.
I'd take my soul and sell it to the Devil
To be revenged upon him! I'll get level.
O God, why did I let myself be fooled?'
    The fiery heat of love by now had cooled,
For from the time he kissed her hinder parts
He didn't give a tinker's curse for tarts;
His malady was cured by this endeavour
And he defied all paramours whatever.

The study of the sun, moon and stars had engaged astronomers since centuries before the birth of Christ and was pursued earnestly in the medieval monasteries. Here an illuminated manuscript records in simple diagram form an eclipse of the sun.

Thy zodiak of þin astrelabye ys schapen as a com-
pas which þat conteneþ a large brede as after the
quitite of þin astrelabye. In ensample þat þe zodiak in
heuene ys ymagyned to ben a surface conteynynge a
latitude of 12 degrees. Where as alle þe remenaunt
of cercles in þe heuene ben ymagyned uerrey lynes
wiþ outen eny latitude. & Amyddes þis celestial zodi-
ak ys ymagyned a lyne which þat is cleped þe eclip-
tik lyne under which lyne ys euermo þe wey of þe
sune. Thus ben þere sixe degrees of þe zodiak on þat

A diagram from *The Treatise on the Astrolabe*
which Chaucer wrote for his son Lewis to explain the use of the instrument.

So, weeping like a child that has been whipped,
He turned away; across the road he slipped
And called on Gervase. Gervase was a smith;
His forge was full of things for ploughing with
And he was busy sharpening a share.

Absalon knocked, and with an easy air
Called, 'Gervase! Open up the door, come on!'
'What's that? Who's there?' 'It's me, it's Absalon.'
'What, Absalon? By Jesu's blessed tree
You're early up! Hey, *benedicite*,
What's wrong? Some jolly girl as like as not
Has coaxed you out and set you on the trot.
Blessed St Neot! You know the thing I mean.'

But Absalon, who didn't give a bean
For all his joking, offered no debate.
He had a good deal more upon his plate
Than Gervase knew and said, 'Would it be fair
To borrow that coulter in the chimney there,
The hot one, see it? I've a job to do;
It won't take long, I'll bring it back to you.'
Gervase replied, 'Why, if you asked for gold,
A bag of sovereigns or for wealth untold,
It should be yours, as I'm an honest smith.
But, Christ, why borrow that to do it with?'
'Let that,' said Absalon, 'be as it may;
You'll hear about it all some other day.'

He caught the coulter up – the haft was cool –
And left the smithy softly with the tool,
Crept to the little window in the wall
And coughed. He knocked and gave a little call
Under the window as he had before.

Alison said, 'There's someone at the door.
Who's knocking there? I'll warrant it's a thief.'
'Why, no,' said he, 'my little flower-leaf,
It's your own Absalon, my sweety-thing!
Look what I've brought you – it's a golden ring
My mother gave me, as I may be saved.
It's very fine, and prettily engraved;
I'll give it to you, darling, for a kiss.'

Now Nicholas had risen for a piss,
And thought he could improve upon the jape
And make him kiss his arse ere he escape,
And opening the window with a jerk,
Stuck out his arse, a handsome piece of work,

Threshing with flails.

Buttocks and all, as far as to the haunch.
   Said Absalon, all set to make a launch,
'Speak, pretty bird, I know not where thou art!'
This Nicholas at once let fly a fart
As loud as if it were a thunder-clap.
He was near blinded by the blast, poor chap,
But his hot iron was ready; with a thump
He smote him in the middle of the rump.

   Off went the skin a hand's-breath round about
Where the hot coulter struck and burnt it out.
Such was the pain, he thought he must be dying
And, mad with agony, he started crying,
'Help! Water! Water! Help! For Heaven's love!'

   The carpenter, startled from sleep above,
And hearing shouts for water and a thud,
Thought, 'Heaven help us! Here comes Nowel's Flood!'
And up he sat and with no more ado
He took his axe and smote the ropes in two
And down went everything. He didn't stop
To sell his bread and ale, but came down flop
Upon the floor and fainted right away.

   Up started Alison and Nicholay
And shouted, 'Help!' and 'Murder!' in the street.
The neighbours all came running up in heat
And stood there staring at the wretched man.
He lay there fainting, pale beneath his tan;
His arm in falling had been broken double.
But still he was obliged to face his trouble,
For when he spoke he was at once borne down
By Nicholas and his wife. They told the town
That he was mad, there'd got into his blood
Some sort of nonsense about 'Nowel's Flood',
That vain imaginings and fantasy
Had made him buy the kneading-tubs, that he
Had hung them in the rafters up above
And that he'd begged them both for heaven's love
To sit up in the roof for company.

   All started laughing at this lunacy
And streamed upstairs to gape and pry and poke,
And treated all his suffering as a joke.
No matter what the carpenter asserted
It went for nothing, no one was converted;
With powerful oaths they swore the fellow down
And he was held for mad by all the town;

Carrying grain to the mill to be ground into flour.

Even the learned said to one another,
'The fellow must be crazy, my dear brother.'
So to a general laughter he succumbed.
   That's how the carpenter's young wife was plumbed
For all the tricks his jealousy could try,
And Absalon has kissed her nether eye
And Nicholas is branded on the bum.
And God bring all of us to Kingdom Come.

The Reeve's Prologue

When all had laughed at the preposterous lark
Of Absalon and Nicholas the Spark,
Various folk made various comment after;
But the majority dissolved in laughter,
Nor did I see a soul it seemed to grieve
Unless it might be Oswald, the old Reeve,
For, as he was a carpenter by trade,
He was a little angry still and made
Grumbling remarks and scolded for a bit.
   'As I'm a man I'd pay you back for it,'
He said, 'with how they bleared a Miller's eye,
If I liked dirt and wished to argufy.
But I am old. Dirt doesn't go with doddering,
Grass-time is done and I'm for winter foddering.
My hoary top-knot writes me down for old;
Same as my hair, my heart is full of mould,
Unless I be like them there medlar-fruit,
Them that gets rottener as they ripen to't,
Till they be rotted down in straw and dung.
That's how we get to be, no longer young.
Till we be rotten we can never ripe.
We hop along, as long as world will pipe;
Our will is always catching on the nail,
Wanting a hoary head and a green tail,
Like leeks have got; the strength to play that game
Is gone, though we love foolishness the same.
What we can't do no more we talk about
And rake the ashes when the fire is out.
   'Yet we have four live coals, as I can show;
Lies, boasting, greed and rage will always glow.
Those are the sparks among the ancient embers
Though we be nigh unwelded in our members.
Desire never fails, and that's the truth,
For even now I have a coltish tooth,
Many as be the years now dead and done
Before my tap of life began to run.

Certain, when I was born, so long ago,
Death drew the tap of life and let it flow;
And ever since the tap has done its task,
And now there's little but an empty cask.
My stream of life's but drops upon the rim.
An old fool's tongue will run away with him
To chime and chatter of monkey-tricks that's past;
There's nothing left but dotage at the last!'
    Our Host, on hearing all this sermoning,
Began to speak as lordly as a king,
And said, 'What does it come to, all this wit?
What! Spend the morning talking Holy Writ?
The devil that makes a preacher of a Reeve
Turns cobblers into doctors, I believe.
Give us your story, if you've one in stock.
Why, look! Here's Deptford and it's nine o'clock!
And Greenwich too, with many a blackguard in it.
High time to tell your story, so begin it.'
    'Now, gentlemen,' Oswald the Reeve replied,
'I hope as none will be dissatisfied
Though I should tweak the Miller by the cap,
For lawful 'tis to give him tap for tap.
    'This drunken Miller we've had so much drool of,
Told how a carpenter was made a fool of,
Maybe to score off me, for I am one.
By y'r leave, I'll pay him back before I've done
In his own filthy words, you may expec'.
I hope to God he breaks his bloody neck.
He sees the mote in my eye, if there is un,
But cannot see the beam there is in his'n.'

The Reeve's Tale

At Trumpington, not far from Cambridge town,
A bridge goes over where the brook runs down
And by that brook there stands a mill as well.
And it's God's truth that I am going to tell.
   There was a miller lived there many a day
As proud as any peacock and as gay;
He could play bag-pipes too, fish, mend his gear,
And turn a lathe, and wrestle, and poach deer.
And at his belt he carried a long blade,
Trenchant it was as any sword that's made,
And in his pouch a jolly little knife.
No one dared touch him, peril of his life.
He had a Sheffield dagger in his hose.
Round was his face and puggish was his nose;
Bald as an ape he was. To speak more fully,
He was a thorough-going market bully

Whom none dared lay a hand on or come near
Without him swearing that they'd buy it dear.
　　He was a thief as well of corn and meal,
And sly at that; his habit was to steal.
Simpkin the Swagger he was called in scorn.
He had a wife and she was nobly born;
Her father was the parson of the town;
A dowery of brass dishes he put down
In order to have Simpkin his relation.
The nuns had given her an education.
Simpkin would take no woman, so he said,
Unless she were a virgin and well-bred,
To save the honour of his yeoman stock;
And she was proud, pert as a magpie cock.
　　It was a proper sight to see the pair
On holidays, what with him strutting there
In front of her, his hood about his head,
And she behind him all decked out in red,
Like Simpkin's hose, for scarlet-red he had 'em.
No one dared call her anything but 'Madam',
And there was no one bold enough to try
A bit of fun with her or wink an eye,
Unless indeed he wanted Sim the Swagger
To murder him with cutlass, knife or dagger,
For jealous folk are dangerous, you know,
At least they want their wives to think them so.
And then her birth was smirched to say the least;
Being the daughter of a celibate priest
She must maintain her dignity, of which
She had as much as water in a ditch.
She was a sneering woman and she thought
That ladies should respect her, so they ought,
What with her well-connected family,
And education in a nunnery.
　　They had a daughter too between them both,
She was a girl of twenty summers' growth;
But that was all except a child they had
Still in the cradle, but a proper lad.
The wench was plump, well-grown enough to pass,
With a snub nose and eyes as grey as glass;
Her rump was broad, her breasts were round and high;
She'd very pretty hair, I will not lie.
The parson of the town, for she was fair,
Intended to appoint the girl as heir

A scene familiar through the ages.
An irate farmer waits for the boy
who has been caught stealing
cherries to come down from the
tree. The boy's shoes, which he has
removed to help him climb, can be
seen at the foot of the tree.

To all his property in house and land
And he was stiff with suitors to her hand.
He purposed to bestow her if he could
Where blood and ancient lineage made it good.
For Holy Church's goods should be expended
On Holy Church's blood, so well-descended,
And holy blood should have what's proper to it
Though Holy Church should be devoured to do it.
    This miller levied toll beyond a doubt
On wheat and malt from all the land about,
Particularly from a large-sized College
In Cambridge, Solar Hall.* 'Twas common knowledge
They sent their wheat and malt to him to grind it.
Happened one day the man who ought to mind it,
The college manciple, lay sick in bed,
And some reported him as good as dead.
On hearing which the miller robbed him more
A hundred times than he had robbed before;
For up till then he'd only robbed politely,
But now he stole outrageously, forthrightly.
    The Warden scolded hard and made a scene,
But there! The miller didn't give a bean,
Blustered it out and swore it wasn't so.
    Two poor young Bible-clerks or students, though,
Lived in this College (that of which I spoke).
Headstrong they were and eager for a joke,
And simply for the chance of sport and play
They went and plagued the Warden night and day
Just for a little leave to spend the morn
Watching the miller grind their meal and corn,
And each was ready to engage his neck
The miller couldn't rob them half a peck
Of corn by trickery, nor yet by force;
And in the end he gave them leave of course.
    One was called John and Alan was the other,
Both born in the same village, name of Strother,
Far in the north, I cannot tell you where.
    Alan collected all his gear with care,
Loaded his corn upon a horse he had,
And off he went with John the other lad,
Each with his sword and buckler by his side.
John knew the way – he didn't need a guide –
Reaches the mill and down the sack he flings.
    Alan spoke first: 'Well, Simon, lad, how's things?

And how's your canny daughter* and your wife?'
Says Simpkin, 'Welcome, Alan! Odds my life,
It's John as well! What are you up to here?'
'By God,' said John, 'Needs-must has got no peer,
And it behoves a man that has nie servant
To work, as say the learned and observant.
Wor Manciple is like enough to dee,
Such aches and torments in his teeth has he;
So Alan here and I have brought wor sack
Of corn for grinding and to bring it back.
Help us get home as quickly as ye can.'
'It shall be done,' said he, 'as I'm a man.
What'll you do while I've the job in hand?'
'By God,' said John, 'I have a mind to stand
Right by the hopper here and watch the corn
As it gans in. Never since I was born
Saw I a hopper wagging to and fro.'
    Alan spoke up: 'Eh, John, and will ye so?
Then I shall stand below a short way off
And watch the meal come down into the trough;
I need no more than that by way of sport,
For John, in faith, I'm one of the same sort
And diven't knaa nowt of milling, same as ye.'
    The miller smiled at their simplicity
And thought, 'It's just a trick, what they're about
They think that nobody can catch them out,
But by the Lord I'll blear their eyes a bit
For all their fine philosophy and wit.
The more they try to do me on the deal,
When the time comes, the more I mean to steal.
Instead of flour they shall be given bran.
"The greatest scholar is not the wisest man",
As the wolf said in answer to the mare.
Them and their precious learning! Much I care.'
    And when he saw his chance he sidled out
Into the yard behind and looked about
Without their noticing until at last
He found their horse where they had made him fast
Under an arbour just behind the mill.
    Up to the horse he goes with quiet skill
And strips the bridle off him there and then.
And when the horse was loose, off to the fen
Through thick and thin, and whinneying 'Weehee!'
He raced to join the wild mares running free.

The miller then went back and did not say
A word of this, but passed the time of day
With John and Alan till their corn was ground;
And when the meal was fairly sacked and bound,
John wandered out and found their horse was gone.
'Good Lord! Help! Help! Come quickly!' shouted John,
'Wor horse is lost, Alan! The devil's in it!
God's bones, man, use your legs! Come out this minute!
Lord save us all, the Warden's palfrey's lost.'
    Alan forgot his meal and corn and cost,
Abandoning frugality and care.
'What's that?' he shouted. 'Palfrey? Which way? Where?'
    The miller's wife ran clucking like a hen
Towards them, saying, 'Gone off to the fen
To the wild mares as fast as he can go.
Curse on the clumsy hand that tied him so!
Should have known better how to knit the reins.'
John said, 'Bad luck to it. Alan, for Christ's pains,
Put down your sword, man; so will I; let's gan!
We'll rin him like a roe together, man!
God's precious heart! He cannot scape us all!
Why didn't you put the palfrey in the stall?
You must be daft, bad luck to you! Haway!'
And off ran John and Alan in dismay,
Towards the fen as fast as they could go.
    And when the miller saw that this was so,
A good half-bushel of their flour he took
And gave it over to his wife to cook.
'I think,' he said, 'these lads have had a fright.
I'll pluck their beards. Yes, let 'em read and write,
But none the less a miller is their match.
Look at them now! Like children playing catch.
Won't be an easy job to get him, though!'
    These foolish Bible-clerks ran to and fro
And shouted, 'Woa, lad, stand! . . . Look out behind!
Whistle him up . . . I've got him . . . watch it . . . *mind!*'
But to be brief, it wasn't until night
They caught the palfrey, hunt him as they might
Over the fens, he ran away so fast;
But in a ditch they captured him at last.
    Weary and wet, like cattle in the rain,
Came foolish John and Alan back again.
Said John, 'Alas the day that I was born!
We've earned nowt here but mockery and scorn.

Labour-intensive work on the grindstone. Two knife-grinders turn the handles of the stone while a third holds the blade against it.

Wor corn is stolen and they'll call us fools,
Warden and all wor meäts in the Schools,
And most of all the miller. What a day!'
    So back they went, John grousing all the way,
Towards the mill and put the horse in byre.
They found the miller sitting by the fire,
For it was night, too late for going home,
And, for the love of God, they begged a room
For shelter and they proffered him their penny.
'A room?' the miller said. 'There isn't any.
There's this, such as it is; we'll share it then.
My house is small, but you are learned men
And by your arguments can make a place
Twenty foot broad as infinite as space.
Take a look round and see if it will do,
Or make it bigger with your parley-voo.'
'Well, Simon, you must have your little joke
And, by St Cuthbert, that was fairly spoke!
Well, people have a proverb to remind them
To bring their own, or take things as they find them,'
Said John. 'Dear host, do get us out the cup;
A little meat and drink would cheer us up.
We'll give ye the full payment, on my word.
No empty-handed man can catch a bird;
See, here's the silver, ready to be spent.'
    Down into Trumpington the daughter went
For bread and ale; the miller cooked a goose,
And tied their horse up lest it should get loose
Again, and in his chamber made a bed
With clean white sheets and blankets fairly spread,
Ten foot from his, upon a sort of shelf.
His daughter had a bed all by herself
Quite close in the same room; they were to lie
All side by side, no help for it, and why?
Because there was no other in the house.
    They supped and talked and had a fine carouse
And drank a lot of ale, the very best.
Midnight or thereabout they went to rest.
    Properly pasted was this miller's head,
Pale-drunk he was, he'd passed the stage of red;
Hiccupping through his nose he talked and trolled
As if he'd asthma or a heavy cold.
To bed he goes, his wife and he together;
She was as jolly as a jay in feather,

Having well wet her whistle from the ladle.
And by her bed she planted down the cradle
To rock the baby or to give it sup.
   When what was in the crock had been drunk up,
To bed went daughter too, and thereupon
To bed went Alan and to bed went John.
That was the lot; no sleeping-draught was needed.
The miller had taken so much booze unheeded,
He snorted like a cart-horse in his sleep
And vented other noises, loud and deep.
His wife joined in the chorus hot and strong;
Two furlongs off you might have heard their song.
The wench was snoring too, for company.
   Alan the clerk in all this melody
Gave John a poke and said, 'Are ye awake?
Did ye ever hear sich sang for guidness sake?
There's family prayers for ye among they noddies!
Wild fire come doon and burn them up, the bodies!
Who ever heard a canny thing like that?
The devil take their souls for what they're at!
All this lang neet I shall na get nie rest.
   'But never ye mind, all shall be for the best;
I tell ye, John, as sure as I'm a man,
I'm going to have that wench there, if I can!
The law grants easement when things gan amiss,
For, John, there is a law that gans like this:
"If in one point a person be aggrieved,
Then in another he shall be relieved."
   'Wor corn is stolen, nivvor doubt of that;
Ill-luck has followed us in all we're at,
And since no compensation has been offered
Against wor loss, I'll take the easement proffered.
God's soul, it shall be so indeed, none other!'
   John whispered back to him, 'Be careful, brother,
The miller is a torble man for slaughter;
If he should wake and find ye with his daughter
He might do injury to you and me.'
'Injury? Him! I coont him nat a flea!'
   Alan rose up; towards the wench he crept.
The wench lay flat upon her back and slept,
And ere she saw him, he had drawn so nigh
It was too late for her to give a cry.
To put it briefly, they were soon at one.
Now, Alan, play! For I will speak of John.

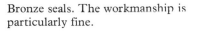

Bronze seals. The workmanship is
particularly fine.

John lay there still for quite a little while,
Complaining and lamenting in this style:
'A bloody joke . . . Lord, what a chance to miss!
I shall be made a monkey of for this!
My meät has got some comfort for his harms,
He has the miller's daughter in his arms;
He took his chance and now his needs are sped,
I'm but a sack of rubbish here in bed.
And when this jape is told in time to come
They'll say I was a softie and a bum!
I'll get up too and take what chance I may,
For God helps those that help theirsels, they say.'
    He rises, steals towards the cradle, lifts it,
And stepping softly back again, he shifts it
And lays it by his bed upon the floor.
    The miller's wife soon after ceased to snore,
Began to wake, rose up, and left the room,
And coming back she groped about in gloom,
Missing the cradle John had snatched away.
'Lord, Lord,' she said, 'I nearly went astray
And got into the student's bed. . . . How dreadful!
There would have been foul doings. What a bed-ful!'
    At last she gropes to where the cradle stands,
And so by fumbling upwards with her hands
She found the bed and thinking nought but good,
Since she was certain where the cradle stood,
Yet knew not where she was, for it was dark,
She well and fairly crept in with the clerk,
Then lay quite still and tried to go to sleep.
John waited for a while, then gave a leap
And thrust himself upon this worthy wife.
It was the merriest fit in all her life,
For John went deep and thrust away like mad.
It was a jolly life for either lad
Till the third morning cock began to sing.
    Alan grew tired as dawn began to spring;
He had been hard at work the long, long night.
'Bye-bye,' he said, 'sweet Molly. . . . Are ye a'right?
The day has come, I cannot linger here,
But ever mair in life and death, my dear,
I am your own true clerk, or strike me deid!'
'Good-bye, my sweet,' she whispered, 'take good heed
But first I'll tell you something, that I will!
When you are riding homewards past the mill

By the main entrance-door, a bit behind it,
There's the half-bushel cake – you're sure to find it –
And it was made out of the very meal
You brought to grind and I helped father steal. . .
And, dearest heart, God have you in his keeping!'
And with that word she almost burst out weeping.

Alan got up and thought, 'Dawn's coming on,
Better get back and creep in beside John.'
But there he found the cradle in his way.
'By God,' he thought, 'I nearly went astray!
My heid is tottering with my work to-neet,
That'll be why I cannot gan areet!
This cradle tells me I have lost my tether;
Yon must be miller and his wife together.'

And back he went, groping his weary way
And reached the bed in which the miller lay,
And thinking it was John upon the bed
He slid in by the miller's side instead,
Grabbing his neck, and with no more ado
Said, 'Shake yourself, wake up, you pig's-head, you!
For Christ's soul, listen! O such noble games
As I have had! I tell you, by St James,
Three times the neet, from midnight into morn,
The miller's daughter helped me grind my corn
While you've been lying in your cowardly way . . .'
'You scoundrel!' said the miller. 'What d'you say?
You beast! You treacherous blackguard! Filthy rat!
God's dignity! I'll murder you for that!
How dare you be so bold as to fling mud
Upon my daughter, come of noble blood?'

He grabbed at Alan by his Adam's apple,
And Alan grabbed him back in furious grapple
And clenched his fist and bashed him on the nose.
Down miller's breast a bloody river flows
Onto the floor, his nose and mouth all broke;
They wallowed like two porkers in a poke,
And up and down and up again they go
Until the miller tripped and stubbed his toe,
Spun round and fell down backwards on his wife.

She had heard nothing of this foolish strife,
For she had fallen asleep with John the clerk,
Weary from all their labours in the dark.
The miller's fall started her out of sleep.
'Help!' she screamed. 'Holly cross of Bromeholme* keep

Chaucer wrote of the Friar: 'and certainly his voice was gay and sturdy, for he sang well and played the hurdy-gurdy'. This instrument also had the more impressive name of symphonia or symphony.

Us! Lord! Into thy hands! To Thee I call!
Simon, wake up! The devil's among us all!
My heart is bursting, help! I'm nearly dead,
One's on my stomach, and another's on my head.
Help, Simpkin, help! These nasty clerks are fighting!'
   Up started John, he needed no inciting,
And groped about the chamber to and fro
To find a stick; she too was on the go
And, knowing the corners better than them all,
Was first to find one leaning by the wall;
And by a little shaft of shimmering light
That shone in through a hole – the moon was bright –
Although the room was almost black as pitch
She saw them fight, not knowing which was which;
But there was something white that caught her eye
On seeing which she peered and gave a cry,
Thinking it was the night-cap of the clerk.
   Raising her stick, she crept up in the dark
And, hoping to hit Alan, it was her fate
To smite the miller on his shining pate,
And down he went, shouting, 'O God, I'm dying!'
   The clerks then beat him well and left him lying
And throwing on their clothes they took their horse
And their ground meal and off they went, of course,
And as they passed the mill they took the cake
Made of their meal the girl was told to bake.
   And thus the bumptious miller was well beaten
And done out of the supper they had eaten,
And done out of the money that was due
For grinding Alan's corn, who beat him too.
His wife was plumbed, so was his daughter. Look!
That comes of being a miller and a crook!
   I heard this proverb when I was a kid,
'Do evil and be done by as you did'.
Tricksters will get a tricking, so say I;
And God that sits in majesty on high
Bring all this company, great and small, to Glory!
Thus I've paid out the Miller with my story!

The Skipper's Tale

There was a merchant in St Denys once
Who being rich was held to be no dunce,
He had a wife, unusually fair,
One of a gay, companionable air,
A thing which causes more pecunial dearth
Than all the foppish compliments are worth
That menfolk offer them at feasts and dances.
Such nods and becks and party countenances
Pass as a shadow passes on a wall.
But woe to him that has to pay for all!
The silly husband always has to pay,
He has to clothe us, he has to array★
Our bodies to enhance his reputation,
While we dance round in all this decoration.
And if he cannot pay, as it may chance,
Or won't submit to such extravagance,
Thinking his money thrown away and lost,
Then someone else will have to bear the cost

Or lend us money, and that's dangerous.
   This noble merchant kept a splendid house
And all day long so many guests there were
– For he was generous and his wife was fair –
You would have been surprised; but to my tale.
   His guests from up and down the social scale
Included a young monk, well-made and bold;
I judge he was some thirty winters old,
And he was always visiting the place.
   Now this young monk, with his delightful face,
Was on such friendly terms with this good man
Ever since their acquaintance first began
That he was welcomed as familiarly
As it is possible for a friend to be.
   And for as much as this good-natured man,
He and the monk, of whom my tale began,
Were born in the same village, the monk stated
That they were cousins, very near related;
The claim was neither questioned nor withdrawn;
Both were as glad of it as bird of dawn.
It pleased the merchant's heart, and his compliance
Had furthered this unbreakable alliance,
And each was happy to assure the other
He always would regard him as a brother.
   This monk Sir John was very free in spending
Whenever he stayed there, carefully attending
To what should please; he poured out tips like wages,
Forgetting not the meanest of the pages
About the house; to each in his degree,
Master or man, he gave a gift or fee
Whenever he came – some honest kind of present –
And so, to them, his coming was as pleasant
As sunrise is to bird upon the nest.
I must have said enough, so let it rest.
   The merchant, as it happened, one fine day,
Began to make arrangements for a stay
Somewhere near Bruges to further his affairs
And buy a fresh consignment of his wares.
And so he sent a message thereupon
To Paris, and invited good Sir John
Down to St Denys, so as to give pleasure
To him and to his wife, and spend his leisure
With them agreeably, a day or two,
Before he left – as he would have to do –

The fox, a menace to poultry then as now, was regarded as vermin and was not hunted in the formal sense but killed by any means. Here the artist has caught the alertness of a fox in the undergrowth as it watches the approach of a man with his dogs.

For Bruges. This noble monk I am describing
Was glad enough, and needed little bribing;
He saw his Abbot and he got permission,
Being a man of prudence and position,
In fact a superintendent, one to ride
Inspecting abbey granges far and wide.
    Off to St Denys, then, the monk has gone.
Who was so welcome as my lord Sir John,
So full of courtesy and 'cousin mine'?
He brought with him a jug of Malmsey wine
And also one of sweet Italian juice,
With these a brace of birds as was his use.
And thus I leave them at their meat and drink,
Merchant and monk, a day or two, I think.
    On the third morning up the merchant gets
In serious thought about his needs and debts
And up into his counting-house he goes
To reckon up, as you may well suppose,
All the past year and how things stood with him,
What he had spent, how the accounts would trim,
And whether his business had increased or not.

    Many a ledger and money-bag he got
And laid them out upon his counting-board.
He had a deal of treasure in his hoard
And so he locked the door with an abrupt
Command that no one was to interrupt
His casting of accounts; he worked away
Sitting up there till past the prime of day.
    Sir John had risen early too, to go
Into the garden. Walking to and fro
He said his office, courteous and devout.
This excellent wife then stealthily came out
Where he was walking softly in the sun
And greeted him, as she had often done.
    A little girl was there for company
Beside her, under her authority,
Still subject to the rod; her mistress said:
'Ah, my dear cousin John! What, not in bed?
What's wrong with you that you are up so soon?'
'Niece,' he replied, 'a man can keep in tune
On five good hours of sleep, as I should judge,
Unless he is a poor old pallid drudge
Like all those married men who cower there
In bed, as in her form a weary hare

When she has had the hounds upon her tail.
But, my dear niece, why do you look so pale?
I cannot but imagine our good man
Has been at work and with you since night began;
You really ought to go and take a rest.'
And he laughed merrily at his little jest,
And for his private thoughts his face turned red.
 This pretty wife began to shake her head
And answered thus: 'Ah, God knows all!' said she.
'No, cousin mine, things aren't like that with me;
For, by the Lord that gave me soul and life,
In all the realm of France there is no wife
That has less pleasure in that sorry play.
For I may sing "Alas, and woe the day
That ever I was born!" I daren't,' said she,
'Tell anyone how matters go with me.
If only I could get away, or end
It all – Oh, I could kill myself, dear friend,
I am so terrified, so full of care. . .'
 On hearing this the monk began to stare
And said, 'Alas, dear cousin, God forbid
That fear or grief, whatever else they did,
Should make you kill yourself! Unfold your grief;
It may be I can give you some relief,
Advice or help, perhaps; and therefore, come,
Tell me about your trouble, I'll keep mum.
Look, on this prayer-book I will take a vow
Never by chance or choice, no matter how,
To give away what you may say to me.'
'I say the same again to you,' said she,
'By God and by this prayer-book I can swear,
Though I were torn in pieces, to play fair
And never breathe a syllable or tell
A living soul, not though I went to Hell;
Not on account of cousinship, but just
Out of affection for you, love and trust.'
And having sworn, they kissed to seal the oath
And then conversed as impulse prompted both.
 'Cousin,' she said, 'if I had time and space
And I have none, especially in this place,
I could unfold a legend of my life
And what I've had to suffer as a wife.
As for my husband, though he's your relation . . .'
'No!' said the monk. 'By God and my salvation!

An embroidered purse with a draw
string. It would have been attached
to the belt.

Cousin indeed! He's no more cousin to me
Than is this leaf, here hanging on the tree.
I call him so, but by the saints of France
I do so only for a better chance
Of seeing you – because I love you dearly,
Above all other women, most sincerely.
I swear it you on my profession, love!
Tell me your troubles while he's still above,
Quick, don't hang back! and then you can be gone.'
'O my dear love,' she answered, 'sweet Sir John,
I hate to tell you... O if I were stronger!
But it must out, I cannot bear it longer.
My husband is the very meanest man,
To me at any rate, since the world began.
It's unbecoming, since I am his wife,
To tell a soul about our private life,
Whether in bed or any other place,
And God forbid I sank to such disgrace!
I know a wife should only speak in honour
About her husband, or else fie upon her!
Only to you, the only one on earth,
This much I'll say. God help me, he's not worth
A fly upon the wall! In no respect.
But his worst fault is niggardly neglect.
For you must know that women naturally
Need to have sixty things, the same as me;
They want to have their husbands, to be candid,
Sturdy and prudent, rich and open-handed,
Obedient to their wives and fresh in bed.
But by the Lord that died for us and bled,
By Sunday next, if I am to look smart
And do my husband honour I must part
With – well, a hundred francs; or I'm undone.
Far better not be born than to be one
That people slander and say cheap things about.
Yet if my husband were to find it out
I were as good as lost – ah, don't deny!
Lend me this little sum or I shall die.
Sir John, I say, lend me these hundred francs!
Trust me I will not fail you in my thanks
If only you'll oblige me as I say.
I'll pay you back, and you shall name the day,
And if there's anything else – some little task
That I can do for you – well, only ask.

A pair of medieval shoes. The soles
have been worn or have rotted away
and all that remains are the uppers
with the holes where they were
stitched to the soles clearly visible.

Elaborate and stylish armour for
horse and man, fashioned in
Germany in the fifteenth century.
Note the long spur and the mace
held in the right hand.

And if I don't, God send as foul mischance
To me as fell to Ganelon of France!'★
 The monk gave answer in his well-bred way:
'My own dear lady, I can truly say
I weep in sympathy for what I've heard,
And here I promise you and plight my word
That when your husband has gone off to Flanders
I will deliver you from fear of slanders
For I will bring you down a hundred francs.'
And on the word he caught her by the flanks
And clasped her closely, giving her a riot
Of kisses, saying softly, 'Keep things quiet . . .
And now let's have some dinner if we may,
My dial says it's past the prime of day;
You'd best be off. And be as true to me
As I to you.' 'God forbid else!' said she.
 And off she went as jolly as a lark
And told the cooks to hurry off the mark
So that they all could dine without delay.
Up to her husband then she made her way
And boldly knocked upon the counter-door.
'*Qui la?*' he said. 'It's me, dear. How much more
Have you to do up there,' she said, 'and fasting?
How long will you be reckoning up and casting
All those accounts of yours and books and things?
The devil run off with all such reckonings!
Heavens, you've had enough of it, my Own!
Come down and leave those money-bags alone.
Aren't you ashamed to leave that poor Sir John
Fasting all day while you go on and on?
What? . . . Let's hear Mass, and then go in to dine.'
 'Dear wife,' he said, 'how little you divine
The complicated nature of affairs!
God save us all! Of such as deal in wares,
There's hardly two of us, as I'm alive,
Not two in twelve, I say, can hope to thrive★
Till they retire, showing a steady clearance.
All very well to make a good appearance,
To drive about the world and make a mark,
But our affairs must always be kept dark
Till we are dead, unless we are to play
At pilgrimage and keep out of the way
Of creditors. It's vital to consider
This curious world and find the highest bidder;

There's always chance to fear, and many a slip
Makes for anxiety in salesmanship.
　'I have to go to Bruges at break of day;
I shall come home as quickly as I may.
Therefore, dear wife, I beg of you to be
Courteous and meek to all in place of me.
Look after all our property with care,
See to the house; here's plenty and to spare.
Govern it well. I'll see you have enough,
But still, be thrifty over household stuff.
You've all the clothes you need, and all the stores.
I'll put some silver in that purse of yours.'
　And with that word he shut the counter-door
And came downstairs, he lingered there no more.
Quickly they all went off to Mass and prayed,
And quickly too the tables then were laid;
The merchant and his wife attacked the spread,
Sir John the monk was sumptuously fed.
　Soon after dinner, soberly, Sir John
Took him aside – this merchant – and went on
To say as follows: 'Cousin, as I see,
You're off to Bruges for some commodity.
May God and St Augustine be your guide!
Now do be careful, cousin, how you ride,
And moderate in your diet; in this heat
You should be temperate in what you eat.
Well, don't let's stand on ceremony! Good-bye,
Dear cousin! God protect you from on high!
And if there's anything by night or day
That I can do to help you, only say.
Command me, and whatever be the task
It shall be done exactly as you ask.
　'Oh . . . One thing. May I ask you as a friend
Before you go . . . Could you contrive to lend
A hundred francs? Just for a week or two?
I have to buy some cattle to renew
A farm of ours with animals and stores.
So help me God I wish the place were yours!
You may be sure I will not fail my day,
Not if it were a thousand francs, I say.
But please tell no one of this little debt.
– You see, I haven't bought the cattle yet.
And now, good-bye to you, my own dear cousin,
And for your kindness to me, thanks a dozen!'

Medieval manuscripts show that
games familiar in children's
playgrounds today have been played
for centuries. Here, for example, is
a vigorous game of pick-a-back
depicted in the Luttrell Psalter.

This noble-hearted merchant thereupon
Replied, 'Good heavens, cousin! Dear Sir John,
This is indeed a very small request!
My gold is yours whenever you think best.
And not my gold alone, but all my stuff;
Take what you please, be sure you take enough.
Of course – I hardly need remind you now –
We merchants use our money like a plough.
We can get credit while our name will run,
But to be short of money is no fun;
So pay me back when you've the cash about.
Meanwhile I'm very glad to help you out.'
   He fetched a hundred francs out of his trunk
And handed them in secret to the monk,
So secretly the deal was only known
To him – this merchant – and Sir John alone.
They drank and talked and loitered for a spell;
Sir John rode back then to his abbey cell.
   Day came; the merchant started on his ride
To Flanders with a prentice as his guide
And came at last to Bruges in good condition.
Once there he worked in haste without remission
And did his business, borrowed, made advances,
And never turned aside for dice or dances,
But purely as a merchant, let me say,
He spent his time, and there I let him stay.
   The very Sunday after he had gone,
Back to St Denys came the good Sir John
New-tonsured and with freshly-shaven face.
There was no little boy in all the place
Nor any other person, it was plain,
But was rejoiced to see Sir John again.
And to go shortly to the point indeed
This lovely woman readily agreed
To take his hundred francs and to requite
Sir John by lying in his arms all night.
And just as was agreed, so it was done.
All night they led a life of busy fun
Till dawn came up. Then with a kindly laugh
He left, wishing good luck to all the staff,
For not a soul, there or in town about,
Had formed the least suspicion or slightest doubt
Of what had happened. Homewards, or where whim
Directed, off he rode; no more of him.

This merchant, having finished his affairs,
Turned for St Denys; thither he repairs
And cheers his wife with fun and feast and such,
But said his merchandise had cost so much
That he must needs negotiate an advance
For he was bound by a recognisance
For twenty thousand crowns he had to pay.
He'd have to go to Paris the next day
To borrow certain sums among his friends
Which, with his ready cash, would meet his ends.
　　No sooner had he come into the town
Than, out of pure affection, he got down
And called upon Sir John for simple pleasure
And not at all to claim the borrowed treasure,
But just to see him, ask how he was doing
And tell him what affairs he was pursuing
As friends will do on their occasional meetings.
Sir John was most effusive in his greetings
And he as blithely chatted back and told
How prosperously he had bought and sold,
Thanks be to God, in all his merchandise,
Save that it was incumbent to devise
The raising of a loan at interest;
That done, he could afford to take a rest.
　　Sir John replied, 'Indeed, I am delighted
That you are safely back with matters righted;
If I were rich – we all have ups and downs –
You should not lack for twenty thousand crowns,
You were so kind to me the other day
Lending me money; all I have to say
Is many, many thanks! God give you life!
But I returned the money to your wife
– The sum you lent – and put it in your till
At home. She'll know about it all, she will.
By double entry. She will understand.
And now you must excuse me. It's been planned
For me to join the Abbot here to-day,
He's going out of town, I cannot stay.
Best greetings to my pretty little niece,
Your wife! Good-bye, dear cousin, go in peace!
Let's hope it won't be long before we meet.'
　　This merchant, who was wary and discreet,
Soon managed to negotiate his loan;
The bond that he had signed became his own

Suffering the penalty of public humiliation, a customary feature of medieval punishment, we see a strangely assorted pair – a monk and a lady in the stocks. Their offence is a matter for conjecture.

For he paid down the money to a franc
To certain Lombards at their Paris Bank.
He left as merry as a popinjay
For home, his business done in such a way
That he was bound to make, to the extent
Of fully a thousand francs, more than he'd spent.

His wife was there and met him at the gate
Just as she always did, and they sat late
That night and had a feast. He did not fret,
Knowing that he was rich and out of debt.

At dawn this merchant started to embrace
His wife afresh, and kissed her on the face,
And up he went and made it pretty tough.
'No more!' she said. 'By God, you've had enough!'
And wantonly she gambolled for a while,
Until at last the merchant with a smile
Said, 'I'm a little cross with you, my dear,
Though I am loth to be so, never fear.
Do you know why? By God, or so I guess,
You've brought about a sort of awkwardness
Between myself, I say, and Cousin John.
You should have warned me, dear, before I'd gone,
That he had paid you back my hundred francs
By ready token. It was little thanks
He gave me when I spoke of borrowing money.
His face showed plainly that it wasn't funny.
But all the same, by God our Heavenly King,
I had no thought to ask for anything!
I beg you not to do it any more.
When off on business I must know before

149

If any debtor has paid you back my pence
Unknown to me, in case your negligence
Should make me ask for what's been paid already.'
    So far from being frightened or unsteady,
This wife retorted boldly thereupon:
'Then I defy that treacherous monk Sir John!
Him and his entries! I don't care a bit!
He gave me a sum of money, I admit.
So what? A curse upon his monkish snout!
God knows I had imagined, out of doubt,
That he had given it me because of you,
To spend on looking smart, on what is due
To your position and the friendly cheer
You've always shown him as a cousin here!
But now it seems that things are out of joint.
Well then! I'll answer briefly to the point;
You've many slacker debtors than myself!
I'll pay you readily, and as for pelf,
If that should fail, from sunset to revally
I am your wife, so score it on my tally.★
I'll pay you back as promptly as I may.
I promise you I spent it in the way
Of pretty clothes; it didn't go in waste,
But I assure you, in the best of taste
To honour you; for goodness' sake I say
Don't be so angry, dear, let's laugh and play.
My jolly body's pledged to you instead;
By God I'll never pay except in bed.
Forgive me, dearest husband, just this while;
Turn round again and let me see you smile!'
    This merchant saw that there was no redress
And that to chide her was but foolishness
Since nothing could be done, and was content
To say 'Well, I forgive you what you spent,
But don't be so extravagant again;
You must economize, let that be plain.'
    And now my story's done, and may God send us
Plenty of entries until death shall end us!
                                        Amen.

Words of the Host to the Monk

'My lord the Monk, don't look so woe-begone,
For it's your turn to tell a story, sir.
Why, look! We've almost got to Rochester!
Forward, my lord, and don't hold up our game.
But, on my honour, I don't know your name;
Sir John, perhaps? Why have you kept it from us?
Or should I say Sir Alban, or Sir Thomas?
What monastery have they shut you in?
I vow to God you have a pretty skin!
There was fine pasturage where you were sent,
You're nothing like a ghost or penitent!
My! You must surely be some officer,
Some worthy Sexton, or some Cellarer.
For by my father's soul, in my opinion,
When you're at home, you're in your own dominion.
You are no novice, cloistered in retreat,
But in control, and wily as discreet.
Moreover when it comes to brawn and bone,
You seem to be well-cared-for, you must own.
God send confusion on the fellow who
First had the thought to make a monk of you!
You would have put a hen to pretty use,
Had you permission, as you have the juice,
To exercise your pleasure in procreation!
You could have done your part to build the nation.
Alas, who put you in so wide a cope?
Damnation take me, but if I were Pope,
Not only you but many a mighty man
Going about the world with tonsured pan
Should have a wife; for look, the world's forlorn!
Religion has got hold of all the corn
Of procreation, laymen are but shrimps.
Weak trees make sorry seedlings! That's what skimps
Our heirs and children, makes them all so slender
And feeble that they hardly can engender.
And that's what makes our wives so apt to cope
Religious people; there they have some hope

Of honest coin to pay the debts of Venus;
We laymen hardly have a groat between us!
    'But don't be angry, sir, at what I say;
Many a true word has been said in play!'
    This worthy Monk took all without offence
And said, 'Sir, I will do my diligence
To tell you all a tale or two, or three,
As far as may conform with decency.
And if you care to hear, as our assessor,
I'll tell the *Life of Edward the Confessor*;
Or else I have some tragedies to tell;
I have at least a hundred in my cell.
    '*Tragedy* means a certain kind of story,
As old books tell, of those who fell from glory,
People that stood in great prosperity
And were cast down out of their high degree
Into calamity, and so they died.
Such tales are usually versified
In six-foot lines they call *Hexameter*.
Many are told in prose, if you prefer,
And other metres suited to the stuff;
This explanation ought to be enough.
    'Now listen, therefore, if you care to hear.
But first I beg you not to be severe
If my chronology in all these things,
Be they of popes, of emperors or kings,
Forsakes the order in which they fell of yore
And I put some behind and some before;
They come to my remembrance but by chance;
Accept excuses for my ignorance.'

The Monk's Tale

In Tragic Manner I will now lament
The griefs of those who stood in high degree
And fell at last with no expedient
To bring them out of their adversity.
For sure it is, if Fortune wills to flee,
No man may stay her course or keep his hold;
Let no one trust a blind prosperity.
Be warned by these examples, true and old.

LUCIFER

With Lucifer, although an angel he
And not a man, I purpose to begin.
For notwithstanding angels cannot be
The sport of Fortune, yet he fell through sin

153

Down into hell, and he is yet therein.
O Lucifer, brightest of angels all,
Now thou art Satan, and canst never win
Out of thy miseries; how great thy fall!

ADAM

Consider Adam, made by God's own finger,
And not begotten of man's unclean seed,
He that in Eden was allowed to linger
– Now called Damascus – and had power at need
Over all Paradise, save that decreed
And single tree prohibited. Than he
None ever on earth stood higher, till his deed
Drove him to labour, Hell and misery.

SAMSON

A lady plays the timbrel, which we now know as the tambourine.

Long ere his birth, by an annunciation,
Samson was heralded by an angel bright
Who marked him out for God in consecration.
He stood forth nobly while he had his sight;
There never was another of such might,
Or hardihood of mind for might to borrow;
And yet he let his secret come to light,
He told his wife, and killed himself for sorrow.

Samson, this noble warrior of Zion,
Having no weapon by him for the fray
But his bare hands, yet slew and tore a lion
While walking to his wedding, on the way.
His treacherous wife so pleased him with her play,
She coaxed his secrets forth; with double face
She then betrayed them to his foes that lay
In wait, and took another in his place.

And Samson took, in his avenging ire,
And lashed three hundred foxes in a band,
Tying their tails, then set the tails on fire
(To every tail he bound a fiery brand)

And burnt up every cornfield in the land
And every vine and olive in a mass
Of flame, and slew a thousand with his hand,
No weapon but the jaw-bone of an ass;

But having slain them was so parched with thirst
He was near lost, yet prayed the Lord on high
To show that favour He had showed at first
And send His servant water lest he die;
Then from that very jaw-bone which was dry
Out of a molar-tooth there sprang a well,
And there he drank enough to satisfy
His thirst; God sent His help, as *Judges* tell.

And then at Gaza on a certain night
By force he rent apart the city gate,
Bore off the pieces on his back, in spite
Of what the Philistines in fierce debate
Could do, and then he set them up in state
High on a hill. O Samson, dear thy worth!
Hadst thou not blabbed thy secrets to thy mate
None ever could have matched thee upon earth!

This Samson never drank of mead or wine,
His head no razor ever touched, or shear;
This precept was enjoined by the divine
Messenger-angel – all his strength lay here,
Lodged in his locks. And fully twenty year
He was a Judge and ruler of Israel;
Yet the day came to him for many a tear
And it was by a woman that he fell.

It was his love, Delilah, even she;
To her he owned that all his power lay
Within his hair, and to the enemy
She sold her lover sleeping, as he lay
Upon her breast, and bade them cut away
His locks, revealed his secret to those spies,
And so they found him there an easy prey.
They bound him fast and put out both his eyes.

But yet before his hair was clipped and shaved
There was no thong or lashing that could bind
His arm; and now they took him and encaved
Him in a prison, set him there to grind
A quern! O Samson, strongest of mankind.
O sometime Judge in glory and in power,
Now mayst thou weep although thine eyes are blind!
Fled is thy joy and come thy bitter hour.

Perished this captive wretch as I shall say;
His foes prepared a feast, and for their jeers
Made him their fool and bade him to display
Amidst a temple, thronged in crowded tiers,
His strength; and yet he set them by the ears.
He grasped two pillars, shook and made them fall,
And the whole temple, shaken from its piers,
Crashed down and slew him, and his foemen all.

That is to say, not Magistrates alone
But some three thousand others also slain
In the huge ruin of their temple of stone.
Of Samson I will say no more; but gain
A warning from his story, old and plain:
Men should keep counsel and not tell their wives
Secrets that it concerns them to retain,
Touching the safety of their limbs and lives.

HERCULES

For Hercules, victor of sovereign power,
His labours sing his praise and lasting fame,
Who in his time was human strength in flower.
He slew a lion and he skinned the same;
He robbed the Centaurs of their boasted name;
He slew the Harpies, cruel birds and fell;
He robbed the golden apples, overcame
Their dragon-guard, drove Cerberus from Hell,

And slew Busiris the tyrannical,
And made his horses eat him, flesh and bone;
He brought about the fiery serpent's fall,
Made one of Acheloüs' horns his own,

Killed the fierce Cacus in his cave of stone
And left Antaeus the Gigantic dead;
He met the grisly boar and laid it prone,
And last he shouldered heaven overhead.

Was never hero since the world began
That slew so many monsters as did he.
Throughout the world his reputation ran,
What with his strength and magnanimity.
All kingdoms of the earth he went to see,
None said him nay, none equalled him in worth,
And the Chaldean prophet named Trophee
Says he set pillars up to bound the earth.

He had a lover, this redoubted man,
Her name was Deianira, fresh as May;
And as the learned tell us, she began
To fashion him a shirt, to make him gay.
O fatal shirt! Alas, alas, I say!
Poison was subtly woven in its mesh;
Ere he had worn it scarcely half a day
From every bone there fell away his flesh.

This touching picture depicts a
double christening in two fonts,
perhaps of twins.

But some authorities would thus excuse her,
Saying that Nessus made the shirt, not she;
Let that be as it may, I won't accuse her;
He wore it anyhow, and certainly
Blackness began to rot his flesh, and he
Raked burning coals upon himself and died,
Having perceived there was no remedy
And scorning death by poison, out of pride.

Thus fell the famous, mighty Hercules.
Who then may trust the dice at Fortune's throw,
Who in this thronging world delights to seize
On the unwary and to lay him low?
Wise is the man that well has learnt to know
Himself; beware! When Fortune would elect
To trick a man, she plots his overthrow
By such a means as he would least expect.

NEBUCHADNEZZAR

The mighty throne, the precious stores of treasure,
The glorious sceptre and the diadem
That once belonged to King Nebuchadnezzar
Tongue cannot tell, hard to describe one gem
Among them! Twice he took Jerusalem
And, from the Temple, bore the vessels plighted
To God, and to his realm he carried them
In Babylon, where he gloried and delighted.

The fairest children of the royal line
Of Israel he gelded, and this done,
Made each of them a thrall and let them pine
In servitude. Daniel of these was one,
Wisest among them all, or under sun.
He could expound the dreams whose visitation
Troubled the King; Chaldean there was none
That could interpret their signification.

This proud king made an image out of gold;
Its height was sixty cubits and its frame
Seven in breadth. He ordered young and old
To bow before this idol and acclaim
Its glory; in a furnace of red flame
Any that disobeyed him should be flung.
But Daniel would not stoop to such a shame
Nor would his two companions. They were young.

This king of kings, so mighty and elate,
Supposed that God who sits in majesty
Could never rob him of his kingly state,
Yet he was cast from it, and suddenly.
Forth in the rain, thinking himself to be
An animal, he went and fed without
On hay as oxen do; and there dwelt he
Among the beasts till time had come about.

And like an eagle's feathers grew his hair,
His nails were like the talons of a bird,
Till God released him of his madness there
For certain years and the king's heart was stirred

In thanks to God; with many a tearful word
He swore to sin no more, until the hour
Of death when at the last he was interred,
He recognized God's mercy and his power.

BELSHAZZAR

He had a son, Belshazzar was his name,
Who held the throne after his father's day,
But took no warning from him all the same,
Proud in his heart and proud in his display,
And an idolater as well, I say.
His high estate on which he so had prided
Himself, by Fortune soon was snatched away,
His kingdom taken from him and divided.

He made a feast and summoned all his lords
A certain day in mirth and minstrelsy,
And called a servant, as the Book records,
'Go and fetch forth the vessels, those,' said he,
'My father took in his prosperity
Out of the Temple of Jerusalem,
That we may thank our gods for the degree
Of honour he and I have had of them.'

His wife, his lords and all his concubines
Drank on as long as appetite would last
Out of these vessels, filled with sundry wines.
The king glanced at the wall; a shadow passed
As of an armless hand, and writing fast.
He quaked for terror, gazing at the wall;
The hand that made Belshazzar so aghast
Wrote *Mene, Tekel, Peres*, that was all.

In all the land not one magician there
Who could interpret what the writing meant;
But Daniel soon expounded it, 'Beware,'
He said, 'O king! God to your father lent
Glory and honour, kingdom, treasure, rent;
But he was proud and did not fear the Lord.
God therefore punished that impenitent
And took away his kingdom, crown and sword.

Many monasteries bred fish in their own ponds. Here we see the steward of a monastery being presented with a handsome fish for the table.

'He cast him from the company of men
To make his habitation in the dew
Among the beasts, eat grass and tread the fen
In rain and drought, until at last he knew
By grace and reason God alone is true
And has dominion over crowns and creatures.
Then God at last was minded to renew
His mercy and restored his realm and features.

'But you, his son, are proud, though well you know
The truth of all these things that I have told;
You are a rebel before God, his foe,
Having defiled his vessels of pure gold;
Your wife and all your wenches have made bold
To do the like and drink of many a wine
In honour of false gods, accurst of old.
But God will punish you, and this his sign!

'That hand was sent of God, that on the wall
Wrote *Mene, Tekel, Peres*, as you see;
Your reign is done, you have been weighed, and fall;
Your kingdom is divided and shall be
Given to Persians and to Medes,' said he.
They slew the King Belshazzar the same night,
Darius took his throne and majesty,
Though taking them neither by law nor right.

My lords, from this the moral may be taken
That there's no lordship but is insecure.
When Fortune flees a man is left forsaken
Of glory, wealth and kingdom; all's past cure.
Even the friends he has will not endure,
For if good fortune makes your friends for you
Ill fortune makes them enemies for sure,
A proverb very trite and very true.

ZENOBIA*

Palmyra (say the Persians) had a queen,
Zenobia; one accounted to possess
A noble nature, and in arms so keen
And hardy, none could match her, they profess.

Her lineage and her breeding were no less
Than of a Persian royally descended;
I will not call her first in loveliness
But say her beauty could not be amended.

I find that from her childhood she had fled
The offices of women, for she went
Off to the wildness of the woods to shed
The blood of forest deer, her bow she bent
On them, still swift of foot when they were spent;
And as she grew to woman she would kill
Leopard and lion too, and once she rent
A bear apart; she ruled the beasts at will.

She dared them all, would thrust into a den,
Or course upon the mountains through the night,
Taking her sleep in bushes; as for men
She was a wrestler and could win a fight
Against a stripling of whatever might;
None could resist her arm and none elude.
And she had kept her maiden honour bright,
Not deigning to be vanquished or subdued.

At last her friends prevailed and she was married
To one Prince Odenathus of that land,
Albeit that she long refused and tarried;
And yet it is as well to understand
He was reluctant too to give his hand,
Having like fantasies. When knit together
Nevertheless their union proved a bland
And happy one, they came to love each other,

Hunting was by no means confined to the menfolk but in many forms was a favourite pastime of the ladies. Here a lady, gaily blowing her horn, is pursuing a stag with the hounds in full cry.

Save for one thing: she never would consent
To let him lie with her, except it be
Once only, for it was her clear intent
To have a child, to leave posterity;
And therefore when she knew that certainly
She had conceived no child from such an act,
She then permitted him his fantasy
Again, but only once; and that is fact.

And when she was with child by him at last
She suffered no more toying at that game
Until the fortieth day was fully past,
Then she permitted him to do the same;
And Odenathus, whether wild or tame,
Could get no more of her. She would aver
It was no more than lechery and shame
To woman for a man to play with her.

Two sons she had by Odenathus then,
Whom she brought up in virtue and in learning.
Now let us turn back to our tale again;
I say once more a creature so discerning,
So much esteemed, so lavish and so burning
In warlike zeal, so courteous by her birth,
You never could have found although returning
From search in all the corners of the earth.

Her splendour of array may not be told,
Whether in clothing or in store of treasure,
For she was clad in jewelry and gold.
In spite of all her hunting she found leisure
For languages and learnt them in full measure
And she applied herself to many, feeling
The study of a book to be a pleasure
That taught the way to power and high dealing.

And briefly to continue with my story,
Her husband was as powerful as she;
They conquered many kingdoms of great glory
Far in the Orient, they held in fee
Cities belonging to the majesty
Of Rome itself, and made their conquests thrive.
They never fled before an enemy
So long as Odenathus was alive.

A bronze and ivory carving of the period.

As for her battles (should you wish for reading)
Against Shapur the King, and more as well,
With all the details of the whole proceeding,
What title won, what captured citadel,
And how at length she came to grief and fell
Besieged, made captive – all that she endured –
Study my master Petrarch, he can tell;
He wrote enough about her, be assured.

When Odenathus died, she mightily
Held all those kingdoms in her sovereign hand,
And was so cruel to her enemy
There was no king or prince in all the land
But felt that it was grace enough to stand
In safety and secured from war and riot,
And treated with her, that they might disband;
Let her make wars so long as they had quiet.

And neither Claudius the Emperor
Nor his successor Gallienus ran
The danger of provoking her to war;
No, nor Armenian or Egyptian,
No Syrian either or Arabian
Dared take the field against her in a fight
Lest she should slay them, or her conquering van
Put them in all its multitude to flight.

In royal robe her sons were wont to go,
Heirs of their father's kingdoms, one and all
Their names Hermanno and Thymalaö,
Or such at least are what the Persians call
The pair. But Fortune's honey turns to gall,
Fortune withdrew her shining countenance
From this great queen and brought about her fall,
And she was plunged in sorrow and mischance.

For when Aurelian came upon the scene
With Rome beneath his government and sway,
He planned a mighty vengeance on the queen,
And, gathering his legions, took his way
Against Zenobia; to be brief, I say,
He routed her, enslaved and brought her home
In fetters with her children, there they lay!
And having conquered, he returned to Rome.

Amongst the other trophies of the war
There was her golden chariot, richly gemmed;
And great Aurelian, Roman emperor,
Returned with it in glory and condemned
The queen to walk before his Triumph, hemmed
By shouting crowds, gold chains about her throat,
And still, as rank allowed her, diademed
And there were jewels crusted on her coat.

O alas, Fortune! She that once had been
Terror of kings and of imperial powers,
Jeered at and gaped upon! A noble queen
That oft had worn the helmet through long hours
Of battle, and had taken towns and towers,
Now wears a mob-cap on her royal head,
She that had held a sceptre wreathed with flowers
Carries a distaff in her hand instead!

KING PETER OF SPAIN *

O noble, worthy Peter, glory of Spain,
Whom Fortune held so high in majesty,
How bitterly should we lament thy pain,
Who, by thy brother driven forth to flee,
After a siege wert caught by treachery,
And thus betrayed wert taken to his tent
Where with his own bare hands he murdered thee
And gained succession to thy throne and rent!

Upon an argent field an eagle sable*
Caught on a line-rod gules (if you can read
This riddle) brewed the treason and was able
– O 'wicked nest'! – to do a wicked deed!
No Oliver of Charlemagne he, to heed
Honour and truth, but Brittany's mishap,
A Ganelon-Oliver corrupt in greed
It was that brought this King to such a trap!

KING PETER OF CYPRUS *

O Peter King of Cyprus, fine and true,
That conqueredst Alexandria by the right
Of arms, and didest woe on heathens too,
Thy very liegemen envied thee, and spite
(No other cause) against thy chivalrous might
Moved them to murder thee upon the morrow
There, on thy bed! Thus Fortune with a light
Turn of her wheel brings men from joy to sorrow.

BERNABO VISCONTI OF LOMBARDY *

Great Bernabo Visconti of Milan,
God of indulgence, scourge of Lombardy,
Should I not tell of thee, unhappy man,
That scaled the summit of felicity?
Thy brother's son, so doubly bound to thee,
Being thy nephew and thy son-in-law,
Yet in his prison wrought thy misery
And death, but how or why I never saw.

COUNT UGOLINO OF PISA

There is no tongue of pity that has power
To tell Count Ugolino's tragedy.
A little out of Pisa stands a tower;
There in that tower he was imprisoned, he
And all his little children. There were three,
Of whom the eldest-born was barely five.
O Fortune! It was grievous cruelty
To put such birds in such a cage, alive!

He was condemned to perish in that prison,
For Bishop Ruggieri had framed lies
Against him, and the city folk had risen,
Believing all the Bishop could devise,
And jailed him, as I said, without supplies
Save for some water and a little meat,
But these so scant and poor, you may surmise
That there was scarce enough for them to eat.

A chalice with a solid base consisting of six discs.

And on a certain day when came the hour
At which their food was usually brought,
The jailer shut the portals of the tower.
He heard it well enough, but he said nought;
There came into his heart at once the thought
That they were minded he should starve to death.
'Alas that I was born!' he said, and sought
In vain to check his tears and calm his breath.

His younger son – just three – ah, it is cruel
To think of him! – said, 'Father dear, why weep?
When will the prison-jailer bring our gruel?
Is there no bread, a morsel, in the keep?
I am so hungry that I cannot sleep.
If only I could sleep till I were dead!
Hunger no more would then have power to creep.
There's nothing I should like so much as bread.'

Thus day by day the little child would cry
Till on his father's bosom down he lay,
And said, 'Farewell, dear father, I must die!'
And kissed him; and he died that very day.
Seeing him dead his father, ashen-grey,
Bit on his arm and cried, 'Ah, wretched me!
Bitterest Fortune, thou hast had thy way,
Thy false wheel turns against me, as I see!'

The other children thought it must be hunger
That made him bite upon his arm, not pain.
'Ah father, don't, don't do it!' cried the younger,
'But rather eat the flesh upon us twain;
Our flesh you gave us, take it back again
And eat enough!' Thus both the children cried,
But in a day or two, their grief in vain,
They crept into his lap and there they died.

He in despair sat on, and slowly starved.
Thus, mighty once, he met his end in jail;
Fortune foreclosed on his estate and carved
His greatness from him. Of this tragic tale,
Those who wish more, and on a nobler scale,
Should turn and read the great Italian poet★
Dante by name; they will not find him fail
In any point or syllable, I know it.

NERO

Though Nero was a vicious man who lusted
As fiercely as a fiend who treads the deep
(Says Suetonius, and he may be trusted),
He ruled the whole wide world; 'twas his to keep.
East, west, north, south, he scoured it o'er to reap
Its rubies, sapphires, pearls of orient white . . .
And his embroidered garments, heap on heap,
Blazed with them richly; gems were his delight.

A prouder, more fastidious ostentation
Of pomp no emperor has ever shown;
A dress once worn he had no inclination
To see again, would scarcely seem to own.
His many nets of golden mesh were thrown
To fish the Tiber with, just to amuse him.
His pleasures were his laws, he made it known
That there was nothing Fortune could refuse him.

And Rome, to please his palate for sensations,
He burnt; he killed his senators in play,
Just for the fun of hearing lamentations
And shrieks of pain; with his own sister lay;
Murdered his brother; carved his dreadful way
Into his mother's womb, only to know
Where he had been conceived. Alas the day
That ever man should treat his mother so!

Yet at the sight of it he shed no tear
But 'A fine woman once, she was,' he said.
Wonder it is that he could so appear
To sit in judgement on her beauty dead.
And then he bade a table to be spread
And drank some wine but showed no other grief.
Where power and a cruel heart are wed
How deep the poison, challenging belief!

In youth they gave him an instructor; he
Taught him to read and taught him gentle breeding.
He was the flower of morality
At that far time, according to my reading.

The duties of the cellarer in a great
religious house may have been
onerous but that they had some
compensations is evident from this
picture.

167

Religion

The Church, which was of course the Roman Catholic Church, played a significant part in English life in Chaucer's time. The abbeys and monasteries were among the greatest land-owners, the Chancellor of the Realm was usually a prelate, and many bishops held high secular office under the king. Only recently had laymen begun to replace clerics in what was the early civil service. But so deeply had the Church become entrenched and privileged that it was highly conservative in its attitude and often negligent in its spiritual work. Corruption, intrigue, worldliness and greed were rife and obvious and as a consequence a great deal of anti-clericalism developed. It was during Chaucer's lifetime that John Wycliff, the English reformer who was once called 'the Morning Star of the Reformation', translated the Bible into English and stressed the need for preaching directly to the people. At first he was helped by the orders of wandering friars and later his ideas were taken over by the Lollards. But although it was a time of re-thinking over religion most people were still deeply pious and inspired by a profound belief in Heaven and Hell as the only alternatives facing them after death. The horrors awaiting sinners are compellingly illustrated in the medieval conception of Hell (2). It is not without significance that about to be tipped into the pit is a barrowload of priests including one wearing a bishop's mitre. Picture (1) shows a funeral. The coffin is being lowered into a vault while the priest reads the service from a book and sprinkles holy water over the grave.

It is perhaps indicative of the penetrating role of the Church at the time that over one third of Chaucer's tale-tellers were connected in some way or another with religion. There was the prioress, and the poet's description of her in the 'Prologue' reminds us that the women who were made the heads of the great convents were appointed, frequently, not so much for their piety as for their aristocratic connections. There was her chaplain, the monk, the second

1

nun, the summoner (an official of an ecclesiastical court), the parson, the friar, the Oxford clerk (who had found 'no preferment in the Church') and the pardoner. The nun's priest and the parson, reproduced from the Ellesmere Chronicle, are shown in (3) and (4).

On the whole Chaucer in his description of these worthies reflects the growing cynicism about the Church as it was then. The monk 'took the modern world's more spacious way', the friar was 'a wanton one and merry', the summoner 'as hot and lecherous as a sparrow', the pardoner he judged to be 'a gelding or a mare', and so on. Only the parson 'rich in holy thought and work' and the Oxford clerk who 'would gladly learn and gladly teach' come in for praise. Yet, despite the anti-clericalism which was developing the people were generally deeply pious. The craftsmen of the day were usually inspired in their work by a genuine feeling for religion as we can see from the enamelled roundel of a mazer or bowl (5) of the time, and the beautiful piece of carved alabaster (9) now in an English church (alabaster and ivory were materials for artists). In the great monasteries monks worked lovingly

omine ne in furo
re tuo arguas me
neq; in ira tua cor

ripias me.

2

3

4

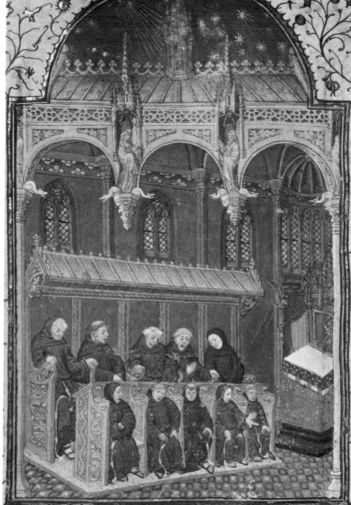

5

7

on their richly illuminated manuscripts (from which many of the illustrations in this book come), toiled in the grounds producing food for themselves and their fellows (7), attended the countless services in the great church to which each monastery was attached. In (6) we see a semi-choir of Franciscan friars singing the Divine Office. One or two are beating time. The picture brings out the beauty of the interior of the church. Although the clergy had their stalls congregations usually sat on the floor as can be seen in (8) where an Archbishop is preaching.

By Chaucer's time the great orders of friars – they have been described as 'home missionaries' – had lost a good deal of their early holiness and zeal but they were still familiar figures about the countryside. The original monastic idea was based on a life of contemplation and therefore involved separation from worldly affairs. The orders of friars were based on the principle of active religious duties among mankind. Their religious houses were built near to centres of population rather than in lonely, isolated places, and from them the friars would journey through the neighbouring areas preaching in parish churches and market squares. Some were called *limitours* because the field of their operations was limited geographically. Others were called *listers* because they could exercise their ministries where they listed. Because they sometimes usurped the role of the local clergy by preaching from their pulpits, hearing confessions etc., they were often believed to be turning the people against the established church: on the other hand they made a considerable contribution in the spiritual field when the local priest was lazy and neglectful. There were four principal orders – the Dominicans and Franciscans, which were founded about the same time, the Carmelites and the Augustines – but there were other smaller orders such as the Austin Friars, the Crutched Friars and the Friars of the Sack. The various orders were distinctively clothed. The Crutched Friars were so called because of the crosses on the front and back of their blue habits, the Dominicans became known as the Black Friars and the Franciscans as the Grey Friars. In (10) are depicted from left to right Cistercians, Dominicans and Premonstratensians – the last an order founded in France.

The fact that in Chaucer's time pilgrims were still making their way to Canterbury in their thousands is itself evidence of the deeply religious feeling of the people. The pilgrims were travelling to pay their respects at the shrine of Thomas à Becket, the Archbishop who had been murdered within the Cathedral in 1170. Becket had excommunicated some bishops who were supporters of King Henry II and the monarch's outburst of anger was misinterpreted by four of his knights who rode to Canterbury and murdered the Archbishop while he was at prayer (11).

It was the Church which played the leading role in education. England's oldest public school, the King's School, Canterbury, founded in A.D. 600, is actually in the precincts of the Cathedral, but many children were taught by their village priest. Oxford was the cultural centre of the country. During Chaucer's lifetime William of Wykeham, who rose from serfdom to become a bishop and Chancellor of England, founded two famous English educational establishments – Winchester College, a school, and New College, Oxford, one of the earliest of the university's colleges. Picture (12) shows the college with its 'hundred clerks'.

12

And for a while he mastered him, succeeding
In putting his intelligence to use
With suppleness and wisdom. Tyranny
And vice in him were not as yet let loose.

This Seneca – the man of whom I speak –
Made Nero fear him, but he went in dread
Of Seneca because he chose to speak
In the rebuke of wickedness instead
Of punishing him. 'An emperor,' he said,
'Shuns tyranny and follows virtue's path.'
So Nero cut his veins for him and bled
The man to death, he killed him in a bath.

It had been Nero's practice, I should judge,
When he was young, to mutiny and rise
Against his master; he could bear a grudge
And killed him for it, so we may surmise.
Nevertheless this Seneca the wise
Preferred to perish thus lest worse disaster
Should overtake him in another guise.
Thus Nero murdered his beloved master.

But as it happened Fortune cared no longer
To cherish Nero in his soaring pride.
Though he was strong enough yet she was stronger
And thus she thought: 'By God, I let him ride
Far too indulgently upon the tide
Of vice, and lend the title that protects
An emperor. By heaven, he shall slide
Out of his seat, and when he least expects.'

One night the citizens of Rome revolted
Against his tyrannies and mad ambition
And when he heard them mutiny he bolted
Alone and sought his friends for coalition.
The more he knocked and begged them for admission
The more they shut their doors and said him nay.
And then he saw that of his own perdition
He was sole author and he fled away.

olle Erle Richard in the wares of ffraunce toke Leufront and entred first into Came/but asmothe as he was there wt Andrs lord Thoms Duc of Clarance the kynge next other/ he sette on the walle the kynge Armys/and the Dukes/and made crye a Clarance Clarance/And then entred the Duke and yave the Erle many great thankes/After e Erle besegd Cubblick on the water of Seyn/and they appoynted to stonde adres owne of Roon/And then brought he up ressels by water to Roon/And then by his policy/wise it beseged both by lond & water/After he wan mount seynt mighell & many other stronge tounes/And the kyng made hym Erle of Aumarle.

A town under siege. The besiegers are encamped in tents and appear to have erected a palisade behind which a large cannon threatens the town. At the bottom right three arbesters or crossbowmen, outside the city wall but protected by shields on rests, seem about to fire at an attacking ship.

The people yelled for him and rumbled round
So that their shouts were dinning in his ear:
'Where's Nero? Where's the tyrant? Treacherous houn(
He almost went out of his mind for fear.
Pitifully he prayed the gods to hear
And succour him; in vain, they would not shield him.
Distraught, and knowing that his end was near,
He ran into a garden that concealed him.

He found two peasants in the garden there
Seated beside a bonfire glowing red
And he approached these peasants with a prayer
To kill him and by smiting off his head
To shield his body after he was dead
From mutilation or an act of shame.
And then he slew himself, for all was said.
And Fortune laughed at having made her game.

HOLOFERNES*

There never was a captain served a king
Who brought so many countries in subjection
Or one more famous then for everything
Touching the fields of war and insurrection,
Or more presumptuous by predilection
Than Holofernes. Fortune ever fair
Kissed him with such a lecherous affection
He lost his head before he was aware.

It was not only that he made a wraith
Of the world's wealth and plundered liberty,
He made his enemies renounce their faith:
'Nebuchadnezzar is your God,' said he,
'You shall adore none other that may be!'
There was no city dared stand up to him
Save one that proved a rebel to decree,
Bethulia, and her priest Eliachim.

But watch how Holofernes met his fate;
Drunken amid his host he lay one night
In his enormous barn-like tent of state.
For all his pomp, his majesty and might,

Judith, a woman, had the strength to smite.
Off went his sleepy head and from the tent
She crept away before the morning light
Bearing his head with her, and home she went.

KING ANTIOCHUS THE ILLUSTRIOUS *

What need to tell of King Antiochus
Or to describe his royal panoply,
His overweening pride, his venomous
Ill-doing? There was never such as he.
Read what is said of him in *Maccabee*,
Read those proud words so arrogantly spoken
And why he fell from his felicity
Upon a hill-side, festering and broken.

Fortune indeed had so enhanced his pride
That verily he thought to take his stand
Among the stars themselves or turn aside
To lift and weigh a mountain in his hand
Or warn the flood of ocean from the land.
But it was God's own people he most hated
And slew by torture, steel and firebrand.
He thought his pride could never be abated.

Because Nicanor once and Timothy
Had by the Jews been mightily defeated
His hatred swelled for Israel. Hastily
He made his chariot ready and when seated
He vowed and swore that they should all be treated
To something of his spite, that they should rue it;
Jerusalem he said should be deleted.
He was prevented ere he came to do it.

God smote him for these menacing recitals
With an invisible and cureless blain
That carved his guts and bit into his vitals.
Afflicted with intolerable pain
He yet had little reason to complain;
It was a just revenge, for he had often
Carved out the guts of other men to gain
His ends; their tortures did not make him soften.

Song birds were often kept as pets. Here we see one being caught as the net is about to be closed on it.

Brass rubbing
of a priest in St Albans.

He gave the word to summon all his hosts
When suddenly, before he was aware,
God daunted his presumption and his boasts,
And down he fell out of his chariot there.
It tore his limbs and flesh, the bone lay bare;
No longer could he either walk or ride
But only could be carried in a chair
All bruised and lacerated, back and side.

The vengeance of the Lord smote cruelly;
Pestilent worms within his body crept
So that he stank with such obscenity
Not one of all the servants that he kept
To guard him when awake or when he slept
Could bear the stench or look upon his features.
And in this agony he wailed and wept
And knew that God was lord of all his creatures.

To all his host and to himself no less
The carrion stench that rose from every vent
Was unendurable in loathsomeness;
They could not carry him. In redolent
And agonizing pain within his tent
Upon a hill this thief and homicide
Who made so many suffer and lament
Wretchedly perished, the reward of pride.

ALEXANDER*

The story of Alexander is so famous
That it is known to everyone at least
In part, unless he be an ignoramus.
He conquered the wide world from west to east
By force of arms, and as his fame increased
Men gladly sued to have him for their friend.
He brought to naught the pride of man and beast
Wherever he came, as far as the world's end.

And never can comparison be made
Of him with any other; at his face
Kingdoms would quake, the whole world was afraid.
He was the flower of knighthood and of grace,

Brass rubbing
of a nun in St Albans.

The heir of Fortune and in nothing base;
Save wine and women there was naught could part
Him from his high designs or take their place,
He was a man so leonine of heart.

What praise were it to him though I should tell
Of great Darius and a thousand more
Kings, princes, generals, dukes and earls as well
Conquered by him and brought to grief in war?
As far as men may ride from shore to shore
Of the wide world, the world was his to hold.
Though I should speak for ever on the score
Of knightly honour, his could not be told.

Twelve years he reigned, so say the *Maccabees*,
And was King Philip's son, of Macedon,
First to be king over the land of Greece.
Alas that Alexander, such a son,
So gentle, so magnanimous, were one
To die by poison from the men he kept!
But Fortune threw him aces for the run ⋆
Of sixes thrown before. She little wept.

Who then will give me tears that I may plain
The death of greatness that was never rough,
Of generous feeling that had held domain
Over the world and thought it not enough?
His was a spirit brimming with the stuff
Of high design. Ah, help me to speak shame
Of poisoners and of the foul rebuff
Of fickle Fortune, whom alone I blame.

JULIUS CAESAR

By wisdom, manhood and the works of war
From humble bed to royal majesty
Arose great Julius Caesar, conqueror,
Who won the occident by land and sea
By strength of arms or by diplomacy
And made of each a Roman tributary
And last was emperor himself till he
Was picked by Fortune for her adversary.

O Caesar that in Thessaly excelled
Against your father-in-law great Pompey's sway,
The whole of orient chivalry was held
In whose command, far as the dawn of day!
Your valour was enough to take and slay
All but a few that fled with him, your spell
Held the whole east in terror and dismay.
Give thanks to Fortune for she served you well!

Yet for a little while I will bewail
This Pompey's fate, the noble governor
Of Rome who fled the battle, for the tale
Tells of a man of his, a perjurer
Who smote his head off, for he hoped to stir
Some gratitude in Caesar, so he brought
The head to him. O Pompey, Justicer
Of all the east, alas that thou wert caught!

To Rome once more this Julius turned, to don
The laurel-wreath, triumphant and elate.
But Brutus Cassius* as time went on,
One that had ever envied his estate,
Made a conspiracy in subtle hate
Against this Julius, gave the treacherous vow,
And chose the place where he should meet his fate
By dagger-thrust, and I shall tell you how.

Up to the Capitol this Julius went
A certain day as he was wont to do.
There he was taken by the malcontent
False-hearted Brutus and his scheming crew,
They stabbed him there with daggers through and throu
Many the wounds, and there they let him die.
After one dagger-stroke or maybe two
He never groaned, unless the stories lie.

He was a soldier with a manly heart;
So dear to him was honest decency
That deeply as he felt his gashes smart
He sought to shroud his person, casting free
His cloak about his hips and privity,
And in the trance of dying, though he knew
It was his death, he held in memory
The things of seemliness and order due.

I recommend you Lucan for this story
And Suetonius and Valerius too.
They write of these two conquerors in their glory
And in their end, how both of them once knew
Fortune to be their friend, and how she grew
To be their foe. No man may trust her long,
Beware of her in everything you do
And think of these great leaders, once so strong.

CROESUS

Rich Croesus, King of Lydia long ago,
Whom even Persian Cyrus held in dread
Was yet cut short in all his pride and show
And led out to be burnt; but as they led
Him to the stake such rain from overhead
Came down it quenched the fire and he escaped.
He failed to take the warning, be it said;
Fate kept him for the gallows, where he gaped.

For having thus evaded death by fire
Nothing would stop him making war again.
He thought that Fortune meant to raise him higher,
After his luck in being saved by rain,
And he presumed he never could be slain.
Moreover being favoured by a vision
That cockered up his heart, he felt so vain
He set himself to vengeance and derision.

He dreamt that he was perching in a tree
With Jupiter to wash him, back and side,
While Phoebus with a towel fair to see
Was drying him. This was what swelled his pride.
He told his daughter who was at his side,
Knowing her versed in mysteries, it would seem,
And asked her what the vision signified.
And thus she started to expound his dream:

'This tree,' she told him, 'signifies a gibbet
And Jupiter betokens snow and rain,
While Phoebus with his towel must exhibit
The streaming sun, to dry you off again.

Some heraldic pendants and
roundels.

You will be hanged, my father, that is plain;
The rain shall wash you and the sun shall bake.'
And thus his daughter warned him, but in vain;
Her name Phanya, if I not mistake.

Hanged, then, was Croesus, this tremendous king;
His royal sceptre was of no avail.
Tragedy is no other kind of thing
Nor tunes her song save only to bewail
How Fortune, ever fickle, will assail
With sudden stroke the kingdoms of the proud,
And when men trust in her she then will fail
And cover her bright face as with a cloud. . . .

Words of the knight and the Host

'Ho, my good sir, no more!' exclaimed the Knight.
What you have said so far no doubt is right,
And more than right, but still a little grief
Will do for most of us, in my belief.
As for myself, I take a great displeasure
In tales of those who once knew wealth and leisure
And then are felled by some unlucky hit.
But it's a joy to hear the opposite,
For instance tales of men of low estate
Who climb aloft and growing fortunate
Remain secure in their prosperity;
That is delightful as it seems to me
And is a proper sort of tale to tell.'
  'That's certain, by St Paul's and by its bell!'
Our Host joined in. 'This Monk, he talks too loud;
All about "Fortune covered with a cloud"
– I don't know what – and as for "Tragedy",
You heard just now, what has to be must be.
It does no good to grumble and complain,
What's done is done. Moreover, it's a pain,
As you have said, to hear about disaster;
Let's have no more of it. God Bless you, master,
It's an offence, you're boring us, that's why!
Such talk as that's not worth a butterfly,
Gives no enjoyment, doesn't help the game.
In short Sir Monk – Sir Peter – what's-your-name –
I heartily beg you'll talk of something else.
But for the clink and tinkle of those bells
That hang your bridle round on every side,
By my salvation, by the Lord that died,
I simply should have fallen down asleep
Into the mud below, however deep.
Your story then would have been told in vain,
For, quoting the authorities again,
"When lecturers find their audiences decrease
It does them little good to say their piece."

Give us a word or two on hunting, say.'
'No,' said the Monk, 'I'm in no mood to-day
For fun. Ask someone else, I've said enough.'
   Our Host, whose language was a little rough,
Seeing a Priest beside the Nun, went on:
'Come here, you priest, step forward, you, Sir John,
And tell a tale to make our troubles pack.
Cheer yourself up although you ride a hack.
What if your ugly horse is poor and thin?
If it will serve you, never care a pin!
And always keep your heart up – that's the test!'
'Yes,' he replied, 'yes, Host, I'll do my best,
Not to be merry would deserve reproach.'
And he immediately began to broach
His story to us as we all rode on,
This charming priest and kindly man, Sir John.

The Nun's Priest's Tale

Once long ago, there dwelt a poor old widow
In a small cottage, by a little meadow
Beside a grove and standing in a dale.
This widow-woman of whom I tell my tale
Since the sad day when last she was a wife
Had led a very patient, simple life.
Little she had in capital or rent,
But still, by making do with what God sent,
She kept herself and her two daughters going.
Three hefty sows – no more – were all her showing,
Three cows as well; there was a sheep called Molly.
  Sooty her hall, her kitchen melancholy,
And there she ate full many a slender meal;
There was no *sauce piquante* to spice her veal,
No dainty morsel ever passed her throat,
According to her cloth she cut her coat.
Repletion never left her in disquiet
And all her physic was a temperate diet,

Hard work for exercise and heart's content.
And rich man's gout did nothing to prevent
Her dancing, apoplexy struck her not;
She drank no wine, nor white nor red had got.
Her board was mostly served with white and black,
Milk and brown bread, in which she found no lack;
Broiled bacon or an egg or two were common,
She was in fact a sort of dairy-woman.

    She had a yard that was enclosed about
By a stockade and a dry ditch without,
In which she kept a cock called Chanticleer.
In all the land for crowing he'd no peer;
His voice was jollier than the organ blowing
In church on Sundays, he was great at crowing.
Far, far more regular than any clock
Or abbey bell the crowing of this cock.
The equinoctial wheel and its position*
At each ascent he knew by intuition;
At every hour – fifteen degrees of movement –
He crowed so well there could be no improvement.
His comb was redder than fine coral, tall
And battlemented like a castle wall,
His bill was black and shone as bright as jet,
Like azure were his legs and they were set
On azure toes with nails of lily white,
Like burnished gold his feathers, flaming bright.

    This gentlecock was master in some measure
Of seven hens, all there to do his pleasure.
They were his sisters and his paramours,
Coloured like him in all particulars;
She with the loveliest dyes upon her throat
Was known as gracious Lady Pertelote.
Courteous she was, discreet and debonair,
Companionable too, and took such care
In her deportment, since she was seven days old
She held the heart of Chanticleer controlled,
Locked up securely in her every limb;
O such happiness his love to him!
And such a joy it was to hear them sing,
As when the glorious sun began to spring,
In sweet accord *My Love is far from land**
– For in those far off days I understand
All birds and animals could speak and sing.

    Now it befell, as dawn began to spring,

When Chanticleer and Pertelote and all
His wives were perched in this poor widow's hall
(Fair Pertelote was next him on the perch)
This Chanticleer began to groan and lurch
Like someone sorely troubled by a dream,
And Pertelote who heard him roar and scream
Was quite aghast and said, 'O dearest heart,
What's ailing you? Why do you groan and start?
Fie, what a sleeper! What a noise to make!'
'Madam,' he said, 'I beg you not to take
Offence, but by the Lord I had a dream
So terrible just now I had to scream;
I still can feel my heart racing from fear.
God turn my dream to good and guard all here,
And keep my body out of durance vile!
I dreamt that roaming up and down a while
Within our yard I saw a kind of beast,
A sort of hound that tried or seemed at least
To try and seize me . . . would have killed me dead!
His colour was a blend of yellow and red,
His ears and tail were tipped with sable fur
Unlike the rest; he was a russet cur.
Small was his snout, his eyes were glowing bright.
It was enough to make one die of fright.
That was no doubt what made me groan and swoon.'
   'For shame,' she said, 'you timorous poltroon!
Alas, what cowardice! By God above,
You've forfeited my heart and lost my love.
I cannot love a coward, come what may.
For certainly, whatever we may say,
All women long – and O that it might be! –
For husbands tough, dependable and free,
Secret, discreet, no niggard, not a fool
That boasts and then will find his courage cool
At every trifling thing. By God above,
How dare you say for shame, and to your love,
That anything at all was to be feared?
Have you no manly heart to match your beard?
And can a dream reduce you to such terror?
Dreams are a vanity, God knows, pure error.
Dreams are engendered in the too-replete
From vapours in the belly, which compete
With others, too abundant, swollen tight.
   'No doubt the redness in your dream to-night

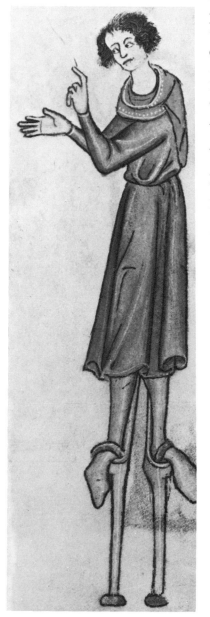

An itinerant performer parades on stilts.

Comes from the superfluity and force
Of the red choler in your blood. Of course.
That is what puts a dreamer in the dread
Of crimsoned arrows, fires flaming red,
Of great red monsters making as to fight him,
And big red whelps and little ones to bite him;
Just so the black and melancholy vapours
Will set a sleeper shrieking, cutting capers
And swearing that black bears, black bulls as well,
Or blackest fiends are haling him to Hell.
And there are other vapours that I know
That on a sleeping man will work their woe,
But I'll pass on as lightly as I can.

　　'Take Cato now, that was so wise a man,
Did he not say, "Take no account of dreams"?
Now sir,' she said, 'on flying from these beams,
For love of God do take some laxative;
Upon my soul that's the advice to give
For melancholy choler; let me urge
You free yourself from vapours with a purge.
And that you may have no excuse to tarry
By saying this town has no apothecary,
I shall myself instruct you and prescribe
Herbs that will cure all vapours of that tribe,
Herbs from our very farmyard! You will find
Their natural property is to unbind
And purge you well beneath and well above.
Now don't forget it, dear, for God's own love!
Your face is choleric and shows distension;
Be careful lest the sun in his ascension
Should catch you full of humours, hot and many.
And if he does, my dear, I'll lay a penny
It means a bout of fever or a breath
Of tertian ague. You may catch your death.

　'Worms for a day or two I'll have to give
As a digestive, then your laxative.
Centaury, fumitory, caper-spurge
And hellebore will make a splendid purge;
And then there's laurel or the blackthorn berry,
Ground-ivy too that makes our yard so merry;
Peck them right up, my dear, and swallow whole.
Be happy, husband, by your father's soul!
Don't be afraid of dreams. I'll say no more.'

　　'Madam,' he said, 'I thank you for your lore,

But with regard to Cato all the same,
His wisdom has, no doubt, a certain fame,
But though he said that we should take no heed
Of dreams, by God, in ancient books I read
Of many a man of more authority
Than ever Cato was, believe you me,
Who say the very opposite is true
And prove their theories by experience too.
Dreams have quite often been significations
As well of triumphs as of tribulations
That people undergo in this our life.
This needs no argument at all, dear wife,
The proof is all too manifest indeed.
   'One of the greatest authors one can read
Says thus: there were two comrades once who went
On pilgrimage, sincere in their intent.
And as it happened they had reached a town
Where such a throng was milling up and down
And yet so scanty the accommodation,
They could not find themselves a habitation,
No, not a cottage that could lodge them both.
And so they separated, very loath,
Under constraint of this necessity
And each went off to find some hostelry,
And lodge whatever way his luck might fall.
   'The first of them found refuge in a stall
Down in a yard with oxen and a plough.
His friend found lodging for himself somehow
Elsewhere, by accident or destiny,
Which governs all of us and equally.
   'Now it so happened, long ere it was day,
This fellow had a dream, and as he lay
In bed it seemed he heard his comrade call,
"Help! I am lying in an ox's stall
And shall to-night be murdered as I lie.
Help me, dear brother, help or I shall die!
Come in all haste!" Such were the words he spoke;
The dreamer, lost in terror, then awoke.
But once awake he paid it no attention,
Turned over and dismissed it as invention,
It was a dream, he thought, a fantasy.
And twice he dreamt this dream successively.
   'Yet a third time his comrade came again,
Or seemed to come, and said, "I have been slain!

Barrel-making was a thriving business. Here a cooper stands in his half-finished work.

Look, look! my wounds are bleeding wide and deep.
Rise early in the morning, break your sleep
And go to the west gate. You there shall see
A cart all loaded up with dung," said he,
"And in that dung my body has been hidden.
Boldly arrest that cart as you are bidden.
It was my money that they killed me for."
   'He told him every detail, sighing sore,
And pitiful in feature, pale of hue.
This dream, believe me, Madam, turned out true;
For in the dawn, as soon as it was light,
He went to where his friend had spent the night
And when he came upon the cattle-stall
He looked about him and began to call.
   'The innkeeper, appearing thereupon,
Quickly gave answer, "Sir, your friend has gone.
He left the town a little after dawn."
The man began to feel suspicious, drawn
By memories of his dream – the western gate,
The dung-cart – off he went, he would not wait,
Towards the western entry. There he found,
Seemingly on its way to dung some ground,
A dung-cart loaded on the very plan
Described so closely by the murdered man.
So he began to shout courageously
For right and vengeance on the felony,
"My friend's been killed! There's been a foul attack,
He's in that cart and gaping on his back!
Fetch the authorities, get the sheriff down
– Whosoever job it is to run the town –
Help! My companion's murdered, sent to glory!"
   'What need I add to finish off the story?
People ran out and cast the cart to ground,
And in the middle of the dung they found
The murdered man. The corpse was fresh and new.
   'O blessed God, that art so just and true,
Thus thou revealest murder! As we say,
"Murder will out." We see it day by day.
Murder's a foul, abominable treason,
So loathsome to God's justice, to God's reason,
He will not suffer its concealment. True,
Things may lie hidden for a year or two,
But still "Murder will out", that's my conclusion.
   'All the town officers in great confusion

A priest hears a lady's confession as she sheds tears of contrition. It is interesting that the priest wears not only a purse at his belt but a knife too.

Seized on the carter and they gave him hell,
And then they racked the innkeeper as well,
And both confessed. And then they took the wrecks
And there and then they hanged them by their necks.
   'By this we see that dreams are to be dreaded.
And in the self-same book I find embedded,
Right in the very chapter after this
(I'm not inventing, as I hope for bliss)
The story of two men who started out
To cross the sea – for merchandise no doubt –
But as the winds were contrary they waited.
It was a pleasant town, I should have stated,
Merrily grouped about the haven-side.
A few days later with the evening tide
The wind veered round so as to suit them best;
They were delighted and they went to rest
Meaning to sail next morning early. Well,
To one of them a miracle befell.
   'This man as he lay sleeping, it would seem,
Just before dawn had an astounding dream.
He thought a man was standing by his bed
Commanding him to wait, and thus he said:
"If you set sail to-morrow as you intend
You will be drowned. My tale is at an end."
   'He woke and told his friend what had occurred
And begged him that the journey be deferred
At least a day, implored him not to start.
But his companion, lying there apart,
Began to laugh and treat him to derision.
"I'm not afraid," he said, "of any vision,
To let it interfere with my affairs;
A straw for all your dreamings and your scares.
Dreams are just empty nonsense, merest japes;
Why, people dream all day of owls and apes,
All sorts of trash that can't be understood,
Things that have never happened and never could.
But as I see you mean to stay behind
And miss the tide for wilful sloth of mind
God knows I'm sorry for it, but good day!"
And so he took his leave and went his way.
   'And yet, before they'd covered half the trip
– I don't know what went wrong – there was a rip
And by some accident the ship went down,
Her bottom rent, all hands aboard to drown

In sight of all the vessels at her side,
That had put out upon the self-same tide.
    'So, my dear Pertelote, if you discern
The force of these examples, you may learn
One never should be careless about dreams,
For, undeniably, I say it seems
That many are a sign of trouble breeding.
    'Now, take St Kenelm's life which I've been reading;
He was Kenulphus' son, the noble King
Of Mercia. Now, St Kenelm dreamt a thing
Shortly before they murdered him one day.
He saw his murder in a dream, I say.
His nurse expounded it and gave her reasons
On every point and warned him against treasons
But as the saint was only seven years old
All that she said about it left him cold.
He was so holy how could visions hurt?
    'By God, I willingly would give my shirt
To have you read his legend as I've read it;
And, Madam Pertelote, upon my credit,
Macrobius wrote of dreams and can explain us
The vision of young Scipio Africanus,
And he affirms that dreams can give a due
Warning of things that later on come true.
    'And then there's the Old Testament – a manual
Well worth your study; see the *Book of Daniel*.
Did Daniel think a dream was vanity?
Read about Joseph too and you will see
That many dreams – I do not say that all –
Give cognizance of what is to befall.
    'Look at Lord Pharaoh, king of Egypt! Look
At what befell his butler and his cook.
Did not their visions have a certain force?
But those who study history of course
Meet many dreams that set them wondering.
    'What about Croesus too, the Lydian king,
Who dreamt that he was sitting in a tree,
Meaning he would be hanged? It had to be.
    'Or take Andromache, great Hector's wife;
The day on which he was to lose his life
She dreamt about, the very night before,
And realized that if Hector went to war
He would be lost that very day in battle.
She warned him; he dismissed it all as prattle

A priest in his pulpit preaching to his congregation which is either squatting or standing.

And sallied forth to fight, being self-willed,
And there he met Achilles and was killed.
The tale is long and somewhat overdrawn,
And anyhow it's very nearly dawn,
So let me say in very brief conclusion
My dream undoubtedly foretells confusion,
It bodes me ill, I say. And, furthermore,
Upon your laxatives I set no store,
For they are venomous. I've suffered by them
Often enough before and I defy them.
 'And now, let's talk of fun and stop all this.
Dear Madam, as I hope for Heaven's bliss,
Of one thing God has sent me plenteous grace,
For when I see the beauty of your face,
That scarlet loveliness about your eyes,
All thought of terror and confusion dies.
For it's as certain as the Creed, I know,
Mulier est hominis confusio
(A Latin tag, dear Madam, meaning this:
"Woman is man's delight and all his bliss"),
For when at night I feel your feathery side,
Although perforce I cannot take a ride
Because, alas, our perch was made too narrow,
Delight and solace fill me to the marrow
And I defy all visions and all dreams!'
 And with that word he flew down from the beams,
For it was day, and down his hens flew all,
And with a chuck he gave the troupe a call
For he had found a seed upon the floor.
Royal he was, he was afraid no more.
He feathered Pertelote in wanton play
And trod her twenty times ere prime of day.
Grim as a lion's was his manly frown
As on his toes he sauntered up and down;
He scarcely deigned to set his foot to ground
And every time a seed of corn was found
He gave a chuck, and up his wives ran all.
Thus royal as a prince who strides his hall
Leave we this Chanticleer engaged on feeding
And pass to the adventure that was breeding.
 Now when the month in which the world began,
March, the first month, when God created man,
Was over, and the thirty-second day
Thereafter ended, on the third of May

It happened that Chanticleer in all his pride,
His seven wives attendant at his side,
Cast his eyes upward to the blazing sun,
Which in the sign of *Taurus* then had run
His twenty-one degrees and somewhat more,
And knew by nature and no other lore
That it was nine o'clock. With blissful voice
He crew triumphantly and said, 'Rejoice,
Behold the sun! The sun is up, my seven.
Look, it has climbed forty degrees in heaven,
Forty degrees and one in fact, by this.
Dear Madam Pertelote, my earthly bliss,
Hark to those blissful birds and how they sing!
Look at those pretty flowers, how they spring!
Solace and revel fill my heart!' He laughed.
   But in that moment Fate let fly her shaft;
Ever the latter end of joy is woe,
God knows that worldly joy is swift to go.
A rhetorician with a flair for style
Could chronicle this maxim in his file
Of Notable Remarks with safe conviction.
Then let the wise give ear; this is no fiction.
My story is as true, I undertake,
As that of good Sir Lancelot du Lake
Who held all women in such high esteem.
Let me return full circle to my theme.
   A coal-tipped fox of sly iniquity
That had been lurking round the grove for three
Long years, that very night burst through and passed
Stockade and hedge, as Providence forecast,
Into the yard where Chanticleer the Fair
Was wont, with all his ladies, to repair.
Still, in a bed of cabbages, he lay
Until about the middle of the day
Watching the cock and waiting for his cue,
As all these homicides so gladly do
That lie about in wait to murder men.
O false assassin, lurking in thy den!
O new Iscariot, new Ganelon!
And O Greek Sinon,* thou whose treachery won
Troy town and brought it utterly to sorrow!
O Chanticleer, accursed be that morrow
That brought thee to the yard from thy high beams!
Thou hadst been warned, and truly, by thy dreams

The seal of the City of Canterbury.
It depicts on one side the murder of
St Thomas à Becket.

That this would be a perilous day for thee.
    But that which God's foreknowledge can foresee
Must needs occur, as certain men of learning
Have said. Ask any scholar of discerning;
He'll say the Schools are filled with altercation
On this vexed matter of predestination
Long bandied by a hundred thousand men.
How can I sift it to the bottom then?
The Holy Doctor St Augustine shines
In this, and there is Bishop Bradwardine's*
Authority, Boethius'* too, decreeing
Whether the fact of God's divine foreseeing
Constrains me to perform a certain act
– And by 'constraint' I mean the simple fact
Of mere compulsion by necessity –
Or whether a free choice is granted me
To do a given act or not to do it.
Though, ere it was accomplished, God foreknew it,
Or whether Providence is not so stringent
And merely makes necessity contingent.
    But I decline discussion of the matter;
My tale is of a cock and of the clatter
That came of following his wife's advice
To walk about his yard on the precise
Morning after the dream of which I told.
    O woman's counsel is so often cold!
A woman's counsel brought us first to woe,
Made Adam out of Paradise to go
Where he had been so merry, so well at ease.
But, for I know not whom it may displease
If I suggest that women are to blame,
Pass over that; I only speak in game.
Read the authorities to know about
What has been said of women; you'll find out.
These are the cock's words, and not mine, I'm giving;
I think no harm of any woman living.
    Merrily in her dust-bath in the sand
Lay Pertelote. Her sisters were at hand
Basking in sunlight. Chanticleer sang free,
More merrily than a mermaid in the sea
(For *Physiologus* reports that thing*
And says how well and merrily they sing).
And so it happened as he cast his eye
Towards the cabbage at a butterfly

A wandering tinker with his bellows strapped to the pack on his back. Utensils were valuable possessions and were patched and mended many times. The picture suggests that such itinerant craftsmen were objects of suspicion to house-dogs, one of which is nipping the tinker's leg.

It fell upon the fox there, lying low.
Gone was all inclination then to crow.
'Cok cok,' he cried, giving a sudden start,
As one who feels a terror at his heart,
For natural instinct teaches beasts to flee
The moment they perceive an enemy,
Though they had never met with it before.
   This Chanticleer was shaken to the core
And would have fled. The fox was quick to say
However, 'Sir! Whither so fast away?
Are you afraid of me, that am your friend?
A fiend, or worse, I should be, to intend
You harm, or practise villainy upon you;
Dear sir, I was not even spying on you!
Truly I came to do no other thing
Than just to lie and listen to you sing.
You have as merry a voice as God has given
To any angel in the courts of Heaven;
To that you add a musical sense as strong
As had Boethius who was skilled in song.
My Lord your Father (God receive his soul!),
Your mother too – how courtly, what control! –
Have honoured my poor house, to my great ease;
And you, sir, too, I should be glad to please.
For, when it comes to singing, I'll say this
(Else may these eyes of mine be barred from bliss),
There never was a singer I would rather
Have heard at dawn than your respected father.
All that he sang came welling from his soul
And how he put his voice under control!
The pains he took to keep his eyes tight shut
In concentration – then the tip-toe strut,
The slender neck stretched out, the delicate beak!
No singer could approach him in technique
Or rival him in song, still less surpass.
I've read the story in *Burnel the Ass*,*
Among some other verses, of a cock
Whose leg in youth was broken by a knock
A clergyman's son had given him, and for this
He made the father lose his benefice.
But certainly there's no comparison
Between the subtlety of such a one
And the discretion of your father's art
And wisdom. Oh, for charity of heart,

Can you not emulate your sire and sing?'
   This Chanticleer began to beat a wing
As one incapable of smelling treason,
So wholly had this flattery ravished reason.
Alas, my lords! there's many a sycophant
And flatterer that fill your courts with cant
And give more pleasure with their zeal forsooth
Than he who speaks in soberness and truth.
Read what *Ecclesiasticus* records
Of flatterers. 'Ware treachery, my lords!
   This Chanticleer stood high upon his toes,
He stretched his neck, his eyes began to close,
His beak to open; with his eyes shut tight
He then began to sing with all his might.
   Sir Russel Fox then leapt to the attack,
Grabbing his gorge he flung him o'er his back
And off he bore him to the woods, the brute,
And for the moment there was no pursuit.
   O Destiny that may not be evaded!
Alas that Chanticleer had so paraded!
Alas that he had flown down from the beams!
O that his wife took no account of dreams!
And on a Friday too to risk their necks!
O Venus, goddess of the joys of sex,
Since Chanticleer thy mysteries professed
And in thy service always did his best,
And more for pleasure than to multiply
His kind, on thine own day is he to die?
   O Geoffrey, thou my dear and sovereign master*
Who, when they brought King Richard to disaster
And shot him dead, lamented so his death,
Would that I had thy skill, thy gracious breath,
To chide a Friday half so well as you!
(For he was killed upon a Friday too.)
Then I could fashion you a rhapsody
For Chanticleer in dread and agony.
   Sure never such a cry or lamentation
Was made by ladies of high Trojan station,
When Ilium fell and Pyrrhus with his sword
Grabbed Priam by the beard, their king and lord,
And slew him there as the *Aeneid* tells,
As what was uttered by those hens. Their yells
Surpassed them all in palpitating fear
When they beheld the rape of Chanticleer.

A musician playing double pipes.

Here we see an acrobat painfully balancing himself on the points of two swords.

Dame Pertelote emitted sovereign shrieks
That echoed up in anguish to the peaks
Louder than those extorted from the wife
Of Hasdrubal, when he had lost his life
And Carthage all in flame and ashes lay.
She was so full of torment and dismay
That in the very flames she chose her part
And burnt to ashes with a steadfast heart.
O woeful hens, louder your shrieks and higher
Than those of Roman matrons when the fire
Consumed their husbands, senators of Rome,
When Nero burnt their city and their home,
Beyond a doubt that Nero was their bale!
    Now let me turn again to tell my tale;
This blessed widow and her daughters two
Heard all these hens in clamour and halloo
And, rushing to the door at all this shrieking,
They saw the fox towards the covert streaking
And, on his shoulder, Chanticleer stretched flat.
'Look, look!' they cried, 'O mercy, look at that!
Ha! Ha! the fox!' and after him they ran,
And stick in hand ran many a serving man,
Ran Coll our dog, ran Talbot, Bran and Shaggy,
And with a distaff in her hand ran Maggie,
Ran cow and calf and ran the very hogs
In terror at the barking of the dogs;
The men and women shouted, ran and cursed,
They ran so hard they thought their hearts would burst,
They yelled like fiends in Hell, ducks left the water
Quacking and flapping as on point of slaughter,
Up flew the geese in terror over the trees,
Out of the hive came forth the swarm of bees;
So hideous was the noise – God bless us all,
Jack Straw and all his followers in their brawl*
Were never half so shrill, for all their noise,
When they were murdering those Flemish boys,
As that day's hue and cry upon the fox.
They grabbed up trumpets made of brass and box,
Of horn and bone, on which they blew and pooped,
And therewithal they shouted and they whooped
So that it seemed the very heavens would fall.
    And now, good people, pay attention all.
See how Dame Fortune quickly changes side
And robs her enemy of hope and pride!

This cock that lay upon the fox's back
In all his dread contrived to give a quack
And said, 'Sir Fox, if I were you, as God's
My witness, I would round upon these clods
And shout, "Turn back, you saucy bumpkins all!
A very pestilence upon you fall!
Now that I have in safety reached the wood
Do what you like, the cock is mine for good;
I'll eat him there in spite of every one."'
    The fox replying, 'Faith, it shall be done!'
Opened his mouth and spoke. The nimble bird,
Breaking away upon the uttered word,
Flew high into the tree-tops on the spot.
And when the fox perceived where he had got,
'Alas,' he cried, 'alas, my Chanticleer,
I've done you grievous wrong, indeed I fear
I must have frightened you; I grabbed too hard
When I caught hold and took you from the yard.
But, sir, I meant no harm, don't be offended,
Come down and I'll explain what I intended;
So help me God I'll tell the truth – on oath!'
'No,' said the cock, 'and curses on us both,
And first on me if I were such a dunce
As let you fool me oftener than once.
Never again, for all your flattering lies,
You'll coax a song to make me blink my eyes;
And as for those who blink when they should look,
God blot them from his everlasting Book!'
'Nay, rather,' said the fox, 'his plagues be flung
On all who chatter that should hold their tongue.'
    Lo, such it is not to be on your guard
Against the flatterers of the world, or yard,
And if you think my story is absurd,
A foolish trifle of a beast and bird,
A fable of a fox, a cock, a hen,
Take hold upon the moral, gentlemen.
    St Paul himself, a saint of great discerning,
Says that all things are written for our learning;
So take the grain and let the chaff be still.
And, gracious Father, if it be thy will
As saith my Saviour, make us all good men,
And bring us to his heavenly bliss.
                                        Amen.

The Pardoner's Prologue

'My lords,' he said, 'in churches where I preach
I cultivate a haughty kind of speech
And ring it out as roundly as a bell;
I've got it all by heart, the tale I tell.
I have a text, it always is the same
And always has been, since I learnt the game,
Old as the hills and fresher than the grass,
Radix malorum est cupiditas.
    'But first I make pronouncement whence I come,
Show them my bulls in detail and in sum,
And flaunt the papal seal for their inspection
As warrant for my bodily protection,
That none may have the impudence to irk
Or hinder me in Christ's most holy work.
Then I tell stories, as occasion calls,
Showing forth bulls from popes and cardinals,
From patriarchs and bishops; as I do,
I speak some words in Latin – just a few –
To put a saffron tinge upon my preaching
And stir devotion with a spice of teaching.
Then I bring all my long glass bottles out
Cram-full of bones and ragged bits of clout,
Relics they are, at least for such are known.
Then, cased in metal, I've a shoulder-bone,
Belonging to a sheep, a holy Jew's.
"Good men," I say, "take heed, for here is news.
Take but this bone and dip it in a well;
If cow or calf, if sheep or ox should swell
From eating snakes or that a snake has stung,
Take water from that well and wash its tongue,
And it will then recover. Furthermore,
Where there is pox or scab or other sore,
All animals that water at that well
Are cured at once. Take note of what I tell.
If the good man – the owner of the stock –
Goes once a week, before the crow of cock,

Fasting, and takes a draught of water too,
Why then, according to that holy Jew,
He'll find his cattle multiply and sell.
   '"And it's a cure for jealousy as well;
For though a man be given to jealous wrath,
Use but this water when you make his broth,
And never again will he mistrust his wife,
Though he knew all about her sinful life,
Though two or three clergy had enjoyed her love.
   '"Now look; I have a mitten here, a glove.
Whoever wears this mitten on his hand
Will multiply his grain. He sows his land
And up will come abundant wheat or oats,
Providing that he offers pence or groats.
   '"Good men and women, here's a word of warning;
If there is anyone in church this morning
Guilty of sin, so far beyond expression
Horrible, that he dare not make confession,
Or any woman, whether young or old,
That's cuckolded her husband, be she told
That such as she shall have no power or grace
To offer to my relics in this place.
But those who can acquit themselves of blame
Can all come up and offer in God's name,
And I will shrive them by the authority
Committed in this papal bull to me."
   'That trick's been worth a hundred marks a year
Since I became a Pardoner, never fear.
Then, priestlike in my pulpit, with a frown,
I stand, and when the yokels have sat down,
I preach, as you have heard me say before,
And tell a hundred lying mockeries more.
I take great pains, and stretching out my neck
To east and west I crane about and peck
Just like a pigeon sitting on a barn.
My hands and tongue together spin the yarn
And all my antics are a joy to see.
The curse of avarice and cupidity
Is all my sermon, for it frees the pelf.
Out come the pence, and specially for myself,
For my exclusive purpose is to win
And not at all to castigate their sin.
Once dead what matter how their souls may fare?
They can go blackberrying, for all I care!

'Believe me, many a sermon or devotive
Exordium issues from an evil motive.
Some to give pleasure by their flattery
And gain promotion through hypocrisy,
Some out of vanity, some out of hate;
Or when I dare not otherwise debate
I'll put my discourse into such a shape,
My tongue will be a dagger; no escape
For him from slandering falsehood shall there be,
If he has hurt my brethren or me.
For though I never mention him by name
The congregation guesses all the same
From certain hints that everybody knows,
And so I take revenge upon our foes
And spit my venom forth, while I profess
Holy and true – or seeming holiness.

   'But let me briefly make my purpose plain;
I preach for nothing but for greed of gain
And use the same old text, as bold as brass,
Radix malorum est cupiditas.
And thus I preach against the very vice
I make my living out of – avarice.
And yet however guilty of that sin
Myself, with others I have power to win
Them from it, I can bring them to repent;
But that is not my principal intent.
Covetousness is both the root and stuff
Of all I preach. That ought to be enough.

   'Well, then I give examples thick and fast
From bygone times, old stories from the past.
A yokel mind loves stories from of old,
Being the kind it can repeat and hold.
What! Do you think, as long as I can preach
And get their silver for the things I teach,
That I will live in poverty, from choice?
That's not the counsel of my inner voice!

A decorative strip from the
Luttrell Psalter showing a dog
chasing a rabbit.

No! Let me preach and beg from kirk to kirk
And never do an honest job of work,
No, nor make baskets, like St Paul, to gain
A livelihood. I do not preach in vain.
Why copy the apostles? Why pretend?
I must have wool, cheese, wheat, and cash to spend,
Though it were given me by the poorest lad
Or poorest village widow, though she had
A string of starving children, all agape.
No, let me drink the liquor of the grape
And keep a jolly wench in every town!
　'But listen, gentlemen; to bring things down
To a conclusion, would you like a tale?
Now as I've drunk a draught of corn-ripe ale,
By God it stands to reason I can strike
On some good story that you all will like.
For though I am a wholly vicious man
Don't think I can't tell moral tales. I can!
Here's one I often preach when out for winning;
Now please be quiet. Here is the beginning.'

The Pardoner's Tale

In Flanders once there was a company
Of youngsters, haunting vice and ribaldry,
Riot and gambling, stews and public-houses
Where each with harp, guitar or lute carouses,
Dancing and dicing day and night, and bold
To eat and drink far more than they can hold,
Doing thereby the devil sacrifice
Within that devil's temple of cursed vice,
Abominable in superfluity,
With oaths so damnable in blasphemy
That it's a grisly thing to hear them swear.
Our dear Lord's body they will rend and tear
As if the Jews had rent Him not enough;
And at the sin of others every tough

201

Will laugh, and presently the dancing-girls,
Small pretty ones, come in and shake their curls,
With youngsters selling fruit, and ancient bawds,
And girls with cakes and music, devil's gauds
To kindle and blow the fires of lechery
That are so close annexed to gluttony.
Witness the Bible, which is most express
That lust is bred of wine and drunkenness.
　　Look how the drunken and unnatural Lot
Lay with his daughters, though he knew it not;
He was too drunk to know what he was doing.
　　Take Herod too, his tale is worth pursuing.
Replete with wine and feasting, he was able
To give the order at his very table
To kill the innocent Baptist, good St John.
　　Seneca has a thought worth pondering on;
No difference, he says, that he can find
Between a madman who has lost his mind
And one who is habitually mellow,
Except that madness when it takes a fellow
Lasts longer, on the whole, than drunkenness.
O cursed gluttony, our first distress!
Cause of our first confusion, first temptation,
The very origin of our damnation,
Till Christ redeemed us with his blood again!
O infamous indulgence! Cursed stain
So dearly bought! And what has it been worth?
Gluttony has corrupted all the earth.
　　Adam, our father, and his wife no less,
From Paradise to labour and distress
Were driven for that vice, they were indeed.
While she and Adam fasted, so I read,
They were in Paradise; when he and she
Ate of the fruit of that forbidden tree
They were at once cast forth in pain and woe.
O gluttony, it is to thee we owe
Our griefs! O if we knew the maladies
That follow on excess and gluttonies,
Sure we would diet, we would temper pleasure
In sitting down at table, show some measure!
Alas the narrow throat, the tender mouth!
Men labour east and west and north and south
In earth, in air, in water – Why, d'you think?
To get a glutton dainty meat and drink!

A leather inkwell with an intricate
tooled design.

How well of this St Paul's Epistle treats!
'Meats for the belly, belly for the meats,
But God shall yet destroy both it and them.'
Alas, the filth of it! If we contemn
The name, how far more filthy is the act!
A man who swills down vintages in fact
Makes a mere privy of his throat, a sink
For cursed superfluities of drink!
   So the Apostle said, whom tears could soften:
'Many there are, as I have told you often,
And weep to tell, whose gluttony sufficed
To make them enemies of the cross of Christ,
Whose ending is destruction and whose God
Their belly!' O thou belly! stinking pod
Of dung and foul corruption, that canst send
Thy filthy music forth at either end,
What labour and expense it is to find
Thy sustenance! These cooks that strain and grind
And bray in mortars, transubstantiate
God's gifts into a flavour on a plate,
To please a lecherous palate. How they batter
Hard bones to put some marrow on your platter,
Spicery, root, bark, leaf – they search and cull it
In the sweet hope of flattering a gullet!
Nothing is thrown away that could delight
Or whet anew lascivious appetite.
Be sure a man whom such a fare entices
Is dead indeed, though living in his vices.
   Wine is a lecherous thing and drunkenness
A squalor of contention and distress.
O drunkard, how disfigured is thy face,
How foul thy breath, how filthy thy embrace!
And through thy drunken nose a stertorous snort
Like 'samson-samson' – something of the sort.
Yet Samson never was a man to swig.
You totter, lurch and fall like a stuck pig,
Your manhood's lost, your tongue is in a burr.
Drunkenness is the very sepulchre
Of human judgement and articulation.
He that is subject to the domination
Of drink can keep no secrets, be it said.
Keep clear of wine, I tell you, white or red,
Especially Spanish wines which they provide
And have on sale in Fish Street and Cheapside.

That wine mysteriously finds its way
To mix itself with others – shall we say
Spontaneously? – that grow in neighbouring regions.★
Out of the mixture fumes arise in legions,
So when a man has had a drink or two
Though he may think he is at home with you
In Cheapside, I assure you he's in Spain
Where it was made, at Lepé I maintain,
Not even at Bordeaux. He's soon elate
And very near the '*samson-samson*' state.

But seriously, my lords, attention, pray!
All the most notable acts, I dare to say,
And victories in the Old Testament,
Won under God who is omnipotent,
Were won in abstinence, were won in prayer.
Look in the Bible, you will find it there.

Or else take Attila the Conqueror;
Died in his sleep, a manner to abhor,
In drunken shame and bleeding at the nose.
A general should live sober, I suppose.
Moreover call to mind and ponder well
What was commanded unto Lemuel
– Not Samuel, but Lemuel I said –
Read in the Bible, that's the fountain-head,
And see what comes of giving judges drink.
No more of that. I've said enough, I think.

Having put gluttony in its proper setting
I wish to warn you against dice and betting.
Gambling's the very mother of robbed purses,
Lies, double-dealing, perjury, and curses,
Manslaughter, blasphemy of Christ, and waste
Of time and money. Worse, you are debased
In public reputation, put to shame.
'A common gambler' is a nasty name.

The more exalted such a man may be
So much the more contemptible is he.
A gambling prince would be incompetent
To frame a policy of government,
And he will sink in general opinion
As one unfit to exercise dominion.

Stilbon, that wise ambassador whose mission
Took him to Corinth, was of high position;
Sparta had sent him with intent to frame
A treaty of alliance. When he came,

Hoping for reinforcement and advice,
It happened that he found them all at dice,
Their very nobles; so he quickly planned
To steal away, home to his native land.
He said, 'I will not lose my reputation,
Or compromise the honour of my nation,
By asking dicers to negotiate.
Send other wise ambassadors of state,
For on my honour I would rather die
Than be a means for Sparta to ally
With gamblers; Sparta, glorious in honour,
Shall take no such alliances upon her
As dicers make, by any act of mine!'
He showed his sense in taking such a line.
 Again, consider King Demetrius;
The King of Parthia – history has it thus –
Sent him a pair of golden dice in scorn,
To show he reckoned him a gambler born
Whose honour, if unable to surmount
The vice of gambling, was of no account.
Lords can amuse themselves in other ways
Honest enough, to occupy their days.
 Now let me speak a word or two of swearing
And perjury; the Bible is unsparing.
It's an abominable thing to curse
And swear, it says; but perjury is worse.
Almighty God has said, 'Swear not at all',
Witness St Matthew, and you may recall
The words of Jeremiah, having care
To what he says of lying: 'Thou shalt swear
In truth, in judgement and in righteousness.'
But idle swearing is a sin, no less.
Behold and see the tables of the Law
Of God's Commandments, to be held in awe;
Look at the third where it is written plain,
'Thou shalt not take the name of God in vain.'
You see He has forbidden swearing first;
Not murder, no, nor other thing accurst
Comes before that, I say, in God's commands.
That is the order; he who understands
Knows that the third commandment is just that.
And in addition, let me tell you flat,
Vengeance on him and all his house shall fall
That swears outrageously, or swears at all.

Leather knife sheaths with heraldic
markings.

'God's precious heart and passion, by God's nails
And by the blood of Christ that is at Hailes,*
Seven's my luck, and yours is five and three;
God's blessed arms! If you play false with me
I'll stab you with my dagger!' Overthrown
By two small dice, two bitching bits of bone,
Their fruit is perjury, rage and homicide.
O for the love of Jesus Christ who died
For us, abandon curses, small or great!
But, sirs, I have a story to relate.
　　It's of three rioters I have to tell
Who long before the morning service bell
Were sitting in a tavern for a drink.
And as they sat, they heard the hand-bell clink
Before a coffin going to the grave;
One of them called the little tavern-knave
And said 'Go and find out at once – look spry! –
Whose corpse is in that coffin passing by;
And see you get the name correctly too.'
'Sir,' said the boy, 'no need, I promise you;
Two hours before you came here I was told.
He was a friend of yours in days of old,
And suddenly, last night, the man was slain,
Upon his bench, face up, dead drunk again.
There came a privy thief, they call him Death,
Who kills us all round here, and in a breath
He speared him through the heart, he never stirred.
And then Death went his way without a word.
He's killed a thousand in the present plague,
And, sir, it doesn't do to be too vague
If you should meet him; you had best be wary.
Be on your guard with such an adversary,
Be primed to meet him everywhere you go,
That's what my mother said. It's all I know.'
　　The publican joined in with, 'By St Mary,
What the child says is right; you'd best be wary,
This very year he killed, in a large village
A mile away, man, woman, serf at tillage,
Page in the household, children – all there were.
Yes, I imagine that he lives round there.
It's well to be prepared in these alarms,
He might do you dishonour.' 'Huh, God's arms!'
The rioter said, 'Is he so fierce to meet?
I'll search for him, by Jesus, street by street.

God's blessed bones! I'll register a vow!
Here, chaps! The three of us together now,
Hold up your hands, like me, and we'll be brothers
In this affair, and each defend the others,
And we will kill this traitor Death, I say!
Away with him as he has made away
With all our friends. God's dignity! To-night!'

They made their bargain, swore with appetite,
These three, to live and die for one another
As brother-born might swear to his born brother.
And up they started in their drunken rage
And made towards this village which the page
And publican had spoken of before.
Many and grisly were the oaths they swore,
Tearing Christ's blessed body to a shred;
'If we can only catch him, Death is dead!'

When they had gone not fully half a mile,
Just as they were about to cross a stile,
They came upon a very poor old man
Who humbly greeted them and thus began,
'God look to you, my lords, and give you quiet!'
To which the proudest of these men of riot
Gave back the answer, 'What, old fool? Give place!
Why are you all wrapped up except your face?
Why live so long? Isn't it time to die?'

The old, old fellow looked him in the eye
And said, 'Because I never yet have found,
Though I have walked to India, searching round
Village and city on my pilgrimage,
One who would change his youth to have my age.
And so my age is mine and must be still
Upon me, for such time as God may will.

'Not even Death, alas, will take my life;
So, like a wretched prisoner at strife
Within himself, I walk alone and wait
About the earth, which is my mother's gate,
Knock-knocking with my staff from night to noon
And crying, "Mother, open to me soon!
Look at me, mother, won't you let me in?
See how I wither, flesh and blood and skin!
Alas! When will these bones be laid to rest?
Mother, I would exchange – for that were best –
The wardrobe in my chamber, standing there
So long, for yours! Aye, for a shirt of hair

A lady beats a gong to rouse game
from an ornamental lake.

To wrap me in!" She has refused her grace,
Whence comes the pallor of my withered face.
   'But it dishonoured you when you began
To speak so roughly, sir, to an old man,
Unless he had injured you in word or deed.
It says in holy writ, as you may read,
"Thou shalt rise up before the hoary head
And honour it." And therefore be it said
"Do no more harm to an old man than you,
Being now young, would have another do
When you are old" – if you should live till then.
And so may God be with you, gentlemen,
For I must go whither I have to go.'
   'By God,' the gambler said, 'you shan't do so,
You don't get off so easy, by St John!
I heard you mention, just a moment gone,
A certain traitor Death who singles out
And kills the fine young fellows hereabout.
And you're his spy, by God! You wait a bit.
Say where he is or you shall pay for it,
By God and by the Holy Sacrament!
I say you've joined together by consent
To kill us younger folk, you thieving swine!'
   'Well, sirs,' he said, 'if it be your design
To find out Death, turn up this crooked way
Towards that grove, I left him there to-day
Under a tree, and there you'll find him waiting.
He isn't one to hide for all your prating.
You see that oak? He won't be far to find.
And God protect you that redeemed mankind,
Aye, and amend you!' Thus that ancient man.
   At once the three young rioters began
To run, and reached the tree, and there they found
A pile of golden florins on the ground,
New-coined, eight bushels of them as they thought.
No longer was it Death those fellows sought,
For they were all so thrilled to see the sight,
The florins were so beautiful and bright,
That down they sat beside the precious pile.
The wickedest spoke first after a while.
'Brothers,' he said, 'you listen to what I say.
I'm pretty sharp although I joke away.
It's clear that Fortune has bestowed this treasure
To let us live in jollity and pleasure.

A stained glass window showing a medieval pedlar, his wares in a sort of chest strapped to his back.

Light come, light go! We'll spend it as we ought.
God's precious dignity! Who would have thought
This morning was to be our lucky day?
　'If one could only get the gold away,
Back to my house, or else to yours, perhaps –
For as you know, the gold is ours, chaps –
We'd all be at the top of fortune, hey?
But certainly it can't be done by day.
People would call us robbers – a strong gang,
So our own property would make us hang.
No, we must bring this treasure back by night
Some prudent way, and keep it out of sight.
And so as a solution I propose
We draw for lots and see the way it goes;
The one who draws the longest, lucky man,
Shall run to town as quickly as he can
To fetch us bread and wine – but keep things dark –
While two remain in hiding here to mark
Our heap of treasure. If there's no delay,
When night comes down we'll carry it away,
All three of us, wherever we have planned.'
　He gathered lots and hid them in his hand
Bidding them draw for where the luck should fall.
It fell upon the youngest of them all,
And off he ran at once towards the town.
　As soon as he had gone the first sat down
And thus began a parley with the other:
'You know that you can trust me as a brother;
Now let me tell you where your profit lies;
You know our friend has gone to get supplies
And here's a lot of gold that is to be
Divided equally amongst us three.
Nevertheless, if I could shape things thus
So that we shared it out – the two of us –
Wouldn't you take it as a friendly turn?'
　'But how?' the other said with some concern,
'Because he knows the gold's with me and you;
What can we tell him? What are we to do?'
　'Is it a bargain,' said the first, 'or no?
For I can tell you in a word or so
What's to be done to bring the thing about.'
'Trust me,' the other said, 'you needn't doubt
My word. I won't betray you, I'll be true.'
　'Well,' said his friend, 'you see that we are two,

A bronze figure of Christ from a crucifix.

And two are twice as powerful as one.
Now look; when he comes back, get up in fun
To have a wrestle; then, as you attack,
I'll up and put my dagger through his back
While you and he are struggling, as in game;
Then draw your dagger too and do the same.
Then all this money will be ours to spend,
Divided equally of course, dear friend.
Then we can gratify our lusts and fill
The day with dicing at our own sweet will.'
Thus these two miscreants agreed to slay
The third and youngest, as you heard me say.

The youngest, as he ran towards the town,
Kept turning over, rolling up and down
Within his heart the beauty of those bright
New florins, saying, 'Lord, to think I might
Have all that treasure to myself alone!
Could there be anyone beneath the throne
Of God so happy as I then should be?'

And so the Fiend, our common enemy,
Was given power to put it in his thought
That there was always poison to be bought,
And that with poison he could kill his friends.
To men in such a state the Devil sends
Thoughts of this kind, and has a full permission
To lure them on to sorrow and perdition;
For this young man was utterly content
To kill them both and never to repent.

And on he ran, he had no thought to tarry,
Came to the town, found an apothecary
And said, 'Sell me some poison if you will,
I have a lot of rats I want to kill
And there's a polecat too about my yard
That takes my chickens and it hits me hard;
But I'll get even, as is only right,
With vermin that destroy a man by night.'

The chemist answered, 'I've a preparation
Which you shall have, and by my soul's salvation
If any living creature eat or drink
A mouthful, ere he has the time to think,
Though he took less than makes a grain of wheat,
You'll see him fall down dying at your feet;
Yes, die he must, and in so short a while
You'd hardly have the time to walk a mile,

The poison is so strong, you understand.'
    This cursed fellow grabbed into his hand
The box of poison and away he ran
Into a neighbouring street, and found a man
Who lent him three large bottles. He withdrew
And deftly poured the poison into two.
He kept the third one clean, as well he might,
For his own drink, meaning to work all night
Stacking the gold and carrying it away.
And when this rioter, this devil's clay,
Had filled his bottles up with wine, all three,
Back to rejoin his comrades sauntered he.

    Why make a sermon of it? Why waste breath?
Exactly in the way they'd planned his death
They fell on him and slew him, two to one.
Then said the first of them when this was done,
'Now for a drink. Sit down and let's be merry,
For later on there'll be the corpse to bury.'
And, as it happened, reaching for a sup,
He took a bottle full of poison up
And drank; and his companion, nothing loth,
Drank from it also, and they perished both.

    There is, in Avicenna's long relation*
Concerning poison and its operation,
Trust me, no ghastlier section to transcend
What these two wretches suffered at their end.
Thus these two murderers received their due,
So did the treacherous young poisoner too.

Women snaring birds. This border
detail from a manuscript in the
Bodleian Library, Oxford, shows a
song bird being used as a lure to
attract other birds into an ingenious
net trap.

    O cursed sin! O blackguardly excess!
O treacherous homicide! O wickedness!
O gluttony that lusted on and diced!
O blasphemy that took the name of Christ

With habit-hardened oaths that pride began!
Alas, how comes it that a mortal man,
That thou, to thy Creator, Him that wrought thee,
That paid His precious blood for thee and bought thee,
Art so unnatural and false within?

    Dearly beloved, God forgive your sin
And keep you from the vice of avarice!
My holy pardon frees you all of this,
Provided that you make the right approaches,
That is with sterling, rings, or silver brooches.
Bow down your heads under this holy bull!
Come on, you women, offer up your wool!
I'll write your name into my ledger; so!
Into the bliss of Heaven you shall go.
For I'll absolve you by my holy power,
You that make offering, clean as at the hour
When you were born. . . That, sirs, is how I preach.
And Jesu Christ, soul's healer, aye, the leech
Of every soul, grant pardon and relieve you
Of sin, for that is best, I won't deceive you.

    One thing I should have mentioned in my tale,
Dear people. I've some relics in my bale
And pardons too, as full and fine, I hope,
As any in England, given me by the Pope.
If there be one among you that is willing
To have my absolution for a shilling
Devoutly given, come! and do not harden
Your hearts but kneel in humbleness for pardon;
Or else, receive my pardon as we go.
You can renew it every town or so
Always provided that you still renew
Each time, and in good money, what is due.
It is an honour to you to have found
A pardoner with his credentials sound
Who can absolve you as you ply the spur
In any accident that may occur.
For instance – we are all at Fortune's beck –
Your horse may throw you down and break your neck.
What a security it is to all
To have me here among you and at call
With pardon for the lowly and the great
When soul leaves body for the future state!
And I advise our Host here to begin,
The most enveloped of you all in sin.

Come forward, Host, you shall be the first to pay,
And kiss my holy relics right away.
Only a groat. Come on, unbuckle your purse!'
    'No, no,' said he, 'not I, and may the curse
Of Christ descend upon me if I do!
You'll have me kissing your old breeches too
And swear they were the relic of a saint
Although your fundament supplied the paint!
Now by St Helen and the Holy Land
I wish I had your ballocks in my hand
Instead of relics in a reliquarium;
Have them cut off and I will help to carry 'em.
We'll have them shrined for you in a hog's turd.'
    The Pardoner said nothing, not a word;
He was so angry that he couldn't speak.
'Well,' said our Host, 'if you're for showing pique,
I'll joke no more, not with an angry man.'
    The worthy Knight immediately began,
Seeing the fun was getting rather rough,
And said, 'No more, we've all had quite enough.
Now, Master Pardoner, perk up, look cheerly!
And you, Sir Host, whom I esteem so dearly,
I beg of you to kiss the Pardoner.
    'Come, Pardoner, draw nearer, my dear sir.
Let's laugh again and keep the ball in play.'
They kissed, and we continued on our way.

The Wife of Bath's Prologue

'If there were no authority on earth
Except experience; mine, for what it's worth,
And that's enough for me, all goes to show
That marriage is a misery and a woe;
For let me say, if I may make so bold,
My lords, since when I was but twelve years old,
Thanks be to God Eternal evermore,
Five husbands have I had at the church door;
Yes, it's a fact that I have had so many,
All worthy in their way, as good as any.
    'Someone said recently for my persuasion
That as Christ only went on one occasion
To grace a wedding – in Cana of Galilee –
He taught me by example there to see
That it is wrong to marry more than once.
Consider, too, how sharply, for the nonce,
He spoke, rebuking the Samaritan
Beside the well, Christ Jesus, God and man.
"Thou hast had five men husband unto thee
And he that even now thou hast," said He,
"Is not thy husband." Such the words that fell;
But what He meant thereby I cannot tell.
Why was her fifth – explain it if you can –
No lawful spouse to the Samaritan?
How many might have had her, then, to wife?
I've never heard an answer all my life
To give the number final definition.
People may guess or frame a supposition,
But I can say for certain, it's no lie,
God bade us all to wax and multiply.
That kindly text I well can understand.
Is not my husband under God's command
To leave his father and mother and take me?
No word of what the number was to be,
Then why not marry two or even eight?
And why speak evil of the married state?

Domestic Life · Games and Pastimes

Medieval manuscripts contain a wealth of illustrations which convey a vivid impression of the way people behaved in their homes and how they amused themselves in their leisure hours. In the field of games and pastimes there is a remarkable similarity with the leisure pursuits of today. Picture (1) shows a game of bowls, from the position of the participants, played much the same as today. But not all the artists of the period were so skilful. The painter of picture (2) was able to draw in perspective the seat on which the two kings are playing chess but was defeated by the same problem with the chessboard. Chess seems to have been very popular and Chaucer himself appears in one of his poems playing chess with Fortune. There are countless pictures of chess games in medieval manuscripts. Sometimes the boards have eight squares on each side as now but the number often varies—perhaps because of impressionistic drawing—and this one has only sixteen squares. Gambling was widespread. Says the Pardoner in his tale 'I wish to warn you against dice and betting. Gambling's the very mother of robbed purses, Lies, double-dealing, perjury and curses . . .'. Picture (3) shows a gambling school anxiously watching the throw of the dice at hazard.

Outdoor sports, such as wrestling, were common, but so important was archery at this time of war that official proclamations called for constant practice at the target at the cost of other activities. Nevertheless these other activities were pursued. We have already seen that bowls was played and the colourful picture (4) shows what resembles a game of hockey although the ball is much larger than that used today. Bull- and bear-baiting were a common form of entertainment. Bear-baiting is illustrated in (5). The bear, chained to a stake, is muzzled but seems to be protected by a sort of metal net over its rear, and the keeper, to whom the bear must have been a valuable asset, seems ready to beat off the dogs if they look like doing too much damage. Not so the owners of the dogs, for the one who is kneeling

appears to be spurring his dog on with a dagger. Passing to slightly less robust pursuits we see in picture (6) a band of musicians.

Picture (7) shows a tranquil scene in a birth-chamber. The artist's purpose was to record the birth of St Edmund, King of East Anglia. He lived 500 years before Chaucer but as was common practice at the time the artist has portrayed a medieval room with the people in the picture dressed in medieval costume. From it we gain the impression of the comparative

1

luxury of a bedchamber in a rich household of Chaucer's time. The mother, attended by her ladies, lies in a richly covered, curtained bed. Beds and bedding were precious possessions. One of the Black Prince's bequests was his 'great bed of red camaca [a sort of silk] together with the whole canopy, curtain, cushions, coverlet, coverings of tapestry and the whole of the rest of the apparel'. But on the whole furniture in the Middle Ages was sparse. There were few chairs—coffers, stools and benches serving mainly as seats—and tables were rare. It will be noticed that the high table in a grand house, depicted top right on the next page, is in fact only a trestle-table which could be removed after the meal.

Rich people ate well, even grossly. Often many courses were served including different kinds of fish, venison, beef, mutton, game birds, rabbits etc., roasted, stewed and made into pies. There was a wide variety of desserts and a good deal of fruit was eaten. The Luttrell

6

7

8   9

Icy commence le quart volume de Guiron le courtois / Et dist comme

Psalter in the pictures (8) and (10) takes us behind the scenes of such a feast. In the first we see food being stirred in great pots over open fires. The centre figure seems to be chopping the ingredients and the man on the right grinding, perhaps flour. Next in the series, picture (10), shows the dishes being prepared for table by what looks like the head cook wearing something very like a modern chef's hat; and, finally, the ample portions are being conveyed to the high table. The household which had to be maintained must have been huge and its members must have eaten well, though many of them would have received only the left-overs. An even grander high table is shown in (11). Here the lord and lady are being entertained as they eat by musicians and a singer. Very different from the gastronomic pleasures of the rich was the food eaten by the poor. The villeins ate very little meat, unless it was bacon from the pigs which most kept, or a rabbit poached from the lord's land at great risk. Their diet consisted mainly of bread, cheese, vegetables and,

occasionally, eggs. The small picture (9) shows members of a household gathered round a fireplace with a chimney. An interesting feature is the perch for the falcons or hawks used by the menfolk in the pursuit of hawking. These birds seem to have been kept in the main half of the house.

Picture (12) gives a good idea of the bustle of a great house – probably a royal palace. While the king or master of the house sits at table in solitary splendour life goes on around him. The clothes of the upper classes were rich and colourful, and not always very practical. But it will be noticed that a feature of men's dress was the heavy, rather voluminous robe – something very necessary even for indoor wear, for the interiors of the great houses were very cold. While the upper classes dressed frequently as gaily as peacocks (which they occasionally ate) the poorer classes generally wore clothes of a drab grey or brown.

Very different from the sophisticated splendour of the interior shown opposite is the simple picture (13) of a group of girls dancing.

3

4

Group games and particularly dancing were, from the pictures in many manuscripts of the time, a favourite leisure pursuit of the young. But for the ladies it was by no means all play. Even in the great houses spinning, weaving, knitting, embroidery and sewing were serious domestic occupations. Picture (14) shows a woman using a spinning wheel, a comparatively new invention in Chaucer's time, for until the thirteenth century the spindle had been rotated by hand.

'Take wise King Solomon of long ago;
We hear he had a thousand wives or so.
And would to God it were allowed to me
To be refreshed, aye, half so much as he!
He must have had a gift of God for wives,
No one to match him in a world of lives!
This noble king, one may as well admit,
On the first night threw many a merry fit
With each of them, he was so much alive.
Blessed be God that I have wedded five!
Welcome the sixth, whenever he appears.
I can't keep continent for years and years.
No sooner than one husband's dead and gone
Some other christian man shall take me on,
For then, so says the Apostle, I am free
To wed, o' God's name, where it pleases me.
Wedding's no sin, so far as I can learn.
Better it is to marry than to burn.

'What do I care if people choose to see
Scandal in Lamech for his bigamy?
I know that Abraham was a holy man,
And Jacob too, for all that I can scan,
Yet each of them, we know, had several brides,
Like many another holy man besides.
Show me a time or text where God disparages,
Or sets a prohibition upon marriages
Expressly, let me have it! Show it me!
And where did He command virginity?
I know as well as you do, never doubt it,
All the Apostle Paul has said about it;
He said that as for precepts he had none.
One may advise a woman to be one;
Advice is no commandment in my view.
He left it in our judgement what to do.

'Had God commanded maidenhood to all
Marriage would be condemned beyond recall,
And certainly if seed were never sown,
How ever could virginity be grown?
Paul did not dare pronounce, let matters rest,
His Master having given him no behest.
There's a prize offered for virginity;
Catch as catch can! Who's in for it? Let's see!

'It is not everyone who hears the call;
On whom God wills He lets His power fall.

Women in medieval dress, from a book by Chaucer's disciple John Lydgate.

The Apostle was a virgin, well I know;
Nevertheless, though all his writings show
He wished that everyone were such as he,
It's all mere counsel to virginity.
And as for being married, he lets me do it
Out of indulgence, so there's nothing to it
In marrying me, suppose my husband dead;
There's nothing bigamous in such a bed.
Though it were good a man should never touch
A woman (meaning here in bed and such)
And dangerous to assemble fire and tow
– What this allusion means you all must know –
He only says virginity is fresh,
More perfect than the frailty of the flesh
In married life – except when he and she
Prefer to live in married chastity.
 'I grant it you. I'll never say a word
Decrying maidenhood although preferred
To frequent marriage; there are those who mean
To live in their virginity, as clean
In body as in soul, and never mate.
I'll make no boast about my own estate.
As in a noble household, we are told,
Not every dish and vessel's made of gold,
Some are of wood, yet earn their master's praise,
God calls His folk to Him in many ways.
To each of them God gave His proper gift,
Some this, some that, and left them to make shift.
Virginity is indeed a great perfection,
And married continence, for God's dilection,
But Christ, who of perfection is the well,
Bade not that everyone should go and sell
All that he had and give it to the poor
To follow in His footsteps, that is sure.
He spoke to those that would live perfectly,
And by your leave, my lords, that's not for me.
I will bestow the flower of life, the honey,
Upon the acts and fruit of matrimony.
 'Tell me to what conclusion or in aid
Of what were generative organs made?
And for what profit were those creatures wrought?
Trust me, they cannot have been made for naught.
Gloze as you will and plead the explanation
That they were only made for the purgation

Of urine, little things of no avail
Except to know a female from a male,
And nothing else. Did somebody say no?
Experience knows well it isn't so.
The learned may rebuke me, or be loath
To think it so, but they were made for both,
That is to say both use and pleasure in
Engendering, except in case of sin.
Why else the proverb written down and set
In books: "A man must yield his wife her debt"?
What means of paying her can he invent
Unless he use his silly instrument?
It follows they were fashioned at creation
Both to purge urine and for propagation.
    'But I'm not saying everyone is bound
Who has such harness as you heard me expound
To go and use it breeding; that would be
To show too little care for chastity.
Christ was a virgin, fashioned as a man,
And many of his saints since time began
Were ever perfect in their chastity.
I'll have no quarrel with virginity.
Let them be pure wheat loaves of maidenhead
And let us wives be known for barley-bread;
Yet Mark can tell that barley-bread sufficed
To freshen many at the hand of Christ.
In that estate to which God summoned me
I'll preserve; I'm not pernickety.
In wifehood I will use my instrument
As freely as my Maker me it sent.
If I turn difficult, God give me sorrow!
My husband, he shall have it eve and morrow
Whenever he likes to come and pay his debt,
I won't prevent him! I'll have a husband yet
Who shall be both my debtor and my slave
And bear his tribulation to the grave
Upon his flesh, as long as I'm his wife.
For mine shall be the power all his life
Over his proper body, and not he,
Thus the Apostle Paul has told it me,
And bade our husbands they should love us well;
There's a command on which I like to dwell . . .'
    The Pardoner started up, and thereupon
'Madam,' he said, 'by God and by St John,

That's noble preaching no one could surpass!
I was about to take a wife; alas!
Am I to buy it on my flesh so dear?
There'll be no marrying for me this year!'
    'You wait,' she said, 'my story's not begun.
You'll taste another brew before I've done;
You'll find it isn't quite so nice as beer.
For while the tale is telling you shall hear
Of all the tribulations man and wife
Can have; I've been an expert all my life,
That is to say, myself have been the whip.
So please yourself whether you want to sip
At that same cask of marriage I shall broach.
Be cautious before making the approach,
For I'll give instances, and more than ten.
And those who won't be warned by other men
By other men shall suffer their correction.
So Ptolemy has said in this connexion.*
You read his *Almagest*; you'll find it there.'
    'Madam, I put it to you as a prayer,'
The Pardoner said, 'go on as you began!
Tell us your tale, spare not for any man.
Instruct us younger men in your technique.'
'Gladly,' she answered, 'if I am to speak.
But still I hope the company won't reprove me
Though I should speak as fantasy may move me,
And please don't be offended at my views;
They're really only offered to amuse.
    'Now, gentlemen, I'll on and tell my tale
And as I hope to drink good wine and ale
I'll tell the truth. Those husbands that I had,
Three of them were good and two were bad.
The three that I call 'good' were rich and old.
They could indeed with difficulty hold
The articles that bound them all to me;
(No doubt you understand my simile).
So help me God, I have to laugh outright
Remembering how I made them work at night!
And faith I set no store by it; no pleasure
It was to me. They'd given me their treasure,
I had no need to do my diligence
To win their love or show them reverence.
They loved me well enough, so, heavens above,
Why should I make a dainty of their love?

A woman shearing a sheep. Fine wool, for which England was famous, played an important part in the country's economy. In Chaucer's time domestic scissors were smaller versions of the shears used here.

'A knowing woman's work is never done
To get a lover if she hasn't one,
But as I had them eating from my hand
And as they'd yielded me their gold and land,
Why then take trouble to provide them pleasure
Unless to profit and amuse my leisure?
I set them so to work, I'm bound to say;
Many a night they sang, "Alack the day!"
Never for them the flitch of bacon though
That some have won in Essex at Dunmow!*
I governed them so well and held the rein
So firmly they were rapturously fain
To go and buy me pretty things to wear;
They were delighted if I spoke them fair.
God knows how spitefully I used to scold them.
      'Listen, I'll tell you how I used to hold them,
You knowing women, who can understand.
First put them in the wrong, and out of hand.
No one can be so bold – I mean no man –
At lies and swearing as a woman can.
This is no news, as you'll have realized,
To knowing ones, but to the misadvised.
A knowing wife if she is worth her salt
Can always prove her husband is at fault,
And even though the fellow may have heard
Some story told him by a little bird
She knows enough to prove the bird is crazy
And get her maid to witness she's a daisy,
With full agreement, scarce solicited.
But listen. Here's the sort of thing I said:
      '"Now, sir old dotard, what is that you say?
Why is my neighbour's wife so smart and gay?
She is respected everywhere she goes.
I sit at home and have no decent clothes.
Why haunt her house? What are you doing there?
Are you so amorous? Is she so fair?
What, whispering secrets to our maid? For shame,
Sir ancient lecher! Time you dropped that game.
And if I see my gossip or a friend
You scold me like a devil! There's no end
If I as much as stroll towards his house.
Then you come home as drunken as a mouse,
You mount your throne and preach, chapter and verse
– All nonsense – and you tell me it's a curse

A medieval schoolroom scene.
The pupils, as was the custom also
with church congregations, are
seated on the floor and only the
teacher has a chair. A kneeling pupil
appears to be submitting an
exercise for approval.

A marginal decoration from a
medieval manuscript in the
Bodleian Library, Oxford.

To marry a poor woman – she's expensive;
Or if her family's wealthy and extensive
You say it's torture to endure her pride
And melancholy airs, and more beside.
And if she has a pretty face, old traitor,
You say she's game for any fornicator
And ask what likelihood will keep her straight
With all those men who lie about in wait.
  '"You say that some desire us for our wealth,
Some for our shapeliness, our looks, our health,
Some for our singing, others for our dancing,
Some for our gentleness and dalliant glancing,
And some because our hands are soft and small;
By your account the devil gets us all.
  '"You say what castle wall can be so strong
As to hold out against a siege for long?
And if her looks are foul you say that she
Is hot for every man that she can see,
Leaping upon them with a spaniel's airs
Until she finds a man to buy her wares.
Never was goose upon the lake so grey
But that she found a gander, so you say.
You say it's hard to keep a girl controlled
If she's the kind that no one wants to hold.
That's what you say as you stump off to bed,
You brute! You say no man of sense would wed,
That is, not if he wants to go to Heaven.
Wild thunderbolts and fire from the seven
Planets descend and break your withered neck!
  '"You say that buildings falling into wreck,
And smoke, and scolding women, are the three
Things that will drive a man from home. Dear me!
What ails the poor old man to grumble so?
  '"We women hide our faults to let them show
Once we are safely married, so you say.
There's a fine proverb for a popinjay!
  '"You say that oxen, asses, hounds and horses
Can be tried out on various ploys and courses;
And basins too, and dishes when you buy them,
Spoons, chairs and furnishings, a man can try them
As he can try a suit of clothes, no doubt,
But no one ever tries a woman out
Until he's married her; old dotard crow!
And then you say she lets her vices show.

'"You also say we count it for a crime
Unless you praise our beauty all the time,
Unless you're always poring on our faces
And call us pretty names in public places;
Or if you fail to treat me to a feast
Upon my birthday – presents at the least –
Or to respect my nurse and her grey hairs,
Or be polite to all my maids upstairs
And to my father's cronies and his spies.
That's what you say, old barrelful of lies!

'"Then there's our young apprentice, handsome John,
Because he has crisp hair that shines as bonny
As finest gold, and squires me up and down
You show your low suspicions in a frown.
I wouldn't have him, not if you died to-morrow!

'"And tell me this, God punish you with sorrow,
Why do you hide the keys of coffer doors?
It's just as much my property as yours.
Do you want to make an idiot of your wife?
Now, by the Lord that gave me soul and life,
You shan't have both, you can't be such a noddy
As think to keep my goods and have my body!
One you must do without, whatever you say.
And do you need to spy on me all day?
I think you'd like to lock me in your coffer!
'Go where you please, dear wife,' you ought to offer,
'Amuse yourself! I shan't give ear to malice,
I know you for a virtuous wife, Dame Alice.'
We cannot love a husband who takes charge
Of where we go. We like to be at large.

'"Above all other men may God confer
His blessing on that wise astrologer
Sir Ptolemy who, in his *Almagest*,
Has set this proverb down: 'Of men, the best
And wisest care not who may have in hand
The conduct of the world.' I understand
That means, 'If you've enough, you shouldn't care
How prosperously other people fare.'
Be sure, old dotard, if you call the bluff,
You'll get your evening rations right enough.
He's a mean fellow that lets no man handle
His lantern when it's just to light a candle;
He has lost no light, he hasn't felt the strain;
And you have light enough, so why complain?

Carrying babies in a double pannier
borne across the shoulders.

'"And when a woman tries a mild display
In dress or costly ornament, you say
It is a danger to her chastity,
And then, bad luck to you, start making free
With Bible tags in the Apostle's name;
'And in like manner, chastely and with shame,
You women should adorn yourselves,' said he,
'And not with braided hair or jewelry,
With pearl or golden ornament.' What next!
I'll pay as much attention to your text
And rubric in such things as would a gnat.

'"And once you said that I was like a cat,
For if you singe a cat it will not roam
And that's the way to keep a cat at home.
But when she feels her fur is sleek and gay
She can't be kept indoors for half a day
But off she takes herself as dusk is falling
To show her fur and go a-caterwauling.
Which means if I feel gay, as you suppose,
I shall run out to show my poor old clothes.

'"Silly old fool! You and your private spies!
Go on, beg Argus with his hundred eyes
To be my bodyguard, that's better still!
But yet he shan't, I say, against my will.
I'll pull him by the beard, believe you me!

'"And once you said that principally three*
Misfortunes trouble earth, east, west and north,
And no man living could endure a fourth.
My dear sir shrew, Jesu cut short your life!
You preach away and say a hateful wife
Is reckoned to be one of these misfortunes.
Is there no other trouble that importunes
The world and that your parables could condemn?
Must an unhappy wife be one of them?

'"Then you compared a woman's love to Hell,
To barren land where water will not dwell,
And you compared it to a quenchless fire,
The more it burns the more is its desire
To burn up everything that burnt can be.
You say that just as worms destroy a tree
A wife destroys her husband and contrives,
As husbands know, the ruin of their lives."

'Such was the way, my lords, you understand
I kept my older husbands well in hand.

Carrying babies in a double pannier
strapped across the shoulders.

I told them they were drunk and their unfitness
To judge my conduct forced me to take witness
That they were lying. Johnny and my niece
Would back me up. O Lord, I wrecked their peace,
Innocent as they were, without remorse!
For I could bite and whinny like a horse
And launch complaints when things were all my fault;
I'd have been lost if I had called a halt.
First to the mill is first to grind your corn;
I attacked first and they were overborne,
Glad to apologize and even suing
Pardon for what they'd never thought of doing.

'I'd tackle one for wenching, out of hand,
Although so ill the man could hardly stand,
Yet he felt flattered in his heart because
He thought it showed how fond of him I was.
I swore that all my walking out at night
Was just to keep his wenching well in sight.
That was a dodge that made me shake with mirth;
But all such wit is given us at birth.
Lies, tears and spinning are the things God gives
By nature to a woman, while she lives.
So there's one thing at least that I can boast,
That in the end I always ruled the roast;
Cunning or force was sure to make them stumble,
And always keeping up a steady grumble.

'But bed-time above all was their misfortune;
That was the place to scold them and importune
And baulk their fun. I never would abide
In bed with them if hands began to slide
Till they had promised ransom, paid a fee:
And then I let them do their nicety.
And so I tell this tale to every man,
"It's all for sale and let him win who can."
No empty-handed man can lure a bird.
His pleasures were my profit; I concurred,
Even assumed fictitious appetite
Though bacon never gave me much delight.
And that's the very fact that made me chide them.
And had the Pope been sitting there beside them
I wouldn't have spared them at their very table,
But paid them out as far as I was able.
I say, so help me God Omnipotent,
Were I to make my will and testament

A 'weeper' on the tomb of King
Edward III in Westminster Abbey.
It was the custom to perpetuate
mourners with such figures. This
weeper is Joan de la Tour.

I owe them nothing, paid them word for word
Putting my wits to use, and they preferred
To give it up and take it for the best
For otherwise they would have got no rest.
Though they might glower like a maddened beast
They got no satisfaction, not the least.
    'I then would say, "My dear, just take a peep!
What a meek look on Willikin our sheep!
Come nearer, husband, let me kiss your cheek;
You should be just as patient, just as meek;
Sweeten your heart. Your conscience needs a probe.
You're fond of preaching patience out of Job,
And so be patient; practise what you preach,
And if you don't, my dear, we'll have to teach
You that it's nice to have a quiet life.
One of us must be master, man or wife,
And since a man's more reasonable, he
Should be the patient one, you must agree.

Another weeper from the same
tomb – William of Hatfield.

    '"What ails you, man, to grumble so and groan?
Just that you want my what-not all your own?
Why, take it all, man, take it, every bit!
St Peter, what a love you have for it!
For if I were to sell my *belle chose*,
I could go walking fresher than a rose;
But I will keep it for your private tooth.
By God, you are to blame, and that's the truth."
    'That's how my first three husbands were undone.
Now let me tell you of my last but one.
    'He was a reveller, was number four;
That is to say he kept a paramour.
And I was young, ah, ragery's the word,
Stubborn and strong and jolly as a bird.
Play me the harp and I would dance and sing,
Believe me, like a nightingale in spring,
If I had had a draught of sweetened wine.
    'Metellius, that filthy lout – the swine
Who snatched a staff and took his woman's life
For drinking wine – if I had been his wife
He never would have daunted me from drink.
Whenever I take wine I have to think
Of Venus, for as cold engenders hail
A lecherous mouth begets a lecherous tail.
A woman in her cups has no defence,
As lechers know from long experience.

'But Christ! Whenever it comes back to me,
When I recall my youth and jollity,
It fairly warms the cockles of my heart!
This very day I feel a pleasure start,
Yes, I can feel it tickling at the root.
Lord, how it does me good! I've had my fruit,
I've had my world and time, I've had my fling!
But age that comes to poison everything
Has taken all my beauty and my pith.
Well, let it go, the devil go therewith!
The flour is gone, there is no more to say,
And I must sell the bran as best I may;
But still I mean to find my way to fun...
Now let me tell you of my last but one.

'I told you how it filled my heart with spite
To see another woman his delight,
By God and all His saints I made it good!
I carved him out a cross of the same wood,
Not with my body in a filthy way,
But certainly by seeming rather gay
To others, frying him in his own grease
Of jealousy and rage; he got no peace.
By God on earth I was his purgatory,
For which I hope his soul may be in glory.
God knows he sang a sorry tune, he flinched,
And bitterly enough, when the shoe pinched.
And God and he alone can say how grim,
How many were the ways I tortured him.

'He died when I came back from Jordan Stream
And he lies buried under the rood-beam,
Albeit that his tomb can scarce supply us
With such a show as that of King Darius
– Apelles sculped it in a sumptuous taste –
But costly burial would have been mere waste.
Farewell to him, God give his spirit rest!
He's in his grave, he's nailed up in his chest.

'Now of my fifth, last husband let me tell.
God never let his soul be sent to Hell!
And yet he was my worst, and many a blow
He struck me still can ache along my row
Of ribs, and will until my dying day.

'But in our bed he was so fresh and gay,
So coaxing, so persuasive...Heaven knows
Whenever he wanted it – my *belle chose* –

Though he had beaten me in every bone
He still could wheedle me to love, I own.
I think I loved him best, I'll tell no lie.
He was disdainful in his love, that's why.
We women have a curious fantasy
In such affairs, or so it seems to me.
When something's difficult, or can't be had,
We crave and cry for it all day like mad.
Forbid a thing, we pine for it all night,
Press fast upon us and we take to flight;
We use disdain in offering our wares.
A throng of buyers sends prices up at fairs,
Cheap goods have little value, they suppose;
And that's a thing that every woman knows.

   'My fifth and last – God keep his soul in health!
The one I took for love and not for wealth,
Had been at Oxford not so long before
But had left school and gone to lodge next door,
Yes, it was to my godmother's he'd gone.
God bless her soul! *Her* name was Alison.
She knew my heart and more of what I thought
Than did the parish priest, and so she ought!
She was my confidante, I told her all.
For had my husband pissed against a wall
Or done some crime that would have cost his life,
To her and to another worthy wife
And to my niece, because I loved her well,
I'd have told everything there was to tell.
And so I often did, and Heaven knows
It used to set him blushing like a rose
For shame, and he would blame his lack of sense
In telling me secrets of such consequence.

   'And so one time it happened that in Lent,
As I so often did, I rose and went
To see her, ever wanting to be gay
And go a-strolling, March, April and May,
From house to house for chat and village malice.

   'Johnny (the boy from Oxford) and Dame Alice
And I myself, into the fields we went.
My husband was in London all that Lent;
All the more fun for me – I only mean
The fun of seeing people and being seen
By cocky lads; for how was I to know
Where or what graces Fortune might bestow?

Two men give assistance to the
oarsmen by towing their boat.

And so I made a round of visitations,
Went to processions, festivals, orations,
Preachments and pilgrimages, watched the carriages
They use for plays and pageants, went to marriages,
And always wore my gayest scarlet dress.
     'These worms, these moths, these mites, I must confe
Got little chance to eat it, by the way.
Why not? Because I wore it every day.
     'Now let me tell you all that came to pass.
We sauntered in the meadows through the grass
Toying and dallying to such extent,
Johnny and I, that I grew provident
And I suggested, were I ever free
And made a widow, he should marry me.
And certainly – I do not mean to boast –
I ever was more provident than most
In marriage matters and in other such.
I never think a mouse is up to much
That only has one hole in all the house;
If that should fail, well, it's good-bye the mouse.
     'I let him think I was as one enchanted
(That was a trick my godmother implanted)
And told him I had dreamt the night away
Thinking of him, and dreamt that as I lay
He tried to kill me. Blood had drenched the bed.
     '"But still it was a lucky dream," I said,
"For blood betokens money, I recall."
It was a lie. I hadn't dreamt at all.
'Twas from my godmother I learnt my lore
In matters such as that, and many more.
     'Well, let me see ... what had I to explain?
Aha! By God, I've got the thread again.
     'When my fourth husband lay upon his bier
I wept all day and looked as drear as drear,
As widows must, for it is quite in place,
And with a handkerchief I hid my face.
Now that I felt provided with a mate
I wept but little, I need hardly state.
     'To church they bore my husband on the morrow
With all the neighbours round him venting sorrow,
And one of them of course was handsome Johnny.
So help me God, I thought he looked so bonny
Behind the coffin! Heavens, what a pair
Of legs he had! Such feet, so clean and fair!

I gave my whole heart up, for him to hold.
He was, I think, some twenty winters old,
And I was forty then, to tell the truth.
But still, I always had a coltish tooth.
Yes, I'm gap-toothed; it suits me well I feel,
It is the print of Venus and her seal.
So help me God I was a lusty one,
Fair, young and well-to-do, and full of fun!
And truly, as my husbands said to me
I had the finest *quoniam* that might be.
For Venus sent me feeling from the stars
And my heart's boldness came to me from Mars.
Venus gave me desire and lecherousness
And Mars my hardihood, or so I guess,
Born under Taurus and with Mars therein.
Alas, alas, that ever love was sin!
I ever followed natural inclination
Under the power of my constellation
And was unable to deny, in truth,
My chamber of Venus to a likely youth.
The mark of Mars is still upon my face
And also in another privy place.
For as I may be saved by God above,
I never used discretion when in love
But ever followed on my appetite,
Whether the lad was short, long, black or white.
Little I cared, if he was fond of me,
How poor he was, or what his rank might be.
    'What shall I say? Before the month was gone
This gay young student, my delightful John,
Had married me in solemn festival.
I handed him the money, lands and all
That ever had been given me before;
This I repented later, more and more.
None of my pleasures would he let me seek;
By God, he smote me once upon the cheek
Because I tore a page out of his book,
And that's the reason why I'm deaf. But look,
Stubborn I was, just like a lioness;
As to my tongue, a very wrangleress.
I went off gadding as I had before
From house to house, however much he swore.
Because of that he used to preach and scold,
Drag Roman history up from days of old,

A fourteenth-century wrought-iron alms box bearing the arms of England.

How one Simplicius Gallus left his wife,
Deserting her completely all his life,
Only for poking out her head one day
Without a hat, upon the public way.
    'Some other Roman – I forget his name –
Because his wife went to a summer's game
Without his knowledge, left her in the lurch.
    'And he would take the Bible up and search
For proverbs in Ecclesiasticus,
Particularly one that has it thus:
"Suffer no wicked woman to gad about."
And then would come the saying (need you doubt?)
    A man who seeks to build his house of sallows,
    A man who spurs a blind horse over fallows,
    Or lets his wife make pilgrimage to Hallows,
    Is worthy to be hanged upon the gallows.
But all for naught. I didn't give a hen
For all his proverbs and his wise old men.
Nor would I take rebuke at any price;
I hate a man who points me out my vice,
And so, God knows, do many more than I.
That drove him raging mad, you may rely.
No more would I forbear him, I can promise.
    'Now let me tell you truly by St Thomas
About that book and why I tore the page
And how he smote me deaf in very rage.
    'He had a book, he kept it on his shelf,
And night and day he read it to himself
And laughed aloud, although it was quite serious.
He called it *Theophrastus and Valerius.**
There was another Roman, much the same,
A cardinal; St Jerome was his name.
He wrote a book against Jovinian,
Bound up together with Tertullian,
Chrysippus, Trotula and Heloise,
An abbess, lived near Paris. And with these
Were bound the parables of Solomon,
With Ovid's *Art of Love* another one.
All these were bound together in one book
And day and night he used to take a look
At what it said, when he had time and leisure
Or had no occupation but his pleasure,
Which was to read this book of wicked wives;
He knew more legends of them and their lives

The fifteenth-century picture
(opposite) shows not only the
panoply of the law but how firmly it
was established in the social fabric.
A shackled prisoner, guarded
by a court official, stands before
the judges of the Court of the King's
Bench while the jury on the left
is being sworn in. An array of clerks
prepare to record the proceedings.
In the foreground six more
shackled prisoners, two of them
showing boredom, await their turn,
guarded by officials armed
with staves.

Than there are good ones mentioned in the Bible.
For take my word for it, there is no libel
On women that the clergy will not paint,
Except when writing of a woman-saint,
But never good of other women, though.
Who called the lion savage? Do you know?
By God, if women had but written stories
Like those the clergy keep in oratories,
More had been written of man's wickedness
Than all the sons of Adam could redress.
Children of Mercury* and we of Venus
Keep up the contrariety between us;
Mercury stands for wisdom, thrift and science,
Venus for revel, squandering and defiance.
Their several natures govern their direction;
One rises when the other's in dejection.
So Mercury is desolate when halted
In *Pisces*, just where Venus is exalted,
And Venus falls where Mercury is raised,
And women therefore never can be praised
By learned men, old scribes who cannot do
The works of Venus more than my old shoe.
These in their dotage sit them down to frowse
And say that women break their marriage-vows!

'Now to my purpose as I told you; look,
Here's how I got a beating for a book.
One evening Johnny, glowering with ire,
Sat with his book and read it by the fire.
And first he read of Eve whose wickedness
Brought all mankind to sorrow and distress,
Root-cause why Jesus Christ Himself was slain
And gave His blood to buy us back again.
Aye, there's the text where you expressly find
That woman brought the loss of all mankind.

'He read me then how Samson as he slept
Was shorn of all his hair by her he kept,
And by that treachery Samson lost his eyes.
And then he read me, if I tell no lies,
All about Hercules and Deianire;
She tricked him into setting himself on fire.

'He left out nothing of the miseries
Occasioned by his wives to Socrates.
Xantippe poured a piss-pot on his head.
The silly man sat still, as he were dead,

Decorated pitchers which have
survived provide evidence of the skill
and artistry of medieval potters.

Wiping his head, but dared no more complain
Than say, "Ere thunder stops, down comes the rain."
   'Next of Pasiphaë the Queen of Crete;*
For wickedness he thought that story sweet;
Fie, say no more! It has a grisly sting,
Her horrible lust. How could she do the thing!
   'And then he told of Clytemnestra's lechery
And how she made her husband die by treachery.
He read that story with a great devotion.
   'He read me what occasioned the commotion
By which Amphiaraüs lost his life;
My husband had a legend about his wife
Eriphyle, who for a gaud in gold
Went to the Greeks in secret, and she told
Them where to find him, in what hiding-place.
At Thebes it was; he met with sorry grace.
   'Of Livia and Lucilia then he read,
And both of course had killed their husbands dead,
The one for love, the other out of hate.
Livia prepared some poison for him late
One evening and she killed him out of spite,
Lucilia out of lecherous delight.
For she, in order he might only think
Of her, prepared an aphrodisiac drink;
He drank it and was dead before the morning.
Such is the fate of husbands; it's a warning.
   'And then he told how one Latumius
Lamented to his comrade Arrius
That in his orchard-plot there grew a tree
On which his wives had hanged themselves, all three,
Or so he said, out of some spite or other;
To which this Arrius replied, "Dear brother,
Give me a cutting from that blessed tree
And planted in my garden it shall be!"
   'Of wives of later date he also read,
How some had killed their husbands when in bed,
Then night-long with their lechers played the whore,
While the poor corpse lay fresh upon the floor.
   'One drove a nail into her husband's brain
While he was sleeping, and the man was slain;
Others put poison in their husbands' drink.
He spoke more harm of us than heart can think
And knew more proverbs too, for what they're worth,
Than there are blades of grass upon the earth.

A particularly intricate and
pleasing design.

'"Better," says he, "to share your habitation
With lion, dragon, or abomination
Than with a woman given to reproof.
Better," says he, "take refuge on the roof
Than with an angry wife, down in the house;
They are so wicked and cantankerous
They hate the things their husbands like," he'd say.
"A woman always casts her shame away
When she casts off her smock, and that's in haste.
A pretty woman, if she isn't chaste,
Is like a golden ring in a sow's snout."

'Who could imagine, who could figure out
The torture in my heart? It reached the top
And when I saw that he would never stop
Reading this cursed book, all night no doubt,
I suddenly grabbed and tore three pages out
Where he was reading, at the very place,
And fisted such a buffet in his face
That backwards down into our fire he fell.

'Then like a maddened lion, with a yell
He started up and smote me on the head,
And down I fell upon the floor for dead.

'And when he saw how motionless I lay
He was aghast and would have fled away,
But in the end I started to come to.
"O have you murdered me, you robber, you,
To get my land?" I said. "Was that the game?
Before I'm dead I'll kiss you all the same."

'He came up close and kneeling gently down
He said, "My love, my dearest Alison,
So help me God, I never again will hit
You, love; and if I did, you asked for it.
Forgive me!" But for all he was so meek
I up at once and smote him on the cheek
And said, "Take that to level up the score!
Now let me die, I can't speak any more."

'We had a mort of trouble and heavy weather
But in the end we made it up together.
He gave the bridle over to my hand,
Gave me the government of house and land,
Of tongue and fist, indeed of all he'd got.
I made him burn that book upon the spot.
And when I'd mastered him, and out of deadlock
Secured myself the sovereignty in wedlock,

And when he said, "My own and truest wife,
Do as you please for all the rest of life,
But guard your honour and my good estate,"
From that day forward there was no debate.
So help me God I was as kind to him
As any wife from Denmark to the rim
Of India, and as true. And he to me.
And I pray God that sits in majesty
To bless his soul and fill it with his glory.
Now, if you'll listen, I will tell my story.'

Words between the Summoner and the Friar

The Friar laughed when he had heard all this.
'Well, Ma'am,' he said, 'as God may send me bliss,
This is a long preamble to a tale!'
But when the Summoner heard the Friar rail,
'Just look at that!' he cried. 'God's arms and skin!
These meddling friars are always butting in!
Don't we all know a friar and a fly
Go buzzing into every dish and pie!
What do you mean with your "preambulation"?
Amble yourself, trot, do a meditation!
You're spoiling all our fun with your commotion.'
The Friar smiled and said, 'Is that your notion?
I promise on my word before I go
To find occasion for a tale or so
About a summoner that will make us laugh.'
'Well, damn your eyes, and on my own behalf,'
The Summoner answered, 'mine be damned as well
If I can't think of several tales to tell
About the friars that will make you mourn
Before we get as far as Sittingbourne.
Have you no patience? Look, he's in a huff!'
    Our Host called out, 'Be quiet, that's enough!
Shut up, and let the woman tell her tale.
You must be drunk, you've taken too much ale.
Now, Ma'am, you go ahead and no demur.'
'All right,' she said, 'it's just as you prefer,
If I have licence from this worthy friar.'
'Nothing,' said he, 'that I should more desire.'

The Wife of Bath's Tale

When good King Arthur ruled in ancient days
(A king that every Briton loves to praise)
This was a land brim-full of fairy folk.
The Elf-Queen and her courtiers joined and broke
Their elfin dance on many a green mead,
Or so was the opinion once, I read,
Hundreds of years ago, in days of yore.
But no one now sees fairies any more.
For now the saintly charity and prayer
Of holy friars seem to have purged the air;
They search the countryside through field and stream
As thick as motes that speckle a sun-beam,
Blessing the halls, the chambers, kitchens, bowers,
Cities and boroughs, castles, courts and towers,
Thorpes, barns and stables, outhouses and dairies,
And that's the reason why there are no fairies.
Wherever there was wont to walk an elf
To-day there walks the holy friar himself

239

As evening falls or when the daylight springs,
Saying his mattins and his holy things,
Walking his limit round from town to town.
Women can now go safely up and down
By every bush or under every tree;
There is no other incubus but he,
So there is really no one else to hurt you
And he will do no more than take your virtue.

   Now it so happened, I began to say,
Long, long ago in good King Arthur's day,
There was a knight who was a lusty liver.
One day as he came riding from the river
He saw a maiden walking all forlorn
Ahead of him, alone as she was born.
And of that maiden, spite of all she said,
By very force he took her maidenhead.

   This act of violence made such a stir,
So much petitioning of the king for her,
That he condemned the knight to lose his head
By course of law. He was as good as dead
(It seems that then the statutes took that view)
But that the queen, and other ladies too,
Implored the king to exercise his grace
So ceaselessly, he gave the queen the case
And granted her his life, and she could choose
Whether to show him mercy or refuse.

   The queen returned him thanks with all her might,
And then she sent a summons to the knight
At her convenience, and expressed her will:
'You stand, for such is the position still,
In no way certain of your life,' said she,
'Yet you shall live if you can answer me:
What is the thing that women most desire?
Beware the axe and say as I require.

   'If you can't answer on the moment, though,
I will concede you this: you are to go
A twelvemonth and a day to seek and learn
Sufficient answer, then you shall return.
I shall take gages from you to extort
Surrender of your body to the court.'

   Sad was the knight and sorrowfully sighed,
But there! All other choices were denied,
And in the end he chose to go away
And to return after a year and a day

The three ladies seated on the settle
have not been translated into the
Inferno but are watching a masque
being performed in a great house.

Armed with such answer as there might be sent
To him by God. He took his leave and went.
  He knocked at every house, searched every place,
Yes, anywhere that offered hope of grace.
What could it be that women wanted most?
But all the same he never touched a coast,
Country or town in which there seemed to be
Any two people willing to agree.
  Some said that women wanted wealth and treasure,
'Honour,' said some, some 'Jollity and pleasure,'
Some 'Gorgeous clothes' and others 'Fun in bed,'
'To be oft widowed and remarried,' said
Others again, and some that what most mattered
Was that we should be cossetted and flattered.

The monastery bell-ringer.

That's very near the truth, it seems to me;
A man can win us best with flattery.
To dance attendance on us, make a fuss,
Ensnares us all, the best and worst of us.
  Some say the things we most desire are these:
Freedom to do exactly as we please,
With no one to reprove our faults and lies,
Rather to have one call us good and wise.
Truly there's not a woman in ten score
Who has a fault, and someone rubs the sore,
But she will kick if what he says is true;
You try it out and you will find so too.
However vicious we may be within
We like to be thought wise and void of sin.
Others assert we women find it sweet
When we are thought dependable, discreet
And secret, firm of purpose and controlled,
Never betraying things that we are told.
But that's not worth the handle of a rake;
Women conceal a thing? For Heaven's sake!
Remember Midas? Will you hear the tale?
  Among some other little things, now stale,
Ovid relates that under his long hair
The unhappy Midas grew a splendid pair
Of ass's ears; as subtly as he might,
He kept his foul deformity from sight;
Save for his wife, there was not one that knew.
He loved her best, and trusted in her too.
He begged her not to tell a living creature
That he possessed so horrible a feature.

And she – she swore, were all the world to win,
She would not do such villainy and sin
As saddle her husband with so foul a name;
Besides to speak would be to share the shame.
Nevertheless she thought she would have died
Keeping this secret bottled up inside;
It seemed to swell her heart and she, no doubt,
Thought it was on the point of bursting out.
    Fearing to speak of it to woman or man,
Down to a reedy marsh she quickly ran
And reached the sedge. Her heart was all on fire
And, as a bittern bumbles in the mire,
She whispered to the water, near the ground,
'Betray me not, O water, with thy sound!
To thee alone I tell it: it appears
My husband has a pair of ass's ears!
Ah! My heart's well again, the secret's out!
I could no longer keep it, not a doubt.'
And so you see, although we may hold fast
A little while, it must come out at last,
We can't keep secrets; as for Midas, well,
Read Ovid for his story; he will tell.
    This knight that I am telling you about
Perceived at last he never would find out
What it could be that women loved the best.
Faint was the soul within his sorrowful breast
As home he went, he dared no longer stay;
His year was up and now it was the day.
    As he rode home in a dejected mood
Suddenly, at the margin of a wood,
He saw a dance upon the leafy floor
Of four and twenty ladies, nay, and more.
Eagerly he approached, in hope to learn
Some words of wisdom ere he should return;
But lo! Before he came to where they were,
Dancers and dance all vanished into air!
There wasn't a living creature to be seen
Save one old woman crouched upon the green.
A fouler-looking creature I suppose
Could scarcely be imagined. She arose
And said, 'Sir knight, there's no way on from here.
Tell me what you are looking for, my dear,
For peradventure that were best for you;
We old, old women know a thing or two.'

This small border decoration from a manuscript in the Bodleian Library, Oxford, illustrates fighting between game cocks which are being spurred on by their owners who are no doubt wagering on the outcome.

'Dear Mother,' said the knight, 'alack the day!
I am as good as dead if I can't say
What thing it is that women most desire;
If you could tell me I would pay your hire.'
'Give me your hand,' she said, 'and swear to do
Whatever I shall next require of you
– If so to do should lie within your might –
And you shall know the answer before night.'
'Upon my honour,' he answered, 'I agree.'
'Then,' said the crone, 'I dare to guarantee
Your life is safe; I shall make good my claim.
Upon my life the queen will say the same.
Show me the very proudest of them all
In costly coverchief or jewelled caul
That dare say no to what I have to teach.
Let us go forward without further speech.'
And then she crooned her gospel in his ear
And told him to be glad and not to fear.

   They came to court. This knight, in full array,
Stood forth and said, 'O Queen, I've kept my day
And kept my word and have my answer ready.'

   There sat the noble matrons and the heady
Young girls, and widows too, that have the grace
Of wisdom, all assembled in that place,
And there the queen herself was throned to hear
And judge his answer. Then the knight drew near
And silence was commanded through the hall.

   The queen then bade the knight to tell them all
What thing it was that women wanted most.
He stood not silent like a beast or post,

An intimate picture of a sick room. The elderly patient lies on a raised, panelled and not very comfortable-looking bed. At the fire a nurse on a low stool prepares perhaps a nourishing dish, perhaps a healing brew. The book she has on her knee could contain recipes or a guide to magic potions.

But gave his answer with the ringing word
Of a man's voice and the assembly heard:
  'My liege and lady, in general,' said he,
'A woman wants the self-same sovereignty*
Over her husband as over her lover,
And master him; he must not be above her.
That is your greatest wish, whether you kill
Or spare me; please yourself. I wait your will.'
  In all the court not one that shook her head
Or contradicted what the knight had said;
Maid, wife and widow cried, 'He's saved his life!'
  And on the word up started the old wife,
The one the knight saw sitting on the green,
And cried, 'Your mercy, sovereign lady queen!
Before the court disperses, do me right!
'Twas I who taught this answer to the knight,
For which he swore, and pledged his honour to it,
That the first thing I asked of him he'd do it,
So far as it should lie within his might.
Before this court I ask you then, sir knight,
To keep your word and take me for your wife;
For well you know that I have saved your life.
If this be false, deny it on your sword!'
  'Alas!' he said, 'Old lady, by the Lord
I know indeed that such was my behest,
But for God's love think of a new request,
Take all my goods, but leave my body free.'
'A curse on us,' she said, 'if I agree!
I may be foul, I may be poor and old,
Yet will not choose to be, for all the gold
That's bedded in the earth or lies above,
Less than your wife, nay, than your very love!'
  'My love?' said he. 'By heaven, my damnation!
Alas that any of my race and station
Should ever make so foul a misalliance!'
Yet in the end his pleading and defiance
All went for nothing, he was forced to wed.
He takes his ancient wife and goes to bed.
  Now peradventure some may well suspect
A lack of care in me since I neglect
To tell of the rejoicings and display
Made at the feast upon their wedding-day.
I have but a short answer to let fall;
I say there was no joy or feast at all,

Nothing but heaviness of heart and sorrow.
He married her in private on the morrow
And all day long stayed hidden like an owl,
It was such torture that his wife looked foul.
    Great was the anguish churning in his head
When he and she were piloted to bed;
He wallowed back and forth in desperate style.
His ancient wife lay smiling all the while;
At last she said 'Bless us! Is this, my dear,
How knights and wives get on together here?
Are these the laws of good King Arthur's house?
Are knights of his all so contemptuous?
I am your own beloved and your wife,
And I am she, indeed, that saved your life;
And certainly I never did you wrong.
Then why, this first of nights, so sad a song?
You're carrying on as if you were half-witted.
Say, for God's love, what sin have I committed?
I'll put things right if you will tell me how.'
    'Put right?' he cried. 'That never can be now!
Nothing can ever be put right again!
You're old, and so abominably plain,
So poor to start with, so low-bred to follow;
It's little wonder if I twist and wallow!
God, that my heart would burst within my breast!'
    'Is that,' said she, 'the cause of your unrest?'
    'Yes, certainly,' he said, 'and can you wonder?'
    'I could set right what you suppose a blunder,
That's if I cared to, in a day or two,
If I were shown more courtesy by you.
Just now,' she said, 'you spoke of gentle birth,
Such as descends from ancient wealth and worth.
If that's the claim you make for gentlemen
Such arrogance is hardly worth a hen.
Whoever loves to work for virtuous ends,
Public and private, and who most intends
To do what deeds of gentleness he can,
Take him to be the greatest gentleman.
Christ wills we take our gentleness from Him,
Not from a wealth of ancestry long dim,
Though they bequeath their whole establishment
By which we claim to be of high descent.
Our fathers cannot make us a bequest
Of all those virtues that became them best

And earned for them the name of gentlemen,
But bade us follow them as best we can.
    'Thus the wise poet of the Florentines,
Dante by name, has written in these lines,
For such is the opinion Dante launches:
"Seldom arises by these slender branches
Prowess of men, for it is God, no less,
Wills us to claim of Him our gentleness."
For of our parents nothing can we claim
Save temporal things, and these may hurt and maim.
    'But everyone knows this as well as I;
For if gentility were implanted by
The natural course of lineage down the line,
Public or private, could it cease to shine
In doing the fair work of gentle deed?
No vice or villainy could then bear seed.
    'Take fire and carry it to the darkest house
Between this kingdom and the Caucasus,
And shut the doors on it and leave it there,
It will burn on, and it will burn as fair
As if ten thousand men were there to see,
For fire will keep its nature and degree,
I can assure you, sir, until it dies.
    'But gentleness, as you will recognize,
Is not annexed in nature to possessions,
Men fail in living up to their professions;
But fire never ceases to be fire.
God knows you'll often find, if you enquire,
Some lording full of villainy and shame.
If you would be esteemed for the mere name
Of having been by birth a gentleman
And stemming from some virtuous, noble clan,
And do not live yourself by gentle deed
Or take your father's noble code and creed,
You are no gentleman, though duke or earl.
Vice and bad manners are what make a churl.
    'Gentility is only the renown
For bounty that your fathers handed down,
Quite foreign to your person, not your own;
Gentility must come from God alone.
That we are gentle comes to us by grace
And by no means is it bequeathed with place.
    'Reflect how noble (says Valerius)
Was Tullius surnamed Hostilius,

Who rose from poverty to nobleness.
And read Boethius, Seneca no less,
Thus they express themselves and are agreed:
"Gentle is he that does a gentle deed."
And therefore, my dear husband, I conclude
That even if my ancestors were rude,
Yet God on high – and so I hope He will –
Can grant me grace to live in virtue still,
A gentlewoman only when beginning
To live in virtue and to shrink from sinning.

'As for my poverty which you reprove,
Almighty God Himself in whom we move,
Believe and have our being, chose a life
Of poverty, and every man or wife
Nay, every child can see our Heavenly King
Would never stoop to choose a shameful thing.
No shame in poverty if the heart is gay,
As Seneca and all the learned say.
He who accepts his poverty unhurt
I'd say is rich although he lacked a shirt.
But truly poor are they who whine and fret
And covet what they cannot hope to get.
And he that, having nothing, covets not,
Is rich, though you may think he is a sot.
True poverty can find a song to sing.

'Juvenal says a pleasant little thing:
"The poor can dance and sing in the relief
Of having nothing that will tempt a thief."
Though it be hateful, poverty is good,
A great incentive to a livelihood,
And a great help to our capacity
For wisdom, if accepted patiently.
Poverty is, though wanting in estate,
A kind of wealth that none calumniate.
Poverty often, when the heart is lowly,
Brings one to God and teaches what is holy,
Gives knowledge of oneself and even lends
A glass by which to see one's truest friends.
And since it's no offence, let me be plain;
Do not rebuke my poverty again.

'Lastly you taxed me, sir, with being old.
Yet even if you never had been told
By ancient books, you gentlemen engage
Yourselves in honour to respect old age.

Seated one day at the organ!
This organist, singing as he plays,
is clearly thoroughly enjoying
himself, but the same may not
perhaps be said about the organ boy
keeping up with the hand bellows.

Countryside

Life in the country was a mixture of hard work, the lot of the villeins, and such pursuits as hunting and hawking, the recreations of the nobles and their households. For the villeins the work was hard indeed for they had not only to scrape a living from their own strips of land provided by the lord of the manor but for two or three days a week, and more at harvest and other special times, they were bound to work on the lord's land as well. The land around a castle or manor house usually consisted of forest, cultivated farmland and common land. Hunting in the forest was reserved for the lord of the manor, although, doubtless, a little poaching was not unknown. The villeins were permitted to collect firewood and could put in the pigs which most of them kept to grub up acorns. The farmland was divided into the lord's land, worked by the villeins and providing the huge quantities of food needed for a large household, and the strips allotted to the villeins. The farmland was generally split into three sections, one of which would lie fallow for a year while crops were rotated on the other two. The lord's cattle would be grazed on the commonland as would be the sheep and pigs of the villeins. As well as a sheep and a pig or two most villeins would keep a few chickens. From these sparse resources the villein would not only have to feed himself and his family but occasionally surrender some of his produce to the lord of the manor. Picture (1) shows a farm worker engaged in the age-old occupation of sowing seed. His dog is excitedly chasing away a bird which has been trying to eat the grain, but unbeknown to the dog and his master another bird is feeding off the sack of seed.

Far more sophisticated is the scene depicted in (2). It shows the activities in the month of March on the land surrounding the château of a French nobleman of the period, the Duke de Berry. In the foreground a ploughman cuts a furrow with a plough drawn by two oxen. In other fields sheep are grazing, workers are tending an orchard, and we see a neatly laid out vineyard. In pictures (3), (4) and (5) we see more everyday country scenes. In (3) a man is driving a goose and her goslings, using a stick and a cloth to steer them on a straight

1

4

6

8-15▶

path. In (4) a horse, restrained in a wooden frame, is being shod. Chaucer, in 'The Miller's Tale', compares someone to 'a skittish colt boxed in a frame for shoeing'. Picture (5) shows sheep in a pen with shepherds tending them. The manufacture of woollen cloth was to become England's greatest industry but in Chaucer's time it was the export of raw wool to Europe that was the greatest single source of the king's revenue. As the villeins won their freedom they lost their land holdings and many of them turned to the sheep farms which were growing in number. Others turned to weaving and their wives to spinning, thus establishing a form of cottage industry.

Hunting not only provided boisterous sport for the nobility but served a useful purpose, providing fresh meat through most of the year. Wild boar which roamed the forests, and deer, provided the main sport in the chase; hawking provided game birds, herons etc. for the tables of the rich. Venery, a sport of gentlemen, developed like heraldry its own traditions and its own language. Wolves were hunted of necessity and were eventually eliminated from the forests, and foxes, as 'vermyne', were not hunted as they are today but were killed by any means, fair or foul. In (6) we see the 'kill' as a stag, surrounded by hounds, is at bay in

a pool, while the hunt, which includes ladies, watches in the background. In (7) is depicted the end of a wild boar chase in a clearing of the forest by the Duke de Berry's château. One of the huntsmen is triumphantly blowing his horn. Boar hunting was probably the most dangerous of the sports.

Typical country scenes are shown in the series of pictures (8 to 15) from the richly illuminated Bedford Book of Hours which dates from the early part of the fifteenth century and is preserved in the British Museum. Pruning is to be seen in (8), and sowing in (9). A villein is reaping with a sickle in (10), and in (11) another is threshing with a flail, a hinged stave with which the grain was beaten from the husk. In (12) we see a peasant carrying away a tree. Villeins, as has been said, were allowed to let their pigs loose in the lord's forests to root out acorns, and (13) shows a peasant beating a tree to knock the acorns to the ground. In (14) a man is killing a pig with a long-handled mallet not unlike a croquet stick. Finally, the mounted gentleman in (15) is engaged in hawking or falconry, his highly trained falcon resting on his wrist, waiting to be released for the chase.

The month of September in the grounds of the Duke de Berry's château is illustrated in (16). The grapes are being gathered from the vineyards – one of the peasants engaged in the work is tasting a bunch. Mules with panniers make their own way towards the château with its fairy-story towers, and we see an oxcart carrying two great containers of grapes. Wine was extensively drunk in England in the Middle Ages. Some was grown and made in England but the quality of French wines was more appreciated. Indeed French wines in a way were themselves English, for the wine-growing areas around Bordeaux belonged to the English kings, as, for a time, did those of Burgundy.

In the communities of the time the miller was an important figure and generally not a very popular one. The grain grown by the villeins had to be taken to his mill to be ground into flour so that bread could be made. The miller kept back a proportion of the grain or flour as payment for his services. Here he had the whip hand and was popularly believed to cheat regularly. Chaucer in the Prologue paints a very unflattering picture of his miller. In (17) we see a miller placing a sack of flour on a woman's back.

17

To call an old man "father" shows good breeding,
And this could be supported from my reading.
   'You say I'm old and fouler than a fen.
You need not fear to be a cuckold, then.
Filth and old age, I'm sure you will agree,
Are powerful wardens upon chastity.
Nevertheless, well knowing your delights,
I shall fulfil your worldly appetites.
   'You have two choices; which one will you try?
To have me old and ugly till I die,
But still a loyal, true, and humble wife
That never will displease you all her life,
Or would you rather I were young and pretty
And chance your arm what happens in a city
Where friends will visit you because of me,
Yes, and in other places too, maybe.
Which would you have? The choice is all your own.'
   The knight thought long, and with a piteous groan
At last he said, with all the care in life,
'My lady and my love, my dearest wife,
I leave the matter to your wise decision.
You make the choice yourself, for the provision
Of what may be agreeable and rich
In honour to us both, I don't care which;
Whatever pleases you suffices me.'
   'And have I won the mastery?' said she,
'Since I'm to choose and rule as I think fit?'
'Certainly, wife,' he answered her, 'that's it.'
'Kiss me,' she cried. 'No quarrels! On my oath
And word of honour, you shall find me both,
That is, both fair and faithful as a wife;
May I go howling mad and take my life
Unless I prove to be as good and true
As ever wife was since the world was new!
And if to-morrow when the sun's above
I seem less fair than any lady-love,
Than any queen or empress east or west,
Do with my life and death as you think best.
Cast up the curtain, husband. Look at me!'
   And when indeed the knight had looked to see,
Lo, she was young and lovely, rich in charms.
In ecstasy he caught her in his arms,
His heart went bathing in a bath of blisses
And melted in a hundred thousand kisses,

And she responded in the fullest measure
With all that could delight or give him pleasure.
　　So they lived ever after to the end
In perfect bliss; and may Christ Jesus send
Us husbands meek and young and fresh in bed,
And grace to overbid them when we wed.
And – Jesu hear my prayer! – cut short the lives
Of those who won't be governed by their wives;
And all old, angry niggards of their pence,
God send them soon a very pestilence!

The Friar's Prologue

Our worthy limiter, the noble Friar,
Kept glancing with a lowering sort of ire
Towards the Summoner, but, to keep polite,
As yet had said no ugly word outright.
At last he turned towards the Wife of Bath.
'Madam,' he said, 'God be about your path!
You here have touched on many difficult rules
Debated, I assure you, in the Schools.
Much you advanced was excellent, I say!
But, Madam, as we ride along the way
We're only called upon to speak in game.
Let's leave the authorities, in Heaven's name,
To preachers and to schools for ordinands.
    'But if it meets the company's demands,
I'll talk about a summoner, for a game,
Lord knows, one can be certain from the name
A summoner isn't much to be commended.
I hope that none of you will be offended.
    'A summoner's one who runs about the nation
Dealing out summonses for fornication,
Is beaten up by every villager
At the town's end . . .' 'Now, mind the manners, sir,'
Our Host called out, 'befitting your estate.
In company we do not want debate.
You tell your tale and let the Summoner be.'
'Nay,' said the Summoner, 'makes no odds to me.
Say what he likes, and when my turn's to come
I'll pay him back, by God! I'll strike him dumb!
I'll tell him what an honour it is, none higher,
To be a limiter, a flattering friar!
I'll tell him all about that job of his.'
    Our Host replied, 'Let's have no more of this.'
Then turning to the Friar, 'We prefer,'
He said, 'to hear your story, my dear sir.'

The Friar's Tale

In my own district once there used to be
A fine archdeacon, one of high degree,
Who boldly did the execution due
On fornication and on witchcraft too,
Bawdry, adultery and defamation,
Breaches of wills and contract, spoliation
Of church endowment, failure in the rents
And tithes and disregard of sacraments,
All these and many other kinds of crime
That need have no rehearsal at this time,
Usury, simony too. But he could boast
That lechery was what he punished most.
They had to sing for it if they were caught,
Like those who failed to pay the tithes they ought.
As for all such, if there was an informant,
Nothing could save them from pecunial torment.

For those whose tithes and offerings were small
Were made to sing the saddest song of all,
And ere the bishop caught them with his crook
They were all down in the archdeacon's book,
And he had jurisdiction, on inspection,
And powers to administer correction.
   He had a summoner ready to his hand.
There was no slyer boy in all the land,
For he had subtly formed a gang of spies
Who taught him where his profit might arise,
And he would spare one lecher from his store
To teach the way to four-and-twenty more.
Though it may drive him mad as a March hare,
Our Summoner here, I mean, I will not spare
His harlotries. He has no jurisdiction
On friars and he cannot make infliction
Upon us, now or ever, or take dues
From friars . . . 'Nor from women of the stews!'
The Summoner shouted, 'We have no control
On either lot.' 'The devil take your soul!'
Called out the Host, 'I say I won't have squalls.
On with your story, sir, and if it galls
The Summoner, spare him not, my worthy master! . . .
   This treacherous thief (the Friar said) was pastor
To certain bawds that ate out of his hand,
Lures for a hawk, none such in all the land.
They told him all the secret things they drew
From sinners; their acquaintance was not new.
Each was his agent, say, his private spy;
He drew large profits to himself thereby.
Even the archdeacon didn't always know
How much he got. He didn't have to show
A warrant when he chose to make things hot
For some obscure, uneducated sot;
For he could summon under threat of curse
And they were glad enough to fill his purse
Or give him banquets at the *Lamb and Flag*.
   And just as Judas kept a little bag
And was a thief, just such a thief was he.
His master got no more than half the fee.
To give the man his due and not to skimp,
He was a thief, a summoner, and a pimp.
   And he had wenches in his retinue,
So when the Reverend Robert or Sir Hugh

A mace head. In medieval times a
mace, later to become a ceremonial
symbol of office, was a deadly
weapon when wielded by a knight
on a horse. A mace similar to this
can be seen in the picture on
page 144.

Or Jack or Ralph, whoever it was, drew near
And lay with them, they told it in his ear.
He and these wenches made a gang of it.
Then he would fetch forth a fictitious writ,
Summon them both before the Chapter-bench
And skin the man while letting off the wench,
Saying, 'Dear friend, I know you would prefer
Her name were struck from our black register;
Trouble yourself no further, my good man,
On her account. I'll help you all I can.'
   He knew so much of bribery and blackmail
I should be two years telling you the tale.
There is no sporting dog that's more expert
At knowing a wounded deer from one unhurt
Than was this summoner who could spot for sure
Lecher, adulterer or paramour.
Indeed on that his whole attention went
Because it was the source of all his rent.
   So it befell that on a certain day
This summoner rode forth to catch his prey,
A poor old fiddle of the widow-tribe
From whom, on a feigned charge, he hoped a bribe.
Now as he rode it happened that he saw
A gay young yeoman under a leafy shaw;
He bore a bow with arrows bright and keen
And wore a little jacket of bright green
And had a black-fringed hat upon his head.
'Hail, welcome and well met!' the summoner said.
'Welcome to you and all good lads,' said he.
'Whither away under the greenwood tree?'
Pursued the yeoman, 'Have you far to go?'
   The summoner paused a moment and said, 'No,
Just here, close by. In fact I'm only bent
On going for a ride, to raise a rent
That's owing to my lord, a little fee.'
'Why then you are a bailiff?' 'Yes,' said he.
He did not dare, for very filth and shame,
Say that he was a summoner, for the name.
   'Well, I'll be damned!' the yeoman said. 'Dear brother,
You say you are a bailiff? I'm another.
But I'm a stranger round about this part.
I'll beg acquaintance with you for a start,
And brotherhood, if that is fair to offer.
I have some gold and silver in my coffer

A hound giving chase.

And should you chance to cross into our shire
All shall be yours, as much as you desire.'
'My word!' the summoner answered, 'Thanks a lot!'
The pair of them shook hands upon the spot,
Swore to be brothers to their dying day
And, chatting pleasantly, rode on their way.
    This summoner, always ready with a word,
As full of venom as a butcher-bird,
And sticking his nose into one thing or other
Went on, 'And where do you live at home, dear brother
I might come calling there some other day.'
    The yeoman said in his soft-spoken way,
'O, far away up north; I'll tell you where.
I hope that some time I shall see you there.
Before we part I shall be so explicit
About my home I'm sure you'll never miss it.'
    'Brother,' the summoner said, 'I'd like to know
If you can teach me something as we go.
Since you're a bailiff just the same as me,
Tell me your subtler tricks. Now, seriously,
How can I win most money at the game?
Keep nothing back for conscience, or from shame.
Talk like a brother. How do you make out?'
    'Well, I break level, brother, just about.
I'll tell a truthful story; all in all
My wages are extremely tight and small.
My master's hard on me and difficult,
My job laborious and with poor result,
And so it's by extortion that I live.
I take whatever anyone will give.
At any rate by tricks and violences
From year to year I cover my expenses.
I can't say better, speaking truthfully.'
    The summoner said, 'It's just the same with me.
I'm ready to take anything, God wot,
Unless it is too heavy or too hot.
What I can get out of a little chat
In private – why should conscience boggle at that?
Without extortion, how could I make a living?
My little jokes are hardly worth forgiving.
Bowels of pity, conscience, I have none.
Plague on these penance-fathers every one!
We make a pair, by God and by St James!
But, brother, what do you say to swopping names?'

The summoner paused; the yeoman all the while
The summoner spoke had worn a little smile.
'Brother,' he answered, 'would you have me tell?
I am a fiend, my dwelling is in Hell.
I ride on business and have so far thriven
By taking anything that I am given.
That is the sum of all my revenue.
You seem to have the same objective too,
You're out for wealth, acquired no matter how,
And so with me. I'll go a-riding now
As far as the world's end in search of prey.'
    'Lord!' said the summoner. 'What did I hear you say?
I thought you were a yeoman, certainly
You have the body of a man like me.
And have you, then, another shape as well
Appointed for your high estate in Hell?'
    'No,' he replied, 'for Hell admits of none.
But when we like we can appropriate one,
Or rather make you think we have a shape;
Sometimes it's like a man, sometimes an ape,
Even an angel riding into bliss.
There's nothing very wonderful in this;
A lousy conjuror can trick your eye,
And he, God knows, has far less power than I.'
    'But why,' pursued the summoner, 'track your game
In various shapes? Why don't you stay the same?'
'Just to appear,' he said, 'in such a way
As will enable us to snatch our prey.'
'But why do you have to go to all this bother?'
'For very many reasons, my dear brother;

You shall know all about it in good time.
The day is short and it is long past prime,
And yet I've taken nothing the whole day,
And I must think of business, if I may,
Rather than air my intellectual gift;
Besides, you lack the brains to catch my drift.
If I explained you wouldn't understand;
Yet since you ask why we're a busy band,
It's thus: at times we are God's instruments,
A means of forwarding divine events,
When He so pleases, that concern His creatures,
By various arts, disguised by various features.
We have no power without Him, that's a fact,
If it should please Him to oppose some act.

Sometimes, at our request, He gives us leave
To hurt the body, though we may not grieve
The soul. Take Job; his is a case in point.
At other times the two are not disjoint,
That is to say, the body and the soul.
Sometimes we are allowed to take control
Over a man and put his soul to test,
But not his body; all is for the best;
For every time a man withstands temptation
It is a partial cause of his salvation,
Though our intention is, when we beset him,
Not that he should be saved, but we should get him.
At times we slave for men without complaint
As on Archbishop Dunstan, now a saint;
Why, I was servant to the Apostle* once.'
   'Tell me,' the summoner said, '– I'm just a dunce –
But do you make new bodies as you go
Out of the elements?' The fiend said, 'No;
We just create illusions, or we raise
A corpse and use it; there are many ways.
And we can talk as trippingly and well
As, to the Witch of Endor, Samuel.
And yet some people say it wasn't he;
I have no use for your theology.
   'One thing I warn you of, it is no jape;
You will be learning all about our shape
In any case, hereafter, my dear brother,
Where you will not need me, nor yet another,
To teach you; for your own experience
Will furnish you sufficient evidence
To give a lecture on it, and declare
As much as from a professorial chair,
Better than Virgil when he was alive,
Or Dante either. Now, if we're to thrive
Let's hurry on; I'll keep you company
Unless it chance that you abandon me.'
   'What?' said the summoner, 'Leave you on your own
I am a yeoman, pretty widely known;
I'll hold to my engagement, on the level,
Though you were Satan's self, the very Devil!
I keep my word of honour to a brother,
As I have sworn, and so shall each to other;
True brothers we shall be; the bargain's made
And both of us can go about our trade.

You take your share – whatever people give –
And I'll take mine, and that's our way to live.
If either should do better than the other,
Let him be true and share it with his brother.'
    'Agreed,' the devil answered. 'As you say.'
And on the word they trotted on their way.
Just at the entry of the very village
The summoner had it in his mind to pillage
They saw a farm-cart loaded up with hay.
There was a carter driving, but the way
Was deep and muddy and the cart stood still.
The carter lashed and shouted with a will,
'Hey, Brock! Hup, Scottie! Never mind the stones!
The foul fiend come and fetch you, flesh and bones,
As sure as you were foaled! Mud, ruts and rubble!
Lord, what a team! I've never known such trouble!
The devil take all, cart, horse and hay in one!'
    The summoner said, 'Now we shall have some fun!'
And, as if nothing were happening, he drew near
And whispered softly in the devil's ear:
    'Listen to that, dear brother, use your head!
Didn't you hear what the old carter said?
Take it at once, he gave them all to you,
His hay, his cart and his three horses too.'
    'Don't you believe it!' said the fiend. 'I heard,
But he meant nothing by it, take my word.
Go up and ask him if you don't trust me,
Or else keep quiet for a bit and see.'
    The carter thwacked his horses, jerked the rein,
And got them moving; as they took the strain,
'Hup, there!' he shouted, 'Jesus bless you, love,
And all His handiwork! Hey! Saints above!
Well tugged, old fellow, that's the stuff, Grey Boy!
God save you all, my darlings, send you joy!

Rabbits were a useful source of food, especially for the peasants, and here we see one method of catching them that was still used until recently. A woman thrusts a ferret (?) into a conveniently heaped burrow and a rabbit quickly emerges into a net held by another woman on the other side.

That's lifted the old cart out of the slough!'
   'What did I tell you,' said the fiend, 'just now?
That ought to make it clear to you dear brother,
The chap said one thing but he meant another.
So let's go on a bit. You mustn't scoff,
But here there's nothing I can carry off.'
   When they were out of town a little way
The summoner whispered to the fiend to say,
'There's an old fiddle here, an ancient wreck,
Dear brother, who would rather break her neck
Than lose a penny of her goods. Too bad,
She'll have to pay me twelve-pence. She'll be mad,
But if she doesn't pay she'll face the court.
And yet, God knows there's nothing to report,
She has no vices. But as you failed just now
To earn your keep, I'd like to show you how.'
   The summoner battered at the widow's gate.
'Come out,' he said, 'you old inebriate!
I'll bet you've got a friar or priest inside!'
   'Who's knocking? Bless us, Lord!' the widow cried,
'God save you, sir, and what is your sweet will?'
   'Here!' said the summoner. 'I've a summons-bill.
On pain of excommunication, see
That you're at court at the archdeacon's knee
To-morrow morning. There are certain things
To answer for.' 'Christ Jesus, King of Kings,'
She said, 'have mercy! What am I to say?
I can't! I'm ill, and have been many a day.
I couldn't walk so far, nor even ride,
'Twould kill me. There's a pricking in my side.
Couldn't you write it down and save a journey,
And let me answer it through my attorney,
The charge I mean, whatever it may be?'
   'Yes, if you pay at once,' he said. 'Let's see.
Twelve pence to me and I'll secure acquittal.
I get no profit from it – very little.
My master gets the profit and not me.
Come off it, I'm in haste. It's got to be.
Give me twelve pence. No time to wait, old fairy.'
   'Twelve pence!' said she. 'O blessed Virgin Mary,
Help me and keep me clear of sin and dearth!
Why, if you were to offer me the earth
I couldn't! There's not twelve pence in my bag!
You know I'm nothing but a poor old hag,

Show kindness to a miserable wretch!'
'If I excuse you may the devil fetch
Me off! Though it should break you! Come along,
Pay up!' he said. 'But I've done nothing wrong!'
'You pay at once, or by the sweet St Anne,'
He said, 'I'll carry off your frying-pan
For debt, the new one, owed me since the day
You cuckolded your husband. Did I pay
For your correction then or did I not?'
   'You lie!' she said. 'On my salvation! What?
Correction? Whether as widow or as wife
I've never had a summons in my life;
I never cuckolded my poor old man!
And as for you and for your frying-pan
The hairiest, blackest devil out of Hell
Carry you off and take the pan as well!'
   Seeing her kneel and curse, the devil spoke:
'Now, Mother Mabel, is this all a joke,
Or do you really mean the things you say?'
   'The devil,' she said, 'can carry him away
With pan and all unless he will repent!'
'No, you old cow, I have no such intent,'
The summoner said, 'there's no repentance due
For anything I ever had of you.
I'd strip you naked, smock and rag and clout!'
   The devil said, 'What are you cross about,
Dear brother? You and this pan are mine by right.
You yet shall be in Hell with me to-night,
Where you'll know more about our mystery
Than any Doctor of Divinity.'
   And on the word this foul fiend made a swoop
And dragged him, body and soul, to join the troupe
In Hell, where summoners have their special shelf.
And God, who in the image of Himself
Created man, guide us to Abraham's lap,
And make this Summoner here a decent chap!
   My lords, I could have told you, never fear,
Had I the time to save this Summoner here,
Following texts from Christ and Paul and John
And many teachers who are dead and gone,
Of torments that are fit to terrorize
Your hearts, though tongue of man can scarce devise
Such things, or in a thousand winters tell
The pain of that accursed house of Hell.

A medieval bronze ewer. This one is decorated with the names of Tomas and Wyllem Elyot.

Watch therefore, and pray Jesus of his grace
To keep us out of that accursed place
And ward off Satan, tempting us from glory;
Ponder my words, reflect upon my story.
The lion's always on the watch for prey
To kill the innocent, if so he may;
And so dispose your heart that it withstand
The fiend who would enslave you in his band.
He may not tempt you, though, above your might,
For Christ will be your champion and your knight.
And, Summoners, flee the sins that so beset you,
And learn repentance ere the devil get you.

The Summoner's Prologue

The Summoner rose in wrath against the Friar
High in his stirrups, and he quaked with ire.
He stood there trembling like an aspen leaf.
'I've only one desire,' he said, 'it's brief,
And one your courtesy will not deny;
Since you have heard this filthy friar lie,
Let me refute him. I've a tale to tell!
This friar boasts his knowledge about Hell,
And if he does, God knows it's little wonder;
Friars and fiends are seldom far asunder.
Lord knows you must have often heard them tell
Of how a friar was ravished down to Hell
Once in a vision, taken there in spirit.
An angel led him up and down to ferret
Among the torments – various kinds of fire –
And yet he never saw a single friar,
Though he saw plenty of other kinds of folk
In pain enough. At last this friar spoke:
"Sir, are the friars in such a state of grace,"
He said, "none ever come into this place?"
"Why, yes," the angel answered, "many a million!"
And led him down to Lucifer's pavilion.
"Satan," the angel said, "has got a tail
As broad or broader than a carrack sail.
Hold up thy tail, thou Satan!" then said he,
"Show forth thine arse and let the friar see
The nest ordained for friars in this place!"
Ere the tail rose a furlong into space
From underneath it there began to drive,
Much as if bees were swarming from a hive,
Some twenty thousand friars in a rout
And swarmed all over Hell and round about,
And then came back as fast as they could run
And crept into his arse again, each one.
He clapped his tail on them and then lay still.
And after when the friar had looked his fill

On all the torments in that sorry place
His spirit was restored by Heaven's grace
Back to his body again and he awoke.
But all the same the terror made him choke,
So much the devil's arse was in his mind,
The natural heritage of all his kind.
God save you all except this cursed Friar,
For that is all the prologue I require.'

The Summoner's Tale

My lords, there lies—in Yorkshire, as I guess—
A marshy district known as Holderness,
In which a friar, a limiter, went about
To preach his sermons and to beg, no doubt.
And on a certain day it so befell,
When he had preached in church, and cast his spell
With one main object, far above the rest,
To fire his congregation with a zest
For buying trentals,* and for Jesu's sake
To give the wherewithal for friars to make
Their holy houses, where the Lord is dowered
With truest honour, not to be devoured
By those to whom there is no need to give
Like those endowed already, who can live,
Thanks be to God, in affluence and glory,
'Trentals,' he said, 'can fetch from Purgatory
The souls of all your friends, both old and young,
Yes, even when they're very quickly sung

265

– Not that a priest is frivolous or gay
Because he only sings one mass a day –
Release the souls,' he thundered, 'from the pit,
Deliver them from the flesh-hook and the spit!
What agony to be clawed, to burn, to bake!
Be quick, exert yourselves, for Jesu's sake!'
    When he had finished all he had to say,
With *qui cum Patre*★ off he went his way.
When folk had put their pennies in the plate
He used to go away, he wouldn't wait.
With scrip and pointed staff uplifted high
He went from house to house to poke and pry
And beg a little meal and cheese, or corn.
His comrade had a staff was tipped with horn,
And bore a pair of ivory tablets, jointed,
Also a stylus elegantly pointed.
He always wrote the names down as he stood
Of those who gave him offerings or food
(Pretence of praying for them by and by).
    'Give us a bushel of barley, malt or rye,
A wee God's cookie, then, a slice of cheese,
It's not for us to choose, but as you please;
A penny to say mass, or half a penny,
Some of your brawn perhaps – you haven't any? –
Well then, a bit of blanket, worthy dame,
Our well-beloved sister! There's your name,
It's down. Beef? Bacon? Anything you can find!'
    A sturdy varlet followed them behind,
The servants for their guests, and bore a sack,
And what they gave he carried on his back.
Once out of doors again and business done
He used to plane the names out, every one,
That he had written on his ivory tables.
He'd served them all with fairy-tales and fables...
    'No, there you lie, you Summoner!' said the Friar.
'Shut up! For Christ's sake be a little shyer
Of interruption,' said our Host, 'keep still!
Summoner, go on, spare nothing.' 'Nor I will.'
    On went this friar from house to house till he
Came up to one where he was wont to be
Better refreshed than anywhere in town.
The householder was sick and lying down;
Bedridden on a couch the fellow lay.
'*Deus hic!* Well, Thomas, how are we to-day?'

The friar said, taking great pains to soften
His voice politely, 'God protect you! Often,
How often, I've sat upon this bench to steal
Your kindness, eaten many a merry meal!'
And from the bench he drove away the cat,
And laying down his pointed staff and hat,
His scrip as well, he settled softly down.
His comrade was off walking in the town
Together with the varlet, to get sight
Of where it was he meant to spend the night.

  'O my dear master,' said the sick old man,
'How have things been with you since March began?
Ain't seen you for a fortnight now, or more.'

    'God knows,' he answered, 'I have laboured sore
And more especially have said in care
Of your salvation many a precious prayer,
And for our other friends, but let that pass.
I went this morning to your Church for mass
And preached according to my simple wit;
It wasn't all on texts from Holy Writ,
For that's too hard for you as I suppose,
And I prefer to paraphrase or glose.
Glosing's a glorious thing, and anyway
"The letter killeth" as we clerics say.
And so I taught them to be charitable
And spend their goods where it is reasonable;
And there I saw your wife – Ah, where is she?'

    'Out in the yard, I think, or ought to be,'
The fellow said; 'she'll come, she can't be far.'

    'Why, sir, you're welcome, by St John you are!'
The woman said, 'I hope you're keeping sprightly?'
Up from his bench the friar rose politely
Embracing her – the clasp was somewhat narrow –
And kissed her sweetly, chirping like a sparrow
As his lips parted. 'Ma'am,' he said, 'I'm fine.
Your servant, Ma'am,' he said, 'in all that's mine.
Thanks be to God that gave you soul and life
I haven't seen a prettier little wife
In all the church to-day, upon my word!'
'Well, God amend defects!' the woman purred.
'At any rate you're welcome, I'll be bound.'
'My warmest thanks! That's what I've always found.
If I may trespass – you're so very kind –
On your good nature, if you wouldn't mind,

An alms bowl found in Bermondsey,
London.

I want to talk to Thomas here; you know
These curates are so negligent and slow
At groping consciences with tenderness.
I study how to preach and to confess,
Earnestly read St Peter and St Paul
And walk about to fish and make a haul
Of christian souls, pay Christ his proper rent,
And if I spread His word I am content.'
    'Now, my dear master, by your leave,' said she,
'Scold the man well, for by the Trinity,
He is as irritable as an ant,
Though he has everything a man can want.
I try to keep him warm at night, I squeeze him,
Put my leg over him, or arm, to please him,
And all he does is grunt, like boar in sty!
I get no other sport of him, not I.
No way of pleasing him at all, I promise.'
    'O Thomas, *je vous dis*, O Thomas, Thomas!
That is the devil's work and must be chidden.
Anger's a thing by Heavenly God forbidden;
I mean to speak of that, a word or so.'
    'Now, master,' said the wife, 'before I go,
What would you like for dinner? What would suit?'
'Well, Ma'am,' he answered, '*je vous dis sans doute*,
If I could have a little chicken-liver
And some of your soft bread – the merest shiver –
And then a pig's head roasted – but, do you see?
I won't have any creature killed for me –
It would be homely and sufficient fare.
The sustenance I take is very spare;
You see, my spirit draws its nourishment
Out of the Bible, and my body's spent
In pains and prayers; my stomach is destroyed.
    'However, Ma'am, you mustn't be annoyed
To hear me speak as frankly as I do,
For these are things I tell to very few.'
    'Before I leave you, sir, you ought to know,'
She said, 'my baby died two weeks ago,
Just after you left town on visitation.'
    'I know. I saw his death by revelation,'
Replied the friar, 'in our dormitory.
I saw the little fellow borne to glory,
I dare say it was less than half an hour
After his death indeed. To God the power!

Bagpipes were by no means
confined to Scotland, then a
separate country with its own
monarch.

Our sexton and our infirmarian,
They saw it too, both friars boy and man
These fifty years, thank God. They now are free
To walk alone, they've reached their jubilee.★
I rose at once, in fact the entire place
Rose, and the tears were trickling down my face.
There was no noise, no clattering bells were rung,
But a *Te Deum* – nothing else – was sung,
Save that I made an act of adoration
To Christ, to thank Him for His revelation.
For I assure you both, believe me well,
Our orisons are more effectual
And we see more of Christ's most secret things
Than common people do, or even kings.
We live in poverty and abstinence
But common folk in riches and expense
On food and drink, and other foul delight;
But we contemn all worldly appetite.
    'Dives and Lazarus lived differently,
And different their guerdon had to be.
Whoever prays must fast, he must keep clean,
Fatten his soul and make his body lean.
We follow the Apostle; clothes and food
Suffice us though they may be rough and rude,
Our purity and fasting have sufficed
To make our prayers acceptable to Christ.
    'Moses had fasted forty days and nights
Before Almighty God, upon the heights
Of Sinai, came down to speak with him,
And with an empty stomach, frail of limb,
Moses received the law Jehovah drew
With his own finger; and Elijah too
When in Mount Horeb, ere he could have speech
With that Almighty Lord, who is the leech
Of life, had fasted long in contemplation.
    'Aaron no less, under whose domination
The temple was, and other Levites too,
When they approached the temple to renew
Their services and supplications, they
Refrained from drinking – drinking, that's to say,
That might have made them drunk – attending there
In abstinence, in watching and in prayer
Lest they should die. Take heed of what I say;
Unless the priest is sober who would pray

For you – but there! I've said enough of it.
   'Jesus our Lord, it says in Holy Writ.
Fasted and prayed, and patterned our desires,
And so we mendicants, we simple friars
Have wedded poverty and continence,
Charity, humbleness and penitence,
And persecution too for righteousness;
Pure, merciful, austere, but quick to bless
Though weeping often. Therefore our desires
– I'm speaking of ourselves, mendicant friars –
Are more acceptable to God, more able
Than yours, with all your feasts upon the table.
   'I speak the truth; gluttony was the vice
That first flung Adam out of Paradise;
And man was chaste in Eden, I may mention.
   'But listen to me, Thomas, pay attention.
Though there's no text exactly, I suppose,
Yet in a manner of speaking, if I glose
A little, you will see our Lord referred
Especially to friars in the word
"Blessed are the poor in spirit." Think and look,
Study the gospels, search the Holy Book,
And see if it be liker our profession
Than theirs who swim in riches and possession.
Fie on their pomp! Fie on their gluttony!
Their ignorance is a disgrace to see.
   'Jovinian makes a good comparison,
"Fat as a whale and waddling like a swan,"
They stink of wine like bottles in a bar;
How reverent their supplications are!
When they say prayers for souls their psalm of David
Is just a "Burp! *Cor meum eructavit!*"★
Who follows on the gospel, tracks the spoor
Of Christ, but we the humble, chaste and poor,
The doers of the word, not hearers only?
And as a hawk springs up into the lonely
Regions of heaven, so the prayer aspires
Of charitable, chaste and busy friars,
Takes flight and enters in at God's two ears.
O Thomas, Thomas! Let me say with tears
And by that patron who is called St Ives,
Where were your hope to be as one that thrives
If you were not our brother? Day and night
Our Chapter prays the Lord to send you might,

Strengthen your body, girdle it and belt it!'
'God knows,' the fellow said, 'I haven't felt it.
So help me Christ, I've spent a lot in hire,
These last few years, on various kinds of friar,
Aye, many a pound; and yet I'm none the better.
I've poured it out. I'm very near a debtor.
Farewell my gold, it's gone; no more to go!'
　'O Thomas!' said the friar. 'Did you so?
What need to seek out "various kinds of friar"?
Who, with a perfect doctor, could require
To seek out other doctors in the town?
Your own inconstancy has let you down.
Do you suppose our convent, and I too,
Are insufficient, then, to pray for you?
Thomas, that joke's not good. Your faith is brittle.
You're ill because you've given us too little.
"Ah! give that convent half a quarter of oats!"
"Ah! give that convent four and twenty groats!"
"Ah! give that friar a penny and let him go?"
No, Thomas, Thomas, it should not be so!
What is a farthing worth if split in twelve?
An undivided thing is (if you delve
Into your wits) stronger than when it's scattered.
Thomas, by me you never shall be flattered.
You're trying to get our work for nothing, eh?
What does Almighty God – who made us – say?
"The labourer is worthy of his hire."
Thomas, you know it's not that I desire
Your treasure for myself; it should be spent,
Seeing our convent is so diligent
In prayer for you, to build the church of Christ.
Thomas! If you would learn or be enticed
To learn what good there is in building churches,
Your namesake's life will further your researches,
St Thomas of India. There you lie in ire,
The devil having set your heart on fire,
And chide this foolish, innocent woman here,
Your wife, so meek, so patient, so sincere.
So, Thomas, please let this be understood;
No wrangling with your wife! It's for your good.
And take this thought away to fill your head
Touching this matter; wisely was it said:
"Then be not as a lion in thy house,
A terror to thy household, tyrannous,

Nor such that thine acquaintance flees away."
I charge you, Thomas, once again and say,
Beware of her that in your bosom sleeps;
Beware the serpent that so slyly creeps
Amidst the grass and stings with subtlety.
Beware, my son, and listen patiently,
For twenty thousand men have lost their lives
For wrangling with their lovers and their wives.
And since you have so holy and meek a wife,
What, Thomas, is the need for all this strife?
No serpent is so cruel, truth to tell,
If one should tread upon his tail, so fell
As women who have given way to ire.
Vengeance is then the sum of their desire.
Ire is a sin, one of the deadly seven,
Abominable unto God in Heaven,
And a destruction to yourself, none quicker.
Every illiterate parson, every vicar
Can tell that ire engenders homicide.
For ire is the executor of pride.
Were I to say what ire can bring in sorrow
To man, my tale would last until to-morrow.
So day and night I pray as best I can
God send no power to an angry man!
Great harm can come of it, great misery,
When angry men are set in high degree.
    'Once on a time an angry potentate,
Seneca says, bore rule over a state.
A certain day two knights went riding out
And fortune willed that it should come about
That one of them returned, the other not.
The knight was brought to judgement on the spot;
This judge gave sentence: "You have killed your friend.
You are condemned to death and that's the end."
And to another knight was standing by
He turned and said, "Go, lead him out to die."
And so it happened as they went along
To the appointed place, towards the throng
There came the knight that was reported dead.
So it seemed best that both of them be led
Together back before the judge again.
"My lord," they said, "the knight has not been slain;
His friend is guiltless. As you see, they thrive."
"You all shall die," said he, "as I'm alive!

Alchemy, a mixture of science, magic and religion, was widely practised throughout the Middle Ages. The alchemists sought either to change base metals into gold or silver, or to discover the elixir of life. (Opposite) an alchemist presides over the work in his medieval 'laboratory'.

You first, the second, you, and you the third!"
And turning to the first he said this word:
"I have condemned you. You must therefore die."
Then to the next, "You too, and this is why:
Your comrade clearly owes his death to you."
Then to the third he turned and said, "You too;
You had my orders; they were not fulfilled."
And so it was the three of them were killed.

   'An angry man and drunken was Cambyses,
Who took great joy in showing off his vices.
A knight, it happened, in his company,
Given to virtue and morality,
In private conference with him began:
"A lord is lost if he's a vicious man,
And drunkenness is filthy to record
Of any man, especially a lord.
Many the eye and ear that takes good care
To spy on lords, they can't be certain where.
For God's love be more temperate in your drink,
For wine will rob you of your power to think
And incapacitate your members too."

   '"You'll see," said he, "the opposite is true,
And prove it by your own experience
That wine has no such power of offence.
There is no wine so strong as to deny

Killing a pig. Villeins on the great estates relied largely on the few pigs they kept on their own strips for meat and bacon. Although the man is wielding an axe he appears to be using the blunt end of the axehead to stun the animal.

Strength to my hand or foot or sight of eye."

   'And out of spite he drank as much, nay, more
A hundred times than he had drunk before
And right away this angry, cursed wretch
Gave an immediate command to fetch
This noble's son, and there he made him stand;
Then snatching up a bow into his hand
Drew string to ear, and aiming it with care
He shot him with an arrow then and there.
"Now have I got a steady hand or not?
Now have my mental powers gone to rot?"
The tyrant said, "Has wine destroyed my sight?"

   'Why should I tell the answer of the knight?
His son was slain, there is no more to say.
Dealing with lords be careful in your play;
You sing *Placebo*! I shall if I can,
Except when talking to some poor old man.
To tell their vices to the poor is well,
But not to lords, though they should go to Hell.

274

'Cyrus the Persian was an evil-liver
And given to anger; he destroyed the river
Gyson in which his horse was drowned, upon
His expedition to take Babylon.
That river in his rage was so diminished
Women could wade it by the time he'd finished.
    'Solomon teaches us as no one can:
"Make thou no friendship with an angry man;
And with a furious man take not thy way,
Lest thou repent it"; there's no more to say.
    'Leave anger, Thomas; brother, have a care!
You'll find me just. I'm like a joiner's square.
That devil's knife, O draw it from your heart!
It is your anger causes you to smart.
Make your confession to me if you can.'
    'No, by St Simon,' said the ailing man,
'The curate came and shrived me here to-day.
I told him everything I had to say.
There's no more need to speak of it,' said he,
'Unless I care to, from humility.'
    'Then give me of your gold to make our cloister,'
Said he, 'for many a mussel, many an oyster,
When other men eat well and fill their cup,
Has been our food, to build our cloister up.
And yet we've hardly finished the foundation.
There's not a tile as yet or tessellation
Upon the pavement that we hope to own,
And forty pound is owing still for stone.
    'Now, Thomas, help, for Him that harrowed Hell,
For otherwise we shall be forced to sell
Our books, and if you lacked our predication
The world would quickly fall to desolation.
To cheat it of our sermons and bereave
The world of us, dear Thomas, by your leave,
Were worse than to bereave it of the sun.
Who teaches and who works as we have done?
And for a long, long time,' he said, 'because
There have been friars since Elijah was;
Elisha too was one, the books record,
In charity with us, I thank our Lord.
Now Thomas, help, for holy charity!'
And down at once he went upon his knee.
    The ailing man was nearly mad with ire;
He would have very gladly burnt the friar,

Butchering a pig.

A glimpse of medieval building
methods. Among the workers, who
seem to be building a church,
can be seen a mason shaping stone
and a plasterer: one man (right)
seems to be mixing cement. On the
left a bearded foreman appears
to be explaining the operation
to a priest.

Him and his lying speech and false profession.
  'I'll give you what I have in my possession,
Such as it is,' he said, 'I have none other.
You said a moment back I was your brother?'
'Believe it,' said the friar, 'and none better;
I brought your wife our letter – our sealed letter!'
  'Well now,' he said, 'there's something I can give
Your holy convent, if I am to live.
And you shall have it in your hand to own
On one condition and on one alone,
That you divide it equally, dear brother,
And every friar to have as much as other.
But swear by your profession to the thing,
And without fraudulence or cavilling.'
  'I swear it by my faith!' the friar said,
Clasping the hand of the poor man in bed.
'My hand on it! In me shall be no lack.'
  'Well, then, reach down your hand along my back,'
The sick man said, 'and if you grope behind,
Beneath my buttocks you are sure to find
Something I've hidden there for secrecy.'
  'Ah!' thought the friar, 'that's the thing for me!'
And down he launched his hand and searched the cleft
In hope of finding what he had been left.
When the sick man could feel him here and there
Groping about his fundament with care,
Into that friar's hand he blew a fart.
There never was a farm-horse drawing cart
That farted with a more prodigious sound.
  Mad as a lion then the friar spun round,
'You treacherous lout!' he cried, 'God's bones and blig
You did it on purpose! It was done for spite!
You shall pay dearly for that fart, I say!'
  The sick man's servants, hearing the affray,
Came leaping in and chased away the friar,
And off he went still spluttering with ire
To find his comrade where he kept his goods.
He looked like a wild boar out of the woods,
Gnashing his teeth, he was so furious.
  He strode along towards the manor-house
Where lived a man of honour and possession
Who used to seek the friar in confession.
This worthy man was the manorial lord;
As he was sitting eating at his board

In came the friar in a towering rage
Almost past speech for anger by that stage,
But in the end 'God bless you, sir,' said he.
    The lord stared back. 'Hey, *benedicite*!
It's Friar John! What sort of world is this?
It's plain to see that something's gone amiss.
You look as if the wood were full of thieves;
Sit down and tell me what it is that grieves
You so! I'll settle it for you if I can.'
    'I've had the greatest insult,' said the man.
'Down in your town to-day – God give you joy –
No guttersnipe in all the world, no boy
But would be shocked at it, no serf at tillage,
At what I've had to suffer in your village.
It's an abomination, *most* unpleasant;
What shocks me most of all, this hoary peasant
Even blasphemed our holy convent too!'
    'Now, master,' said the lord, 'I beg of you –'
'No master, sir,' he said, 'your servitor!
Although the Schools did me that honour, sir,
But still God wishes not that men should call
Us "Rabbi" either here in your large hall
Or in the market.' 'Never mind,' said he,
'Tell me your trouble.' 'Sir, there was done to me,
And to my Order too, an odious wrong;
Per consequens to all that may belong
To Holy Church itself. May God amend it.'
    'Sir,' said the lord, 'you know the way to end it.
Keep calm, you're my confessor; I know your worth.
You are the salt and savour of the earth.
For love of God be patient and unfold
The matter of your grief.' So then he told
The story (you have heard it) with a will.
    The lady of the house sat very still
Till she had heard the friar's whole tirade.
'Mother of God,' she said, 'O blessed Maid!
And is there nothing else? Now tell me true.'
    'Madam,' he answered, 'May I hear your view?'
'My view?' she said. 'God help us! What's the need?
I say a churl has done a churlish deed.
What should I say? May God deny him ease!
His poor sick head is full of vanities.
I think he must have had some kind of fit.'
    'Madam,' said he, 'I'll pay him out for it,

By God I will! There are within my reach
Several ways; for instance I can preach,
I can defame him! I won't be derided
Or bidden divide what cannot be divided
In equal parts – God damn his ignorance!'
    The lord had sat like someone in a trance,
Rolling in heart the problem up and down,
How the imagination of a clown
Had hit on this conundrum for the friar.
'I never before heard such a thing transpire;
I think the devil put it in his mind.
In all arithmetic you couldn't find
Until to-day so tricky an equation.
How could one set about a demonstration
Where every man alike should have his part
Both of the sound and savour of a fart?
Proud churl! O nice distinction! Damn his nerve!'
He then went on more gravely to observe,
'Who ever heard of such a thing till now!
"To every man alike?" Good Lord, but how?
It is impossible, it cannot be!
Aha, nice churl! God send him misery!
The rumbling of a fart or any sound
Is only air reverberating round,
What's more, diminishingly, bit by bit.
Upon my word! No one could have the wit
To see it was divided equally.
To think a churl, a churl of mine, could be
So shrewd, and to my own confessor too!
He's certainly demoniac in my view!
Now eat your food and leave the churl alone
And let the devil hang him for his own!'
    Now the lord's squire was standing by and heard
The tale as he was carving, word for word,
And saw the problem you have heard defined.
'My lord,' he said, 'I hope you will not mind,
But, for a piece of cloth to make a gown,
I'd tell the friar – but he musn't frown –
How such a fart could equally be shared
Between him and his convent, if I cared.'
    His lord replied, 'Well, tell us then, go on,
And you shall have your gown-cloth, by St John.'
    'Well, when the weather, sir,' he said, 'is fair,
When there's no wind or movement in the air,

Then have a cartwheel brought into this hall,
But see the spokes are fitted – twelve in all,
A cartwheel has twelve spokes – then, by and by,
Bring me twelve friars. You will ask me why?
Well, thirteen make a convent, as I guess.
And this confessor here, for worthiness,
Shall bring the number to thirteen, my lord.
Then they shall all kneel down with one accord;
To each spoke's end a friar, I propose,
Shall very seriously lay his nose.
Your excellent confessor, whom God save,
Shall put his nose right up under the nave.
And then the churl, with belly stiff and taut
As drum or tabor, hither shall be brought,
Set on the wheel thus taken from the cart
Above the nave, and made to let a fart.
Then you will see, as surely as I live,
And by a proof that is demonstrative,
That equally the sound of it will wend,
Together with the stink, to the spokes' end,
Save that this worthy friar, your confessor,
Being of great honour, they of lesser,
Shall have the first-fruits, as is only right.
A noble custom, in which friars unite,
Is that a worthy man should first be served
And certainly it will be well-deserved.
To-day his preaching did us so much good,
Being beneath the pulpit where he stood,
That I'd allow him, if it fell to me,
First smell of every fart, say up to three,
And so would all his convent I am sure,
His bearing is so holy, fair and pure.'
    The lord and lady – all except the friar –
Thought Jacky's answer all they could desire,
As wise as Euclid or as Ptolemy.
As for the churl, it was his subtlety,
His wit, they said, to think of such a crack.
'He is no fool, he's no demoniac!'
And Jacky has acquired a new gown.
My tale is done; we've almost come to town.

The Studley Bowl, dating from the late fourteenth century. It is fashioned of silver gilt, chased and engraved, and provides a fine example of the skilled workmanship of the time.

The Merchant's Prologue

'Weeping and wailing, care and other sorrow,
I know them well enough by eve and morrow,'
The Merchant said; 'like others I suppose
That have been married, that's the way it goes;
I know too well that's how it goes with me.
I have a wife, the worst that there could be;
For if a fiend were coupled to my wife,
She'd overmatch him, you can bet your life.
Why choose a special instance to recall
Her soaring malice? She's a shrew in all.
There's a wide difference I'm bound to say
Between Griselda's patience and the way
My wife behaves; her studied cruelty
Surpasses everything. If I were free,
Never again, never again the snare!
We married men, our life is grief and care.
Try it who will, and he will find, I promise
That I have spoken truly, by St Thomas,
For most of us – I do not say for all,
And God forbid that such a thing befall.

  'Ah, my good Host, I have been wedded now
These two months past, no more than that I vow,
Yet I believe no bachelor alive,
Not if you were to take a knife and rive
Him to the heart, could tell of so much grief
As I could tell you of; beyond belief,
The curst malignity I get from her!'

  Our Host replied, 'God bless you, my dear sir!
But since you know so much about the art
Of marriage, let me beg you to impart.'

  'With pleasure,' he said, 'but on the personal score
I'm so heart-scalded I shall say no more.'

The Merchant's Tale

There was a knight one time of good renown
In Lombardy, Pavia was the town.
He'd lived there very prosperously for more
Than sixty years and was a bachelor,
Though always taking bodily delight
On women, such as pleased his appetite,
As do these foolish worldlings, never fear.
Now when this knight had passed his sixtieth year
–Whether for holiness, or from a surge
Of dotage, who can say?–he felt an urge
So violent to be a wedded man
That day and night his eager fancies ran
On where and how to spy himself a bride,
Praying the Lord he might not be denied
Once to have knowledge of that blissful life
There is between a husband and his wife,

And live within the holy bond and tether
In which God first bound woman and man together.
'No other life,' he said, 'is worth a bean;
For wedlock is so easy and so clean
It is a very paradise on earth.'
Thus said this ageing knight, so full of worth.
   And certainly, as sure as God is King,
To take a wife is a most glorious thing,
Especially if a man is old and hoary;
Then she's the fruit of all his wealth and glory.
It's then he ought to take her, young and fair,
One upon whom he might beget an heir,
And lead a life of rapture and content,
Whereas these bachelors can but lament
And suffer, when in some adversity
From love, which is but childish vanity.
And it's no more than right it should be so
If bachelors are beset by grief and woe:
On brittle ground they build, so all is ready
For brittle love, though they expect a steady.
Their liberty is that of bird or beast,
They've no restraint, no discipline at least,
Whereas a married man achieves a state
Of bliss that's orderly and fortunate.
Under the yoke of matrimony bowed,
The heart, in bliss abounding, sings aloud.
For who is so obedient as a wife?
Who is so true, so careful for his life
Whether in health or sickness, as his mate?
For weal or woe she tends upon his state,
In service, and in love, she never tires,
Though he lie bedridden till he expires.
   And yet some writers say this isn't so;
One such was Theophrastus long ago.
Who cares if Theophrastus was a liar?
'Don't take a wife,' he said, 'from a desire
To make economies and spare expense.
A faithful servant shows more diligence
In guarding your possessions than a wife
For she claims half you have throughout her life;
And if you're sick, as God may give me joy,
Your very friends, an honest serving-boy,
Do more than she, who's watching for a way
To corner your possessions night and day;

And if you take a wife into your bed
You're very likely to be cuckolded.'
   Opinions such as these and hundreds worse
This fellow wrote, God lay him under curse!
But take no heed of all such vanity,
Defy foul Theophrastus and hear me.
   A wife is verily the gift of God.
All other kinds of gift, the fruitful sod
Of land, fair pastures, movables in store,
Rents – they're the gifts of fortune, nothing more,
That pass as does a shadow on a wall.
   Still, if I must speak plainly, after all
A wife does last some time, and time may lapse
A good deal slower than one likes, perhaps.
   Marriage is a momentous sacrament,
Bachelordom contemptible, and spent
In helpless desolation and remorse
– I'm speaking of the laity, of course.
I don't say this for nothing; listen why.
Woman was made to be a man's ally.
When God created Adam, flesh and bone,
And saw him belly-naked and alone,
He of His endless goodness thus began:
'Let us now make a help-meet for this man
Like to himself.' And He created Eve.
Here lies the proof of what we all believe,
That woman is man's helper, his resort,
His earthly paradise and his disport.
So pliant and so virtuous is she
They cannot but abide in unity.
One flesh they are; one flesh as I suppose
Has but a single heart in joys and woes.
   A wife! Saint Mary, what a benediction!
How can a man be subject to affliction
Who has a wife? Indeed I cannot say.
There is a bliss between them such as may
No tongue tell forth, such as no heart can judge.
If he be poor she helps her man to drudge,
Sets guard upon his goods and checks the waste;
All that her husband likes is to her taste,
She never once says 'no' when he says 'yes'.
'Do this,' says he; 'already done,' she says.
O blissful state of wedlock, no way vicious
But virtuous and merry, nay, delicious,

A gold penny of Henry III's reign
(1216–1272) and a noble of Edward
III's (1327–1377).

And so commended and approved withal
That any man who's worth a leek should fall
On his bare knees, to thank God, all his life,
For having ordained and given him a wife,
Or else to pray that he vouchsafe to send
A wife to last him to the very end.
    Then he can count upon security
And not be tricked, as far as I can see,
Provided that he works by her advice:
Jacob, the learned tell us, was precise
In following the good counsel of his mother,
And won his father's blessing from his brother,
By binding round his neck a pelt of kid.
Or Judith, one can read of what she did:
Her wisdom held God's people in its keeping
By slaying Holofernes, who was sleeping.
    Take Abigail, what good advice she gave!
It saved her husband Nabal from the grave.
Take Esther too, whose wisdom brought relief
To all God's people, saved them from their grief
And made Ahasuerus grant promotion
To Mordecai for his true devotion.
There's no superlative that ranks in life,
Says Seneca, above a humble wife.
'The tongue of wife,' so Cato was to say,
'Commands the husband: suffer and obey.'
And yet she will obey by courtesy.
A wife is guardian of your husbandry;
Well may a man in sickness wail and weep
Who has no wife to nurse him and to keep
His house for him; do wisely then and search
For one and love her as Christ loves His Church.
For if you love yourself you love your wife,
For no one hates his flesh, nay all his life
He fosters it, and so I bid you wive
And cherish her, or you will never thrive.
Husband and wife, whatever the worldly say
In ribald jest, are on the straight, sure way.
They are so knit no accident or strife
Harms them, particularly not the wife.
    So January thought, of whom I told,
Deeply considering as he grew old
The life of lusty joy and virtuous quiet
That marriage offers in its honey-diet.

A rubbing of a brass memorial of
1391 in Stoke Fleming church,
Devonshire. It is of an elderly man,
John Crip.

And so one day he sent for all his friends
To tell them how he meant to gain his ends.
   With serious face he spoke, and solemn tongue.
'My friends,' he said, 'I am no longer young;
God knows, I'm near the pit, I'm on the brink:
I have a soul, of which I ought to think.
   'My body I have foolishly expended;
Blessed be God, that still can be amended.
I have resolved to be a wedded man.
And that at once in all the haste I can
To some fair virgin; one of tender years.
Prepare yourselves to help as overseers
Against my wedding, for I will not wait.
I for my own part will investigate
And find a hasty match, if there be any:
But in as much as you, my friends, are many,
You may discern more readily than I
Where it would most befit me to ally.
   'But, my dear friends, you may as well be told
The woman must on no account be old,
Certainly under twenty, and demure.
Flesh should be young though fish should be mature;
As pike, not pickerel, makes the tastier meal,
Old beef is not so good as tender veal.
I'll have no woman thirty years of age;
That's only fodder, bean-straw for a cage.
God knows these ancient widows know their trade,
They are as tricky as the Boat of Wade★
With so much trouble breaking when they please
To fight, I should not have a moment's ease.
Subtle is the scholar taught in several schools;
And women taught in many are no fools
–Half-scholars one might say; but when they're young
A man can still control them with his tongue
And guide them, should their duty seem too lax,
Just as a man may model in warm wax.
So let me sum the matter in a clause;
I will have no old woman, for this cause.
For were I so unlucky as to marry
Where I could take no pleasure, I'd miscarry,
I should commit adultery and slide
Straight downwards to the devil when I died.
I could beget no child on her to greet me,
Yet I had rather that the dogs should eat me

Than that my fine inheritance should fall
Into strange hands, that let me tell you all.
  'I'm not a fool, I know the reason why
People should wed, though I could specify
Many who prate of it, but I engage
They know about as little as my page
Touching the reasons one should take a wife.
A man unable to be chaste in life
Should take a wife in holy dedication
And for the sake of lawful procreation
Of children, to the honour of God above,
Not as a paramour or lady-love,
But to curb lechery, which he should eschew,
Paying his debt whenever it falls due,
Or each a willing helper to the other
In trouble, like sister to a brother
And live a life of holy chastity;
But, by your leave, sirs, that would not suit me,
For, God be thanked, I dare to make the claim,
I feel my limbs sufficient, strong and game
For all that is belonging to a man,
And am my own best judge in what I can.
I may seem hoary, but I'm like a tree
That blossoms white before the fruit can be;
Blossoming trees are neither dry nor dead
And I am only hoary on my head.
My heart and all my members are as green
As laurel is; all the year round, I mean.
And now you are informed of my intention
I beg you to agree without dissension.'
  Various men gave various examples
Of classic marriages, convincing samples;
Some praised it certainly, some reprehended,
But at the last (to get the matter ended),
As altercation happens every day
Among good friends who mean to say their say,
An argument was presently begun
Between two friends of his, Placebo one,
Justinus, as I recollect, the other.
  Placebo said, 'O January, dear brother,
You have no need, sweet lord, it must appear,
To take advice from anybody here,
Save that your sapience, after meditation,
Would prudently resist the inclination

286

A merchant gives alms to a beggar in the street.

To set aside the word of Solomon,
For this is what he said for everyone:
"Do all things by advice," his saying went,
"And then you'll have no reason to repent."
Though that may be what Solomon commends,
Dear lord, my brother, nay my best of friends,
As surely as the Lord may give me rest
I think your own opinion is the best.
Take it from me – if I can find the phrase –
You know I've been a courtier all my days,
God knows unworthily, I make admission,
Yet I have stood in quite a high position
And among lords of very great estate;
But I have never joined in a debate
With them, or offered contradiction. Why?
Well, obviously, my lord knows more than I,
And what he says I hold as firm and stable;
I echo it as far as I am able.
No counsellor is such a fool as he
That, serving on a lord of high degree,
Dares to presume or even thinks it fit
To be superior to him in wit.
Lords are no fools, believe me . . . May I say
That you have also shown yourself to-day
A man of lofty views, an eloquent,
A holy-minded man, and I consent
To all you said. It should be written down.
A speech like that – there isn't one in town,
No, nor all Italy, able to supply it!
Christ holds himself more than rewarded by it.
In anyone at all advanced in age
It shows a lively spirit to engage
In taking a young wife. Ah, Lord of grace!
You've pinned your heart up in a jolly place;
Follow your inclination; I protest
Whatever you decide on will be best.'
    Justinus who sat silent, having heard
Placebo speaking, then took up the word.
'Brother,' he said, 'be patient with me, pray;
You spoke your mind, now hear what I would say;
Seneca gave a lot of sound advice;
He says it's always better to think twice
Before you give away estate or pelf.
And therefore if you should advise yourself

In giving property away or land,
If it's important you should understand
Who is to get your goods, how much the more
You ought to think things over well before
You give away your body. If I may
I'd like to warn you; it is no child's play
Choosing a wife. It needs consideration,
In fact it asks a long investigation.

    'Is she discreet and sober? Or a drinker?
Or arrogant? Or shrewish like a tinker?
A scolder? Or extravagant? Too clannish?
Too poor? Too rich? Unnaturally mannish?
Although we know there isn't to be found
In all the world one that will trot quite sound,
Whether it's man or beast, the way we'd like it,
It were sufficient bargain, could we strike it,
In any woman, were one sure she had
More good among her qualities than bad.

    'But all this asks some leisure to review;
God knows that many is the tear I too
Have wept in secret since I had a wife.
Praise whoso will the married state of life
I find it a routine, a synthesis
Of cost and care, and wholly bare of bliss.
And yet the neighbours round about, by God,
Especially the women – in a squad –
Congratulate me that I chose to wive
The constantest, the meekest soul alive.
I know where the shoe pinches; but for you,
Why, you must please yourself in what you do.
You're old enough – that's not what I disparage –
To think before you enter into marriage,
Especially if your wife is young and fair.
By Him that made earth, water, fire and air,
The youngest man in this distinguished rout
Will have a busy task – you need not doubt –
To keep a woman to himself. Trust me,
You will not please her more than for, say, three
Years – that is, please her to the point of fervence.
Wives ask a lot in matters of observance.
I beg you not to take it the wrong way.'

    'Well,' said old January, 'have you said your say?
Straw for your Seneca and proverbial tags;
Not worth a basketful of weeds and rags,

Fishermen hauling in their catch.
Fish played an important part in
the medieval diet.

Your pedant-jargon! Wiser men than you,
As you have heard, take quite another view
Of my proposal. What would you reply,
Placebo?' 'An accursed man, say I,
It is that offers an impediment,'
Said he, and so, by general consent,
His friends then rose, declaring it was good
That he should marry when and where he would.

   Busy imaginations, strange invention
And soaring fantasy obsessed the attention
Of January's soul about his wedding.
Came many a lovely form and feature shedding
A rapture through his fancies night by night.
As who should take a mirror polished bright
And set it in the common market-place,
And watch the many figures pause and pace
Across his mirror; in the self-same way,
Old January allowed his thoughts to play
Mirroring all the girls that lived nearby,
Still undetermined where his thought should lie.
For were there one with beauty in her face
There was another standing high in grace
With people, for her grave benignity,
Whose voices gave her the supremacy.
Others were rich, but had a tarnished name.

   At last, and half in earnest, half in game,
He fixed on one, and setting her apart,
He banished all the others from his heart.
He chose her on his own authority,
For love is always blind and cannot see,
And when he lay in bed at night his thought
Pictured her in his heart, for he was caught
By her fresh beauty and her age so tender;
Her little waist, her arms so long and slender,
Her wise self-discipline, her gentle ways,
Her womanly bearing and her serious gaze.
His thought, descending on her thus, was fettered,
It seemed to him his choice could not be bettered.
Once he was satisfied in this decision,
He held all other judgement in derision:
It was impossible to disagree
With him in taste, such was his fantasy.

   He sent his friends a very strong request
Begging the pleasure – would they do their best? –

Of an immediate visit. In his belief
They needn't be kept long; he would be brief,
For there was no more need to cast around;
He was restored, the lady had been found.

Placebo came and so did all the rest,
And January began with the request
That none should offer any argument
Against the purpose 'which was his intent,
Pleasing to God Almighty, and,' said he,
'The very ground of his prosperity.'

He said there was a maiden in the town
Whose beauty was indeed of great renown;
Her rank was not so great, to tell the truth,
But still she had her beauty and her youth;
She was the girl he wanted for his wife,
To lead a life of ease, a holy life.
And he would have her all – thank God for this! –
There would be shares for no one in his bliss.
He begged them then to labour in his need
And help to make his enterprise succeed,
For then, he said, his mind would be at rest
'With nothing to annoy me or molest,
But for one thing which pricks my conscience still,
So listen to me kindly if you will.

'I've often,' he continued, 'heard ere this
That none may have two perfect kinds of bliss,
Bliss in this world, I mean, and bliss in Heaven;
Though he keep clear of sin – the deadly seven
And all the branches of their dreadful tree –
Yet there's so perfect a felicity
In marriage, so much pleasure, so few tears,
That I keep fearing, though advanced in years,
I shall be leading such a happy life,
So delicate, with neither grief nor strife,
That I shall have my heaven here in earth,
And may not that cost more than it is worth?
Since that true heaven costs a man so dear
In tribulation and in penance here,
How should I then, living in such delight,
As every married man, by day and night,
Has with his wife, attain to joys supernal
And enter into bliss with Christ Eternal?
That is my terror. Have you a suggestion,
My worthy brothers, to resolve the question?'

Justinus, who despised his nonsense, said,
Jesting as ever, what was in his head;
And wishing not to spin things out in chatter
Used no authorities to support the matter.
'If there's no obstacle,' he said, 'but this,
God by some mighty miracle of His
May show you mercy as He is wont to do,
And long before they come to bury you
May cause you to bewail your married life
In which you say there never can be strife.
And God forbid that there should not be sent
A special grace that husbands may repent,
And sent more often than to single men.
This, sir, would be my own conclusion, then;
Never despair! You still may go to glory,
For she perhaps may prove your purgatory,
God's means of grace, as one might say, God's whip
To send your soul to Heaven with a skip
And swifter than an arrow from the bow!
    'I hope to God that you will shortly know
There's no such paramount felicity
In marriage, nor is ever like to be,
As to disqualify you for salvation,
Provided you observe some moderation,
Tempering down the passions of your wife
With some restriction of your amorous life,
Keeping yourself, of course, from other sin.
My tale is done, but there! My wit is thin.
Be not afraid, dear brother, that's the moral.
Let us wade out, however, of this quarrel;
The Wife of Bath, if you can understand
Her views in the discussion now on hand,
Has put them well and briefly in this case:
And now, farewell, God have you in His Grace!'
    He then took leave of January his brother
And they had no more speech with one another.
And when his friends saw that it needs must be
They made a careful marriage-treaty. She,
The girl agreed upon, whose name was May,
(And with the smallest possible delay)
Was to be married to this January.
    And I assume there is no need to tarry
Over the bonds and documents they planned
To give her possession of his land.

Knocking down acorns to feed pigs.
One pig on the left has dexterously
caught a falling acorn in its snout.

Or make you listen to her rich array,
But finally there came the happy day
And off at last to church the couple went
There to receive the holy sacrament.

Out came the priest, with stole about his neck,
And bade her be like Sarah at the beck
Of Abraham in wisdom, truth and grace,
Said all the prayers were proper to the case,
Then signed them with the cross and bade God bless
Them both, and made all sure in holiness.

Thus they were wedded in solemnity,
And at the wedding-banquet he and she
Sat with their worthier guests upon the dais.
Joy and delight filled the entire place,
Stringed instruments, victuals of every kind,
The daintiest all Italy could find.
Music broke forth as with the sound of Zion,
Not Orpheus nor the Theban king Amphion
Ever achieved so sweet a melody.

At every course there came loud minstrelsy
And Joab's trumpets never took the ear
So forcefuly as this, nor half so clear
Those of Theodamas when Thebes held out.
Bacchus himself was pouring wine about
And Venus smiled on everyone in sight,
For January had become her knight
And wished to try his courage in the carriage
Of his new liberty combined with marriage.
Armed with a fire-brand she danced about
Before the bride and all the happy rout;
And certainly I'll go as far as this,
And say that Hymen, God of wedded bliss,
Never beheld so happy a wedded man.

Hold thou thy peace, O poet Martian,
Give us no more thy marital doxology
For Mercury on wedding with Philology!
Silence the song the Muses would have sung,
Thine is too small a pen, too weak a tongue,
To signalize this wedding or engage
To tell of tender youth and stooping age,
Such joy it is as none may write about:
Try it yourself and you will soon find out
If I'm a liar or not in such a case.

For there sat May with so benign a face

That but to see her was a fairy-tale.
Queen Esther's eye could never so assail
Ahasuerus, never looked so meek;
Of so much loveliness I dare not speak,
Yet thus much of her beauty I will say
That she was like the brightest morn of May
With every grace and pleasure in her glance.
This January sat ravished, in a trance,
And every time he gazed upon her face
His heart began to menace her and race;
That night his arms would strain her with the ardour
That Paris showed for Helen, aye, and harder.
And yet he felt strong qualms of pity stir
To think he soon must do offence to her,
That very night, and thought, 'O tender creature!
Alas, God grant you may endure the nature
Of my desires, they are so sharp and hot.
I am aghast lest you sustain them not.
God hinder me from doing all I might!
But O I wish to God that it were night,
And the night last for ever! Oh, how slow...
I wish these guests would hurry up and go!'
     So he began to dedicate his labours
To getting rid politely of his neighbours,
And to detaching them from food supplies.
At last their reason told them they should rise;
They danced and drank and, left to their devices,
They went from room to room to scatter spices
About the house. Joy rose in every man
Except in one, a squire called Damian,
Who carved for January every day.
     He was so ravished by the sight of May
As to be mad with suffering; he could
Almost have died or fainted where he stood,
So sorely Venus burnt him with the brand
Which, as she danced, she carried in her hand.
And hastily the boy went off to bed;
No more of him at present need be said.
I leave him there to weep and to complain
Till fresh young May have pity on his pain.
     O perilous fire, in the bed-straw started!
Foe in the family, home-like but false-hearted,
Pretending service and a traitor too,
An adder in the bosom, sly, untrue,

A merchant counting his money.
The furniture and the man's
clothes, apart from the full money
chest, are indicative of the increased
prosperity of the growing merchant
and professional classes.

God shield us all from your acquaintanceship!
O January, drunk upon the lip
Of marriage, see your servant, Damian,
Who was your very squire, born your man,
Even now is meditating villainy.
O God unmask your household enemy!
Over the world no pestilence can roam
That is as foul as foe within the home.

    The sun had traced his arc with golden finger
Across the sky, caring no more to linger
On the horizon in that latitude.
Night with her mantle which is dark and rude
Had overspread the hemisphere about,
And gone were all the merry-making rout
Of January's guests, with hearty thanks,
And homeward each convivially spanks
To undertake such business as will keep
Him happy, till it should be time for sleep.

    Soon after this the restive January
Demanded bed; no longer would he tarry
Except to quaff a cordial for the fire
That claret laced with spice can lend desire;
For he had many potions, drugs as fine
As those that monk, accursed Constantine,
Has numbered in his book *De Coitu*.
He drank them all; not one did he eschew,
And to his private friends who lingered on
He said, 'For God's love, hurry and be gone,
Empty the house politely if you can.'
And presently they did so to a man.
A toast was drunk, the curtains back were thrown;
The bride was borne to bed as still as stone.
And when the priest had blessed the wedding-bed
The room was emptied and the guests were sped.

    Fast in the arms of January lay
His mate, his paradise, his fresh young May.
He lulled her, sought to kiss away all trouble;
The bristles of his beard were thick as stubble,
Much like a dog-fish skin, and sharp as briars,
Being newly shaved to sweeten his desires.
He rubbed his chin against her tender cheek
And said, 'Alas, alas that I should seek
To trespass—yet I must—and to offend
You greatly too, my spouse, ere I descend.

A wooden cradle with guardian birds
watching at head and foot.

Nevertheless consider this,' said he,
'No workman, whatsoever he may be,
Can do his work both well and in a flurry;
This shall be done in perfect ease, no hurry.
It's of no consequence how long we play,
We are in holy wedlock and we may.
And blessed be the yoke that we are in
For nothing we can do will count as sin.
A man is not a sinner with his wife,
He cannot hurt himself with his own knife;
We have the law's permission thus to play.'
And so he laboured till the break of day,
Then took a sop of claret-sodden toast,
Sat up in bed as rigid as a post,
And started singing very loud and clear.
He kissed his wife and gave a wanton leer,
Feeling a coltish rage towards his darling
And chattering in the jargon of a starling.
The slack of skin about his neck was shaking
As thus he fell a-chanting and corn-craking.

    God knows what May was thinking in her heart,
Seeing him sit there in his shirt apart,
Wearing his night-cap, with his scrawny throat.
She didn't think his games were worth a groat.

    At last he said, 'I think I'll take a rest;
Now day has come a little sleep were best.'

An English Gothic cupboard.

And down he lay and slept till half-past eight;
Then he woke up, and seeing it was late,
Old January arose; but fresh young May
Kept her apartment until the fourth day
As women will, they do it for the best.
For ever labourer must have time to rest,
For otherwise he can't keep labouring;
And that is true of every living thing,
Be it a fish, a bird, a beast, or man.

    Now I will speak of woeful Damian
Languishing in his love, as will appear.
I would address him thus, if he could hear:
'O silly Damian! Alas, alas!
Answer my question; in your present pass
How are you going to tell her of your woe?
She's absolutely bound to answer no,
And if you speak, she's certain to betray you;
I can say nothing. God be your help, and stay you!'

Chivalry and Romance

haucer's knight, we are told in the 'Prologue', was a man of 'truth, honour, generousness and courtesy' who had never in his life said a boorish thing and was 'a true, a perfect gentle-knight'. These virtues, associated with a deep love for and faith in the Christian religion, were those expected of a knight in the days of chivalry. These ideals had stemmed from the legend of King Arthur and his Knights of the Round Table which was popular through reading and minstrelsy in both England and France. It was on the basis of King Arthur and his knights that Edward III founded the Order of the Garter while Chaucer was alive. An essential ingredient of the ideals of chivalry was a romantic image of woman, at least women of the knightly class of society, and although chivalry as such established and perpetuated a class structure in society it nevertheless had a pronounced civilizing effect on it too. The knight of the Middle Ages was a man of split personality. He was expected to be romantic in his thoughts, courteous in his way of life but tough in battle or in the tourney – it can have been no small ordeal to be unhorsed by the thrust of a sixteen foot lance with the weight and power of a cart horse behind it when the recipient of the blow was encased in heavy plate armour. Yet this risk was undertaken not only at time of war but for fun and with what appears now to be a somewhat perverted form of moral obligation.

1

...sez y ferir et hurtay· Et maintesfois le escoutay	front reluisant sourci uoultie Lentreoeil si nestoit pas petis
Se le oroye scans nulle ame	Ame fut asses mans y mesme
Le guichet qui estoit de charme	Le nes eut bien fait a droiture
Ille ouurit une pucellette	Les yeulx eut uers come faulcone
Qui asses estoit comte et nette	Pour faire enuie a toute home
Cheueulx eut blons come ung bassin	Doulce a fame eut et sauouree
La char plus tendre que ung poussin	La face blanche et coulouree
	La bouche petite et grossette
	Et au menton une fossette

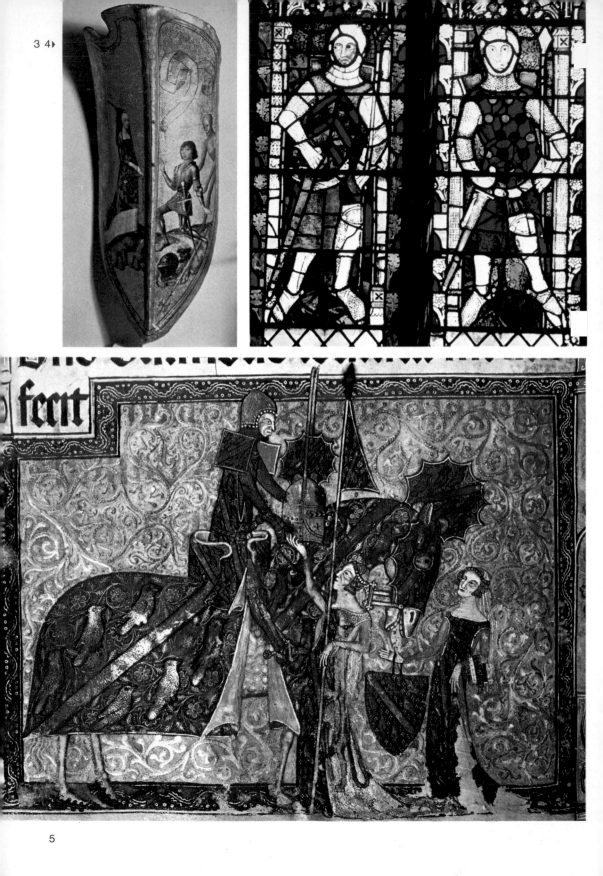

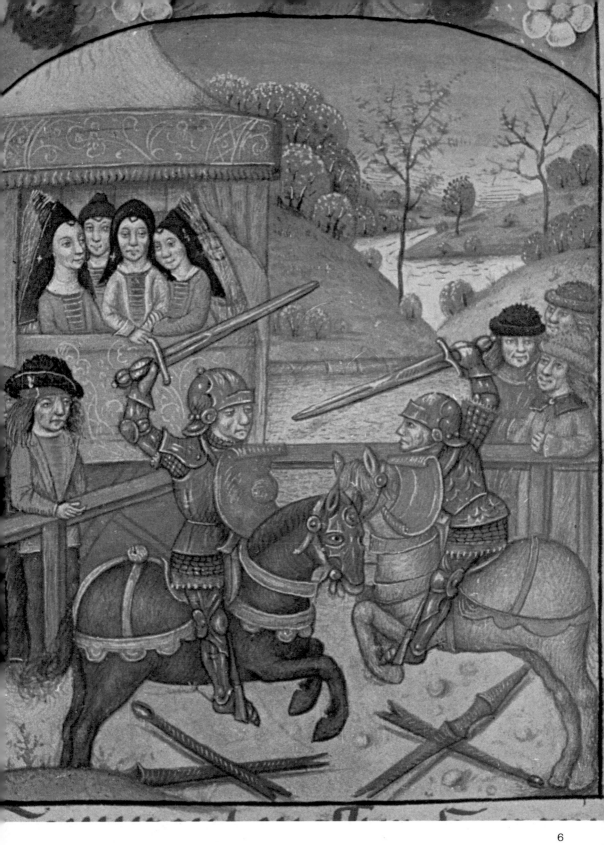

6

7
8▸

Jousts and tournaments took place sometimes to settle affairs of honour but more often for the sheer joy of combat and for the entertainment of others.

There is a distinctly romantic atmosphere in (1) depicting three knights riding back from the wars into a castle as trumpets blare from the battlements. Each knight is being welcomed by his lady. Even more romantic is the scene in (2). The picture comes from a Flemish manuscript, the *Roman de la Rose*, illustrating the medieval idea of chivalry, part of which was translated into English by Chaucer himself. It shows a knight in his 'perfect gentle' role playing and singing to a lady in the idyllic surroundings of a walled garden with

9

fountain playing. In (3) is depicted a parade shield which would be displayed at a tournament. It epitomizes the very spirit of the tournament in which the knight, probably wearing his lady's favour, faced death usually in her presence. We see the figure of Death behind the kneeling knight and above them the words 'You or Death' in French.

Chaucer was certainly familiar with tournaments (6) for in 1390 he was Clerk of the King's Works and was responsible for the erection of the scaffolding for a spectacular tournament held in Smithfield (now London's meat market) in which sixty knights, who were accompanied by their squires and ladies, took part. It was an international affair in which foreign knights joined and, interrupted by feasting and dancing, lasted for a week. In picture (6) the knights are fighting with swords as ladies look on from their pavilion, but under each horse is a broken lance. The first round, as it were, was usually tilting with long lances but if these were broken by the impact, as often happened, there would follow a second round in which swords, sometimes deliberately blunted, would be used. In picture (8) we get a vivid impression of what the first round must have looked like although the picture dates back before Chaucer's time. It is interesting because the horseman on the right (with the green face) depicts the Saracen leader, Saladin, about to be unhorsed.

It is hard today to imagine the feast of colour which the great chivalric occasions presented. The splendour of a knight's apparel, and that of his horse, is richly illustrated in (5). The knight is Sir Geoffrey Luttrell, who ordered the Luttrell Psalter to be made. The Psalter, with its often witty illuminations, is an important source of information on the habits of the time. In the picture Sir Geoffrey is being handed his helmet by his wife while his daughter-in-law stands by with his shield. In (4) we see two armoured knights whose memory is preserved in a fourteenth-century stained glass window in Tewkesbury Abbey.

The ideals of chivalry were fostered by poetry which was a favourite literary form. Troubadours on the continent, minstrels and gleemen in England, travelled from one great house to another reciting and singing the great romances of the past and others of their own composition in verse. The love songs they wrote were often about actual ladies, but these were portrayed usually as pure and ethereal, inspiring spiritual rather than sexual love, and encouraging the knights to greater and more glorious deeds. In (7) we see such a lady rewarding a poet with a crown of laurel. Heralds played an important part in the comings and goings of diplomacy and war. In (9) we see a herald announcing one of the several truces during the Hundred Years War. He is flanked by others bearing standards emblazoned with the royal arms of England and France.

Sick-hearted Damian in Venus' fire
Is so consumed, he's dying with desire;
And so he took his courage in his hand
To end a grief he could no longer stand
And with a pen that he contrived to borrow
He wrote a letter pouring out his sorrow,
After the fashion of a song or lay,
Indited to his lady, dazzling May,
And wrapped it in a purse of silk apart
To hang inside his shirt, upon his heart.
The moon, that stood in Taurus on the day
When January had wedded lovely May,
Had glided into Cancer; she of whom
I speak, fresh May, had meanwhile kept her room,
As is the custom among nobles all.
A bride of course should never eat in hall
Till four days afterwards, or three at least,
But when they're over, let her go and feast.

On the fourth day, from noon to noon complete,
And when high mass was over, in his seat
Sat January in his hall with May,
As fresh and bright as is a summer's day.
And it so happened that this good old man
Remembered Damian, and thus began:
'Where's Damian? Saints above! How can it be
That Damian isn't here to wait on me?
Is he still sick? What's happened? Is he up?'

The squires standing there to fill his cup
Excused him on the grounds that he was ill,
He was in bed, unfit for duty still;
No other reason could have made him tarry.
'I'm very sorry for it,' said January,
'And he's a gentleman, to tell the truth,'
The old man said, 'and if he died, poor youth,
It were a pity; he's a lad of worth.
I don't know anyone of equal birth
So wise, discreet and secret, and so able;
Thrifty and serviceable too at table.
As soon as possible after meat to-day
I'll visit him myself; and so shall May.
We'll give him all the comfort that we can.'

Then everybody blessed the kind old man
So eager in his bounty and good breeding
To offer anything that might be needing

A green glaze pottery whistle.

To comfort a sick squire; a gentle deed.
    'Madam,' said January, 'take good heed
That after meat you and your women all,
When you have sought your room and left the hall,
Go up and have a look at Damian
And entertain him; he's a gentleman.
And tell him too that I shall do my best
To visit him myself, after my rest.
Now hurry on, be quick, and I shall bide me
Here, until you return to sleep beside me.'
And on the word he rose and gave a call
To fetch a squire (the marshal of the hall)
And gave him some instructions. Fresh young May
With all her women took the shortest way
To Damian's room and sat beside his bed;
A warmth of comfort was in all she said,
Benignity and beauty in her glance.
And Damian, when at last he saw his chance,
Secretly took his purse and billet-doux,
Couched in the sweetest phrases that he knew,
And put it in her hand with nothing more
Than a long sigh, as deep as to the core;
But in a whisper he contrived to say,
'Mercy, have mercy! Don't give me away!
I should be killed if this were ever known.'
The purse slid from his bosom to her own
And off she went. You get no more of me.
Back to old January then went she;
He was reclining on his bed by this.
He drew her to his arms with many a kiss,
Then settled back to sleep at once; and so
She then pretended that she had to go
Where everybody has to go at times.
There, after memorizing Damian's rhymes,
She tore them into pieces and she cast
Them softly down the privy-drain at last.
    Who fell into a study then but May?
And down beside old January she lay
Who slept until awoken by his cough.
He begged her then to strip her garments off
For he would have some pleasure of her, he said,
Her clothes were an encumbrance, to be shed.
And she obeyed, whether she would or no.
Lest I offend the precious, I will go

No further into what he did, or tell
Whether she thought it paradise or hell.
I leave them working thus as I suppose
Till it was evensong, and then they rose.
    Whether by destiny or accident,
By starry influence or natural bent,
Or whether some constellation held its state
In heaven to make the hour fortunate
For giving billet-doux and lending wing
To Venus – there's a time for everything,
The learned say – and get a lady's love,
I cannot tell. But God who sits above
And knows that every action has a cause,
Let Him decide, for I can only pause
In silence; this at least is true of May
That such was the impression made that day
And such her pity for the sick young man
She could not rid her heart of Damian,
Or of the wish to see his troubles ended.
'Whoever else,' she thought, 'may be offended,
I do not care; but I can promise this,
To love him more than anyone there is,
Though he mayn't have a shirt. I will be kind.'
Pity flows swiftly in a noble mind.
    Here one may see how excellently free
In bounty women, on taking thought, can be.
Some female tyrants – many I have known –
Are pitiless, their hearts are made of stone
And would have rather let him die the death
Than yield their grace or favour by a breath,
And they exult in showing cruel pride,
Calmly indifferent to homicide.
    Soft May felt pity, you must understand.
She wrote a letter in her own fair hand
In which she granted him her very grace.
There needed nothing but the time and place
To grant the satisfaction he desired;
He was to have whatever he required.
    So when she saw occasion one fine day
To visit him, off went the lovely May
And thrust this letter down with subtle skill
Under his pillow, read it if he will.
She took him by the hand and squeezed it hard
(But secretly, for she was on her guard),

Bade him get well, then went without demur
To January who had called for her.
    And up rose happy Damian on the morrow;
Gone was all trace of malady and sorrow.
He preens himself and prunes and combs his curls
To take the fancy of this queen of girls.
To January his master, in addition,
He was a very spaniel in submission,
And was so pleasant in his general drift
(Craft's all that matters if you have the gift),
That people spoke him well in every way,
But above all he stood in grace with May.
Thus I leave Damian, busy with his needs,
And turn once more to how my tale proceeds.
    Some writers argue that felicity
Wholly consists in pleasure; certainly
This noble January, as best he might
In all that was befitting to a knight,
Had planned to live deliciously in pleasure;
His house and all his finery and treasure
Were fashioned to his rank as are a king's,
And among other of his handsome things
He had a garden, walled about with stone;
So fair a garden never was there known.
For out of doubt I honestly suppose
That he who wrote the *Romance of the Rose*
Could not have pictured such magnificence;
Priapus never had the eloquence,
Though he be god of gardens, to re-tell
The beauty of this garden and the well
Under a laurel, standing ever-green.
Many a time King Pluto and his Queen
Proserpina and all her fairy rout
Disported and made melody about
That well and held their dances, I am told.
This January, so noble, and so old,
Found walking in it such felicity
That no one was allowed to have the key
Except himself, and for its little wicket
He had a silver latch-key to unclick it
Or lock it up, and when his thought was set
Upon the need to pay his wife her debt
In summer season, thither would he go
With May his wife when there was none to know,

A man and a woman cutting down
a tree using a two-handed saw.

John Lydgate, a monk, was the equivalent of the Poet Laureate in the early part of the fifteenth century and described himself as a disciple of Chaucer. He is shown here presenting one of his books to the king.

And anything they had not done in bed
There in the garden was performed instead,
So in this manner many a merry day
Was spent by January and lovely May.
But worldly joys, alas, may not endure
For January or anyone, be sure.
    Changeable Fortune, O unstable Chance,
Thine is the scorpion's treacherous advance!
Thy head all flattery, about to sting,
Thy tail a death, and death by poisoning.
O brittle joy, O venom sweet and strange,
O monster that so subtly canst arrange
Thy gifts and colour them with all the dyes
Of durability to catch the wise
And foolish too! Say, why hast thou deceived
Old January, thy friend, as he believed?
Thou hast bereft him of his sight, his eye
Is dark, and in his grief he longs to die.
    Alas this noble January, he
So generous once in his prosperity
Went blind; quite suddenly he lost his sight.
Pitiful loss! He wept it day and night,
While fires of jealousy seared his melancholy,
For fear his wife might fall into some folly.
His heart burned hot; he had been nothing loth,
Nay glad, if one had come to slay them both.
For neither on his death nor in his life
Was she to be the mistress or the wife
Of any other, but in weeds of state,
True as a turtle that has lost her mate,
She was to live, the garments on her back
A widow's, never anything but black.
    But in the end, after a month or two,
His sorrows cooled a little, it is true,
For when he saw there was no remedy
He took in patience his adversity,
Save that the ineradicable sting
Of jealousy embittered everything,
For so outrageous are the thoughts it rouses
That neither when at home or in the houses
Of his acquaintance, no, nor anywhere
Would he allow his wife to take the air
Unless his hand were on her day and night.
    Ah, how she wept, fresh as she was, and bright,

John Lydgate at work in his study.
As was common the floor is tiled
and the poet has a floor rug to
protect his feet from the cold as he
works at a rather complicated
writing desk.

Who loved her Damian, and with so benign
A love that sudden death was her design
Unless she could enjoy him; so at first
She wept and waited for her heart to burst.
    And Damian too, upon the other part,
Became in turn so sorrowful of heart
That none was ever like him: night or day
There never was a chance to speak to May
As to his purpose, no, nor anything near it,
Unless old January was there to hear it,
Holding her hand and never letting go.
Nevertheless by writing to and fro
And private signals, Damian knew her mind;
And she was well aware what he designed.
O January, what might it thee avail
Though thou couldst see as far as ship can sail?
As well be blind and be deceived as be
Deceived as others are that still can see.
Consider Argus with his hundred eyes
Poring and prying, yet for all these spies
He was deceived, and many more I know,
God wot, who sagely think they are not so.
Least said is soonest mended; say no more.
    Now this fresh May of whom I spoke before
Took some warm wax and fashioned an impression
Of that same key (in January's possession)
Into the garden, where he often went.
Damian, who knew exactly what she meant,
Secretly forged a counterfeited key.
That's all there is to say, but presently
A wonder will befall, if you will wait,
Thanks to this key and to the wicket-gate.
    O noble Ovid, that was truly spoken
When you affirmed there was no cunning token
Or trickery, however long or hot,
That lovers could not find. For did they not
When Pyramus and Thisbe, I recall,
Though strictly watched, held converse through a wall?
There was a trick that none could have forecast!
But to our purpose; ere a week had passed,
Before July was on them, it befell
That January's thoughts began to swell,
Incited by his wife, with eager wishes
To be at play with her among the bushes

In his walled garden, he and she alone,
And so at last one morning he made moan
To May with this intention: 'Ah,' said he,
'Rise up, my wife, my love, my lady free!
The turtle's voice is heard, my dove, my pet.
Winter is gone with all its rain and wet;
Come out with me, bright-eyes, my columbine,
O how far fairer are thy breasts than wine!
Our garden is enclosed and walled about;
White spouse, come forth to me; ah, never doubt
But I am wounded to the heart, dear wife,
For love of you, unspotted in your life
As well I know. Come forth to take our pleasures,
Wife of my choice and treasure of my treasures!'
    He got these lewd old words out of a book.
And May at once gave Damian a look
Signalling he should go before and wait;
So Damian ran ahead, unlocked the gate
And darted in as swiftly as a bird,
He managed to be neither seen nor heard,
And crouched beneath the bushes on his own.
    And then this January, blind as stone,
Came hand in hand with May, but unattended,
And down into the garden they descended
And having entered clapped the wicket to.
    'Now wife,' he said, 'none's here but I and you,
And you are she, the creature I best love.
For by the Lord that sits in Heaven above,
Believe me I would die upon the knife
Rather than hurt you, truest, dearest wife.
Remember how I chose you, for God's sake;
Not covetously nor in hope to make,
But only for the love I had to you.
And though I may be old and sightless too,
Be true to me and I will tell you why.
    'Three things for certain you shall win thereby:
First, love of Christ; next, honour to yourself;
Last, your inheritance, my lands and pelf,
Towers and towns; draw the agreement up,
They're yours, it shall be signed before we sup.
But first, as God may bring my soul to bliss,
I pray you seal the covenant with a kiss.
And though I may be jealous, blame me not;
You are so deeply printed in my thought

That when I see your beauty, and engage
That thought with my dislikable old age,
I cannot – though it might be death to me –
Forbear a moment of your company
For very love; I say it with no doubt.
Now kiss me, wife, and let us roam about.'
　　Fresh-hearted May on hearing what he said
Benignly answered him with drooping head,
But first and foremost she began to weep.
'Indeed,' she said, 'I have a soul to keep
No less than you, and then there is my honour
Which for a wife is like a flower upon her.
I put it in your hands for good or ill
When the priest bound my body to your will,
So let me answer of my own accord
If you will give me leave, beloved lord;
I pray to God that never dawn the day
– Or let me die as foully as I may –
When I shall do my family that shame
Or bring so much dishonour on my name
As to be false. And if my love grow slack,
Take me and strip me, sew me in a sack
And drop me in the nearest lake to drown.
I am no common woman of the town,
I am of gentle birth, I keep aloof.
So why speak thus to me, for what reproof
Have I deserved? It's men that are untrue
And women, women ever blamed anew.
I think it a pretence that men profess;
They hide behind a charge of faithlessness.'
　　And as she spoke she saw a short way off
Young Damian in his bush. She gave a cough
And signalled with a finger quickly where
He was to climb into a tree – a pear
Heavily charged with fruit, and up he went,
Perfectly understanding what she meant,
Or any other signal, I may state,
Better than January could, her mate.
For she had written to him, never doubt it,
Telling him all and how to set about it.
And there I leave him sitting, by your pardon,
While May and January roamed the garden.
　　Bright was the day and blue the firmament,
Down fell the golden flood that Phoebus sent

A bronze cooking pot for hanging over an open fire.

To gladden every flower with his beams;
He was in Gemini at the time, it seems,
And but a little from his declination
In Cancer, which is Jupiter's exaltation.
And so it happened through the golden tide
Into the garden from the further side
Came Pluto, who is king of Fairyland,
And many a lady of his elfin band
Behind his queen, the lady Proserpine,
Ravished by him from Aetna. I incline
To think it is in Claudian you can read
How she was gathering flowers in a mead
And how he fetched her in his grisly cart.
The King of Faery sat him down apart
Upon a little bench of turfy green,
And then he turned and thus addressed his queen:
  'Dear wife,' he said, 'what no one can gainsay
And what experience shows us every day
Are the foul treacheries women do to men.
Ten thousand tales, and multiply by ten,
Record your notable untruth and lightness.
O Solomon in thy wisdom, wealth and brightness,
Replete in sapience as in worldly glory,
How memorable are thy words and story
To every creature capable of reason!
Of man's true bounty and of woman's treason
Thou saidst, "Among a thousand found I one,
And yet among all women found I none."
  'So said the king who knew your wickedness;
And Jesus son of Sirach,* as I guess,
Seldom says much of you in reverence –
Wild fire and a corruptive pestilence
Fall down upon you all to burn and blight!
Do you not see that honourable knight
Who, being blind and old and unobservant,
Is to be cuckolded by his own servant?
Look, there he sits, that lecher in the tree!
Now will I grant it of my majesty
To this blind, old and estimable knight
That he shall instantly receive his sight
Whenever his wife begins her villainy.
He shall know all about her harlotry
Both in rebuke of her and others too.'
  'So that,' the queen replied, 'is what you'll do!

A corbel from a building in Blackfriars, London. Corbels were projections used to support a wall above and the ends were often decorated, sometimes in grotesque style.

Now, by my grandsire's soul, though she is young
I'll put a ready answer on her tongue
And every woman's after, for her sake.
Though taken in their guilt they yet shall make
A bold-faced explanation to excuse them
And bear down all who venture to accuse them;
For lack of answer none of them shall die.
Though a man saw things with his naked eye
We'll face it out, we women, and be bold
To weep and swear, insinuate and scold
As long as men are gullible as geese.
   'What do I care for your authorities?
I'm well aware this Jew, this Solomon
Found fools among us women, many a one;
But if he never found a woman true,
God knows that there are many men who do,
Who find them faithful, virtuous and good.
Witness all those in christian sisterhood
Who proved their constancy by martyrdom.
And Roman history has mentioned some,
Aye many, women of exceeding truth.
Now keep your temper, sir, though he, forsooth,
Said there were no good women, if you can.
Consider the opinion of this man.
He meant it thus that sovereign constancy
Is God's alone who sits in Trinity.
Hey! God knows Solomon is only one;
Why do you make so much of Solomon?
What though he built God's temple in the story?
What though he were so rich, so high in glory?
He made a temple for false gods as well,
And what could be more reprehensible?
Plaster him over as you may, dear sir,
He was a lecher and idolater,
And in his latter days forsook the Lord;
Had God not spared him, as the books record,
Because He loved his father, surely he would
Have lost his kingdom, rather than that he should.
And all the villainous terms that you apply
To women, I value at a butterfly!
I am a woman and I needs must speak
Or swell until I burst. Shall I be meek
If he has said that we were wrangleresses?
As ever I may hope to flaunt my tresses,

I will not spare for manners or politeness
To rail at one who rails at woman's lightness.'
  'Madam,' he said, 'be angry now no more;
I give it up. But seeing that I swore
Upon my oath to grant him sight again,
I'll stand by what I said, I tell you plain.
I am a king, it fits me not to lie.'
'And I'm the Queen of Fairyland, say I!
Her answer she shall have, I undertake.
Let us have no more words, for goodness' sake.
Indeed I don't intend to be contrary.'
  Now let us turn again to January
Who walked the garden with his airy May
And sang more merrily than a popinjay,
'I love you best, and ever shall, my sweet!'
So long among the paths had strayed their feet
That they at last had reached the very tree
Where Damian sat in waiting merrily,
High in his leafy bower of fresh green.
And fresh young May, so shiningly serene,
Began to sigh and said 'Oh! I've a pain!
Oh Sir! Whatever happens, let me gain
One of those pears up there that I can see,
Or I shall die! I long so terribly
To eat a little pear it looks so green.
O help me for the love of Heaven's Queen!
I warn you that a woman in my plight
May often feel so great an appetite
For fruit that she may die to go without.'
  'Alas,' he said, 'that there's no boy about,
Able to climb. Alas, alas,' said he,
'That I am blind.' 'No matter, sir,' said she,
'For if you would consent – there's nothing in it –
To hold the pear-tree in your arms a minute
(I know you have no confidence in me),
Then I could climb up well enough,' said she,
'If I could set my foot upon your back.'
  'Of course,' he said, 'why, you shall never lack
For that, or my heart's blood to do you good.'
And down he stooped; upon his back she stood,
Catching a branch, and with a spring she thence
– Ladies, I beg you not to take offence,
I can't embellish, I'm a simple man –
Went up into the tree, and Damian

Pulled up her smock at once and in he thrust.
    And when King Pluto saw this shameful lust
He gave back sight to January once more
And made him see far better than before.
Never was man more taken with delight
Than January when he received his sight.
And his first thought was to behold his love.
He cast his eyes into the tree above
Only to see that Damian had addressed
His wife in ways that cannot be expressed
Unless I use a most discourteous word.
He gave a roaring cry, as might be heard
From stricken mothers when their babies die.
'Help! Out upon you!' He began to cry.
'Strong Madam Strumpet! What are you up to there?'
'What ails you, sir?' said she, 'what makes you swear?
Have patience, use the reason in your mind,
I've helped you back to sight when you were blind!
Upon my soul I'm telling you no lies;
They told me if I wished to heal your eyes
Nothing could cure them better than for me
To struggle with a fellow in a tree.
God knows it was a kindness that I meant.'
'Struggle?' said he, 'Yes! Anyhow, in it went!
God send you both a shameful death to die!
He had you, I saw it with my very eye,
And if I did not, hang me by the neck!'
    'Why then,' she said, 'my medicine's gone to wreck,
For certainly if you could really see
You'd never say such words as those to me;
You caught some glimpses, but your sight's not good.'
'I see,' he said, 'as well as ever I could,

A familiar form of cooking was by roasting on the spit over an open fire. Here one man turns the spit by hand while the other feeds the fire under what look like sucking pigs.

Thanks be to God! And with both eyes, I do!
And that, I swear, is what he seemed to do.'
  'You're hazy, hazy, my good sir,' said she;
'That's all I get for helping you to see.
Alas,' she said, 'that ever I was so kind!'
  'Dear wife,' said January, 'never mind,
Come down, dear heart, and if I've slandered you
God knows I'm punished for it. Come down, do!
But by my father's soul, it seemed to me
That Damian had enjoyed you in the tree
And that your smock was pulled up over your breast.'
'Well, think,' she said, 'as it may please you best,
But, Sir, when suddenly a man awakes,
He cannot grasp a thing at once, it takes
A little time to do so perfectly,
For he is dazed at first and cannot see.
Just so a man who has been blind for long
Cannot expect his sight to be so strong
At first, or see as well as those may do
Who've had their eyesight back a day or two.
Until your sight has settled down a bit
You may be frequently deceived by it.
Be careful then, for by our heavenly King
Many a man feels sure he's seen a thing
Which was quite different really, he may fudge it;
Misapprehend a thing and you'll misjudge it.'
  And on the word she jumped down from the tree.
And January – who is glad but he? –
Kissed her and clasped her in his arms – how often! –
And stroked her breast caressingly to soften
Her indignation. To his palace then
He led her home. Be happy, gentlemen,
That finishes my tale of January;
God and his Mother guard us, blessed Mary!

Epilogue to the Merchant's Tale

'Ey, mercy of God!' our Host exclaimed thereat,
'May God preserve me from a wife like that!
Just look what cunning tricks and subtleties
There are in woman! Busy little bees
They are, deceiving silly men like us!
They're always sliding and evading thus,
Dodging the truth; the Merchant's tale has shown it
And it's as true as steel – I have to own it.
I have a wife myself, a poor one too,
But what a tongue! She is a blabbing shrew,
And she has other vices, plenty more.
Well, let it go! No sense to rub a sore.
But, d'you know what? In strictest secrecy,
Being tied to her is misery to me.
Were I to reckon her vices one by one,
I'd only be a fool when I had done;
And why? Because it would be sure to be
Reported back to her, by two or three
Among us here; by whom I needn't say;
In all such matters women find a way.
And anyhow my brains would hardly run
To telling you, and so my story's done.'

The Squire's Prologue

'Squire, come up and if you feel disposed
Say something about love – it is supposed
You know as much of that as any man.'
'O no, sir,' he replied, 'but what I can
I'll do with all my heart. I won't rebel
Against your pleasure; I've a tale to tell.
Have me excused if I should speak amiss,
My will is good and, look, my tale is this.'

The Squire's Tale

PART I

At Tzarev in the land of Tartary
There dwelt a king at war with Muscovy
Which brought the death of many a doughty man.
This noble king was known as Cambuskan★
And in his time enjoyed such great renown
That nowhere in that region up or down
Was one so excellent in everything;
Nothing he lacked belonging to a king.
  As to the faith in which he had been born
He kept such loyalties as he had sworn,
Then he was powerful and wise and brave,
Compassionate and just, and if he gave
His word he kept it, being honourable,
The same to all, benevolent, and stable
As is a circle's centre; and in a fight
As emulous as any squire or knight,

315

Young, personable, fresh and fortunate,
Maintaining such a kingliness of state
There never was his match in mortal man.
   This noble king, this Tartar Cambuskan,
Begat two sons on Elpheta his wife.
The elder bore the name of Algarsyf,
The other son, the younger, Cambalo.
He had another child, a daughter though,
Youngest of all; her name was Canace.
To tell her beauty is too much for me,
Lying beyond what tongue of mine can sing;
I dare not undertake so high a thing.
My English too is insufficient for it,
It asks a rhetorician to explore it,
A poet in the colours of that art,
To give a fair account of every part.
I am none such, I speak as best I can.
   Now it so happened that when Cambuskan
Had borne his diadem for twenty years,
As was his usual custom it appears,
He had the feast of his nativity
Proclaimed throughout the land of Tartary.
It was the Ides of March, in the new year;
Phoebus the sun shone happily and clear
For he was near his point of exaltation
In face of Mars, and there he held his station
In *Aries*, and that's a sultry sign.
Cheerful the weather, vigorous and benign,
And all the birds against the sunny sheen,
What with the season and the early green,
Sang the loud canticles of their affection,
For, as it seemed, at last they had protection
Against the sword of winter, keen and cold.
   This noble Cambuskan of whom I told
Sat on his dais in a royal robe,
High on his throne with diadem and globe,
And there held feast in all his power enfurled,
And there was nothing like it in the world.
If I should pause to tell of his array
The task would occupy a summer's day,
Nor is there any need I should enforce
Attention to his banquet, course on course,
Or number the quaint dishes they put on,
The heron-chick, the richly roasted swan,

For in that country veteran knights report
There are some meats esteemed the daintiest sort
Though in this country their esteem is small,
But there is none who could report it all,
So let me not delay you – it is prime
Of day, it would be fruitless loss of time.
   Let me retrace my footsteps to their source.
It happened, close upon the second course,
As the king sat with his nobility
Listening to instruments of minstrelsy
That made delicious music in the hall,
Suddenly at the door in sight of all
There came a knight upon a steed of brass
Bearing a mirror, broad and made of glass.
Upon his thumb he had a golden ring
And at his side a naked sword a-swing,
And up he rode and reached the royal table.
In all that hall not one of them was able
To speak a word for wonder at this knight;
They waited, young and old, and watched the sight.
   This stranger-knight so suddenly presented,
Bare-headed, armed and richly ornamented,
Saluted king and queen and nobles all
In order as they sat about the hall
With such deep reverence and comely grace
Not only in his speech but in his face,
That Gawain,* ever courteous, ever bland,
Though he were come again from fairyland
A greater courtesy could not have shown.
And thus before High Table and the throne
He gave his message in a manly voice
In his own language, with a perfect choice
Of phrase, faultless in syllable or letter;
And, that his story might appear the better,
Gesture and word were fitted each to each,
As taught to those that learn the art of speech,
And though I lack his talent to beguile
And cannot climb over so tall a stile,
I say, as to their general content,
The words I use amount to what he meant,
So far as I can trust my memory.
   'The King of India and Araby,
Who is my sovereign lord, this solemn day
Salutes your Majesty as best he may

A royal game of cards in the fourteenth century. Playing cards do not seem to have reached Western Europe from the East until the thirteenth century and in Chaucer's time were still used mainly only by the upper classes.

And sends you here in honour of your feast,
Through me who am your servant, though the least,
This steed of brass that easily may run
Within the natural circuit of the sun,
That is to say in four and twenty hours,
Wherever you may wish, in drought or showers,
And bear your body to whatever place
Your heart desires, at a gentle pace
And without hurt to you through foul or fair.
If you should wish to fly, and mount the air
As does an eagle when it seeks to soar,
This very steed will bear you as before
In perfect safety on your chosen track,
Though you should fall asleep upon his back,
And, when you twist this pin, return again.
    'He that devised it had a cunning brain;
He watched through many a change of constellation
Ere finding one to suit his operation,
And he knew many a magic seal and spell.
    'This mirror that I have in hand as well
Is such that those who look in it may see
The coming shadow of adversity
Upon yourself and kingdom, it will show
You plainly who is friend and who is foe.
More than all this, if any lady bright
Has set on any man her heart's delight,
If he be false she shall perceive his shady
And treacherous conduct, and the other lady,
So openly, nothing will hide his treason.
And so, against this lusty summer season,
This mirror and this ring are sent by me,
As you behold, to Lady Canace
Your excellent and lovely daughter here.
    'The virtue of the ring, as will appear,
Stands in this point; if she be not averse
To wear it on her thumb or in her purse,
There is no bird that flies beneath the reach
Of heaven but she will understand its speech
And know its meaning openly and plain
And in its language answer it again.
Of every rooted grass that grows on earth
She shall have knowledge too and test its worth
In sickness, or on wounds, however wide.
    'This naked sword here hanging at my side

318

Retains the property to cut and bite
The armour of whatever man you smite,
Though it were thicker than a branching oak;
And when a man is wounded by its stroke,
Nothing can heal him till the sword is laid
In mercy flat upon the wound it made,
Where he was hurt. This is as much to say
Lay the blade flat, turning the edge away,
And stroke the wound, and you will see it close;
This is the very truth in sober prose.
While it is in your hold it cannot fail.'
    The stranger-knight, thus having told his tale,
Rode out of hall, dismounted and had done.
His steed of brass that glittered like the sun
Stood in the courtyard still as any stone.
They gave the knight a chamber of his own,
Unarmed and feasted him, and in a while
His gifts were carried forth in royal style,
That is to say the mirror and the sword,
And brought to the high tower under ward
Of certain officers appointed for it.
    As for the ring, in solemn pomp they bore it
To Canace herself who sat at table.
But I assure you all it is no fable;
That horse of brass could not be raised or slewed
But stood its ground as if it had been glued.
It was of no avail to drive or bully,
Use windlass, engine, artifice or pulley;
And why? Because they didn't know the dodge.
And so they were obliged to let it lodge
Below until the knight had shown them how
To shift him; you shall hear it, but not now.
    Great was the crowd that swarmed about in force
To gaze upon the stationary horse.
It was as tall, as broad, and of a length
Just as proportionable to its strength
As any courser bred in Lombardy,
Quick-eyed, as horsely as a horse can be,
Like an Apulian steed, as highly bred.
And I assure you that from tail to head
Nothing could be improved by art or nature,
So they supposed at least who saw the creature.
But yet the wonder nothing could surpass
Was how it went if it were made of brass.

A bronze cooking pot. A similar
cauldron can be seen in use in
picture (8), in the colour section
'Domestic Life: Games and
Pastimes'.

Some thought it came from fairyland's dominions.
  Various men gave various opinions,
As many heads, so many fallacies.
They murmured round it like a swarm of bees
And guessed according to their fantasy,
Or quoted snatches of old poetry
Saying it was like Pegasus of old,
The fabled horse that flew on wings of gold,
Or it was Sinon's horse by whose employ
The Greeks had brought destruction upon Troy,
As one may read in those old epic tales.
Said one of them, 'My spirit fairly quails
To think there may be men-of-arms within it
Plotting to take our town this very minute.
It would be well if such a thing were known.'
Another, whispering to his friend alone,
Muttered, 'He's wrong. More like some apparition
Or trick-illusion made by a magician,
Like what these jugglers do at feasts of state.'
  Thus they kept up the jangle of debate
As the illiterate are wont to do
When subtler things are offered to their view
Than their unletteredness can comprehend;
They reach the wrong conclusions in the end.
  Some wondered at the mirror and its power
(It had been taken to the master-tower)
And how such things could be foreseen in it.
Another said that such a thing could fit
Quite naturally by the skilled direction
Of angles, by the laws of light-reflection,
And said there was another such in Rome.
Then they referred to many a learned tome
By Aristotle and by Alhazen
And Witelo and other learned men*
Who when alive had written down directives
For use of cunning mirrors and perspectives,
As anyone can tell who has explored
These authors. Others wondered at the sword
That had the power to pierce through anything,
And spoke of Telephus the Mysian king,
And of Achilles and his marvellous spear,
Able to heal no less than it could shear,
Exactly like this sword, that at a word
Could wound a man or heal him, as you heard.

Wrestling in the open air was a
favourite pastime.

They spoke of sundry ways of hardening metal
By various ointments, and they tried to settle
The times and methods for this mystery,
Which are unknown, at any rate to me.
    And then they spoke about the magic ring
Given to Canace, a marvellous thing,
Concluding thus: 'None such, as one supposes,
Was ever known; but Solomon and Moses
Were said to have been cunning in that art.'
Thus people spoke in little groups apart;
And others said how strange it was to learn
That glass is made out of the ash of fern,
Though bearing no resemblances to glass;
But being used to this they let it pass,
The argument declined, they ceased to wonder,
Like those who speculate on what makes thunder,
Ebb, flood or mist, how gossamer is blown,
Or anything until the cause is known.
And so they guessed and judged as they were able
Until the king began to rise from table.
    Phoebus was over the meridian line;
It was the hour of the ascending sign
Of royal *Leo* with his Aldiran,*
And this great Tartar king, this Cambuskan,
Rose from the board in all his majesty.
Before him went a blare of minstrelsy
Until he reached the presence-room surrounded
By divers instruments, and these were sounded
So sweetly it was heaven to those that listened.
Children of Venus glided there and glistened
In happy dance, for she was mounted high
In *Piscis*, and looked down with friendly eye.
    The noble king was seated on his throne;
The stranger-knight was fetched and he alone
Was chosen forth to dance with Canace.
Great was the revelling and jollity,
It went beyond all dull imagination;
Only a man who knows the exaltation
Of serving love, a man as fresh as May,
A gamesome one, could tell of their array.
    For who could paint the circling of their dances,
So foreign to us, or the countenances
So subtle-smooth in their dissimulations
For fear of jealousy's insinuations?

No one but Launcelot and he is dead.
Pass over them and leave them there to tread
Their long delight, beyond all words of mine.
So on they danced till it was time to dine.

    The steward bids them hurry with the spices
And fetch the wine, the minstrelsy entices,
The ushers and the squires in a pack
Run off and bring the wines and spices back.
They ate and drank, and having left the table
They sought the temple, as was reasonable.
The service done, they feasted all day long.
Why should I tell you what they served the throng?
Everyone knows that at a royal feast
There's plenty for the greatest and the least,
And delicacies more than I would know.

    His supper done, the king proposed to go
And see this horse of brass, with all his rout
Of lords and ladies standing round about.

    Such the amazement at this brazen horse,
Not since the siege of Troy had run its course,
At which another horse amazed her men,
Had there been such astonishment as then.
The king at last put question to the knight
As to this courser's properties and might,
Begging him to explain the beast's control.

    This horse began to dance and caracole
Under its master's hand that held the rein;
He answered, 'Sir, there's nothing to explain
But this; if you would ride it far or near,
Just twirl this pin that's standing in its ear,
As when we are alone I soon can show,
Then name the country where you wish to go,
Or else the place, wherever you would ride,
And having reached it, if you so decide,
Bid him descend and twirl another pin,
For all the mechanism lies therein,
And down he'll go to carry out your will
And having reached the ground will stand stock-still.
Whatever then the world may do or say
He cannot thence be dragged or borne away.

    'To make him move or seek some other place
Twirl this pin and he'll vanish into space,
Yes, disappear completely out of sight,
Yet will return to you by day or night

If you should please to summon him again
After a manner that I shall explain
To you alone, and that without delay;
Ride when you will, there is no more to say.'
    The knight informed the king as he had said,
And when he had it firmly in his head
How to control the beast in everything
How blithe, how happy was this doughty king!
And he returned to revel as before.
Then they took off the bridle that it wore
And laid it with his treasures in the tower.
The horse then vanished; it's beyond my power
To tell you how, you get no more from me.
And thus I leave, in joy and jollity,
This Cambuskan, feasting with all his train
Till dawn of day had almost sprung again.

PART II

The nourisher of all digestion, Sleep,
Began to wink upon them. 'Drinking deep,'
He said, 'and heavy toil, for slumber call.'
And with a yawning mouth he kissed them all,
Saying, 'To bed, to bed, it is the hour
Of my dominion, blood is in its power.
Cherish your blood,' he whispered, 'nature's friend.'
    They thanked him yawningly and in the end
By twos and threes they wandered off to rest
As sleep ordained, they took it for the best.
What dreams they had shall not be told, for me;
Their heads were full of the fumosity
That causes dreams which are of no account.
And so they lay and slept until the fount
Of day filled heaven, all but Canace;
For she was temperate and womanly
And having kissed her father, had departed
And sought her rest before the evening started.
She had no wish to pale her lovely cheek
Or greet the morrow colourless and bleak.
    She slept her beauty sleep and then awoke,
And at her waking, in her heart there spoke
Such joy about her glass and magic ring
That twenty times she felt her colour spring.

Elegant dancers representing Mirth,
Gladness, Courtesy and a Lover
from the *Roman de la Rose*.

323

She had dreamed visions from the deep impression
Made by the magic glass, her new possession.
　　So ere the sun began its upward glide
She called the waiting-woman at her side
And told her that it was her wish to rise.
　　Like all old women, glad to be as wise
As are their mistresses, the crone replied,
'What, madam, do you mean to go outside
This early? Everyone is still asleep.'
'I will arise,' she said, 'I cannot keep
In bed or sleep, I want to walk about.'
　　Her woman called the servants in a rout
And up they got – some ten or twelve there were –
And up rose Canace as fresh and fair,
As bright and ruddy as the early sun
When by some four degrees it has begun
To rise into the *Ram*. It was no higher
When she was ready; forth at her desire
With easy pace, and gowned to greet the May,
She lightly went to walk on foot, and play.
Some five or six were with her, and, content,
Forth by an alley through the park she went.
　　There was a mist that glided from the earth
And gave the sun a huge and ruddy girth,
And yet it was so beautiful a sight
That all their hearts were lifted in delight,
What with the season and the dawn-light springing
And noise of all the birds in heaven singing,
For instantly she knew what they were saying
And understood the meaning in their maying.
　　The knot and gist of every tale that's told,
If lingered out till all desire be cold
In those that listen and the moment's past,
Savours the less the longer it may last
By fulsomeness of its prolixity,
And for that reason as it seems to me
I ought to reach that knot of which I'm talking
And make an end, and quickly, of her walking.
　　Amidst a tree so parched it seemed of chalk
Where Canace came dallying in her walk
Above her head a falcon sat on high.
This bird began so piteously to cry
That all the woods re-echoed her distress.
And she had scourged herself with pitiless

Chess is not usually associated with violence but here (opposite) the artist depicts a quarrel in which one of the players has lost his temper, and presumably the game, has picked up the board and smashed it on his opponent's head.

Eigneuro dites chancon dnt les ver
sont plaisant
Gzacieuse et bien faicte veritable et
plaisant
Nest mie de la flable ancelot et tristant.

Beating of her wings; a crimson flood
Poured down and painted all the tree with blood,
As ever and again with scream and shriek
She bent and tore her body with her beak.
There is no tiger, no, nor cruel beast
That dwells in wood or forest, west or east,
But would have wept if weep indeed it could
In pity of her, shrieking as she stood.
And never yet has been a man to tell
– If only I could describe a falcon well! –
Of such another bird, as fair to see
Both in its plumage and nobility
Of form and attribute, or find her twin.

It seemed this falcon was a peregrine
From foreign country; bleeding there she stood,
Fainting from time to time from loss of blood,
Till she had nearly fallen from the tree.

This beautiful king's daughter, Canace,
That on her finger bore the curious ring
By which she understood whatever thing
Birds in their language said, and which could teach
Her how to answer in their natural speech,
Had understood the words the falcon said;
The pity of it almost struck her dead.

Up to the tree she hastened at her cries
And looking with compassion in her eyes
Held out her lap towards it, knowing well
The bird was like to faint, and if she fell
For lack of blood, she would be there at hand
Below the branches. Long she seemed to stand
And wait, and then at last began to talk,
As you shall hear, and thus addressed the hawk.

'What is the cause, if you are free to tell,
That puts you to the furious pain of Hell?'
Said Canace to the poor bird above.
'Is it for grief in death, or loss of love?
For as I think these have the greatest part
Among the sorrows of a noble heart.
Other misfortunes one may well contemn,
The way is open for avenging them,
So that it must be either love or loss
That is occasion for your cruel cross,
For none, I see, has hunted you to-day.
God's love, have pity on yourself, or say

How I can help you. Neither east nor west
Was ever bird or beast so sore distressed
That ever I saw, or in such piteous plight;
It kills my heart to witness such a sight.
I feel such great compassion, come to me,
Come down for love of God and leave the tree,
For as I am the daughter of a king,
If I knew verily the cause and spring
Of your misfortunes, were it in my power
I would make all things well this very hour.
Great God of nature, help me so to do!
I shall find herbs enough and salves for you
To heal your wounds, and quickly if you will.'
    The falcon gave a shriek more piteous still
Than any yet and fell to earth; she lay
Stone-still for she had fainted dead away,
Till, lifted up by Canace and taken
Into her lap, the bird began to waken,
And being recovered had the strength to talk,
Answering in the language of a hawk:
    'That pity is swift to course in noble heart,
Feeling the likeness of another's smart,
Is daily proved, as anyone can see,
Both by experience and authority,
For gentleness of birth and breeding shows
Itself in gentleness; you feel my woes
As I can see, and sure it is a fashion
Well fitting a princess to show compassion
As you have done, my lovely Canace,
In true and womanly benignity
That nature planted in your disposition.
And in no hope to better my condition
But to obey your generosity,
Also that others may be warned by me,
As lions may take warning when a pup★
Is punished, I will therefore take it up
And make a full confession of my woe
While yet there is the time before I go.'
    And ever while the falcon said her say
The other wept as she would melt away
Until the falcon bade her to be still
And sighing spoke according to her will.
    'Where I was bred – alas, the cruel day! –
And fostered in a rock of marble grey

This interior of a rich man's house
again illustrates the sparseness
of the furniture. The master of the
house is giving orders to two
servants.

Travel

The medieval traveller needed to be tough and resourceful whether he moved on foot, on horseback or on a ship at sea. Roads were very poor, for their repair was usually the responsibility of the great landowners, including the monasteries, and was often neglected. The Black Death, the war with France and the resulting shortage of labour led to a general decay in the highways. Once in Chaucer's time (1380) Parliament could not meet because the state of the roads prevented the attendance of sufficient members. Chaucer's pilgrims rode to Canterbury on horseback – the word 'canter' comes from the leisurely pace at which mounted pilgrims rode – but most pilgrims travelled on foot, usually in groups for safety. Trains of packhorses carrying merchants' goods, heavily guarded, were a familiar sight, as must have been bodies of bowmen and spearmen following their leaders to and from the battlefields of France during the Hundred Years War.

2

1

There was a constant traffic to and fro across the English Channel, not only because of the war but in trade with Flanders and elsewhere in Europe. By present standards the ships were mere cockleshells (3) and the passengers, packed on the open decks, must have suffered agonies in the rough seas of the Channel. Although navigational methods were crude, sophisticated instruments were becoming more used. The picture (2) is of a brass quadrant bearing the date 1399 on which is depicted the badge of Richard II. Chaucer himself seems to have been interested in scientific instruments, for in 1391, when he was Clerk of the King's Works, he wrote a prose *Treatise on the Astrolabe* for his son Lewis. The astrolabe, later replaced by the sextant, was an instrument for observing the stars. The instrument shown in (1) is a medieval military sphere made of brass and

4 5▶

6

7

gilt brass with a compass in its base.

Some idea of land travel can be gained from the three pictures at the top of the next page. Picture (4) is of a country cart driven by a monkey – medieval illuminators often used animals, especially monkeys and hares, in human roles. Interesting are the high wheels with large treads, forerunners of the modern caterpillar tracks, useful on muddy fields and roads. Next (5) is a baggage wagon obviously, from the arms displayed, carrying the goods of a nobleman. The picture (6) of transport for royal ladies shows an ornate covered wagon, drawn by five horses and escorted by a group of gentlemen. The lady at the rear of the wagon is handing out a pet dog to one of the escort, probably to give it a run, and another dog released earlier seems to be eating scraps thrown from the wagon. Less regal, but no less impressive, is the form of transport depicted in (7). The passenger, evidently a lady of high rank, is being carried in a horse litter. It is not difficult to imagine the discomfort involved in such a means of transport with no springs and on an ill-kept road. Here again the vehicle is strongly escorted, a necessary precaution in those days. In 1285 King Edward I ordered that the highways to market towns

should be cleared of underwood for 200 feet on each side to make ambush by robbers more difficult.

Travellers sought shelter at night, often according to their station in life, in the local great house, monasteries or inns and taverns. There were many of the latter, usually displaying a sign, often a bush, hung over the door. In the inns travellers were expected to supply their own fuel, bedding (most travellers slept in the nude) and provisions, though there was a plentiful supply of drink which must have led to many a convivial evening. Picture (8) on the preceding page could well illustrate one of them with the tapster being kept fully occupied in the cellar. Despite the difficulties of transport the carriage of wine cost only about one penny per tun per mile. Chaucer himself was knowledgeable about wine as can be seen in 'The Pardoner's Tale' – after all his father was a vintner and he had lived in France – and it was perhaps appropriate that in 1398 the King granted him a tun of wine yearly for his lifetime, alas, only another two years.

Picture (9) shows passengers paying toll on landing at a foreign port. A seated customs officer holds a purse while the fee is taken by one of the armed guards. Customs duties must have been a very familiar subject to Chaucer. The customs duty levied on the export of wool was one of the principal sources of revenue for the King in providing the sinews of war in France and in 1374 the poet was appointed to the important post of Comptroller of the Customs and Subsidy of Wools, Skins and Leathers for the Port of London. The passengers paying the toll in the picture are probably pilgrims, for two of them are carrying the long staff which was one of the badges of a pilgrim. The staff would have been blessed by a priest before the pilgrim's departure with the words, 'Take this staff, the support of your journey, and of the labour of your pilgrimage, that you may be able to conquer all the bands of the enemy, and to come safely to the threshold of the saints to which you desire to go, and, your journey obediently performed, return to us with joy.' The pilgrims in the picture may have been on their way to the Holy Land or to the shrine of St James of Compostella in Spain, a favourite attraction of pilgrims. Picture (10) shows an abbot riding sedately through the countryside, his right hand raised in blessing.

So tenderly that nothing troubled me,
I never knew the word adversity
Till I could wing aloft into the sky.
   'There was a tercelet* that lived nearby
Who seemed a very well of gentle breeding;
Yet he was filled with treachery, exceeding
In all that's false. He wore the humble cloak
And colour of true faith in all he spoke,
An eagerness to please me and to serve.
Who could think such a hawk had power to swerve?
Dyed in the grain they were, those treacherous powers,
Just as a serpent hides itself in flowers,
Ready to strike, and waits the moment fit,
Just so this god of love, this hypocrite,
Kept up all ceremonious obligations,
The sweet observances and protestations
That make the music of a gentle love.
   'But as a sepulchre is white above
The rotting corpse within, as we are told,
Just so this hypocrite blew hot and cold
And in this way pursued his treacherous bent;
None knew, unless the devil, what he meant.
   'So long I heard his weeping and complaining,
So long beheld the service he was feigning,
My heart, too foolish-pitiful to sound him,
All innocent of the treachery that crowned him,
Fearing his death (for so it seemed to me),
Believed his oaths, believed him trustworthy,
And granted him my love, on this condition,
That my good name, my honour and position
In public and in private had no hurt;
That is to say, according to desert
In him, my heart and thought were his for ever,
But otherwise God knows, and he knew, never.
I took his heart, exchanging it for mine.
   'How true the saying in the ancient line,
"Thieves' thoughts are not the thoughts of honest men",
For seeing things had gone so far by then,
That I had fully granted him my love
In such a way as I have told above
And had as freely given my heart as he
Had sworn his own was given up to me,
Straightway this tiger with his double heart
Fell on his knees and played the humble part

This decorative strip from the Luttrell Psalter shows two swans floating serenely on a lake.

With such devout and bashful reverence
He seemed a noble lover, one whose sense
Was ravished, one would think, for very joy.
  'Not Jason, no, nor Paris, Prince of Troy
– Did I say Jason? Sure, no other man
Since Lamech was, Lamech who first began,
So it is said, the game of loving two,
Has ever, since the world itself was new,
Thought or contrived the twenty thousandth part
Of counterfeited sophistry and art
As did my love. None fit to tie his shoe
Where there was double-faced deceit to do,
Not one to pay the thanks he paid to me!
And yet his manner was a heaven to see
For any woman, be she ne'er so wise,
Painted and trim and barbered to the eyes
Both in his words and in his countenance.
  'I loved him, then, for his obedient glance
And for the truth I judged was in his heart,
So that at any time he felt the smart
Of pain, were it so little as a breath,
And I was told, it seemed the twist of death
Tore at my heart. And so it grew to this,
My will became the instrument of his,
That is to say my will obeyed his mood
In everything, as far as reason would,
Within the bounds of honour; nearer, nearer
We grew together, none so dear, none dearer
Than he, God knows, and none shall ever be!
  'This lasted for two years perhaps, or three,
And I supposed nothing of him but good.
But at its final ending thus it stood:
As fortune willed, he had to leave the land
In which I lived. Ah, never make demand
Of what I felt in sorrow, ask no question,
I cannot picture it, for no suggestion

331

Would paint the truth, but this I boldly say,
I knew the pain of death that fatal day,
Such was my grief because he had to go.
　'He took his leave with such a world of woe,
So sorrowfully, that I felt assured
His feelings were no less than I endured
Hearing him speak, seeing his change of hue.
I was so certain he was wholly true,
So certain he would come to me again
And very soon, if ever truth were plain.
　'And there were reasons too for him to go.
Reasons of honour; it is often so.
I made a virtue of necessity
And took it well, knowing it had to be.
I sought to hide my sorrow, as in fitness
I should, and took his hand – St John my witness! –
And said, "Lo, I am yours, and though we sever,
Be such as I have been and shall be ever."
　'What he replied I need not now rehearse;
For who could have said better, or done worse?
Yes, what he said was well enough, and soon
The thing was done. Ah, "long should be your spoon
When supping with the devil!" so they say.
　'And so at last he went upon his way
And forth he flew, whither it seemed him best.
Yet later, when he had a mind to rest,
I think he must have had the text in mind
That "everything, according to its kind,
Seeks its own pleasure", so they say, I guess.
Man by his nature seeks new-fangledness,
As do those birds that people keep in cages;
One cares for them day-long and one engages
To get them straw as fair and soft as silk
And gifts of sugar, honey, bread and milk,
Yet on the instant that the slide is up,
The foot will spurn away the proffered cup
And to the woods they fly for worms to eat,
Such is their longing for new-fangled meat.
The love for novelty their natures gave them;
No royalty of blood has power to save them.
　'So with this tercelet falcon, woe the day!
Although of gentle birth, though fresh and gay,
Handsome, adoring, good in everything,
One day he saw a kite upon the wing

The mitre worn by William of Wykeham who founded Winchester College in 1378 and New College Oxford in 1379. The recognized headgear of bishops, mitres were also worn by certain abbots in the Middle Ages.

And suddenly he felt a love so hot
For this same kite that mine was clean forgot,
And thus he broke his faith in foul delight
And thus my love is servant to a kite
And I am lost and there's no remedy!'
   She ceased and with a scream of agony
She swooned away in her protectress' arms.
Great the lamenting for her falcon's harms
That Canace and all her ladies made,
Not knowing how to soothe her or persuade.
   Canace bore her homeward in her lap;
In softest plasters she began to wrap
The falcon's wounds that her own beak had torn,
And Canace went delving eve and morn
For herbs out of the ground; new salves she made
From precious grasses of the finest shade
To heal her hawk, indeed both day and night
She lavished on her all the care she might.
   Beside her bed she made a little mew
To house the falcon, hung with velvet blue★
To signify fair faith, so often seen
In women, and the mew was painted green
Without, with pictures of these treacherous fowls
Like tytyfers and tercelets and owls,
And there were magpies painted too, to chide
Them spitefully, to chatter and deride.
   Thus I leave Canace to nurse her hawk
And of her ring at present I will talk
No more, till I return to make it plain
How the poor falcon got her love again
Repentant, as the tale I tell will show,
Through the good offices of Cambalo,
Son of the king of whom I have made mention.
But for the moment it is my intention
To tell adventures and the feats of war,
Such marvels as you never heard before.
   First I will tell you about Cambuskan
And all the cities that he overran;
Then I shall speak of Algarsyf his son
And next of Theodora whom he won
To wife, and of the perils he must pass
On her account, helped by the steed of brass.
And after of another Cambalo
Who fought her brothers in the lists and so

At last won Canace by might and main.
And where I stopped I shall begin again.

PART III

Apollo whirled his chariot on high
Up through the house of Mercury, the sly —

Words of the Franklin to the Squire and of the Host to the Franklin

'Well! you have done yourself great credit, Squire,
Most like a gentleman! I do admire
Your powers,' said the Franklin. 'For a youth,
You speak most feelingly, and that's the truth;
In my opinion there is no one here
Will equal you in eloquence, or near,
If you should live. God prosper all that's in you
And may your talents flourish and continue!
It's all so dainty, it delighted me.
 'I have a son, and by the Trinity
I'd rather than have twenty pounds' worth land
(Though it should fall right now into my hand)
That he could show the excellent discretion
That you have shown. A plague upon possession!
What use is property if you're a dunce?
I've spoken to him sharply, more than once
And shall again. He doesn't like advice,
All he can do is squander and play dice
And lose his money, at his present stage.
He'd rather romp and chatter with a page
Than entertain a serious conversation
Or learn to be a gentleman. Vocation –'
'Franklin, a straw for your gentility!'
Remarked our Host, 'You know as well as me
That each must tell a tale or two at least
Or break his word and miss the final feast.'
 'I know it well,' the Franklin said again,
'I beg you not to hold me in disdain,
Just for a word or two to this young man.'
 'Well, no more words, and tell us if you can
Some story of your own.' 'Glad to obey,
Since it's your wish; here's what I have to say.
Nothing could move me to oppose your will,
Save in so far as I may lack the skill;
I hope you may take pleasure in my stuff,
And if you do, I'll know it's good enough.'

The Franklin's Prologue

Of old the noble Bretons in their days
Delighted in adventures and made lays
In rhyme, according to their early tongue,
Which to the sound of instruments were sung,
Or read in silence for their own delight.
And I remember one, if I am right,
Which I will render you as best I can.
    But, sirs, I'm not a cultivated man,
And so from the beginning I beseech
You to excuse me my untutored speech.
They never taught me rhetoric I fear,
So what I have to say is bare and clear.
I haven't slept on Mount Parnassus, no.
Nor studied Marcus Tullius Cithero.★
I can't give colouring to my words – indeed
Such colours as I know adorn the mead,
Or else are those they use in dyes or paint.
'Colours of rhetoric' to me seem quaint,
I have no feeling for such things; but still
Here is my story, listen if you will.

The Franklin's Tale

In Brittany, or as it then was called,
Armorica, there was a knight enthralled
To love, who served his lady with his best
In many a toilsome enterprise and quest,
Suffering much for her ere she was won.
   She was among the loveliest under sun
And came from kindred of so high a kind
He scarce had the temerity of mind
To tell her of his longing and distress.
But in the end she saw his worthiness
And felt such pity for the pains he suffered,
Especially for the meek obedience offered,
That privately she fell into accord
And took him for her husband and her lord
– The lordship husbands have upon their wives.
And to enhance the bliss of both their lives
He freely gave his promise as a knight
That he would never darken her delight

By exercising his authority
Against her will, or showing jealousy,
But would obey in all with simple trust
As any lover of a lady must;
Save that his sovereignty in name upon her
He should preserve, lest it should shame his honour.

    She thanked him, and with great humility
Replied, 'Sir, since you show a courtesy
So fair in proffering me so free a rein,
God grant there never be betwixt us twain,
Through any fault of mine, dispute or strife.
Sir, I will be your true and humble wife,
Accept my truth of heart, or break, my breast!'
Thus were they both in quiet and at rest.

    For there's one thing, my lords, it's safe to say;
Lovers must each be ready to obey
The other, if they would long keep company.
Love will not be constrained by mastery;
When mastery comes the god of love anon
Stretches his wings and farewell! he is gone.
Love is a thing as any spirit free;
Women by nature long for liberty
And not to be constrained or made a thrall,
And so do men, if I may speak for all.

    Whoever's the most patient under love
Has the advantage and will rise above
The other; patience is a conquering virtue.
The learned say that, if it not desert you,
It vanquishes what force can never reach;
Why answer back at every angry speech?
No, learn forbearance or, I'll tell you what,
You will be taught it, whether you will or not.
No one alive – it needs no arguing –
But sometimes says or does a wrongful thing;
Rage, sickness, influence of some malign
Star-constellation, temper, woe or wine
Spur us to wrongful words or make us trip.
One should not seek revenge for every slip,
And temperance from the times must take her schooling
In those that are to learn the art of ruling.

    And so this wise and honourable knight
Promised forbearance to her that he might
Live the more easily, and she, as kind,
Promised there never would be fault to find

An example of the medieval illustrator's use of contemporary settings for classical subjects. The story is of the Rape of Lucrece – the furnishings, etc. are medieval.

In her. Thus in this humble, wise accord
She took a servant when she took a lord,
A lord in marriage in a love renewed
By service, lordship set in servitude;
In servitude? Why no, but far above
Since he had both his lady and his love,
His lady certainly, his wife no less,
To which the law of love will answer 'yes.'

So in the happiness that they had planned
He took his wife home to his native land
With joyful ease and reached his castle there
By Penmarch Point, not far from Finisterre,
And there they lived in amity unharried.

Who can recount, unless he has been married,
The ease, the prosperous joys of man and wife?
A year or more they lived their blissful life
Until it chanced the knight that I have thus
Described and who was called Arveragus
Of Caer-rhud, planned to spend a year or so
In Britain (no, not Brittany), to go
And seek high deeds of arms and reputation
In honour; that was all his inclination.
He stayed two years, at least the book says thus.

Now I will pause about Arveragus
And turn to speak of Dorigen his wife
Who loved her husband as her own heart's life.

She wept his absence, sighed for him and pined
As noble wives will do when so inclined;
She mourned, lay wakeful, fasted and lamented,
Strained by a passion that could be contented
Only by him, and set the world at naught.
Her friends who knew the burden of her thought
Brought her such consolations as they might;
They preached to her, they told her day and night,
'You'll kill yourself for nothing.' Such relief
And comfort as is possible to grief
They fuss about to find, and finding, press
Upon her to relieve her heaviness.

Slow is the process, it is widely known,
By which a carver carves his thought in stone,
Yet cuts at last the figure he intended;
And slowly too, thus soothed and thus befriended,
Her soul received the print of consolation
Through hope and reason, and her long prostration

Turned to recovery, she ceased to languish;
She couldn't be always suffering such anguish.
  Besides, Arveragus as it befell
Sent letters to her saying all was well
And that he shortly would be home again;
Only for that her heart had died of pain.
  Her friends, seeing her grief began to ease,
Begged her for heaven's sake and on their knees
To come and roam about with them and play
And drive her darker fantasies away,
And finally she granted their request
And clearly saw it would be for the best.
  Her husband's castle fronted on the sea
And she would often walk in company
High on the ramparts, wandering at large.
Many a ship she saw and many a barge
Sailing such courses as they chose to go;
But these made part and parcel of her woe
And she would often say, 'Alas for me,
Is there no ship, so many as I see,
To bring me home my lord? For then my heart
Would find a cure to soothe its bitter smart.'
  At other times she used to sit and think
With eyes cast downward to the water's brink
And then her heart endured a thousand shocks
To see such jagged, black and grisly rocks,
So that she scarce could stand upon her feet.
Then she would refuge in some green retreat,
Lie on a lawn, and looking out to sea
With long, cold sighs, would murmur piteously:
  'Eternal God that by thy providence
Guidest the world in wise omnipotence,
They say of Thee that Thou hast nothing made
In vain; but, Lord, these fiendish rocks are laid
In what would rather seem a foul confusion
Of work than the creation and conclusion
Of One so perfect, God the wise and stable;
Why madest Thou thy work unreasonable?
These rocks can foster neither man nor beast
Nor bird, to north or south, to west or east;
Thy are a menace, useless, to my mind.
Lord, seest Thou not how they destroy mankind?
A hundred thousand bodies dead and rotten
Have met their death on them, though now forgotten;

Thy fairest work, wrecked on a rocky shelf,
Mankind, made in the image of Thyself.
It seemed that then Thou hadst great charity
Towards mankind; how therefore may it be
That Thou has fashioned means as these to harm them
That do no good, but injure and alarm them?
   'I know it pleases scholars to protest
In argument that all is for the best,
Though what their reasons are I do not know.
   'But O Thou God that madest wind to blow,
Preserve my husband, that is my petition!
I leave the learned to their disquisition.
But would to God these rocks so black, so grim,
Were sunk in Hell itself for sake of him!
They are enough to kill my heart with fear.'
Thus she would speak with many a piteous tear.
   Her friends could see it gave her no relief
To roam the shore, but added to her grief,
And so they sought amusement somewhere else.
They led her by the water-ways and wells
And many another scene of loveliness;
They danced, they played backgammon, they played chess.
   And so one sunny morning, as they'd planned,
They went into a garden near at hand
Where they had staged a picnic and supplied
Victuals enough and other things beside,
And there they lingered out the happy day.
   It was the morning of the sixth of May
And May had painted with her softest showers
A gardenful of leafiness and flowers;
The hand of man with such a cunning craft
Had decked this garden out in pleach and graft.
There never was a garden of such price
Unless indeed it were in Paradise.
The scent of flowers and the freshening sight
Would surely have made any heart feel light
That ever was born, save under the duress
Of sickness or a very deep distress;
Pleasure and beauty met in every glance.
   And after dinner they began to dance
And there was singing; Dorigen alone
Made her continual complaint and moan
For never among the dancers came to view
Her husband, he that was her lover too.

Serving a king at table.

Nevertheless she had to pass the day
In hope and let her sorrows slide away.
    Now in this dance, among the other men,
There danced a squire before Dorigen,
Fresher and jollier in his array,
In my opinion, than the month of May.
He sang and danced better than any man
There is or has been since the world began.
He was, what's more, if I could but contrive
To picture him, the handsomest man alive,
Young, strong and wealthy, mettlesome, discreet,
And popular as any you could meet;
And shortly, if I am to tell the truth,
All unbeknown to Dorigen, this youth
–A lusty squire and servant in the game
Of Venus, and Aurelius was his name –
Had loved her best of any for two years
And longer so it chanced, but still his fears
Had never let him bring the matter up;
He drank his penance down without cup.*
    He had despaired of her and dared not say
More of his passion than he might convey
In general terms, by saying that he burned
With love but that his love was not returned;
On all such themes he fashioned many a phrase,
Wrote songs, complaints, roundels and virelays
Saying his griefs were more than he dared tell,
He languished as a fury did in Hell,
And he must die, he said, as Echo did
For young Narcissus and the love she hid.
But in no other way, as said above,
Had he the courage to confess his love,
Save that perhaps from time to time at dances,
Where youth pays love's observances, his glances
It well may be would linger on her face
Beseechingly, as is the common case;
But she was unaware of what he meant.
    Nevertheless it happened, ere they went
Out of the garden, since he lived nearby
And was of good position, standing high
In honour and had known her from of old,
They fell in speech and he at last grew bold
And drew towards the purpose in his head.
Taking his opportunity he said:

A blind man with his dog.

342

Ladies, as well as gentlemen, went hawking and were advised by an expert not only to hold the hawk on the wrist but to do so 'day and night as continually as possible'. Here we see a lady tending her perched hawks.

'Madam, by God's green earth and all its treasure,
Had I imagined it could give you pleasure
That day, on which your lord Arveragus
Went over sea, then I, Aurelius,
Would have gone too, and never come again.
I know the service of my love is vain,
My recompense is but a bursting heart.
  'Madam, have pity on the pain and smart
Of love; a word from you can slay or save.
Would God your little feet stood on my grave!
There is no time to say what I would say;
Have mercy, sweetheart, chase me not away.'
  She looked at him with closer scrutiny
And answered, 'Are you saying this to me?
Can you intend it? Never,' she said, 'till now
Had I suspected that – what you avow.
But by the Lord that gave me soul and life
I never mean to prove a faithless wife
In word or deed if I can compass it.
I will be his to whom I have been knit.
Take that for final answer, as for me.'
  But after that she added playfully,
'And yet, Aurelius, by the Lord above
I might perhaps vouchsafe to be your love,
Since I perceive you groan so piteously.
Look; on the day the coasts of Brittany
Are stone by stone cleared of these hateful rocks
By you, so that no ship or vessel docks
In danger, when, I say, you clear the coast
So clean there's not a single stone to boast,
I'll love you more than any man on earth;
Accept my word in truth for all it's worth.'
  'Is there no other way than this?' said he.
  'No, by the Lord,' she said, 'that fashioned me.
For it will never happen, that I know;
So clear your heart of fancies, let them go.
How can a man find daintiness in life
Who goes about to love another's wife,
That can enjoy her body when he pleases?'
  Aurelius sighed again. The long uneases
Of lovers' woe returned on hearing this
And he replied with sorrowing emphasis,
'Madam, it is impossible to do,
So I must die a horrible death, for you.'

And on the word he turned and went away.
  Her other many friends came up to play
And wander with her through the leafy walk
Of alleys pleached, but of her lover's talk
They did not know. Revels began anew,
On till the dazzling sun had lost its hue
For the horizon reft it of its light;
This is as much to say that it was night.
So they went home delighted, all in joy
Except, alas, Aurelius, wretched boy.
  He sought his house, a sigh at every breath,
And could see no way of avoiding death.
Within himself he felt his heart turn cold
And falling on his knees began to hold
His hands to heaven and the upper air
In raving madness, and he said a prayer.
Excessive suffering had turned his head,
He knew not what he spoke, but this he said,
With pleading heart and pitiful, to one
And all the gods, beginning with the sun:
  'Apollo, God and Governor, whose power
Tends over every plant and herb and flower
And tree, appointing unto each by reason
Of thy celestial course, his time and season,
According as thy arc is low or high,
Lord Phoebus, in thy mercy cast an eye
On sad Aurelius, wretched and forlorn.
Look on me, Lord! My lady-love has sworn
To prove my death, though for no fault in me,
Unless, O Lord, in thy benignity
Thou pity a dying heart; for well I know,
Shouldest thou please, Lord Phoebus, to bestow
Thy mercy, thou canst help me best of all
Except my lady; listen to my call,
Vouchsafe to hear me, Lord, if I expound
A means of help and how it may be found.
  'Thy blissful sister, Luna the Serene,
Chief goddess of the ocean and its queen,
Though Neptune have therein his deity,
Is over him and empress of the sea.
Thou knowest, Lord, that just as her desire
Is to be lit and quickened by the fire,
For busily she follows after thee,
Just so the natural longing of the sea

The apothecary (one is shown here) was an important member of the community, compounding medicines and other brews from herbs and drugs hopefully for the comfort of the sick.

Follows on her and so is bound to do;
She is its goddess and the rivers' too.
   'And so, Lord Phoebus, this is my request,
Do me this miracle – or burst, my breast! –
That even now at thy next opposition
Which is to be in *Leo*, thou petition
Thy sister to bring floods so much increased
That they shall rise five fathom at the least
Above the highest rock that now appears
In Brittany, and let this last two years.
Then to my lady I can safely say,
"Keep truth with me, the rocks are all away."
   'Lord Phoebus, do this miracle for me now!
Beg her to go no faster, Lord, than thou;
I say, beseech thy sister that she go
No faster than thyself two years or so,
Then she will stay at full, and at their height
The spring floods will continue, day and night.
And should she not vouchsafe in such a way
The granting of my lady, then I pray
That she may sink the rocks, that they be drowned
Within her own dark region underground
Where Pluto dwells, for while they are above
I cannot hope to win my lady-love.
   'Barefoot to Delphi will I go and seek
Thy temple! See the tears upon my cheek,
Lord Phoebus, have compassion, grant my boon!'
And on the word he fell into a swoon
And long he lay upon the ground in trance.
   His brother who had heard of his mischance
Found him and caught him up, and off to bed
He carried him. With torment in his head
I leave this woeful creature, if to die
In desperation, he must choose, not I.
   Meanwhile Arveragus in health and power
Came honourably home, the very flower
Of chivalry, with other noble men.
How art thou blissful now, my Dorigen!
Thou hast a lusty husband to thy charms,
Thine own fresh knight, thy honoured man-at-arms
That loves thee as his life, in whom there springs
No inclination to imagine things
Or ask if anyone while he was out
Has talked to thee of love. But not a doubt

A jug made in the shape of a ram's head.

Entered his head; he had no thought in life
Except to dance and joust and cheer his wife
In blissful joy; and so I leave him thus
And turn again to sick Aurelius.
　　In furious torment, languishing away,
Two years and more, wretched Aurelius lay
Scarce with the strength to put his foot to ground.
No comfort during all that time he found
Save in his brother, who was a learned man
And privy to his grief since it began,
For to no other could Aurelius dare
Ever to say a word of his affair.
More secretly he guarded his idea
Than ever did Pamphilus for Galatea.*
To all appearances his breast was whole,
But a keen arrow stuck within his soul.
A wound that's only surface-healed can be
A perilous thing, you know, in surgery,
Unless the arrow-head be taken out.
　　His brother wept for him and fell in doubt
Of his recovery until by chance
It came to him that when he was in France
At Orleans – he was a student then –
He lusted in his heart like all young men
To study things prohibited, to read
In curious arts of magic, and indeed
Search every hole and corner with defiance
To learn the nature of that special science.
And he remembered how he took a look
One morning, in his study, at a book
On natural magic, which it chanced he saw
Because a friend, then bachelor-at-law
Though destined later to another trade,
Had hidden it in his desk. This book displayed
The workings of the moon; there were expansions
In detail on the eight-and-twenty mansions
Belonging to her – nonsense such as that,
For nowadays it isn't worth a gnat,
Since holy church has managed to retrieve us
And suffers no illusions now to grieve us.
　　And so, remembering this book by chance,
His heart as suddenly began to dance
For joy within him; quickly reassured,
He said, 'My brother surely shall be cured

For I am certain that there must be sciences
By which illusions can be made, appliances
Such as these subtle jugglers use in play
At banquets. Very often, people say,
These conjurors can bring into a large
And lofty hall fresh water and a barge
And there they seem to row it up and down;
Sometimes a lion, grim and tawny-brown,
Sometimes a meadow full of flowery shapes,
Sometimes a vine with white and purple grapes,
Sometimes a castle which by some device,
Though stone and lime, will vanish in a trice,
Or seem at least to vanish, out of sight.
   'So I conclude that if I only might
Discover some old fellow of the kind
Who has these moony mansions in his mind
At Orleans, or has some power above
All this, my brother might enjoy his love.
A learned man could hoodwink all beholders
With the illusion that the rocks and boulders
Of Brittany had vanished one and all
And ships along the brink could safely call,
Coming and going, and if it but endured
A day or two my brother could be cured.
She will be forced to recognize his claim
Or else she will at least be put to shame.'
   Why draw my story out? What need be said?
He went to where his brother lay in bed
And brought him so much comfort with his plot
To visit Orleans, that up he got
And started off at once upon the road
High in the hope of lightening his load.
   They neared the city; when it seemed to be
About two furlongs off, or maybe three,
They met a youngish scholar all alone
Who greeted them in Latin, in a tone
Of friendly welcome and he struck them dumb
In wonder with 'I know why you have come.'
And ere they went a step upon their way
He told them all they had in mind to say.
   The Breton scholar wanted to be told
About the friends that they had known of old
And he replied that they were all now dead;
He spoke with feeling, many tears were shed.

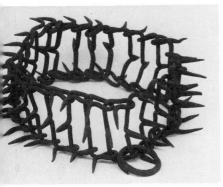

A boarhound collar, designed to protect the hound's throat and jugular vein from the boar's tusks.

Down from his horse Aurelius soon alighted
To follow the magician, who invited
Him and his brother home, set them at ease
And served them victuals; nothing that could please
Was lacking and Aurelius soon decided
He'd never seen a house so well provided.
　　And the magician caused there to appear
Before their supper, parks of forest deer
And he saw stags among them, antlered high,
The greatest ever seen by human eye.
He saw a hundred of them killed by hounds
And others, arrow-wounded, lay in mounds.
Next, when the deer had vanished, he was shown
A river bank and there a hawk was flown
By falconers; they saw a heron slain.
　　Then he saw knights at joust upon a plain
And after that Aurelius was entranced
At seeing his beloved as she danced
And he, it seemed, was dancing with her too.
And when the master of this magic view
Saw it was time he clapped his hands and banished
The figures, and farewell! our revels vanished.
Yet all the time they had not left the house
While being shown these sights so marvellous,
But sat within his study where there lay
His books about them; there were none but they.
　　The master called the squire who was to set
Their meal, and said, 'Is supper ready yet?
It's very near an hour I could swear,'
He added, 'since I told you to prepare,
When these two gentlemen came in with me
To see my study and my library.'
　　'Sir,' said the squire, 'it's ready, and you may
Begin, if it so please you, right away.'
'Then let us eat,' he said; 'that will be best;
These amorous people sometimes need a rest.'
　　After they'd eaten bargaining began;
What payment should this master-artisan
Have to remove the rocks of Brittany
From the Gironde to where the Seine meets sea?
He made it difficult and roundly swore
He'd take a thousand pounds for it or more,
He wasn't too eager even at that price.
Aurelius with his heart in paradise

Readily answered, 'Fie on a thousand pound!
I'd give the world, which people say is round,
The whole wide world, if it belonged to me;
Call it a bargain then, for I agree.
You shall be truly paid it, on my oath.
But look, be sure no negligence or sloth
Delay us here beyond to-morrow, now!'
The scholar gave him answer 'That I vow.'
    Aurelius went to bed in high delight
And rested soundly pretty well all night.
Tired by his journey and with hope retrieved
He slept, the troubles of his heart relieved.

Preparing a meal outside a building
which, from the sign, is an inn.
A servant is basting the geese being
roasted perhaps for some festivity,
while vegetables or a stew are being
prepared in the cauldron. By an
ingenious device the spit is turned
on a hook attached to the base of
the cauldron.

    And morning came; as soon as it was day
They made for Brittany by the nearest way,
The brothers with the wizard at their side,
And there dismounted having done their ride.
It was – so say the books, if I remember –
The cold and frosty season of December.
Phoebus grew old, his coppered face was duller
Than it had been in *Cancer* when his colour
Shone with the burnished gold of streaming morn,
But now descending into *Capricorn*
His face was very pale, I dare maintain.
The bitter frosts, the driving sleep and rain
Had killed the gardens; greens had disappeared.
Now Janus by the fire with double beard,
His bugle-horn in hand, sits drinking wine;
Before him stands a brawn of tusky swine,
And '*Sing Noël!*' cries every lusty man.
    Aurelius, using all the means he can,
Gives welcome to the master, shows respect
And begs his diligence, that no neglect
Or sloth delay the healing of his smart,
Lest he should kill himself, plunge sword in heart.
    This subtle sage had pity on the man
And night and day went forward with his plan
Watching the hour to favour the conclusion
Of his experiment, that by illusion
Or apparition – call it jugglery,
I lack the jargon of astrology –
She and the world at large might think and say
The rocks had all been spirited away
From Brittany or sunk under the ground.
    And so at last the favouring hour was found

To do his tricks and wretched exhibition
Of that abominable superstition.
His calculating tables were brought out
Newly corrected (he made sure about
The years in series and the single years
To fix the points the planets in their spheres
Were due to reach and so assessed their 'root'
In longitude) and other things to suit,
Such as his astrolabe, and argument
From arc and angle, and was provident
Of fit proportionals for the minor motion
Of planets, and he studied with devotion,
Measuring from the point where Alnath* swam
In the eighth sphere, to where the head of the *Ram*
Stood in the ninth, in its eternal station
(As we suppose), and made his calculation.
And finding the first mansion of the moon,
He calculated all the rest in tune
With that. He worked proportionally, knowing
How she would rise and whither she was going
Relative to which planets and their place,
Equal or not, upon the zodiac face.
And thus according to his calculations
He knew the moon in all her operations
And all the relevant arithmetic
For his illusion, for the wretched trick
He meant to play, as in those heathen days
People would do. There were no more delays
And by his magic for a week or more
It seemed the rocks were gone; he'd cleared the shore.
　　Aurelius, still despairing of the plot,
Nor knowing whether he'd get his love or not,
Waited for miracles by night and day,
And when he saw the rocks were cleared away,
All obstacles removed, the plot complete,
He fell in rapture at his master's feet.
'Wretch as I am, for what has passed between us,
To you, my lord, and to my lady Venus
I offer thanks,' he said, 'for by your care,
As poor Aurelius is well aware,
He has been rescued from a long dismay.'
　　And to the temple then he took his way
Where, as he knew, his lady was to be;
And when he saw his opportunity,

With terror in his heart, and humbled face,
He made obeisance to her sovereign grace.
   'My truest lady,' said this woeful man,
'Whom most I dread and love – as best I can –
Last in the world of those I would displease,
Had I not suffered many miseries
For love of you, so many I repeat
That I am like to perish at your feet,
I would not dare approach you, or go on
To tell you how forlorn and woebegone
I am for you; but I must speak or die.
You kill me with your torture; guiltless, I.
Yet if my death could never so have stirred
Your pity, think before you break your word.
Repent, relent, remember God above you
Before you murder me because I love you.
You know what you have promised to requite
– Not that I challenge anything of right,
My sovereign lady, only of your grace –
Yet in a garden yonder, at such a place
You made a promise which you know must stand
And gave your plighted truth into my hand
To love me best, you said, as God above
Knows, though I be unworthy of your love.
It is your honour, madam, I am seeking;
It's not to save my life that I am speaking.
I have performed what you commanded me
As if you deign to look you soon will see.
Do as you please but think of what you said
For you will find me here alive, or dead.
It lies in you to save me or to slay –
But well I know the rocks are all away!'
He took his leave of her and left the place.
   Without a drop of colour in her face
She stood as thunderstruck by her mishap.
'Alas,' she said, 'to fall in such a trap!
I never had thought the possibility
Of such a monstrous miracle could be,
It goes against the processes of nature.'
And home she went, a very sorrowful creature
In deadly fear, and she had much to do
Even to walk. She wept a day or two,
Wailing and swooning, pitiful to see,
But why she did so not a word said she,

A recumbent deer: a tranquil decorative detail from the Luttrell Psalter.

moult de laidures et pour especial aux traistres. Et pour ce que tant les
ennuyoit ils la menoient sur le rivage de la mer en briefs lieu apelle valide
et la la pendoient et furent mourir mauvaisement. Et ainsi finit la vaillan-
tise herculle. lune des plus vaillantes femes et des plus nobles du mode

The end of a stag hunt.

For her Arveragus was out of town.
But to herself she spoke and flinging down
In pitiable pallor on her bed
She voiced her lamentation and she said:
    'Alas, of thee, O Fortune, I complain,
That unawares hast wrapped me in thy chain,
Which to escape two ways alone disclose
Themselves, death or dishonour, one of those,
And I must choose between them as a wife.
Yet I would rather render up my life
Than to be faithless or endure a shame
Upon my body or to lose my name.
My death will quit me of a foolish vow;
And has not many a noble wife ere now
And many a virgin slain herself to win
Her body from pollution and from sin?
    'Yes, surely, many a story we may trust
Bears witness; thirty tyrants full of lust
Slew Phido the Athenian★ like a beast,
Then had his daughters carried to their feast,
And they were brought before them in despite
Stark naked, to fulfil their foul delight,
And there they made them dance upon the floor,
God send them sorrow, in their father's gore.
And these unhappy maidens full of dread,
Rather than they be robbed of maidenhead,
Broke from their guard and leapt into a well
And there were drowned, so ancient authors tell.
    'The people of Messina also sought
Some fifty maidens out of Sparta, brought
Only that they might work their lechery
Upon them, but in all that company
Not one that was not slain; they were content
To suffer death rather than to consent

The end of a boar hunt.

To being forced in their virginity;
What then's the fear of death, I say, to me?
  'Consider Aristoclides for this,
A tyrant lusting after Stymphalis
Who, when her father had been slain one night,
Fled for protection to Diana's might
Into her temple, clung to her effigy
With both her hands and from it could not be
Dragged off, they could not tear her hands away
Till they had killed her. If a virgin may
Be seen to have so loath an appetite
To be defiled by filthy man's delight,
Surely a wife should kill herself ere she
Were so defiled, or so it seems to me.
  'And what of Hasdrubal? Had he not a wife
At Carthage who had rather take her life?
For as she watched the Romans win the town
She took her children with her and leapt down
Into the fire; there she chose to burn
Rather than let them do their evil turn.
  'Did not Lucrece choose death for her escape
In Rome of old when she had suffered rape
For Tarquin's lust? Did not she think it shame
To live a life that had been robbed of name?
  'The seven virgins of Miletus too
Took their own lives – were they not bound to do? –
Lest they be ravished by their Gaulish foes.
More than a thousand stories I suppose
Touching this theme were easy now to tell.
  'Did not his wife, when Abradates fell,
Take her own life and let the purple flood
Glide from her veins to mingle with his blood,
Saying, "My body shall at least not be
Defiled by man, so far as lies in me"?

'Since there are found so many, if one delves,
That gladly have preferred to kill themselves
Rather than be defiled, need more be sought
For my example? Better were the thought
To kill myself at once than suffer thus.
I will be faithful to Arveragus
Or slay myself as these examples bid,
As the dear daughter of Demotion did
Who chose to die rather than be defiled.

'O Skedasus, thou also hadst a child
That slew herself, and sad it is to read
How she preferred her death to such a deed.

'As pitiable or even more, I say,
The Theban maid who gave her life away
To foil Nichanor and a like disgrace.

'Another virgin at that very place
Raped by a Macedonian, it is said,
Died to repay her loss of maidenhead.

'What shall I say of Niceratus' wife
Who being thus dishonoured took her life?

'And O how true to Alcibiades
His lover was! She died no less than these
For seeking to give burial to her dead.

'See what a wife Alcestis was,' she said,
'And what says Homer of Penelope?
All Greece can celebrate her chastity.

'Laodamia, robbed of all her joy
(Protesilaus being killed at Troy),
Would live no longer, seeing that he was slain.

'Of noble Portia let me think again;
She could not live on being forced to part
From Brutus whom she loved with all her heart.

'And Artemisia, faithful to her man,
Is honoured, even by the barbarian.

'O Teuta, queen! Thy wifely chastity
Should be a mirror for all wives to see;
I say the same of Bilia and as soon
Of chaste Valeria and Rhodogoun.'

Thus for a day or two she spent her breath,
Poor Dorigen, and ever purposed death.

On the third day, however, of her plight,
Home came Arveragus, that excellent knight,
And questioned her; what was she crying for?
But she continued weeping all the more.

Gambling was rife and the gamblers were prepared to stake all they possessed. Here the man on the right has staked his clothes on the throw of the dice and has lost.

'Alas,' she said, 'that ever I was born!
Thus have I said,' she answered, 'thus have sworn –'
She told him all as you have heard before.
It need not be repeated here once more.
　　Her husband smiled at her with friendly eyes
And countenance, and answered in this wise:
'And is there nothing, Dorigen, but this?'
'No, no, so help me God!' with emphasis
She answered. 'Is it not enough, too much?'
'Well, wife,' he said, 'it's better not to touch
A sleeping dog, so I have often heard;
All may be well, but you must keep your word.
For, as may God be merciful to me,
I rather would be stabbed than live to see
You fail in truth. The very love I bear you
Bids you keep truth, in that it cannot spare you.
Truth is the highest thing in a man's keeping.'
And on the word he suddenly burst out weeping
And said, 'But I forbid on pain of death,
As long as you shall live or draw your breath,
That you should ever speak of this affair
To living soul; and what I have to bear
I'll bear as best I may; now wash your face,
Be cheerful. None must guess at this disgrace.'
　　He called a maidservant and squire then
And said, 'Go out with Lady Dorigen;
Attend upon her, whither she will say.'
They took their leave of him and went their way
Not knowing why their mistress was to go.
It was his settled purpose none should know.
　　Perhaps a heap of you will want to say,
'Lewd, foolish man to act in such a way,
Putting his wife into such jeopardy!'
Listen before you judge them, wait and see.
She may have better fortune, gentlemen,
Than you imagine; keep your judgements then
Till you have heard my story which now turns
To amorous Aurelius as he burns
For Dorigen; they happened soon to meet
Right in the town, in the most crowded street
Which she was bound to use, however loath,
To reach the garden and to keep her oath.
　　Aurelius gardenwards was going too;
A faithful spy on all she used to do,

The whipping top, as this picture
shows, is one of the children's
games that has come down through
the ages. It has been suggested
that the knots on the thongs may
have been a conventional way
of portraying a whip (horse-whips
are similarly drawn) for a knotted
whip would be difficult to use with
a top.

He kept close watch whenever she went out
And so by accident or luck no doubt
They met each other; he, his features glowing,
Saluted her and asked where she was going,
And she replied as one half driven mad,
'Why, to the garden, as my husband bade
To keep my plighted word, alas, alas!'
    Aurelius, stunned at what had come to pass,
Felt a great surge of pity that arose
At sight of Dorigen in all her woes
And for Arveragus the noble knight
That bade her keep her word of honour white,
So loth he was that she should break her truth.
And such a rush of pity filled the youth
That he was moved to think the better course
Was to forgo his passion than to force
An act on her of such a churlish kind
And against such nobility of mind.
So, in few words, the squire addressed her thus:
    'Madam, say to your lord Arveragus
That since I well perceive his nobleness
Towards yourself, and also your distress,
Knowing the shame that he would rather take
(And that were pity) than that you should break
Your plighted word, I'd rather suffer too
Than seek to come between his love and you.
    'So, Madam, I release into your hand
All bonds or deeds of covenant that stand
Between us, and suppose all treaties torn
You may have made with me since you were born.
I give my word never to chide or grieve you
For any promise given, and so I leave you,
Madam, the very best and truest wife
That ever yet I knew in all my life.
Let women keep their promises to men,
Or at the least remember Dorigen.
A squire can do a generous thing with grace
As well as can a knight, in any case.'
    And she went down and thanked him on her knees.
Home to her husband then with heart at ease
She went and told him all as I've recorded.
You may be sure he felt so well rewarded
No words of mine could possibly express
His feelings. Why then linger? You may guess.

Arveragus and Dorigen his wife
In sovereign happiness pursued their life,
No discord in their love was ever seen,
He cherished her as though she were a queen,
And she stayed true as she had been before;
Of these two lovers you will get no more.

Aurelius, all whose labour had been lost,
Cursing his birth, reflected on the cost.
'Alas,' he said, 'alas that I am bound
To pay in solid gold a thousand pound
To that philosopher. What shall I do?
All I can see is that I'm ruined too.
There's my inheritance; that I'll have to sell
And be a beggar. Then there's this as well;
I can't stay here a shame and a disgrace
To all my family; I must leave the place.
And yet he might prove lenient; I could pay
A yearly sum upon a certain day
And thank him gratefully, I can but try.
But I will keep my truth, I will not lie.'

And sad at heart he went to search his coffer
And gathered up what gold he had to offer
His master, some five hundred pound I guess,
And begged him as a gentleman, no less,
To grant him time enough to pay the rest.

'Sir, I can boast, in making this request,'
He said, 'I've never failed my word as yet,
And I will certainly repay this debt
I owe you, master, ill as I may fare,
Yes, though I turn to begging and go bare.
If you'd vouchsafe me, on security,
A little respite, say two years or three,
All would be fine. If not I'll have to sell
My patrimony; there's no more to tell.'

Then this philosopher in sober pride,
Having considered what he'd said, replied,
'Did I not keep my covenant with you?'
'You did indeed,' he said, 'and truly too.'
'And did you not enjoy your lady then?'
'No...no...' he sighed, and thought of Dorigen.
'What was the reason? Tell me if you can.'

Reluctantly Aurelius then began
To tell the story you have heard before,
There is no need to tell it you once more.

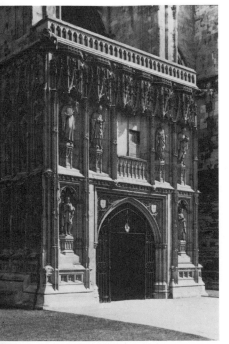

The south-west porch of
Canterbury Cathedral.

He said: 'Her husband, in his nobleness,
Would have preferred to die in his distress
Rather than that his wife should break her word.'
He told him of her grief and what occurred,
How loth she was to be a wicked wife
And how she would have rather lost her life;
'Her vow was made in innocent confusion,
She'd never heard of magical illusion.
So great a sense of pity rose in me,
I sent her back as freely then as he
Had sent her to me, let her go away.
That's the whole story, there's no more to say.'
   Then the magician answered, 'My dear brother,
Each of you did as nobly as the other.
You are a squire, sir, and he a knight,
But God forbid in all His blissful might
That men of learning should not come as near
To nobleness as any, never fear.
   'Sir, I release you of your thousand pound
No less than if you'd crept out of the ground
Just now, and never had had to do with me.
I will not take a penny, sir, in fee
For all my knowledge and my word to rid
The coast of rocks; I'm paid for what I did,
Well paid, and that's enough. Farewell, good-day!'
He mounted on his horse and rode away.
   My lords, I'll put a question: tell me true,
Which seemed the finest gentleman to you?
Ere we ride onwards tell me, anyone!
I have no more to say, my tale is done.

Chaucer's Retractions

Now I beg all those that listen to this little treatise, or
read it, that if there be anything in it that pleases them,
they thank Our Lord Jesu Christ for it, from whom
proceeds all understanding and goodness.

And if there be anything that displeases them, I beg
them also to impute it to the fault of my want of ability,
and not to my will, who would very gladly have said bet-
ter if I had had the power. For our Book says 'all that is
written is written for our doctrine'; and that is my
intention. Wherefore I beseech you meekly for the
mercy of God to pray for me, that Christ have mercy
on me and forgive me my sins: and especially for my
translations and enditings of worldly vanities, which I
revoke in my retractions: as are the book of *Troilus*;★
also the book of *Fame*; the book of *The Nineteen Ladies*;
the book of *The Duchess*; the book of *St Valentine's
Day of the Parliament of Fowls*; *The Tales of
Canterbury*, those that tend towards sin; the book of
The Lion; and many another book, if they were in my
memory; and many a song and many a lecherous lay;
that Christ in his great mercy forgive me the sin.

But the translation of Boethius' *De Consolatione*, and
other books of Saints' legends, of homilies, and
morality and devotion, for them I thank our Lord
Jesu Christ and His blissful Mother, and all the Saints
of Heaven; beseeching them that they henceforth, to
my life's end, send me grace to bewail my sins and to
study the salvation of my soul; and grant me the grace
of true penitence, confession and satisfaction, that I
may perform them in this present life, through the
benign grace of Him that is King of kings and Priest
over all priests, who bought us with the precious blood
of His heart; so that I may be one of those that at the
Day of Judgement shall be saved. *Qui cum Patre*, etc.

Here ends the book of the *Tales of Canterbury* compiled by Geoffrey Chaucer, on whose soul Jesu Christ have mercy.

Amen.

Notes

In preparing this translation I have used the texts as they
appear in the standard editions by W. W. Skeat in seven
volumes (Oxford 1894–7) and by F. N. Robinson in one
volume (Cambridge, Mass., 1933; also Oxford). The texts in
these two editions are naturally not identical. I have generally
referred to both, and where there seemed to be a discrepancy
that could affect a translation I have made my own choice.
I have followed the order of the tales as it is given by Skeat
rather than that given by Robinson.

The notes which follow derive very largely from both these
authorities and from other works of reference I have from
time to time consulted. They correspond to the asterisks in
the text.

Page
22 *Martyr*. St Thomas à Becket of Canterbury.
22 *The Knight's campaigning*.
   Alexandria. Taken and immediately after abandoned by
   Pierre de Lusignan, King of Cyprus, in 1365.
   Algeciras. Besieged and taken from the Moorish King of
   Granada in 1344.
   Ayas in Armenia, taken from the Turks by Pierre de
   Lusignan in about the year 1367.
   Attalia, on the south coast of Asia Minor, taken by Pierre
   de Lusignan soon after 1352.
   Tramissene, now called Tlemcen or Tremessen in western
   Algeria.
   Balat is a conjecture for the original *Palatye* and occupies
   the former site of Miletus.
25 *Gaudies*. Every eleventh bead in a rosary stands for a *pater-
   noster* and is called a 'gaudy'.
26 *A Limiter*. A begging friar who was granted a district to beg
   in, to limit his activities.
26 *Four Orders*. The four Orders of mendicant friars, the
   Dominicans, the Franciscans, the Carmelites, and the
   Augustinian Friars.
29 *St Paul's*. Lawyers used to meet for consultation at the
   portico of St Paul's cathedral.
29 *A Franklin*. A class of land-owner, a freeholder, who is also
   free by birth, but not noble. It is noteworthy that his self-
   conscious chatter about gentility when he politely interrupts
   the Squire is rudely interrupted by the Host.

33   *Dry, cold, moist or hot.* A man's body was conceived as being composed of the four elements, earth, water, air, and fire in due proportions. *Earth* was thought to be cold and dry, *water* cold and moist, *air* hot and moist, *fire* hot and dry. Diseases were thought to be due to an imbalance in one or more of these qualities. A man's character could be roughly defined by reference to them, and their proportion decided his 'humour', e.g. a *sanguine* man (like the Franklin) was held to be hot and moist, which gave him the character of being a laughing, amorous, high-coloured, fleshy, good-natured fellow, with many desires and capacities. A *choleric* man (like the Reeve) was thought to be hot and dry. There were also *melancholy* men (cold and dry) and *phlegmatic* men (cold and moist).

33   *Aesculapius* and other medical authorities.

      Aesculapius, mythical son of Apollo and Coronis, who learnt the art of medicine from Cheiron the Centaur, and whom Zeus struck by lightning for having restored too many people to life. He had a daughter called Hygieia and a temple was built to him, when after death he was deified as the god of medicine, at Epidaurus.

      Hippocrates, the most famous physician of antiquity, born at Cos about 460 B.C.

      Dioscorides, a Greek physician who lived in Cilicia in the first century A.D., with some of whose opinions Chaucer appears, in the *Nun's Priest's Tale* and elsewhere, to have been familiar.

      Galen, a physician and a voluminous author on medical subjects, born at Pergamus in Mysia, who studied at Smyrna, Corinth, and Alexandria and practised in Rome. Approximate dates 130–201 A.D.

      Rhazes, a Spanish Arab doctor of the tenth century.

      Hali, Serapion and *Avicenna* were Arabian physicians and astronomers of the tenth and eleventh centuries.

      Averroes, a Moorish medical author who lived in Morocco in the twelfth century.

      Scotch Bernard. Bernard Gordon, professor of medicine at Montpellier about the year 1300.

      John of Gaddesden, a medical authority educated at Merton College, Oxford, who died in 1361.

      Gilbertine, supposed to be Gilbertus Magnus, an Englishman who flourished towards the middle of the thirteenth century, wrote books about medicine, and is said to have been Chancellor at Montpellier.

37   *A Reeve.* A steward or minor official on an estate, generally an intermediary between a lord and his serfs or tenants.

38   *A Summoner.* One paid to summon sinners to trial before an ecclesiastical court. For further details of his profession see the opening of the *Friar's Tale*.

38   *Cherubinnish.* In medieval art the Cherubin are generally depicted with flame-coloured faces.

38   *Questio quid juris.* 'The question is, what is the point in law?'

42   *A Pardoner.* As the name implies, one who has authority (from the Pope) to sell pardons and indulgences, though not necessarily in holy orders.

78   *Dana*, a modernization of the name *Dane* as it is here found in Chaucer. He meant Daphne of course, who, being so in-human as to flee the embraces of Apollo, was turned into a laurel. Her preserved virginity qualifies her for representation in Diana's temple.

84   *By the three forms:* in Heaven, *Luna*. On earth, *Diana*. In Hell, *Proserpina*. As in Keats' sonnet on Homer:

> Such seeing hadst thou as it once befell
> To Dian, Queen of earth and heaven and hell.

96   *Could not be expelled.* Chaucer is here airing his technical knowledge of contemporary physiology. Three forces or 'virtues' were believed to control the life in a human body: the 'animal' virtues in the brain, the 'natural' in the liver, and the 'vital' in the heart. The 'animal' controlled all muscles, and therefore should have been able to expel the poison from Arcita's liver. But he was too far gone.

105 *A voice like Pilate's.* Miracle plays represented Herod and Pilate as huffing roarers and braggarts. Their lines generally carry heavy alliteration.

112 *Money.* More useful in a town than in the country, where there are fewer things to buy.

115 *Him that harrowed Hell.* When Christ descended into Hell He led away therefrom Adam, Eve, the Patriarchs, St John the Baptist, and others, redeemed and at last released. This act was commonly called 'The harrowing of Hell' in the middle ages and was the subject of several miracle-plays. The original story comes from the *Gospel of Nicodemus* in the Apocryphal New Testament.

131 *Solar Hall.* So called because of its large sunny windows. Its official name was King's Hall, having been founded by Edward III. Later it was merged in what is now called Trinity College.

132 *And how's your canny daughter?* In Chaucer's original the two young northerners from Strother, Alan and John, are made to talk in northern dialect and idiom, for instance, the forms *swa* for *so*, *bathe* for *both*, *raa* for a *roe* are used by them. So far as I know this is the first time dialect occurs for comic effect in English fiction. As a page to the Duchess of Clarence, Chaucer would have spent time in Yorkshire (at Hatfield), and he may have picked up the peculiarities of northern speech there and then. I have attempted to reproduce this peculiarity with the help of Mr H. S. Taylor of Exeter College, Oxford, and Mr J. D. O'Connor, of the Department of Phonetics, University College, London, who have been so kind as to suggest such northern forms as I

have used, e.g. *wor* for *our*. *Canny* here represents *faire* in the original. I am told that in Durham they say *canny* when they mean fair, pretty, or attractive.

137 *Bromeholme*. A piece of wood, said to be of the true cross, known as the Rood of Bromeholme, much venerated in Norfolk.

139 *He has to clothe us*. It is obvious that this passage was meant for a woman speaker, presumably the Wife of Bath. It is likely that Chaucer had at first designed the tale for her, then changed his mind (having found one that suited her even better) and unloaded this one on the Skipper without remembering these tell-tale lines.

145 *Ganelon of France*. The villain of the *Chanson de Roland* that betrayed Roland and Oliver who, with Archbishop Turpin, formed Charlemagne's rearguard at Roncesvalles against the Moors. Ganelon was torn asunder by four horses.

145 *Two in twelve*. The MSS differ as to the proportion; some say ten in twelve, some twelve in twenty.

150 *Tally*. Paying by tally was a common though often unreliable method of buying on credit in the middle ages. A stick was notched with notches to the amount owed and then split. Vendor and purchaser each retained half. When pay day came the sticks were compared to see if they 'tallied'. If they did the sum due was clear.

160 *Zenobia* flourished A.D. 264 as Queen of Palmyra and was married to Odenathus, a Bedouin. Recognized by the Emperor Gallienus, she was attacked and defeated and led in triumph by the Emperor Aurelian, but survived to live in comfort.

164 *King Peter of Spain*. Skeat notes: 'He reigned over Castille and Leon from 1350 to 1362 and his conduct was marked by numerous acts of unprincipled atrocity.' There was a quarrel with his brother Enrique who stabbed him to the heart. This is the murder here lamented, though if Skeat's view be accepted it was no great loss. Chaucer takes his part because the Black Prince fought on his side against Enrique at the battle of Najera, 1367.

164 *Upon an argent field*. The second stanza of this 'tragedy' is written as a sort of heraldic riddle intermixed with puns. The arms described (argent, a double-headed eagle sable, displayed, debruised by a bend gules) are those of Bertrand Du Guesclin who 'brewed' the treason by luring King Peter into his brother's tent. The 'wicked nest' is a pun on the name of Sir Oliver Mauny (*Mau* is Old French for *wicked*, *nid* for *nest*), who was an accomplice according to Chaucer. Chaucer continues that this was not such an Oliver as that in the *Chanson de Roland*, loyal soldier of Charlemagne, but much more like Ganelon (the villain of the *Chanson*).

I suppose this emblematic way of expressing what occurred would have been easily intelligible to Chaucer's first audiences, but can see no way of translating it so as to seem so to the modern reader without adding this long note.

165 *King Peter of Cyprus.* Pierre de Lusignan, ascended to the throne of Cyprus in 1352 and was assassinated in 1369. Chaucer's Knight seems to have seen service with him.

165 *Bernabo Visconti*, Duke of Milan, was deposed and died in prison in 1385. Chaucer knew him personally, though this does not show from what the Monk has to say. He went on the King's business to treat with him in 1378. The death of Bernabo is the most recent historical event mentioned in the *Canterbury Tales*.

166 *Dante.* See *Inferno* xxxii–xxxiii.

172 *Holofernes,* and

173 *Antiochus.* For both of these see the *Book of Judith* and 2 *Maccabees* ix in the *Apocrypha.*

174 *Alexander of Macedon*, the Great, 356–323 B.C. His dazzling career, high intelligence, and astounding magnanimity made him a legendary ideal of knightly soldiership in the middle ages.

175 *Aces.* The lowest possible throw of the dice in the game of *Hazard.*

176 *Brutus Cassius.* Chaucer supposed these two famous assassins to be one and the same.

182 *The equinoctial wheel.* I quote from Professor Robinson: 'A great circle of the heavens in the plane of the equator. According to the old astronomy it made a complete daily revolution so that 15 degrees would "ascend" every hour.' It was a popular belief in the time of Chaucer that cocks crew punctually on the hour.

182 *My Love is far from land.* The original, probably the refrain of a popular song, reads 'my lief is faren in londe' and means 'my love has gone away into foreign parts' but I could not resist the allusion to a song of our own, 'She is far from the land where her young hero sleeps.'

191 *Greek Sinon.* The Greek who tricked King Priam into admitting the Trojan Horse to Troy.

192 *Bishop Bradwardine*, a famous contemporary theologian, Proctor of Oxford University in 1325, and later Professor of Divinity and Chancellor.

192 *Boethius*, author of *De Consolatione Philosophiae* which Chaucer translated, was esteemed not only as a philosopher but also as a musician. In the fifth book of his great work there is a long argument on the subject of Predestination and Free Will on which Chaucer many times pondered and drew as a writer. He was a very learned poet, but carried his learning lightly. Boethius lived *c.* A.D. 470–525.

192 *Physiologus.* I quote from Tyrwhitt, 'a book in Latin metre entitled *Physiologus de Naturis xii Animalium*, by one Theobaldus, whose age is not known. The Chapter *De Sirensis* begins thus:

> *Sirenae sunt monstra maris resonantia magnis vocibus,* etc.

193 *Burnel the Ass.* A poem by Nigel Wireker of the twelfth

century. The tale alluded to is that of a priest's son who broke a rooster's leg by throwing a stone at it. In revenge the bird declined to crow in the morning on the day when the priest was to be ordained and receive a benefice, so the priest failed to wake up in time and being late for the ceremony lost his preferment.

194 *Geoffrey* is Geoffrey de Vinsauf, an author on the art of Rhetoric who flourished in the twelfth century. In this work *De Nova Poetria* there is an intricate passage about the death of Richard Coeur de Lion to exhibit the art of apostrophe and playing upon words. Fridays come in for ingenious abuse. Chaucer, who derived a great deal of his stylistic manner from a sane use of the rules of rhetoric as laid down by his 'dear and sovereign master', is here poking gentle fun at him. It may be observed that the whole of the *Nun's Priest's Tale* is a farrago of rhetorical fireworks which must have made the poem far funnier to the fourteenth century, trained in such matters, than it is to us. I suppose a fair comparison would be between the delight taken in Pope's *Rape of the Lock* by a reader who knew the *Aeneid* and the delight taken in it by one who did not.

195 *Jack Straw* was one of the leaders of the riots in London during the Peasants' Revolt of 1381, according to Walsingham's Chronicle. He and his gang massacred a number of Flemings in the Vintry, and he was later captured and decapitated.

204 *In neighbouring regions.* There were regulations against the mixture of wines. Lepé wine is light by nature, but may have been fortified with spirit for export. He is ironically suggesting that – as one cannot, of course, suspect an honest Fish Street vintner of deliberately mixing his wines – one can only suppose the mixture to occur spontaneously, thanks to the geographical proximity of Spain and France. I am told by Mr Warner Allen that this seems the first mention of the practice of fortifying wines that he has come upon in his researches.

206 *Hailes.* In Gloucestershire; the abbey ruins can still be seen. It formerly possessed a phial of Christ's blood; later publicly destroyed at St Paul's Cross by order of Henry VIII.

212 *Avicenna.* An Arabian physician (A.D. 980–1037) who wrote a work on medicines that includes a chapter on poisons.

221 *Ptolemy.* Claudius Ptolemaeus, an astronomer of the second century whose chief work was known as his *Almagest*, an Arabic corruption of its title in Greek. His astronomical theories are those on which all medieval astronomy was based. His general wisdom also was proverbial.

222 *Dunmow.* The prize of a flitch of bacon for the married pair that have had fewest disputes during the previous year is still annually offered at Dunmow.

225 *Three misfortunes.* She is alluding to Proverbs xxx, 21-8. 'For three things the earth is disquieted, and for four which

it cannot bear; for a servant when he reigneth; and a fool when he is filled with meat; for an odious woman when she is married; and an handmaid that is heir to her mistress.'

232 *Theophrastus and Valerius*. A work attributed to Walter Map, a wit and cynic who flourished about A.D. 1200. The subject of the work here referred to is *De non ducenda uxore*, a satire on matrimony.

234 *Children of Mercury*. Learning was held to be under the protection of Mercury; his 'children' are scholars, who in those days were generally celibate.

235 *Pasiphaë*. Wife of Minos, King of Crete. She fell in love with a white bull and became the mother of the Minotaur, half-man, half-bull.

244 *Sovereignty*. To realize the full force of the Knight's answer it may help to glance at the Introduction, p. 10.

258 *Apostle*. i.e. St Paul.

265 *Trentals*. An office of thirty masses for the souls of those in Purgatory. The gibe about their being 'very quickly sung' a few lines later refers to the official view that the soul in question could not be released until the whole thirty had been sung. Thus it was held reasonable and charitable to sing them one after another, all on the same day if possible, so as not to keep the soul lingering in Purgatory longer than was necessary. Those who sang these masses were naturally paid for their work.

266 *Qui cum Patre*. The conventional close of a sermon, 'Who with the Father,' etc.

269 *Jubilee*. After serving fifty years in a Convent friars were permitted to go about alone.

270 *Cor meum eructavit*. The opening words of Psalm xlv, 'My heart is inditing of a good matter,' which less poetically rendered could mean, 'My heart is belching a good matter.'

285 *The Boat of Wade*. Wade was a hero of Anglo-Saxon antiquity to whom there are several scattered references outside Chaucer, but nothing is known about this subtle boat of his except that its name was *Guingelot*.

308 *Jesus son of Sirach*. The supposed author of *Ecclesiasticus*.

315 *Cambuskan*. I have adopted Milton's spelling for this name from his famous praise of the tale in *Il Penseroso*. Skeat notes that the name in Chaucer (Cambinskan) was intended by him for the name more familiar to us of Genghis Khan, though the account here given of him suits his grandson Kublai Khan better.

317 *Gawain*. A knight of the Round Table, distinguished, though not specially so in Malory, for his extreme courtesy. A noble alliterative romance, contemporary with Chaucer, describes his adventures with a Green Knight of magical powers in whose castle Gawain was staying. The Green Knight's lady makes love to Gawain and he is in a cleft stick, for it would seem as discourteous to refuse her as to cuckold his host.

Gawain's perfect manners, however, are equal to the occasion
and he offends neither.

320 *Alhazen and Witelo.* Alhazen was an Arabian astronomer who
died A.D. 1039. Witelo was a Polish mathematician of the
thirteenth century.

321 *Aldiran.* The name of a star in the constellation of *Leo*,
identified by Skeat as the star θ Hydrae.

327 *A pup.* The proverb here referred to is 'Beat the dog before
the lion,' meaning that if you chastise a smaller creature in
sight of a larger, the larger will take warning. One can see
the application of this in the political field. Repress a minor
rebel and a greater enemy may think twice before attacking.

330 *A tercelet.* The technical term for a male falcon or hawk.

333 *Velvet blue.* Blue for Chaucer's age was the colour of constancy
in love and green of lightness in love. This is echoed in
'Greensleeves is my delight' and elsewhere. The fickle birds
were depicted on the outside to imply that such could never
enter *within* the mew, where all was constancy. So in the
Roman de la Rose, the walls of the garden of love are decorated
on the outside with the figures of poverty, old age, hypocrisy,
etc., which are never to be admitted in the land of true love.

336 *Cithero.* He means Cicero, of course, famous for all the
'figures' and 'colours' of rhetoric. These are technical names
for various known devices of style, such as those referred to
towards the end of the *Nun's Priest's Tale*.

342 *Without cup.* The sense of this proverbial phrase is that he
drank misery straight from the cask and not in small portions,
cup by cup.

346 *Pamphilus for Galatea.* This is not an error for Pygmalion
and Galatea but refers according to Skeat to a long poem in
barbarous Latin by one Pamphilus, declaring his love.

350 *Alnath.* The name still of a star of first magnitude known to
astronomers as α Arietis. Chaucer was himself a considerable
astronomer and wrote a treatise on the Astrolabe. The whole
of this passage about the magician's calculations is highly
technical and exact. Being no astronomer myself I have trans-
lated it with as much understanding as I could bring to bear
on it, with frequent recourse to the full notes on pages 393–5
of the fifth volume of Skeat's large edition of Chaucer's works.
Those interested in medieval science may there learn the
astounding complexity of detail which underlies the bland
verses of Chaucer, though he appears to assume that his
readers will take it all for granted. The Franklin has just
said that he 'lacks the jargon of astrology' ('I can no termes
of astrologye') but all the same he makes no blunders, it
seems. I hope I have been able to follow his example.

352 *Phido.* The whole of this speech is a set piece of medieval
rhetoric in spite of the Franklin's disclaimer in his Prologue.
It begins with the figure of *apostrophe* and passes to a long
digressio built out of *exempla* from ancient history. All the

instances of female fidelity that sprang to Dorigen's mind
rose from authentic sources in Chaucer's reading which can
be found in the notes to Skeat's or Robinson's edition of
his works. On consideration I have thought it would be tedious
to repeat them here.

359 *Troilus*. For a brief account of most of the works here
mentioned by Chaucer see the Introduction (page 12). The
book of *The Lion* has been lost, but it is conjectured to be
a translation from the French of Machault, a work called
Le Dit du Lion, composed in 1342.

Acknowledgements

PICTURE CREDITS

Colour Sections

MAGIC AND MEDICINE: TRADES AND PROFESSIONS
(between pages 40 and 41)

[1] Bodleian Library, Oxford, MS 210 eG; [2] British Library, MS
Roy 17 FII f. 283 verso; [3] British Library, MS Add 42130 f. 61;
[4] Bibliothèque Royal Albert I, Brussels, MS 9392 f. 92 verso;
[5 and 6] London Library, Ellesmere Chronicle facsimile; [7] British
Library, MS Add 27695 f. 7 verso; [8] British Library, MS Cotton
(Tiberius) Avii f. 93 recto; [9] Biblioteca Casatouse, Rome; [10]
British Library, MS Harl 4425 f. 142; [11] British Library, MS Roy
15 EII f. 265.

WAR: THE FEUDAL SYSTEM *(between pages 72 and 73)*

[1] British Library, MS Roy 14 Eiv f. 195; [2] Bodleian Library,
Oxford, MS Laud Misc 653 f. 17; [3] Bodleian Library, Oxford,
MS Laud 653 f. 13; [4] Bodleian Library, Oxford, MS Bod 264
f. 113 verso; [5] British Library, MS Roy 16 G VI f. 178; [6]
British Library, MS Roy 16 G VI f. 74; [7] photo Woodmansterne;
[8] Bodleian Library, Oxford, MS Bod 16 K4; [9] British Library,
MS Add 42130 f. 161; [10] Bibliothèque de l'Arsenal, Paris, Livres
des Prouffits Champestres; [11] British Library, MS Roy 2 Bvii f. 78;
[12] British Library, MS Harl 4379 f. 64.

TOWNS AND BUILDINGS *(between pages 120 and 121)*

[1] British Library, MS Roy 18 DII f. 148; [2] British Library,
MS Roy 16 F ii f. 73; [3] photo. A. F. Kersting; [4] John Clark
Collection; [5] Bibliothèque Nationale, Paris, MS français 364 f. 39;
[6] photo A. F. Kersting; [7] British Library, MS Harl 4376
[150 15792]; [8] photo Woodmansterne; [9] Westminster Abbey.

RELIGION *(between pages 168 and 169)*

[1] Bodleian Library, Oxford, MS 269 f. 76; [3 & 4] London Library,
Ellesmere Chronicle facsimile; [5] London Museum; [6] British
Library, MS Domitian Avii; [8] British Library, MS Harl. 1319
f. 12; [9] photo A. F. Kersting; [10] Sidney Sussex College,
Cambridge; [12] Bodleian Library, Oxford, MS New College 288
f. 32.

DOMESTIC LIFE: GAMES AND PASTIMES
(between pages 216 and 217)

[1] Bodleian Library, Oxford, MS Bod 264 f. 63; [2] British Library, MS Add 2228 f. 23; [3] Bodleian Library, Oxford, MS Bod 264 f. 109 verso; [5] British Library, MS Add 42130 f. 161; [6] Bodleian Library, Oxford, MS Bod 264 f. 180 verso; [7] British Library, MS Harl 2278 f. 13 verso; [8] British Library, MS Add 42130 f. 206; [9] Bodleian Library, Oxford, MS Bod 264 f. 123; [10] British Library, MS Add 42130 f. 207 verso and 208; [11] British Library, MS Harl 2838 f. 45; [12] Bodleian Library, Oxford, MS Doves 383 f. 178; [13] Bodleian Library, Oxford, MS Bod 264 f. 97; [14] British Library, MS Add 42130 f. 193.

COUNTRYSIDE *(between pages 248 and 249)*

[1] British Library, MS Add 42130 f. 170; [2] Musée Condé, Les Très Riches Heures du Duc de Berri (March); [3] British Library, MS Add 42130 f. 169; [4] Bodleian Library, Oxford, MS Bod 264; [5] British Library, MS Add 42130 f. 163; [6] Bodleian Library, Oxford, MS Bod 1698 f. 15; [7–10] British Library, MS Add 18850 (Bedford Book of Hours) ff. 3, 4, 5 and 7; [11] Musée Condé, Les Très Riches Heures du Duc de Berri (December); [12–15] British Library, MS Add 18850 ff. 8, 10–12; [16] Musée Condé, Les Très Riches Heures du Duc de Berri (September).

ROMANCE AND CHIVALRY *(between pages 296 and 297)*

[1] British Library, MS Harl 4379 f. 99; [2] British Library, MS Harl 4425 f. 12; [4] photo Sonia Halliday; [5] British Library, MS Add 42130 f. 202 verso; [6] Bodleian Library, Oxford, MS Bod 167K 15; [7] Trivulziana Library, Milan; [8] Bodleian Library, Oxford, MS Bod 121 18; [9] British Library, MS Roy 18 El.

TRAVEL *(between pages 328 and 329)*

[1 and 2] London Museum; [3] British Library, MS Harl 4425 f. 86; [4–6] British Library, MS Add 42130 f. 162; [7] British Library, MS Harl 4431 f. 153; [8] British Library, MS Add 27695 f. 7 verso; [9] British Library, MS Add 24189; [10] British Library, MS Cotton (Nero) DVII f. 13 verso.

Black and White Pictures

[Page 24] British Library MS Harl. 1319 f. 25; [27] British Library MS Add. 42130 f. 171; [29] British Library MS Harl. 1319; [30, 31] London Museum; [32] British Library MS Domitian A17 f. 74 verso; [33] British Library MS Cotton Dom. XVII f. 12; [35] British Library MS Cotton (Nero) DVII f. 16 verso; [36] Bodleian Library, Oxford, MS Douce 300 f. 38 verso; [38] National Monuments Record; [39] London Museum; [42] British Library MS Harl. 1527 f. 10 verso; [43] MS Roy. (top) 10EIV f. 108 verso; British Library (bottom) MS Roy. 10EIV f. 108 verso; [45] London Library Ellesmere

Chronicle facsimile; [49] British Library MS Add. 10292 f. 21 verso; [50] Bodleian Library, Oxford, MS 264 f. 90; [51] British Library MS Add. 42130 f. 59; [53] British Library MS Add. 42130 f. 63; [54, 55] British Library MS Add. 42130 f. 56; [57] London Museum; [58] Bibliothèque Nationale, Paris, MS français 166; [59] (top) Art Gallery & Museum, Glasgow; (bottom) Victoria & Albert Museum, London; [61] Bodleian Library, Oxford, MS Bod. 264 f. 258 verso; [62] British Library MS Sloane 2435 f. 11 verso; [64/5] London Museum; [67] Art Gallery & Museum, Glasgow; [68/9] British Library Roy. 2BVII f. 177; [71] Glasgow University Library Les cents nouvelles nouvelles;

[74] British Library MS Harl. 4425 f. 11; [75] London Museum; [77] British Library MS Add. 42130 f. 173; [78] National Monuments Record; [79] photo A. F. Kersting; [80] British Library MS Roy. 15EVII f. 209; [83] British Library MS Harl. 1892 f. 68; [85] London Museum; [86] British Library MS Arundel 91 f. 47 verso; [89] British Library MS Add. 42130 f. 13; [90/1] Victoria & Albert Museum, London; [93] British Library MS Roy. 18DII f. 153 verso; [94/5] photo. Aero Films Ltd; [96] British Library MS 18852 f. 235; [99] British Library MS Add. 42130 f. 163; [101] British Library MS Roy. 18DII f. 151; [102] British Library MS Add. 42130 f. 58; [109] British Library MS Add. 42130 f. 190; [110] London Museum; [112/13] Bodleian Library, Oxford, MS Bod. 264 f. 62; [114] British Library MS Add. 42130 f. 166b; [117] British Library MS Add. 42130 f. 173; [118] London Museum; [119] London Museum;

[122] British Library MS Sloane 2435 f. 117; [123] London Museum; [124] British Library MS Add. 42130 f. 70; [125] Bodleian Library, Oxford, MS Bod. 264 f. 81; [130] British Library MS Add. 42130 f. 196b; [133] British Library MS Add. 42130 f. 78b; [135] London Museum; [137] British Library MS Add. 42130 f. 17b; [140/1] British Library MS Add. 42130 f. 64 verso; [142] London Museum; [143] London Museum; [144] Tower of London Armouries; [146] British Library MS Add. 42130 f. 62; [149] British Library MS Roy. 10EIV f. 187; [154] British Library MS Add. 42130 f. 61; [157] British Library MS Harl. 1527 f. 104; [159] British Library MS Harl. 1527 f. 46; [161] Bodleian Library, Oxford, MS Bod. 264 f. 122 verso; [162] London Museum; [165] London Museum; [167] British Library Sloane 2435 f. 44 verso; [171] British Library MS Harl. 2278 f. 6; [173] British Library MS Add. 42130 f. 63; [174/5] London Museum; [177] London Museum; [183] British Library MS Add. 42130 f. 70b; [185] British Library MS Harl. 892 f. 29 verso; [186] British Library MS Harl. 4425 f. 143; [191] Society of Antiquaries, London; [193] British Library MS Add. 42130 f. 7; [194/5] British Library MS Roy. 10EIV f. 58; [199] British Library MS Add. 42130 f. 17b; [202] London Museum;

[205] London Museum; [207] British Library MS Roy. 10EIV f. 77 verso; [209] London Museum; [211] London Museum; [212] Bodleian Library, Oxford, MS Bod. 264 f. 21 verso; [218] British Library MS Roy. 18D11 f. 160; [221] British Library MS Harl. 1892 f. 27 verso; [222/3] Bodleian Library, Oxford, MS Bod. 264 f. 123 verso; [224/5] Bodleian Library, Oxford, MS Bod. 264; [226/7] photos A. F. Kersting; [229] British Library MS Add. 42130 f. 160; [231] London Museum; [233] Society of Antiquaries, London; [234] London Museum; [235] London Museum; [240] British Library MS Roy. 18E2 f. 206; [241] Trinity College,